The UNION

Kyle S. Berkley

Dedication

This book is dedicated to my strong and brave cousin, Tarlethea Gardner, my father, Samuel Berkley; my Uncle Elisha Garland; my cousin Kenneth Bowman; my best friend Chris Burton; my friends Kevin Brown; Antonio Washington, a.k.a. Tony Bones; the amazingly talented Zandy Moore and so many other brothers and sisters we have lost over the years.

Special Thanks

I have to give thanks to my loving and supportive wife, Rebecca, and my three beautiful daughters, Savannah, Sage, and Shiloh. I wish I could put hearts by all of their names. They're my whole world. I also have to thank my parents for all they have poured into me to become the man I am today. Thanks also to my sisters Kyrissa, Kim, Toi, Sharay and Brenda, and my brothers Lamont, Andre, Anthony, Angelo, Charles, John Mark, and Reggie. I would like to give thanks to Stacie Doi, Odessa Rose, Ashley Logan Graham, Cherrie Woods and Cheryl Barton. I would like to give special thanks to my family and friends that have helped me throughout my life. I genuinely love you all. I also want to thank each and every person that purchased *The Wake*, *The Void* and *The Legacy*. I would also like to thank everyone that supported the East Coast Book Tour of 2023. It has meant so much to be supported and promoted the way I have been over the years.

Table of Contents

Prologue

Fair warning, those of you who have not yet read my three previous books, *The Wake*, *The Void*, and *The Legacy*, from this sentence forward, this book contains many spoilers. I urge you to stop here and consider purchasing those books first to get the full story.

Tiffany Gibbons, a beautiful 35-year-old African American woman and her best friend Sasha Green were displaced from their apartment building, thanks to a community redevelopment effort led by Titan Industries. Titan Industries is owned by twin adult siblings, Chandler and Chanel Titan, along with married couple Sedrick and Erica Little. Tiffany's grandmother, community leader Florence Simms, and her former pastor, Donald Avery fought against the efforts of Titan Industries until their untimely deaths.

During the same time, Tiffany's youngest daughter, Kenya, and her baby's father, Keyon, were murdered in a hit-and-run car accident. Tiffany's best friend, Sasha experienced the death of her high-school-age son, Tyrone Clinton at the hands of the Baltimore City Police during a botched robbery. It was later learned that Tyrone did not want to take part in the armed robbery but was bullied into participating. Unfortunately, when he attempted to give himself up to the responding police, he was murdered.

Tyrone Clinton was a star football player for a local high school, who was coached by local police officer, Edward Carter. Edward Carter and Tyrone made a deal that if he improved his grades, Tyrone could use the coach's BMW for the prom. Tyrone had hoped to take his longtime crush, Tina Simms, to the prom. Following the murder of an unarmed high school student, Kannard Lyles-Bey, Edward Carter went to the local hospital to speak to Mr. Lyles-Bey's parents, against Police Commissioner Alex Tillman's orders. Edward Carter was killed by what were assumed to be rioters, following an exchange of gunfire. Alex Tillman murdered the two presumed rioters.

Sadly, Tiffany's aunt, Gina Simms remained deeply entrenched in her drug addiction for several years. During that time, she befriended a young transwoman named Silk, born Simon Little, a former radio personality who was fired for sleeping with the radio station owner's husband during a highly publicized function. Silk's parents, Erica and Sedrick Little were resentful of Silk and being forced to accept her sexual identity. This became the catalyst for the murder of Silk at the hands of Tiffany's father.

Sedrick and Erica attempted to have a private funeral for Silk at the Allen Bradley Funeral Home during the same time that Florence Simms', Donald Avery's, Edward Carter's, Tyrone Clinton's, and Kenya Gibbons' services were held. Gina Simms revealed Silk's birth name, Simon Little, and alerted Anna Cartwright, the local news media personality covering the service for Tyrone Clinton. The City of Baltimore paused the community reconstruction project due to the controversy.

A year after the funeral services, Tiffany and the local community leader-turned-impromptu-pastor, Hakeem Andrews began dating. Tiffany moved into the home her grandmother left her, along with her four remaining children. Tiffany's best friend Sasha began living with her but developed a drinking habit to cope with the grief of her deceased son, Tyrone Clinton.

Hakeem has attempted to overcome the challenges in the Ridgely Square community using advocacy to stop Titan Industries in their new search for community redevelopment. Hakeem tried to partner with his estranged brother Jamar, leader of a local mosque. But there were too many differences in their belief systems; for instance, Jamar is of the opinion that the best way for Ridgely Square to thrive is to alienate itself from the rest of Baltimore City and become sovereign. He also alleges that the community should have its own schools, banks, and police department.

Hakeem disagrees with Jamar's assertions, and the two constantly butt heads on these viewpoints. It soon becomes clear that Jamar's previous criminal past has deep unresolved roots tied to Hakeem. Hakeem never went to prison unlike his brother Jamar. In addition to Jamar's incarceration, he was alienated by the family and the family's church. Jamar understood Tiffany's growing concerns about the worsening conditions in her neighborhood, so he provided her with a gun for protection from the local gang known as the Alphas and the rogue police unit known as the Narcotics and Firearms Taskforce.

Finally taking her sobriety seriously, Tiffany's aunt, Gina Simms, attempted to bond with Tiffany and they attended a grief and loss group gathering at the Allen Bradley Funeral Home. Gina also participated in a documentary about police corruption in the Baltimore City communities, specifically Ridgely Square, where she highlighted the actions of the Narcotics and Firearms Taskforce, also known as NAFA. NAFA has been working with a local gang called the Alphas, raiding the homes of revival gang members, known as the Cabal, taking narcotics and selling them in order to receive cash or gift card payments.

The leader of NAFA, Marshawn Bell, saved the extorted money with the goal of paying for his terminally ill mother's medical treatment at an experimental lab in Virginia. Prior to achieving his goal of paying for her treatment, Marshawn was arrested, thanks to Gina's involvement in the documentary. Marshawn admitted to his illegal actions while expressing his concern about his mother's meager teacher's salary and the fact that Medicare insurance did not provide her a competitive chance to thrive.

Marshawn also admitted he put a hit out on Edward Carter because he believed Alex Tillman used Edward Carter to spy on Marshawn's criminal behavior. He also used Jada Austin to get his case thrown out by agreeing to be a witness in a federal trial against the Alphas. Upon Marshawn's release from jail, he attempted to kidnap Sasha Green to assist with medicating his mother until they could reach the treatment center in Virginia, but Sasha was too intoxicated. Marshawn replaced Sasha with Tiffany with the goal that Tiffany would keep his mother stable until she reached the medical research center in Newport News, Virginia. Marshawn provided Tiffany with millions of dollars in gift cards for the damage he caused her and the Gibbons family. Upon arrival at the treatment center, Marshawn Bell was murdered by Commissioner Alex Tillman.

Upon Tiffany's return to Baltimore, Sasha agreed to go into substance abuse treatment, and move into Gina's home. After having a heart-to-heart talk with Sasha, Tiffany finally felt more comfortable talking to her children about the grief and trauma they endured throughout the last year. Gina was placed in witness protection for her upcoming court testimony against the Alphas and NAFA. While going into the basement, a place where Tiffany frequently heard the voices of her grandmother Florence, her daughter Kenya, her cousin Tina and negative words from her father, Daryl Gibbons, Tiffany learned that someone broke into the back door of her home. Tiffany discovered her father, who had repeatedly molested her and her cousin Tina in the past had broken into her home, with the children right upstairs. Tiffany used the handgun that Jamar had given her weeks before to take the life of her father.

Two years after the murder of Marshawn Bell and Tiffany's father, Daryl "Cube" Gibbons, an FBI investigation was conducted on NAFA and Alpha gang members, causing internal conflicts with the gang. A vigilante serial killer, known as the Action Figure Killer, also called AFK, prowled the streets of Baltimore City, killing crooked politicians, and anyone involved with NAFA or the Alphas. It was later discovered that the Action Figure Killer, was actually the former police commissioner, Alex Tillman.

During the reign of terror caused by AFK, the leader of the Alphas, Paul Douglass, sought vengeance against Gina Simms for publicly outing the illegal dealings of the Alphas, and wanted to funnel his money through Tiffany's community bank, the 10th Bank. Because of Tiffany's decision to stand up to Paul Douglass, Jamar was murdered by the Alpha lieutenant, Roland Wise. Tiffany Gibbons' home was also burned down by Roland Wise as a result of Tiffany standing up to Paul Douglass. The Alphas burned down several buildings in Ridgely Square, including the New Hope Greater Love Church under the order of Paul Douglass. During the night of chaos, Roland Wise and Paul Douglass were murdered by AFK. The FBI and Baltimore City police covered up the fact that AFK was Alex Tillman and pinned all of the AFK murders on Roland Wise and Paul Douglass. They feared that other criminals would be set free if news got out about the former police commissioner being a vigilante serial killer.

Now Tiffany Gibbons' saga continues. Welcome back to Ridgely Square. Welcome to *The Union*.

Chapter 1

It's a beautiful night on the beach area of our Jamaican resort. I can feel the perfect cool breeze of the wind as it gently greets my shoulders, neck, and chest area. The breeze slightly moves the white veil covering my face as I look at my soon-to-be husband Hakeem. Just to think about a destination wedding two years ago would be unheard of. The world was shut down, thanks to a global pandemic caused by the coronavirus. Then face masks and mandatory vaccinations allowed life to go back to semi-normalcy. I guess that's true if you look past the growing murder rate in Baltimore City, a government cover-up to protect a former police commissioner-turned-serial killer and a gang war that turned into a massive riot. We could get all into the weeds of the problems in Ridgely Square, but that would take away from this moment with my soon-to-be husband, Hakeem Andrews. He's standing in a white tuxedo, white shirt, and black bowtie. His brown skin and lean muscular frame are showcased well in the lighting from the gazebos and the overhead lighting. A destination wedding was a great idea; look at how he's glowing on this beach. Hakeem's hair is cut short, with a small amount of gray hair peeking through his beard.

The stars are bright and plentiful in the sky. The clouds and the moon appear perfectly placed by God himself. This is a sight I have never seen in the Baltimore sky. A Caribbean band is playing the guitar, and a steel drum provides the perfect accompaniment in the background. Three singers are harmonizing reggaeton renditions of neo-soul music, but it comes out muffled because of the low-quality speakers the microphones are plugged into.

I turn my attention slightly to see my sons, Darrin and RJ standing behind Hakeem's best man, Allen. Darrin, Allen and Hakeem are all six-foot-even. RJ stands about five-foot-eight. It amuses me that all my children are taller than me, as I stand at five-foot-six. Allen is the biggest person standing at the altar. His muscular arms are visible through the tuxedo jacket. This is actually the longest I have ever seen him go without unbuttoning a shirt or revealing his pectoral muscles. My eyes look back towards Hakeem as the preacher is speaking. I can't hear the words coming from his mouth. I hear the waves from the ocean crashing against the beach. I hear my aunt Gina and my best friend Sasha whispering between themselves as Hakeem's sister, Kesha, tells them to quiet down.

I can't hear the words from the overweight Jamaican preacher, nor can I hear the words of my bridal party, but I know they are saying something. I have lived this moment before. It was in January of this year. Why am I reliving an event? Why does it feel so real? I can smell the food in the background.

"You were so hungry that day," the voice of Marshawn Bell says to me. I can see him clearly in this dream. He's wearing a black suit with a black bulletproof vest overtop.

My maid of honor, Sasha, says, "We need to get back to the United States," as Hakeem moves the veil above my face. It is time for him to kiss the bride as we hear a commotion. The sounds from the ocean stop. The beautiful lighting changes to something dimmer. The beautiful smells from the food cooking change to the sour stench of the alleyway behind my home in Baltimore. People are running in all directions as the sound of gunfire disrupts what was left of the perfect night.

I notice Alex Tillman, the former Baltimore police commissioner, turned serial killer, loading a shotgun and pointing it toward Kesha. At the same time, Gina and Sasha run into Marshawn Bell, a six-foot-one, maybe six-foot-two plain clothes police officer wearing all black, and a bulletproof vest. Moments earlier he was wearing a black suit with a bulletproof vest. As Bell points a handgun at my aunt Gina he is shot by a familiar face, Paul Douglass. Something does not feel right. As Paul turns in my direction, Alex Tillman sneaks behind him and starts choking Paul until he falls lifelessly to the ground. Alex Tillman points a gun at me and fires but kills Jamar, Hakeem's brother in the process.

Wait, none of this is right, I think as an alarm clock goes off. I sit up in a panic and notice that the digital alarm clock next to the nightstand reads 12:34 am. The exact time my grandmother, Florence Simms died several years ago. Hakeem attempts to calm me as I think about the dream I just had. So many people from that dream died, and it felt too real. Hakeem and I were just married in January in Jamaica. I've witnessed many deaths throughout the years, including Marshawn Bell, Paul Douglass, and Hakeem's brother Jamar. As I gather my thoughts, I notice we're in my grandmother's home, well ... the house I inherited from my grandmother. I suddenly smell smoke, as fire engulfs the room. Oh no, not this again. I look to my side and notice Hakeem has vanished.

I run out of the room, followed by my twins, Desha and Darrin, along with my younger children RJ and Trinity. As I arrive at the door, a tall thin-framed African American male is pointing a gun at me. It's Roland

Wise, a lieutenant for the Alpha street gang. He was the right-hand man for Paul Douglass until the two were murdered by Alex Tillman, also known as the Action Figure Killer. Roland Wise fires the gun twice, missing me and striking the steps behind me. My son, Darrin, fires his gun once and kills Roland Wise. The smell of gunpowder and smoke fill the stairway as I attempt to rush to the door.

Darrin pushes me to the side, with a gun in his hand in a protective manner. He opens the door, pointing the pistol to the night sky as I hear a loud blast that knocks my oldest son to the floor. I notice Alex Tillman entering the home with a shotgun in his hand. The shotgun has a pistol grip and is entirely black. He turns towards me as I hear Trinity's loud screams.

"What is it you want out of marriage?" I hear a female's voice ask me. The voice seems familiar. Like the premarital counselor Hakeem and I worked with.

"I want to win. I want to win at life, marriage, and being a mom," I hear myself saying.

"You have millions that I gave to you. At what time do you really want to win?" I hear Marshawn Bell say as everything turns to a black silhouette. The silhouette doesn't have any distinguishable features, it is just a giant blotch of black, in different sizes and shapes.

I wake up again, this time in a smaller bedroom as Hakeem is sleeping. We're at Hakeem's home. Hakeem hates it when I call it *his* house because we are married. It doesn't feel like my house. My home was burned down four years ago when Roland Wise set it on fire with the goal of killing my family. I continue to hear the screams of Trinity as I run to the bedroom she shares with Desha. Trinity has experienced night terrors for the last four years since she was burned severely in her sleep as a result of the firebombing. I walk into the bedroom to find an angry Desha staring me down in disappointment with her fist clenched. Desha is standing over Trinity in a defensive position.

"She's not here," Marshawn Bell's voice says loudly as I awake again. This time for real. Desha and RJ went to the Billie Holiday Arts Camp for the summer. Trinity went into an intensive residential treatment program to help with her untreated trauma and night terrors.

I look at the clock and notice the time says 4:15 am, a time that Trinity normally wakes Hakeem and me with her night terrors. The house is blazing hot. Hakeem's window unit air conditioners stopped working again.

The kids and I moved into Hakeem's home shortly after the firebombing in 2019. We agreed to move back into my home after the rebuild, but the pandemic of 2020, along with a community reconstruction project led by Titan Industries, put our plans on hold.

Hakeem and I were married in January of this year in Jamaica. It was a beautiful destination, but living here in the Ridgely Square community has been a constant rehash of all the trauma I've endured since 2016.

"It's been longer than that if you want to be honest," the voice of Marshawn Bell says in my ear. He's taken up permanent residence in my head since he helped influence me to shoot and kill my father. Well, father isn't the right word for Darryl Gibbons. The sperm donor that had a hand in my creation was a longtime child molester and rapist. He turned me and my cousin Tina Simms into his victims. He infected my cousin Tina with HIV, and the trauma from the rape caused her to commit suicide by swallowing a bunch of my grandmother's pills. One day he broke into my home, don't know why and don't care to know. I sent him to his God. If there's forgiveness for a sinner, I hope he got it on the other side. I had nothing but trauma, anger, and fear, thanks to his deeds. There are always dreams of me killing my father, along with the murders of Jamar Andrews, Roland Wise, and Paul Douglass. I also dream about my son being shot and I can't go an hour without the voice of Marshawn Bell.

"Because you love me," Marshawn says in my ear.

I walk silently down the stairs into the living room, turning on the TV to a low volume. It's a replay of the news that was on yesterday. The police commissioner, Keith Mercer, a tall chubby, gray-haired, African American male, is standing at a podium with the Baltimore official seal displayed on the front. Standing next to Commissioner Keith Mercer is our mayor, Hugo Titan. Mayor Hugo is an average-height, heavy-set, bald man. He was a billionaire business tycoon from Baltimore that founded and operated Titan Industries. The same Titan Industries that was run by his adult twin children, Chanel and Chandler Titan. Also, the same Titan Industries where Erica Little is the chairwoman of the board and has a majority stake in ownership since Hugo stepped down to run for mayor in 2020. Mayor Hugo and Commissioner Mercer are talking to the local press and citizens of Baltimore City.

"We are proud to announce the arrest of Carson Jessup and members of the Right Hand of God Fellowship Church," Mayor Hugo says with his distinctive whiney voice. "This was of course accomplished using the Paul Douglass Law."

The Paul Douglass Law was an executive order Mayor Hugo put in place following his 2020 election into the position. The Paul Douglass Law allowed local law enforcement to gain access to doorbell cameras and surveillance footage from a central command station with the goal of apprehending a dangerous person or group that was endangering the community. This law was created with the hope that the city could stop the next Action Figure Killer without having as many casualties as the City of Baltimore previously suffered. As a result of the Paul Douglass Law, and its effectiveness in catching the remaining high-ranking Alpha gang members in Baltimore, a group of white supremacists, known as the Right Hand of God Fellowship Church, was discovered.

"We the people of Baltimore City have suffered through countless unsolved murders as a direct result of the Right Hand of God Fellowship Church, led by their false prophet pastor, Carson Jessup," Mayor Hugo continued. "It is a shame that this racist organization was allowed to operate in the name of religion and took so many African American lives. This group could have been stopped sooner. So many African Americans' lives could have been spared if previous administrations would have made the hard decision to actually protect this city by any means necessary, instead of playing politics. I would like to thank our fine citizens and our great police department for their efforts in apprehending these thugs. I would now like for our great police commissioner, Keith Mercer to have a word with you all."

Mayor Hugo steps aside as the police commissioner approaches the stand. He clearly is taller than our current mayor. Commissioner Mercer has great posture, and his presence exudes confidence. He's a well spoken man that was born and raised in the Parkville area of Baltimore County. He graduated from University of Baltimore with a bachelor's degree in criminal justice. When he was promoted to the commissioner position, Keith Mercer held a meeting with the mayor, the city council, the school board, local delegates, senators and stakeholders, about his plans to reduce crime in Baltimore City. Commissioner Mercer places a piece of paper on the podium as he is met by several flashes of lights from cameras.

"Thank you, Mayor Hugo, and thank you for supporting our brothers in blue with the technological and financial resources to catch such a dangerous group of criminals," Commissioner Mercer begins. "The Baltimore Police Department, along with a group of concerned citizens in the Ridgely Square Community known as the Knights, helped to bring this criminal terrorist organization down. Carson Jessup and his religious hate group, the Right Hand of God, have haunted and killed African American men without penalty for more than 12 years. The men they targeted were between the ages of 21 and 60 years old. Many of these victims of their pillage of terror were returning home from work, the grocery store, or doing housework. They were completely unaware that they were being hunted like deer or quail. I use the term hunted because that is the term Carson Jessup used. They game-hunted these African American men, with point systems based on age, where they were shot, and what they were wearing. Carson Jessup and his band of demonic evangelicals also took trophies from their victims, sometimes a clothing item, sometimes a piece of hair, and sometimes fingers or toes."

Commissioner Mercer pauses for a brief second to look at the mayor before continuing. "Carson Jessup has cooperated with the Baltimore City police in identifying the members of the Right Hand of God Fellowship Church that are not in police custody. Carson Jessup has also provided complete details about these individuals, including their actions and who they hunted."

"Has the Right Hand of God claimed responsibility for the murder of the teenage boys that were found strangled over the last few months at Leakin Park?" an African American woman in her late 60s asks from the back of the room. She is dark brown skinned, wearing a white and blue patterned dress. Her shiny hair is in an Afro with a white headband covering her forehead and going behind her ears. She's wearing a pair of glasses with thick white frames. Her name is Ms. Jean Pugh. Her grandson was murdered a few months ago and was one of the first identified victims of the person the community calls the Charm City Strangler. All of the victims associated with the Charm City Strangler so far have been African American males, appearing between the ages of 11 and 16 years old and found with a white sheet covering them in Leakin Park. Ms. Pugh began raising her grandson, Miles when her daughter died of cervical cancer in 2019.

Commissioner Mercer turns briefly towards the mayor again before looking at Ms. Pugh, the audience gathered, and the cameras. "While the case of these young children is a top priority, there hasn't been a clear connection to their murders and Carson Jessup. Mr. Jessup has been very clear with our detectives about his role in the multiple murders he and the Right Hand of God Fellowship Church committed. Mr. Jessup has adamantly denied having anything to do with the teenage children that were found strangled throughout the last few months. The Carson Jessup case is still an active investigation. The mayor and I have made this a high priority.”

“Will the Paul Douglass Law stay in effect to catch the Charm City Strangler?” Ms. Pugh asks as the mayor approaches the podium.

“At this time, no. We have tried to establish a connection with the FBI to come in and assist with this case. We also have the best detectives in the world working this case,” Mayor Hugo answers.

Outside of a row of houses, Ms. Pugh is standing next to a tall skinny African American male who is interviewing her. “My grandson was murdered and left covered under a bedsheet,” Ms. Pugh begins. “The mayor has refused to use the Paul Douglass Law to catch this serial killer but wanted to use it to catch the Alphas. The only reason he caught Carson Jessup and the Right Hand of God was by mistake. If those sick racists weren’t caught on camera during the investigation of the Alphas, they would still be game-hunting black people. The number of victims from the Charm City Strangler grows, and nobody is doing anything about it. Who is going to make sure my grandson Miles gets justice?”

Chapter 2

A few hours later, Mayor Hugo found himself in the community center Hakeem's brother Jamar used to run. Since the murder of Jamar, Minister Aleem Muhammad runs the center. Aleem also helps Hakeem run a private patrol group called the Knights. The Knights patrol the Ridgely Square Community, reducing crime, cleaning up trash, helping individuals purchase groceries, fixing items in houses, tutoring students, and walking children to and from school.

Mayor Hugo scans the room of concerned residents, seated behind a long table with a black tablecloth. The room is very chilly. The air is very much appreciated considering the hot June temperature outside. The lighting in the room is bright, but the expression on everyone's face is angry. To be fair, the last white man that was mayor of Baltimore City, Guy Dulaney, taxed the middle- and lower-class citizens, along with trashing the schools in the community. He became governor of Maryland for a brief period of time before having to step down because his name was associated with the Dulaney Crime Family. The crime family allegations didn't stop Guy Dulaney from creating newer taxes that impacted the black communities. Not that his decisions alone created the downfall of Ridgely Square. We've had our share of Black mayors, men and women, that taxed the poor and got involved with political corruption. A lot of the political corruption led to the arrival of the serial killer, the Action Figure Killer, and his vigilante time of terror in the city. Speaking of AFK, the City of Baltimore covered up his crimes, pinned them on Paul Douglass, and the real AFK hasn't been seen since.

"It's been three years since the riotous activity known as the Incident of 2019," Mayor Hugo begins. "Since that time, we've had a global pandemic called the coronavirus, also known as COVID-19. The pandemic changed life as we previously knew it, shutting down many businesses and causing a lot of people that had less to begin with, to struggle without anything at all. That being said, when life started to gain some sense of normalcy last year, we were able to notice a rise in levels of lead in many of the communities directly affected by the Incident of 2019. High traces of lead that traveled from homes and companies set on fire, was found in other homes and pieces of property. In addition to those high levels of lead being found in many of the homes in Ridgely Square, we found high levels of lead and asbestos in the water lines running through the majority of the city.

Truthfully speaking, the pipes in this city are critically outdated, and the Department of Health has informed me of critical levels of Legionella found in the water. This has caused an increase in people being admitted to the hospital from exposures caused by the most basic activities, such as using showers, using ice, or even washing their hands in their home."

Members in the crowd begin to gasp and talk amongst themselves as Hakeem and I look on in shock about this new revelation.

"Sadly, this has placed me in a position where I need to make a difficult decision. The first option is the City of Baltimore can absorb the expenses to fix all the pipes, but we would have to dramatically increase the taxes on our citizens. This would include more red-light camera tickets, more speeding camera tickets, higher bottle cap taxes for those that purchase beverages of any kind, increased junk food tax, increased alcohol tax, a restaurant tax that would include carry-outs, along with increasing water and property taxes. That would also scare away the businesses that I have spent countless hours trying to attract for our new financial district near the Inner Harbor. The second option is to outsource the water and sewage to a private vendor, which would cover the cost of the repairs for these pipes. My office is willing to draft a budget for an outside vendor to fix our outdated pipes and provide our residents with fresh water. Again, we do have homes with extremely high traces of lead that will be condemned and will require demolishing. The demolishing process requires a few steps to ensure public safety from further spread of lead."

"What is the name of the vendor you have in mind?" Hakeem questions with a booming tone.

"Titan Industries," Mayor Hugo answers, barely making eye contact with Hakeem. "They're my former company, I acknowledge that. I do not receive any financial kickbacks from making this referral. I do know the people in charge, and what their goals are to improve this city. The work would begin in the Ridgely Square Community. I would like Erica Little to share a few words with those in attendance."

The thin-framed, light-brown-skinned Erica Little approaches the podium. Her hair is light brown and flows straight back touching her shoulders. She's in her 50s but for some odd reason looks younger than the last time we met. I remember the conversation she and I had the day she brought my mother to the basketball court back in 2019. She was determined to purchase my grandmother's house, by any means necessary. I really can't stand Erica Little. It was because of her and Mayor Hugo's twin children, Chandler and Chanel Titan, that I was displaced and had to move into my mother's home. Titan Industries, led by Erica Little, Chanel, and Chandler Titan, purchased my apartment building and demolished it.

The only reason they were unsuccessful in the past with the community redevelopment process was Erica attempted to have a secret funeral for her child, born Simon Little but changed her name to Silk Diamond during her transition. Erica's transphobic handling of Silk's death was not received well by the citizens of Baltimore City, along with the city council. Silk was a radio personality for a period of time, but she slept with the owner of the radio station's husband and was terminated. Silk would soon become homeless, started sex working with my aunt, Gina Simms, and would later be murdered by my father, Daryl 'Cube' Gibbons. Erica and her now divorced husband, Sedrick Little, attempted to have a private funeral but that failed when my aunt Gina outed them to Hakeem Andrews, the man that would later become my husband.

"Good morning, everyone," Erica Little began, looking in my direction. There's always this weird energy between the two of us. I can't tell if she wants to fight or be friends.

"As many of you know, I'm Erica Little. I'm the current chief executive officer and chairman of the board for Titan Industries. Sadly, I've lost both of my children to the mean streets of the Ridgely Square Community. Years ago, I lost my youngest daughter Sabrina to a hit-and-run. In 2016 my second child was murdered while sex working. No parent should ever have to bury their child. This community has made that a sad but constant reality.

"My mission remains the same, to make Ridgely Square a better place. In the past, I was met with opposition from community leaders like Pastor Donald Avery and Florence Simms. After their untimely deaths in 2016, the 10th Bank Owner, Tiffany Andrews and her wonderful husband and community leader, Dr. Hakeem Andrews continued to meet Titan Industries with opposition. My prayer is on this challenge we can be on the same page."

Erica pauses for a brief moment to observe the faces of the members in attendance before glancing back in my direction. "Titan Industries is currently in the process of purchasing every home, school, and shopping center in the Ridgely Square Community. While this may seem a bit much to many people in attendance, this is a necessity. Titan Industries believes that we can retool and rebuild this community. The 2019 Incident created a series of challenges that this community cannot afford to handle. Ridgely Square has hundreds of dilapidated houses and high amounts of lead have spread throughout the whole community, not just on the outside of the homes, but in the drinking water. In good faith, I think it's criminal to overlook these problems. In the past, the 10th Bank, New Hope Greater Love Church, and the Masjid Allahu Mosque have met us in opposition. I dare to think that we can all work together to fix the challenges of this community and make this a better place to live."

"Why should we believe you?" Ms. Pugh questions from her seat in the front row. She's been oddly quiet up until this point. Normally she questions the mayor about the Charm City Strangler at any function.

Erica answers, "In 2016 the City of Baltimore lost two great community leaders, Pastor Donald Avery and Florence Simms. The community also went through the murder of a decorated police officer who was also a great high school football coach, Edward Carter. During that time, Baltimore City also had a series of riots due to public outrage following the deaths of Tyrone Clinton, a local high school football star, and his classmate Kannard Lyles-Bey. In 2017 a detective named Marshawn Bell, and a group of rogue police officers called the Narcotics and Firearms Taskforce raided the homes of drug dealers to sell to a local gang called the Alphas. This action created an increase in crime and sex trafficking. This action also led to an FBI investigation of the Narcotics and Firearms Taskforce, and a serial killer called the Action Figure Killer.

"While attempting to capture AFK, Baltimore Police learned of a group of racist religious fanatics called the Right Hand of God Fellowship Church, led by Carson Jessup. The group has been killing black hard-working people. It's time to overhaul this community and stop ringing the dinner bell for trouble in this neighborhood. I'm here to give a way out. A fresh start. I'm not the enemy here. The enemy is the Charm City Strangler, Paul Douglass also known as the AFK, and Marshawn Bell. Is fighting me on rebuilding this community worth your children's lives? I'm not just talking murder; I'm talking lead poisoning. You can't take a shower with this water. You can't purchase carryout food—they use this water too. This neighborhood should be condemned. I'm extending an olive branch with the hopes that you will help me help you."

"What do you plan to do?" I ask as everyone looks in my direction.

"First thing we plan to do is take out the outdated pipes and provide fresh water to the community. We are also ready to offer high-dollar payments to the homeowners, with the goal of demolishing the homes in Ridgely Square and getting rid of all of the lead," Erica answers as people in the room nod with the comfort from Erica's statements.

"Titan Industries does not want to do this alone, Mrs. Andrews, we want to work with the 10th Bank in this process if you let us," Erica mentions as I turn to Hakeem who does not acknowledge my glance.

"We can schedule a time to talk," I respond as the room erupts into a bunch of people yelling at me, questioning, "Why wait?"

"I have children!" A young woman seated behind me yells in my direction. "I can't afford for my children to have lead poisoning. My middle child already is special needs, and I can't afford the programs she needs. The 10th Bank can help. Work with Titan and fix this shit."

More people continue to yell as Erica quickly raises her right hand to calm everyone. "I hear your concerns," Erica interjects. "I want to hear all of your concerns. Please download and use the Titan Industries application. We can read your statements and concerns in real-time. We are going to work with Mrs. Tiffany Andrews and the 10th Bank to rebuild Baltimore. Our top priority is this water and lead crisis in Ridgely Square."

Chapter 3

Later that evening, Hakeem and I meet in a small classroom with Hakeem's cousin, Reverend Raymond Nesmith and Aleem Muhammad. Raymond Nesmith is an extremely tall stout, brown-skinned male with shoulder-length locs. Raymond could have been a basketball player, a professional wrestler, or a football player, but he's an elder at Hakeem's family church, Andrews Memorial. Andrews Memorial has been in Hakeem's family for three generations, previously pastored by Hakeem's father and grandfather. Hakeem's sister, Bishop Kesha Stokes currently pastors the church. Raymond is the adopted cousin of Hakeem and Kesha's aunt, Monica Nesmith.

Aleem Muhammad is a light brown skin, average-height male with a thick beard, and a black and red robe that reaches from his neck to his multi-colored socks. Aleem also has wavy hair and welcoming brown eyes. Aleem took over the mosque and the nearby/neighborhood community center after Jamar was murdered three years ago. Aleem wanted to continue the work Jamar and Hakeem started by privatizing a patrol unit in Ridgely Square. That privatized patrol unit is called the Knights.

"They found another 13-year-old boy strangled to death and placed under a white bedsheet in Leakin Park," Aleem says as Raymond glances at his phone.

Hakeem and I make brief eye contact as I question, "Do you think that this was another victim of the Charm City Strangler?"

"This is probably two different things," Raymond says in his deep booming voice. Even though he's speaking in a low tone, it fills the room. As everyone looks toward him, Raymond continues, "The kid they found today is a known gang member. He was a part of the gang known as the Alphas, who are now calling themselves the 2-5. They changed their name to the 2-5 following the FBI investigation that shut down their operations along with the dirty cops that were a part of the Narcotics and Firearms Taskforce. He was a street kid. If he hadn't been found today in the streets, they would have found him dead on someone's doorstep tomorrow."

"Is that appropriate?" I ask as Aleem shakes his head in disgust. Hakeem doesn't make a sound. He sits emotionless, lost in thought. Something that he constantly does. It started with the murder of his brother, Jamar, three years ago. Following the murder of his brother, my home and the New Hope Greater

Love Church were burned down. The church was burned down during the "Incident." The COVID-19 pandemic didn't help. Several of the members of the church died from the virus. Other members lost their jobs, homes, and apartments. Some of his members were married for decades and found themselves getting divorced.

Hakeem blamed himself, stating that he failed the church and Ridgely Square. He went to the gravesite of founding pastor and community leader Donald Avery daily. Kids in the community committed suicide, substance abuse began to rise, Hakeem took each incident/tragedy personally. When the vaccine was released and the world started to open back up, Hakeem appeared happy for a brief moment. We went to Jamaica for our wedding; I forgot how happy he used to be. His smile and the hope in his eyes. Then the Charm City Strangler started taking out the youth of Ridgely Square. Hakeem started to lose himself in his depression and guilt. Nobody blamed him, but he blamed himself. Daily calling himself a failure. Avoiding mirrors or reflections of himself. This is a person who has a master's degree in social work, a doctorate in Christian theology, and a Juris degree in law. He carries the weight of Baltimore City in his head constantly.

"He was a street kid," Raymond responds in an annoyed tone. He glances at his phone for a brief moment before continuing, "The parents need to take better care of their children. These are the same parents that allow their kids to sell pills. They let these kids harass every car at red lights to squeegee the windshields for money. These are the same parents that allow their kids to kill hard-working people. But instead of taking care of their responsibilities as parents, they blame people like the Action Figure Killer, The Narcotics and Firearms Taskforce, the Charm City Strangler, or even Carson Jessup."

"What do you suggest?" Hakeem questions in a direct tone.

"Focus on the hard-working people in Baltimore City," Raymond answers.

"We can't do that," Aleem answers as Raymond stands up, towering over everyone.

"Why not?" Raymond questions. "Because taking care of the lead and water crisis in Ridgely Square isn't enough? Because you guys are running a bank, and that's not enough?"

"No, because we made a commitment to this community," Aleem answers.

"No," Raymond responds quickly. "My cousins Jamar, Hakeem, Tiffany and Kesha made a commitment to the community. The churches and mosques in Ridgely Square made a commitment. You inherited leadership of the mosque and assumed the responsibility that Jamar aligned himself with. Of course, Jamar is dead. You can walk away. I have to run a church because Hakeem's sister, Kesha, is doing more work with the Flamingo Club and is distracted from the church. The same church that Hakeem ran from only to lead Pastor Donald Avery's small ministry. But when that church burned down and the members were scattered, Hakeem ran back to the church that he thought he was too good to be a part of."

"Raymond *enough*," Hakeem screams, standing up to his cousin. Raymond towers over Hakeem, but Hakeem does not appear intimidated.

"Take a deep breath, cousin," Raymond responds, barely above a whisper.

"I can't breathe; people in this community are dying, and you want to antagonize me for the life I live? The work I've done in this community?" Hakeem answers in an angry tone as Aleem stands up and attempts to get between the two. The tension in the room is thick and very uncomfortable.

"Can we get back to trying to problem-solve? People are depending on us for the betterment of the community," Aleem says in a warm and friendly tone.

"You're wasting time," Raymond quickly answers. "The city has real police officers, and you guys are doing double the work. Stopping professional police from doing their jobs. Kids are dying, you're looking for an answer, and it's not your responsibility. Run your mosques, your banks and community centers. Stop trying to do the police officer's job."

"We're helping," I answer as Raymond cuts his eyes toward me.

"Did any of you help Kannard Lyles-Bey? The high school kid that was spray painting "rest in peace" for his friend, Tyrone Clinton and was killed by a police officer responding to the call?" Raymond questions. "Oh, you helped his parents. You sued the city, and they received a beautiful settlement. Here's the problem, Hakeem... money didn't bring Kannard Lyles-Bey or Tyrone Clinton back. It didn't improve the community. The rec centers that Aleem and you run, they don't stop the gangs or the crime. The church you ran down—my apologies—allowed to get burned down, didn't do anything to help the community."

"Raymond, go home, you're not helping," I say as I hear Marshawn Bell's voice laugh loudly in the back of my mind.

"I agree," Aleem seconds. "We can't do anything fighting amongst ourselves."

"You're not accomplishing anything staying here," the voice of Marshawn Bell says in the back of my mind.

"Where's Kesha?" I ask Raymond, as he breaks his gaze from Hakeem. Kesha is Hakeem's sister and the bishop of Andrews Memorial. Kesha is also a member of the Flamingo Club, a group that openly operates as philanthropists who invest in several projects in the city. In private the Flamingo Club is a secret society that controls Baltimore City at every level.

"Who knows? She focuses on everything *but* the church and keeps me in the dark," Raymond answers.

"Thanks, Raymond," I say with a warm smile. Raymond genuinely means well but gets wrapped up in emotions. "Can we focus on a game plan?"

Aleem sits down as Hakeem and Raymond follow suit. "We need to have the Knights searching for clues. Talking to the residents and asking questions," Aleem states in a calm tone. "Kids are being killed by this

Charm City Strangler. We have a water crisis in the city. We can help with that."

"Maybe we should stay out of this whole Charm City Strangler business," Hakeem says in a low tone looking at the ground.

"Dude, what's up with you?" Raymond questions.

"His brother, your cousin Jamar, was murdered by a serial killer. Did you forget that?" I answer. "He has the right to grieve. While you and the rest of the Andrews family were in Africa or Asia on a mission trip, Hakeem and I had our lives threatened by Roland Wise and Paul Douglass. I had my home burned down. My daughter spent weeks in a burn unit and receiving physical therapy because of the house fire. Please understand, Hakeem has a lot on his mind."

"Then why is he here?" Raymond questions

"Because he actually gives a damn," Aleem answers.

"He didn't give a damn about Andrews Memorial when he left us to work with Pastor Avery at New Hope Greater Love Church," Raymond responds as he attempts to get himself comfortable in the chair.

"You know I left because Andrews Memorial preaches prosperity, and since my father was pastor, it was all about status and not really about helping people in the community." Hakeem rebuts, while rubbing his forehead with his right hand.

"Then why did you come crawling back?" Raymond questions.

"Because I wanted to bond with my family," Hakeem instantly responds. "It sucked watching my brother get buried in a hole. Do you know what that's like? Knowing that we all end up in a hole? That's it. Life over. All the arguments, disagreements, snickering, talking behind the back, rumors, and any other dumb divisive difference we have in life don't mean anything, because when you die, you can't get that time back. You just have a bunch of thoughts and wishes. For me, I wish I had more time with Jamar, to really fix the differences we had. Differences that were created by my father, because he was trying to keep a status and save face with Andrews Memorial."

"Can we not do this now?" I interject. "The 10th Bank is going to buy several pallets of bottled water. We are going to donate it to the Knights. The Knights are to give cases to each resident of Ridgely Square. While that's happening, the Knights can talk to the residents, ask questions about the Charm City Strangler, and let the residents know we're doing everything possible to solve the lead crisis without the homeowners having to sell their property to Titan."

"I like the idea of the 10th Bank buying fresh water for the residents," Aleem states as Hakeem and Raymond nod in agreement.

"I'm also going to close the restaurant side of Legacy of Florence until the water crisis has ended," I add. "In good faith, I can't run a restaurant without fresh water. The market side will remain open until we can figure things out."

"Legacy of Florence survived the COVID-19 pandemic, but you're letting a water crisis take you down?" Marshawn Bell's voice says in the back of my mind. It's sharp, aggressive, and unsettling. Normally his voice is more indulging. Of course, it antagonizes me at times, but this time it's more aggressive. "Maybe you should think about this a little more before making this decision," the voice continues.

"Let us know how we can support the restaurant or the staff," Aleem contributes as Hakeem gives a smile. It's not a smile of happiness, more of a person trying to show an emotion that doesn't know what emotion to give.

Chapter 4

The next afternoon Hakeem, Raymond, and I are met at a local Hibachi restaurant by his sister, Bishop Kesha Stokes and his aunt Monica Nesmith. Kesha is a tall, slim built medium brown skin woman. She has shoulder-length light brown colored locs. Kesha made her wealth as a financial advisor and accountant for several companies and local celebrities. Her father, Bishop Andrews, sent Kesha to college with the goal of her taking care of the financial end of the church, while Hakeem would take over the leadership role. Bishop Andrews hoped that his son, Hakeem, would take over Andrews Memorial and take the family spot in the Flamingo Club. As fate would have it, Kesha would step into the role of pastor of Andrews Memorial and financial broker of the Flamingo Club.

Why is this important? you may ask. Andrews Memorial has washed the dirty money of the Flamingo Club for years. In public, the Flamingo Club appears to be philanthropic and all about saving the city, but in private, they are controlling everything, including the drug trade. Kesha was forced into an arranged marriage, a common practice at Andrews Memorial. Her husband, Elder Patrick Stokes was murdered, along with Monica Nesmith's husband and Hakeem's parents on a mission trip. The details about their deaths have been spotty. What is fact is Kesha was placed in full leadership of Andrews Memorial, and she made her cousin, Raymond an elder to assist with the day-to-day business of the church while she ran her accounting firm and continued in her role with the Flamingo Club.

Monica Nesmith is Hakeem's and Kesha's aunt, Bishop Andrews's last surviving sibling. She stands a little over six feet tall, thick but not portly, with short silver-dyed hair. Monica and her deceased husband Kelly ran a motel called the Nesmith Inn. Monica also handles the finances of Andrews Memorial. Monica was not happy to learn that Hakeem chose to marry me instead of one of the women at Andrews Memorial. She believed that Hakeem sullied the good Andrews' name by marrying an unwed mother of 5. She has gone out of her way to talk down to me because I did not grow up in Andrews Memorial.

"You can order anything you like, I know the owner," Kesha says in a deep voice. She has very distinct mannerisms and speech patterns. She pronounces almost every letter in every word. She hardly ever shows emotion, unless she is preaching, which she hardly does. Hakeem has said several times before, 'She wasn't always like this.'

"How is Khin and the rest of the Flamingo Club doing?" Raymond questions as Monica and Hakeem turn to him like he just invited satan into the room.

"Khin is doing well," Kesha answers, unfazed by her cousin. "As you know, Hugo is the mayor. The other members are doing what they need to for the betterment of the city."

"Who are the other members of the Flamingo Club?" I ask as an eerie silence overtakes the restaurant.

"You already know Councilwoman Mya Rodriguez, Erica Little, Mayor Hugo, and me. The other members are Khin Lao, James DeLuca, and Neil Goldberg. No one you need to concern yourself about just yet," Kesha answers. The names sound familiar enough to me. James DeLuca's family migrated to America from Sicily, started a bakery and sold cooking oil. They have one of the largest bakery and oil companies in Maryland. DeLuca has invested his wealth in tech companies and has side ventures with Formula 1, FIFA, and Major League Baseball. Neil Goldberg owns the West Baltimore Hospital, Sinai Hospital and a few outpatient treatment centers. I don't know much about Khin Lao, except he owns several restaurants, and laundromats, along with beauty and hair stores.

"The Flamingo Club accepts the most prominent and influential families in Baltimore City, except for Mya. Councilwoman Mya Rodriguez was a strong advocate who wanted to make changes in the Arts District, and we thought it would be good to bring her into the public affairs side of the business. Well... Councilwoman Mya Rodriguez and Special Agent Parker of the FBI. Agent Parker was a no-brainer to add to the Flamingo Club. Agent Parker was covering the NAFA and Alpha cases, and we were watching them closely," Kesha continues as a young thin-framed Asian woman walks to our table to take our dinner orders.

Moments after the woman leaves our table, Kesha taps her right hand on the table as a fire ignites at the table behind us. The hibachi chef behind us was performing tricks for the guest at that table. The smell of grilled steak, lobster, and ginger, along with the sounds of laughter, fill the air of the restaurant.

"Hakeem, how are you and Tiffany adjusting to being at the church?" Kesha asks as Monica and Raymond look on quietly.

"It feels weird being back at Andrews Memorial," Hakeem answers. Monica and Raymond watch closely as Hakeem continues. "It's great being able to see members of the church I haven't seen since I was a teenager. I just don't know where I fit in. I've done outreach and community work for so long; I'm still not sure where I fit in with the church's mission."

"Your grandfather built Andrews Memorial," Monica chimes in. "He and your father pastored that church for decades. That church is your birthright. Whatever Pastor Avery filled your head with before he died was garbage. You're with family and friends. You have a really important place at Andrews Memorial."

"I've been trying to fit in, I just don't," Hakeem responds. "I tried to get some of the members from Now Hope Greater Love Church to join. They don't like the church."

"Have they said why they don't like the church?" Kesha asks almost immediately after Hakeem made his statement.

Monica, without a moment of hesitation, interjected her thoughts, "Probably because they're sinners. Those people at New Hope Greater Love Church were not Christians. They were not who God wanted to see build his kingdom and they don't have the discipline it takes to be a member of Andrews Memorial."

"They said the church seems like a cult," Hakeem responded to his aunt.

"A cult?" Monica counters sharply, turning her whole body towards Hakeem. "So, because we're a church that promotes greatness, wealth and doesn't allow anything to go on in our church like what you and Pastor Donald Avery did at New Hope Greater Love Church, we're a cult?"

"People have the right to their individual thoughts," Hakeem states as the chef begins placing fried rice on everyone's plate.

"That's a myth and satanic thinking," Monica counters. "God said that your ways are not my ways. You can't have a church full of disobedient sinners with their own thoughts of what God is, or what he said. Kesha and Raymond are prophets, if people don't want to hear what God himself tells them, they deserve to burn in the hell that is promised to them."

"Do you believe that people with independent thoughts and feelings are not of God?" I ask Monica as she shakes her head no.

"God wants disciples," Raymond contributes. "Disciples must have discipline and be willing to serve without individuality. God wants willing servants. The Andrews family was anointed by Christ himself to give his vision and save the world. Those that are not following after the vision Christ gave the Andrews family will face the wrath of God himself."

"What about the people all over the world that haven't gone to this church? Do they go to hell too?" I ask as Monica says yes without hesitation. "What about the people that died before Hakeem's father was able to minister to them, or before Kesha, Raymond or anybody else from Andrews Memorial were able to minister to them?"

"God saw each one of them as cursed to burn in the lake of fire for all eternity," Monica answers. "There's a reason why Christ has blessed this family, the ministry, and why we have been able to provide ministry all over the world. Hakeem, I wish you could turn your attention away from the murders in the cursed City of Baltimore and focus on the vision God blessed your grandfather with many years ago."

"God has blessed us with the ability to help the people of Baltimore," I blurt out as Monica angrily cuts her eyes toward me. I can feel the resentment she has toward me; it's unsettling. "We have a growing water crisis and a constantly increasing murder rate. Hakeem and I are trying to help the people of the city."

"Sodom and Gomorrah were burned by fire for not being of God, and that's exactly what's happening to Baltimore right now," Monica says with an authoritative voice. How many times will you two look at the burning city before you turn to salt or realize God has somewhere greater for you to go?"

"Are you trying to say that a city that our family has served and had a controlling stake in for years is cursed?" Hakeem questions. "Because if that's so, that means that our hands are dirty as well. Whatever I touch is blessed, believe that. God put me in this city to work, not work on some vision that a cult leader grandfather of mine had years ago. We have a water crisis, a lead problem, a growing murder rate, and a serial killer murdering children. It is our responsibility to use our ministry to serve and work."

"No it is not," Monica rebuts. "For all we know that serial killer is one of the racist members of that church, Right Hand of God. The water crisis is on the city; the same city that constantly allows sin to dictate the course of history Baltimore is going in. Hakeem, you, your wife, and her bastard children need to get in alignment with this ministry before you find yourself in the fast lane to hell like your brother."

"Excuse me, Ms. Monica, but you will not disrespect my children," I say angrily. I really want to punch her, and she's dismissive of my existence. This lady has a real problem with me and is comfortable with how she insults me.

"Relax," Monica says looking at Hakeem, never making eye contact with me. "The lady at the well was also a whore, and Jesus saved her from being stoned. The problem is—"

"Who are you calling a whore?" I yell as Monica continues to talk over me, unfazed by my voice.

"The problem is, the woman at the well knew her place. You need to learn yours," Monica concludes as the chef continues to place steak, shrimp, and lobster on her plate.

"Aunt Monica," Kesha says, glancing at her phone before placing it face down on the table. "Tiffany has done a great job advocating and working for the people of Baltimore. She has networked with local mosques, churches and black-owned businesses to open the 10th Bank. In addition to that, she opened the Legacy of Florence restaurant and grocery store. Her businesses survived the COVID-19 pandemic and have continued to provide fresh food to the residents of Ridgely

Square. She's also an outstanding mother of four beautiful children."

"I haven't seen them at the church," Monica grumbles while placing a forkful of food in her mouth. "We have vacation bible school and all kinds of programs going on, and not one of her four fatherless children are at the church."

"My Desha and RJ are at an arts summer camp. Trinity is doing a residential treatment to assist with her trauma and night terrors following the house fire we had in 2019. Darrin hates the church, and people like you are the reason why," I answer as I hear the voice of Marshawn Bell laugh in the back of my mind.

To my surprise, Hakeem and Raymond are both laughing at my statement, as Monica continues to not pay me any mind. "Kesha," I continue, "is it possible that the Flamingo Club can help with the water crisis?"

"I don't want to say no," Kesha answers as she picks up a sushi roll with chopsticks and dips it into soy sauce. "The Flamingo Club is currently working on a few projects. We're partnering with the West Baltimore Hospital to build a new wing to treat opioid addiction. The Flamingo Club is also doing a lot of work renovating theaters and historic homes in the arts district. We're also working to make the Financial District a real thing. Mayor Hugo has done a great job networking with companies and firms from Silicon Valley and Wall Street to Baltimore. One of the big reasons why Titan Industries wanted to flip Ridgely Square was because of the location and the positive impact this Financial District will have on the city."

Hakeem, who hasn't touched his food yet questions, "Why hasn't the Flamingo Club invested in any of the inner-city schools? I've seen what they've done in Canton, Catonsville, Federal Hill, Roland Park, and Towson. Why is it that they can't share those same resources with Cherry Hill, West Port, Mount Winans, Ridgely Square, Harlem Park, Rosemont or Curtis Bay?"

"You raise a good question," Kesha responds. "There's a plan in place. When the Flamingo Club agreed that having Hugo run for office and win was the right thing to do, we wanted to save Baltimore City from Baltimore City. Meaning Baltimore City started becoming an aggressive cancer and killing itself. Look at the Inner Harbor. By design, it's supposed to be a great tourist attraction. You have the football and baseball stadium, the casino, restaurants, hotels, and nice attractions in that area. What else do you see?"

"The homeless people," Raymond answers with a mouth full of food.

"Correct," Kesha affirms. "You have the homeless, panhandling youth, gang members, unruly youth, people driving stolen cars and dirt bikes, drug dealers, drug addicts…"

"Crime, crime, and more crime," Monica proclaims as if she just discovered the cure for cancer.

"That's correct," Kesha again affirms. "The Flamingo Club wants to correct that course of history. Hugo was the best person to put in place, and we knew how to change the course. Baltimore has a growing poverty gap, increased crime, and a ridiculous cost of living problem. What's the first thing you have to do? Change the culture of the city. You create opportunities to thrive. How do you create opportunities to thrive? You bring in thriving businesses and you have them seek employees that want a gainful career. Business owners want to be in Baltimore, they don't want to be associated with crime in Baltimore. They don't want the Baltimore element of crime, poverty, and danger. We have the tools to fix that all at the Flamingo Club. It's a process, but it's a successful process."

"The process should be the word of God," Raymond proclaims, his mouth stuffed with fried rice and mung bean sprouts.

"Raymond," Kesha says in a disappointed tone, still playing with the sushi roll in the soy sauce, "My brother Jamar once said, 'You can't get into the Promised Land until you kill the natives.' The Promised Land is the thriving city of Baltimore. We can pray and pray and pray for something to happen, and it might. Or we can use the tools that we already have and *make* something happen. I believe that God has given us the tools to make a difference. We are in a position with the right people, we have the right resources, and we are operating in the right time. The next step is all about executing the resources."

"I think you're making a mistake," Monica theorizes picking up her cup filled with water and a slice of lemon. "Baltimore is a city that God has cursed. You're wasting your time. I get that my brother, y'all's father, played with the good people of the Flamingo Club, but it comes a time when you know your place. That place is with the church. Not with the heathens of Baltimore, not with some socially elite group, not with some bank, and not with some market. We are living in the end times and you're damning your souls trying to save the damned."

Chapter 5

The next evening I found myself at Andrews Memorial. A large, beautiful cathedral that sits in a large parking lot. The cathedral started out as a tent when Hakeem's grandfather started the church as an outdoor ministry during the civil rights era. He would later purchase two rowhomes, renovate them and run the church from the inside. As time went on, the church evolved into a storefront church, then a small community church, and a few years ago this beautiful monument was built. In the church are different areas such as counseling centers, classrooms, a dining hall and office space.

Inside of one of the large rooms, I'm sitting in the back watching as my aunt Gina Simms completes a session with a substance abuse treatment group. Gina is a beautiful dark brown skin woman, in her late 50s. My aunt Gina has always had a beautiful figure and looks closer to her 20s than her 60s. As the meeting ends, many of the group members congregate, drink coffee, and present slips for my aunt to sign.

My aunt was placed in federal witness protection for 5 years because of her testimony in the Narcotics and Firearms Taskforce case. She had video and first-hand accounts of the illegal dealings of both the Narcotics and Firearms Taskforce, and the gang called the Alphas. Against the FBI's wishes, she came back home to participate in my destination wedding and spend time with me. Since returning home, Aunt Gina has worked for Nubian Media making podcasts, along with running an addiction support group at Andrews Memorial.

"How have you been?" Gina asks, picking up left-behind literature from the chairs and the floor. The Narcotics and Alcoholics Anonymous meetings have been packed since Gina started doing them at the church, but the visitors always leave the pamphlets. The younger members often leave trash, like napkins, carryout boxes, cups, and water bottles.

"I've been. I don't have anything to add behind the *been* part," I answer as Gina chuckles softly.

"I remember that part of marriage all too well," Gina reflects, walking over to spilled coffee on the wooden floor. "The honeymoon phase has ended, now the real work part of marriage starts. Sometimes you want to make him feel like a king, sometimes you're thinking about how to get off from a murder conviction because he didn't put the socks in the hamper. Those days can get rough because you're trying to keep your old habits while making him change the habits that you hate or didn't realize he has."

"How did you know—" I begin to ask as she cuts me off.

"I loved your uncle Larry, but the first two years of our marriage was rough," Gina proclaims as she throws some debris in the black trashcan next to the door. "We had different spending habits, eating habits, and perceptions of romance. Larry thought purchasing flowers or booking a grand vacation was romantic for me. I told him a thousand times, at least, my idea of romance is stuff like him cleaning the kitchen, cleaning the bathroom, folding the clothes I wash, fix the sink, or whatever needed fixing in the house. What did Larry do? Book a trip to Europe so we can vacation and watch a tennis match."

"Did things get better?" I ask. Gina nods yes.

"The first year to year and a half is rough," Gina says in a low tone before her eyes light up. The hope and excitement that just rushed across her face is inspiring. "But after that time passes, you two begin to learn about each other. Dating and living together are totally different from being married. There are compromises, adjustments and learning that happen when you're married. You're committed to building a culture or a legacy together. The honeymoon phase of marriage is beautiful. You want to take pictures everywhere, do anything in the world for him. But when two people become one person, that kind of 'you complete me' part of marriage begins; then you two are really one person. You don't get there by having sex. No, you get there by doing work. Taking care of each other's health, working together to pay bills, choosing your spouse over your family, and struggling financially because of a bad decision. That part of marriage happens, and it turns you into something beautiful, but you have to put the work in."

"How was it bonding with my grandmother before you started using drugs?" I ask as Gina gives a slight smirk. She pauses as if she's at a loss for words and begins picking up more of the trash on the floor.

"Good question," she answers, laughing to herself and walking back to the trashcan to dump the items in. "Your grandmother, Florence Simms, was actually kind to me. We got along well. She had a rule, not to get involved in our marriage and our business. That being said, she could see through me. When I started using drugs, she knew. Your grandfather, her husband, was a cop. He thought everyone was guilty of something. She was the same. When I came to the house high the first time, she knew. The eye contact she gave me made me melt on the inside. Your grandfather, Leon Sr, asked me to leave that day and get myself together. But to answer your question, before I started using, we got along together perfectly."

I begin to help Gina pick up items and clean up the floor as my mind drifts back to the Charm City Strangler and the current water crisis plaguing Ridgely Square. I hear Marshawn Bell's voice speaking in the back of my mind as Gina continues to talk about good memories she has of my grandparents, Uncle Larry, and Uncle Leon. As long as I can remember, Aunt Gina was the only person that would talk about Uncle Leon. It's like a big family secret what happened to him.

"You should do a fish fry and crab feast as a fundraiser for the water crisis," Marshawn's voice says clearly in my mind. "The Bradley Funeral Home owns a forum building near the county line. We can do it there or we can hold it in Harlem Park. The 10th Bank can supply bottled water, sodas, soft drinks, fried fish and crabs."

"That actually sounds like a good idea," I respond out loud catching Gina's attention.

"You good?" Gina asks in a concerned tone.

"I'm ok, just thinking about this water crisis and that Charm City Strangler," I answer. "I feel that the 10th Bank can help, just not sure how. I was thinking about doing a fish fry and crab feast at Harlem Park for a fundraiser."

"That sounds like a great idea. We can probably hire a DJ, get bouncy houses, and partner with the Ridgely Square Hospital to run health workshops. With all these kids affected by the water crisis and traumatized by the Charm City Strangler, we can turn this event into something big. I can talk to Ms. Clair of Nubian Media for sponsorships."

"Are you sure you want your aunt involved?" Marshawn asks in the back of my mind. "She just got out of witness protection for snitching on the Narcotics and Firearms Taskforce and the Alphas. There was a whole FBI investigation because of her. Is this the person you want working with you?"

"She's family," I answer out loud.

"Are you talking to me, Tiffany, or am I missing something?" Gina asks as Raymond Nesmith walks into the room. The room begins to feel unusually cold.

"Good evening, ladies," Raymond starts with his voice deeper than normal. He's dressed in his signature R.

Nesmith brand clothing. I think he created his clothing line because he couldn't find regular clothes to fit him. A lot of the members of the church wear his R. Nesmith brand clothing, and people in the community have begun wearing the clothing brand as well. He created his own factory to mass-produce his clothing and hired many members of the church. Hakeem told me stories in the past about Raymond and Monica hiring people from the homeless outreach to make the clothes in the factory.

"Sister Gina, I can't thank you enough for your help with running the addictions group," Raymond continues. "I wanted to invite you to join my private discipleship bible study group, the Inner Circle. It's a few members from the congregation. We meet a few times a week and dive into the word of Christ and explore how to expand the ministry in the community. We keep a lot of what we do private and confidential. Take some time to think and pray on it."

"That's amazing," I compliment. "Is there a way I can join the Discipleship bible study group?"

"No," Raymond says with a stiff tone. "We're an invitation-only bible study. You're doing a lot right now with your bank and with your husband. I encourage you to attend the open bible study that the church has for all of the members. Also, I noticed your children are not signed up for the summer bible school. I would like more commitment from you and your husband with this ministry if you're really going to be here. One of the first things your family can do is buy into the culture here and wear the clothing line that brings this church revenue."

"R. Nesmith Brand?" I question as Raymond nods in affirmation. He walks out of the room leaving Gina and me alone.

"He can't be serious, right?" I ask as Raymond walks up the hallway.

"Let me check out this bible study. Raymond Nesmith has been really nice to me since my return to Baltimore," Gina responds in a positive tone.

"I'm just saying—" I start as Gina stops me.

"It's church, Tiffany. It's not like it's the Alphas or the Narcotics and Firearms Taskforce. Let's just give things a chance here," Gina suggests as I shrug my shoulders.

Chapter 6

Two days later, Hakeem, my son Darrin and his friend Duck are sitting inside my 10th Bank office. It's barely noon, and it's burning hot outside. The air conditioning is working overtime to keep the temperature at a low 70 degrees. Hakeem, Darrin, and Duck are eating crab cakes, and drinking slushies from a local carryout. Hakeem is clearly in a funky mood about something, but he makes attempts to show excitement and life around my children. The last few nights we video-chatted with my other children. Desha and RJ are still away at their art camp. Trinity is still at her wilderness trauma program. He genuinely was happy to speak with all of them, catch up with them and listen to their stories during the video chat. Even with the craziness related to the Charm City Strangler, Hakeem tries to bond with Darrin and Duck. Darrin absolutely loves the time he spends with Hakeem.

Duck, born J'won Foote, has been Darrin's best friend since they started walking. They lived across the hall from each other when we all stayed in the apartment building years ago. To this day, they've been inseparable. In 2019, our home was firebombed by an Alpha lieutenant named Roland Wise, causing Trinity to be severely burned and have night terrors. Duck came to the hospital that night with blankets and pillows he stole from his home and slept on the floor.

"Do you guys have any input for this fundraiser, or will I have to put this fish fry and crab feast together myself?" I joke as the sounds of chewing and slurping from straws in large Styrofoam cups provide an unlikely response.

Chewing and slow head nodding continue for a few moments until Duck rubs his dark brown hands on his jean shorts as a method to clean his fingertips. Napkins are mere inches away from him on my stained wooden desk, but he chooses to rub his hands on his pants leg. Why? I glance at Darrin to make sure he doesn't follow suit, but he and Hakeem are enjoying their crab cakes too much to pay me any attention.

"Ms. Tiffany," Duck begins, "the crab feast and fish fry is a great idea. I think you're going to need a concert, though. Hear me out. My cousin is Kutter the Poet, and he's about to come off tour. He just won a Grammy Award for his song, "We're Going to Win." Everything he does gets attention from the news and the internet. His following is crazy. I can tell him about the fundraiser, and he'll come, especially since it's about this water crisis."

"Ma," Darrin finally opens his mouth to talk to me instead of eating, "Kutter the Poet is awesome, and he's all about giving back. He hired the guy Jawan from the barber shop to travel with him and cut his hair."

"How much do you think he'll charge, because as of right now, the 10th Bank is paying for everything?" I ask as Duck shakes his head.

"Ms. Tiffany, my cousin ain't gonna charge you nothing. His label would be glad to do something like this for more publicity," Duck answers. "I'll call him in a few minutes."

"Can you tell him we're doing it at Harlem Park?" I ask as Duck nods in agreement.

"Are you sure the mayor will grant us the permits?" Hakeem asks, finally breaking his silence. I swear to God, this guy has been all over the place emotionally for the last few years. He's sad, he's happy, he's a great father figure, a great husband, and then he's depressed. I wish he would do for himself what he's done for so many other people and get help. His brother, Jamar, was murdered by Roland Wise and Paul Douglass back in 2019. A lot of his behavior is related to the grief over the loss of his brother, but I need him present with me handling business. I'm not trying to push him too hard because he also learned that his parents and uncle were murdered during a church mission trip, and the details are sketchy.

"I'm working on that. The mayor wants to meet with me about the fundraiser," I respond. "He's supposed to be here today to talk about it."

"The mayor? Like Mayor Hugo Titan is coming here today to meet with you about the crab feast and fish fry, Ms. Tiffany?" Duck asks with excitement. "That's huge. You created a buzz. When you tell him that Kutter the Poet is going to perform, that's going to make this whole thing go viral on the internet. You should probably call this something. Like the 10th Bank Block Party. Something that people will support and come out and enjoy themselves. It's kind of crazy that *you're* doing all this work to fix the water problem in Ridgely Square and not Mayor Hugo."

"The mayor's trying his best, I'm sure," I respond with a cheerful smile. Duck is a charming young man with a playful spirit, so I can't help but play along. "He's trying to solve the water crisis, the Charm City Strangler, debt challenges, employment opportunities, homelessness and so many more things. It's only fair that we try to help our own community without relying on the government."

"You're starting to sound like Jamar," Hakeem mutters while chewing his crab cake.

"We both agree that Jamar wasn't wrong," I jab back in a low tone as we catch each other's eyes. "The 10th Bank and the Knights were both great ideas that you and Jamar put together after you were shot by Milk."

"I haven't forgotten," Hakeem says in a grumpy voice. "And it's because of this bank he's dead. I wish I hadn't listened to him. Roland Wise and Paul Douglass didn't waste any time trying to put their dirty money in this bank, and they killed him for standing up to them."

"This isn't the place for that conversation," I reply, glancing at Duck and Darrin.

"It's all good, Mom," Darrin says, closing his Styrofoam tray, and nudging Duck with his elbow prior to standing up. Duck quickly follows suit and takes a sip of his drink before he stands up with Darrin and they walk towards the door.

"Stay off them corners," Hakeem says in a warm-hearted tone. "Until we catch this Charm City Strangler, I don't want y'all hanging by that strip of houses you normally be at."

"Yes sir," Darrin says respectfully. As my son opens the office door, he's met eye to eye with Kesha and Mayor Hugo.

"Ayo, that's the mayor!" Duck screams in an excited tone.

"Nice to meet you. What's your name?" Mayor Hugo asks, attempting to shake Duck's hand.

"J'won Foote, but everybody calls me Duck," he answers, shaking the mayor's hand with excitement. "You started the radiology training program at my high school. I'm doing the X-Ray training classes. I can't thank you enough. I'm about to make some real money when I graduate high school. I think I'm going to do the MRI training too."

"Make sure you follow me on social media, Duck, and keep me posted on your progress. After you finish, I'll write you a letter of recommendation to get a job at the West Baltimore Hospital or University of Maryland Medical Center," Mayor Hugo says as Duck and Darrin leave the office with huge smiles on their faces.

Without any hesitation, Mayor Hugo shakes Hakeem's and my hand, and sits down in front of my desk. Kesha sits down next to her brother, Hakeem. The smell of the crab cakes still lingers in the office. Mayor Hugo glances behind him as the door closes. His facial expression changes from excitement to a stern grimace.

"Kesha tells me you've been planning a fundraiser to deal with the water crisis," Mayor Hugo begins. "I was really hoping we could have met and discussed this together instead of you going behind my back."

"Excuse me, Mayor Hugo," I reply without hesitation. "Your company, now run by Erica Little and your children has been planning to take the homes of the citizens of Ridgely Square for almost a decade. Titan Industries' answer to this water crisis is to take the homes of the homeowners of Ridgely Square before fixing the water pipes. We are coming out of the COVID-19 pandemic, people have lost jobs, family members and their normal way of life. Individuals have fallen behind on bills, and taxes, and the city has raised the water bills, property tax, the gas and electricity costs. If this can help my neighbors, my friends and my people, this is what I'm going to do."

"Mrs. Andrews, my goal is not to force the people of Ridgely Square or anywhere in Baltimore City out of their homes," Mayor Hugo counters. "My goal is to bring Baltimore City back to the forefront of great American cities. This city can be a tourist destination, it can be a place where people want to work. I've created a financial district, bringing in Fortune 500 businesses. I want those employees to live in this city, not in Baltimore County, Arundel County, Prince Georges County or Carroll County. Ridgely Square, Harlem Park, Cherry Hill, West Port and Mt. Winans are in a prime area for employees to live and migrate to downtown Baltimore City to work. This work isn't cheap. I've tried to earmark dollars from City Hall to fix this water crisis; do you know what I've run into?"

"What?" Hakeem asks, looking the mayor directly in his eyes with frustration.

"A bunch of resistance from department heads," the mayor answers. "Do you know how many Baltimore City homeowners are behind in their taxes? Let me remind you, the water bill is also counted as property tax in this city. I've seen historic monuments, like African American churches that were built during the Jim Crow Era become city property due to outrageous water bills. Dr. Andrews, you are very familiar with the problems that Pastor Donald Avery was facing while he battled with cancer."

"What's your point?" Hakeem questions.

"My point is, if people can't afford the property, they're living in and will lose it regardless, why not give them a respectable way out, while fixing the city's problems," Mayor Hugo answers.

"One of the goals of the 10th Bank is to prevent that from happening, while providing education and direction to the homeowners," I state. "If the 10th Bank can raise enough money to pay for the water crisis in Ridgely Square and other areas, we will."

"I'm not going to stop you," Mayor Hugo interjects to my surprise "but I want to point out the uphill battle you're facing. Areas like East Monument, Palasky, Green Mount East, Rosemont, Sandtown, Pigtown and Latrobe will need the same attention. If you work on Ridgely Square, Harlem Park, Cherry Hill and Westport, will the 10th Bank survive lawsuits from the communities that did not receive funding to fix their water problems? If the Flamingo Club removes their dollars from the 10th Bank, how much help can the 10th Bank be to the community?"

"Is that a threat?" I ask, about to stand up from my chair. I feel rage running through me. I hear Marshawn's voice screaming in my ear for me to hit Mayor Hugo.

"No," Mayor Hugo responds calmly. "This is the challenge that I've run into. Areas like Canton, Mt.

Vernon, Station North and the northern parts of Park Heights have tax-paying citizens, almost at 88%. That's why I've been able to justify their recent work fixing the water crisis in those areas. I really want to work with both of you. For generations the Andrews family, in partnership with the Andrews Memorial church, have been an important part of the Flamingo Club. Hakeem, your sister Kesha thinks this fundraiser is a great idea. You have my blessing as mayor. You also have the Flamingo Club in your corner. Dr. and Mrs. Andrews, I really want to offer you both a seat at the table of the Flamingo Club. You're doing the philanthropy that the Flamingo Club prides itself on."

"What if we say no?" Hakeem questions.

"Why would you?" Mayor Hugo asks looking at Kesha. "The Flamingo Club's money flows through this bank. Your goal is to improve the black community. Our goal is to improve Baltimore City. Both can exist in the same world, am I correct?"

"My wife and I will talk about it before making a decision," Hakeem responds as Kesha slightly turns toward him.

"I just want to be clear," I reiterate. "We're having this fundraiser; Ridgely Square Medical Center will be one of our sponsors, and Nubian Media has agreed to partner."

"I'm not going to stop you, but I want to point out that West Baltimore Hospital should be involved," Mayor Hugo counters in a relaxed tone.

"No." I sternly reject his suggestion. "The West Baltimore Hospital has profited and taken from Baltimore City for decades. The synthetic opiates they were testing for pain management created a huge uptick in substance abuse in Ridgely Square since 2016. They opened their substance abuse clinics in our neighborhoods, which created more traffic for drug dealers and panhandlers in the community. Their surgeons have been called out on numerous occasions for unethical medical procedures, without penalties. That's just the tip of the iceberg."

"Maybe you should take your concerns up with Neil Goldberg, the CEO of the West Baltimore Hospital," Mayor Hugo suggests with a slight smile.

"I couldn't care less; my answer is still no," I counter, leaning back in my seat.

"That's fine," Mayor Hugo returns. He stands up looking at Kesha still seated and takes a brief glance around my office at my degrees, family pictures then looks back at me. "Will 2 weeks be enough time for you to put together this event?"

"If that's the best you can offer, we can make it work," I retort as the mayor nods in my direction and leaves the office.

Chapter 7

Later that evening I found myself sitting on a rear pew in the balcony area of Andrews Memorial. The pews are cushioned and have a royal purple hue, with shiny stained wood outlining the tops and sides. Standing in the pulpit area is Raymond Nesmith. Seated behind him to the left is Hakeem's sister, Bishop Kesha Stokes, and his aunt Monica Nesmith. It's an open bible study for the church's congregation. Kesha thought it would be a great idea for me to talk to the congregation about the upcoming crab feast and fish fry toward the close of the service. Raymond is talking about the importance of being prosperous in Christ as a young woman ushers an elderly dark-skin woman using a walker near the front of the church to be seated.

"Hey!" Raymond says, screaming into the microphone and pointing at the usher. "Sister Robin! Take Mother Helen to another section. She's not to sit in the VIP section. Only very important members, such as politicians, athletes, music artists, actors or tier 1 tithers are allowed to sit in the VIP section. Mother Helen is a tier 5 tither!"

"I'm sorry, Elder Nesmith," the elderly woman with a large bald spot on her scalp says, barely upright on her walker. "I would love to give more to the church, but I'm on a fixed income because of my disabilities."

"Mother Helen, God loves you no matter what," Raymond responds. "But this is a church of structure. The house of God can't be run any kind of way. And let's not forget, our bodies are temples of the Lord. I'm going to need 100% participation from everyone in this ministry on purchasing our seven-day premade meals. If we're going to live holy, we have to look holy and eat holy. Walking around Baltimore City with high blood pressure, diabetes and a gut will not get you in the kingdom. Not when we have the provisions in place to have an appropriate place for God to dwell within.

"Which brings me back to today's lesson. God wants his people to be prosperous, great, and wealthy. For instance, look at my cousins, Dr. Hakeem Andrews and his beautiful wife, Tiffany Andrews. They run the 10th Bank, a bank designed to start and grow companies in Baltimore. One day the 10th Bank will grow Black owned companies throughout the United States. I'm the prophet of this house, and I see it in the spirit realm."

Raymond pauses for a second as several members of the packed large cathedral begin clapping. I sit in awe of the gold and purple throne-like chairs in the pulpit, along with the stained windows. The band area to Raymond's right is fully staffed. Before my son RJ went away to art camp, he asked about playing the keyboard every Sunday.

"You know why the Dr. and Tiffany Andrews are successful?" Raymond questions as silence fills the congregation. None of the members are allowed to speak or answer questions during the open bible studies at the church. Raymond, Kesha and Monica are the only people with microphones during the bible study services. Raymond also has a private bible study group that is invitation only that he runs with Monica, called Inner Circle.

"The Andrews family is successful because the anointing flows from God to that family. It has flowed for generations through the blood of Hakeem Andrews. His grandfather, his father and now Hakeem has the anointing of God. The same blessing and favor that Abraham, Moses, Daniel, David and Jesus had. That's why the 10th Bank has become successful. God has seen fit for the Andrews Family to be a living testament of his grace and greatness. That grace and anointing flows in the members of the church that humble themselves and serve this mission. How? you may ask. Service, giving, and not questioning the leadership that God has given you."

As several members nod in agreement, I question Raymond's words. Kesha looks on stoically, almost dissociated from Raymond and the church. "As a church, we don't need members, we need partners," Raymond decrees. "We have so many entrepreneurs and leaders. Together, along with the loyal and faithful efforts of the partners of this church, we have served people in need in Africa, South America and Asia. We own private jets, and our outreach ministry travels to different countries, serving and providing services to thousands of people in need, without asking for a dime from outsiders. We have thrived while other churches in this city have struggled, suffered and failed. Why have we become successful? The anointing, the oil that flows from the Andrews family is why. My mother, Monica has that anointing in her veins, my cousin, Bishop Kesha Stokes has that anointing and Dr. Andrews has that anointing. And it flows to you all, but you have to be in the will of God to receive it. How do you get in the will of God? By following after the prophets of this church: Bishop Stokes, my mother and me. You know what happens when you don't follow after the will of God?"

The church grows quiet, members look on patiently as I roll my eyes. I hate being here. I hate the fact that Hakeem came to his family's church. He left after our church was burned down during the incident of 2019. He really wanted to bond with his sister, Kesha, especially after the murder of their brother, Jamar. I don't know how much longer I can stomach this place.

"I had a cousin," Raymond says, changing his tone to a very sober one. "His name was Jamar. He was the son of the late Bishop Andrews. The brother of Hakeem Andrews. He went against the will of Bishop Andrews, selling drugs and running the streets of Baltimore. He turned his back on the prophet of this house, and on God. He was locked up several times. God gave him opportunities to come back. Jamar spat in God's face and changed his religion to Islam. God punished him by taking his life. My other cousin, Dr. Hakeem Andrews left this house of God. Turned his back on his father, Bishop Andrews, and pastored the New Hope Greater Love Church. God gave my cousin a wakeup call, by burning the church down during the riots. My cousin, his wife and her family are here now. They now run a very successful enterprise, that enterprise is the 10th Bank. Who wouldn't want to serve the God of a second chance?"

Members of the church begin to clap, and I want to shoot Raymond the same way I did my father back in 2017. Jamar was a great person who was gunned down in the middle of the Old Market Place area for doing what's right. If that was God's will, or God's wrath, I want nothing to do with it. It doesn't sit right with me that God would have a specific family chosen to run and lead people, while others are just meant to be followers of this family.

"Even now the Andrews family has provided opportunities in the midst of a water crisis," Raymond continues to spew this rhetoric. "Even now, God has led Dr. Andrews's beautiful wife, Tiffany, to own and operate a grocery store and restaurant called The Legacy of Florence, that has hired members of this church. The leaders and entrepreneurs of this church should hire those seeking employment. We should be building wealth within the walls of this church. Tithing in this church, not making excuses. Mother Helen, I love you, but your disability doesn't mean you can't press harder. You should be able to get a job as a bagger, or a greeter at Legacy of Florence. You should promote the R. Nesmith Brand to others. There's always room to do more. Bring yourself closer to the VIP section, not by handouts, but by hard works. You work hard by being in the will of God. The easy way out is the work of satan himself."

Monica begins to stand and clap her hands loudly, praising Raymond. Other members of the congregation begin to follow suit. "Nobody wants to see a Christian struggle," Raymond says, changing the tone of his voice to a more animated tone. Almost like a coach trying to motivate the team to win a big game. "God wants us to walk on water, not stay in the boat. Who's ready to walk on water?"

Members of the church collectively begin to clap and stand to their feet, some smiling, some crying, some hugging one another. I'm still seated, looking on and questioning, *What the hell am I watching*?

"Brother Aaron opened an autobody shop and put the church down as the co-owner of the company," Raymond says pointing to a very dark brown skinned bald-headed man. "Within a few months, his business had to open three more shops in Baltimore City. The next year he met Sister Kamilah at the church. Within 4 months they were married in this building. Three days ago, Sister Nadine helped them close on their first house. That's what this house of God does. It flows in the anointing. We have the resources in this house."

The band begins to play music in the background as members cry and scream in praise. Members are clapping their hands loudly, some are running around the church, while others have passed out on the floor. "Stop the music for a second," Raymond says, extending his right hand towards the church, the left hand holding the microphone firmly near his mouth.

"I want everyone in this church to bring their paystubs next week to bible study," Raymond demands in a soothing tone. "If you receive disability income like Mother Helen, bring your award letter from the Social Security Administration. I don't want you to miss this blessing from God. As the prophet of this house, I want to guide you all on how to walk on water. If you own a business, bring your documentation, if you own a home, bring your lease. Next week, I want to teach everyone here how to walk on water. The City of Baltimore may have a water crisis, but the members of this church are above that because we are operating above them. We are in the will of God. I proclaim victory over the evils of this city. I can proclaim it because we are the anointed church!"

"Can we leave?" Marshawn's voice asks in the back of my mind as the music begins to pump loudly. People begin to clap and sing as a group of people approach the pulpit area leading the members in song. As I walk towards the door, I'm met by the familiar face of Erica Little standing at the door.

Chapter 8

After the open bible study, I find myself with Kesha in her office, joined by Erica Little. Kesha appears livelier in her office than she did in the pulpit during the service. The more I think about it, she never looks comfortable at the church. I get it, she was thrust into the leadership role at the church by Bishop Andrews, Hakeem, Jamar and Kesha's father. Kesha was forced to handle the financial books for Andrews Memorial and the Flamingo Club. It didn't help that Hakeem left Andrews Memorial and worked with Pastor Donald Avery at the New Hope Greater Love Church. Historically, the men ran Andrews Memorial, and Kesha being in leadership was a hard sell, so Bishop Andrews had his adopted nephew, Raymond Nesmith, work as an elder. Raymond's role has been to lead the bible studies, the church sermons, and oversee the actual day-to-day of the church. Kesha's role has been more of a bridge between the church and the Flamingo Club.

"I'm glad to see you've taken a vested interest in Andrews Memorial," Erica says, sitting in the leather office chair. She has perfect posture and the world's most annoying face. My first interaction with Erica was back in 2016 when she purchased my apartment building, displacing my family and so many other people. Since then, she's attempted to purchase all of the property in Ridgely Square for Titan Industries' community reconstruction project.

"You do what you have to do for family," I respond staring her down, looking for a point of weakness in this old broad's face. If I could just get her to blink or look away, I'd take that as a moral victory. Or I could just slap this whore.

"I keep feeling like we're on the wrong side of things," Erica theorizes. "The reconstruction project is for the betterment of Baltimore City. Since the Ridgely Square Incident, Titan Industries has worked tirelessly to rebuild the community, and we have tried to work in concert with the 10th Bank. Now that we have the water crisis, I believe we can help each other."

"I completely agree," Kesha chimes in. "Erica and her ex-husband Sedrick have been long time members of the Flamingo Club. There's a lot of hope that you will join in the efforts to improve this city. Your goal to help pay for the new water lines in the city is great. You're doing the community block party fundraiser the church is on board with supporting. The Flamingo Club is on board with supporting. We want to be honest in this whole process; there's no guarantee that you're going to raise enough to accomplish your goal. Many of these homes will fall to Titan Industries. Many of these residents are behind on their taxes. Many of these homes are unsalvageable."

"We have to try to do something," I plead. "That's my goal."

"You're doing great," Erica assures. "But what happens when you don't have 100% buy in? What happens when you don't receive 50% buy in? This is the challenge with this whole water crisis problem. Titan Industries isn't in the business of wasting money, and neither is the Flamingo Club. From what I've learned about you, the 10th Bank doesn't waste money either. So we're at a fork in the road. How can we help each other?"

"Stay out my way," I answer without thought. Yet, Erica does make a lot of sense.

"I'm not in your way," Erica returns. Her face has no expression. No signs of anger, resentment. She isn't annoyed by me. It's like I really don't matter in her world. "The community reconstruction project will happen. The mayor has goals for this city, and many of those goals are to improve the crime rate, the poverty level and improve economic value. The reconstruction project is a piece of that pie. Currently the mayor has started construction on an indoor water park in the Inner Harbor area. It's going to be one of many new tourist attractions the mayor has been working on. You know the problem with doing the indoor water park right now? Our water is poisonous."

"That is ironic," Marshawn says in the back of my mind, causing me to chuckle out loud.

"Titan has contracts to do the construction in many areas in the city," Erica says, pulling out an iPad Pro from her purse and showing me a map of the city. Many of the areas are highlighted. "Have you heard of the Black Butterfly?" Erica asks as I nod my head yes. "Then you understand the segregated areas shaded in black look like a butterfly. Those areas will become part of the reconstruction project of Titan at some point. Those areas are also facing a health crisis in conjunction with the water crisis. The children are exposed to multiple health challenges, thanks to the high toxicity level of our water due to the lead and asbestos contamination."

"I understand all of that, Erica. My question is at what point are we supposed to join forces?" I directly ask.

"Let's say you're successful with your fundraiser," Erica begins to explain. "Let's say the Harlem Park, West Port, Cherry Hill, Green Mount, and Gwyn Falls communities are helped by your efforts to pay for the new pipes and plumbing. What helps the people rise above the challenges they already face? How do they get out of the poverty? How do they live longer, eat better, get out of the food deserts, avoid becoming a murder victim? Murder, assault, and robbery are constantly on the rise. What's the headline of the day? "The Charm City Strangler has murdered another squeegee kid working in a West Baltimore City community and dumped his body at Leakin Park." How do your efforts stop that?"

"We're trying," I sheepishly say. This well put together businesswoman has beat me at my own game. The thing I've been trying to do, help this city, may be hurting the city in the long run.

"Let's work together, Tiffany," Erica says. "I don't want you to stop helping the Black people of Baltimore City. Hell, I don't want you to stop trying to help the people trying to keep their homes. What I do want you to do is pause from trying to block me in the process and look at what I'm trying to do. You closed the Legacy of Florence restaurant because you couldn't serve that food with poisonous water. You kept the grocery store open because you know the community needs healthy answers for the food desert that is Ridgely Square. We need that kind of thinking. What is in the best interest of the people that will live here?"

"What are the people that will live here going to do when you're done?" I ask.

"People like the members of this church," Erica responds. "People like you and Hakeem. People like the folks in the Arts District. People who are building Baltimore to a brighter future. We have to phase out the problems. That doesn't mean phase out the poor, just the problems."

"What are the problems?" Kesha finally opens her mouth and asks.

"The drug dealers," Erica answers. "The murderers. Have you been at a red light in Baltimore City? People just run them. Have you seen car accidents in the city? People just hit and then run. The high school dropout rate is astronomical. That has to be concerning to you. The mayor partnered with the West Baltimore Hospital and created programs that train high school students in radiology and IT to give these kids a fighting chance at life. What's the problem, though?"

"The kids leave the school and go back to the same environment," Kesha says in a low tone.

"Exactly," Erica affirms. "You have to rid the cities of the problem. The planned communities work. We've done them in other cities. We've posted peer reviewed studies about this. Is it the politically correct left- or right-wing answer you like to hear? No. But it's the answer that's needed to fix this city. The Flamingo Club has a mission: to save this city by any means necessary. You've been trying to save this city with the bank, and it's commendable. The problem is, it's not enough. Not by yourself."

"I have to try," I return. I have nothing else to say. I feel defeated, deflated and like I've been failing the people I tried to help. Maybe I'm in over my head. I should have stopped at running the restaurant and the market. Why did I let Hakeem and Jamar talk me into running this bank?

"There's an easy way, and a hard way," Erica says, showing me an image on the IPad of the Black Butterfly on the Baltimore City Map. She scrolls down the screen to several research articles. "I would love to work with you and make this easier. Think of your children and their friends. Everyone doesn't have a Florence Simms to bail them out when life hits them hard. But they can have a Tiffany Andrews. They can have a 10th Bank. They can have a Mayor Hugo. They can have the Flamingo Club. Together, this city can be greater than it was. Do the fundraiser, see what you can raise. It would be a great way to see how much community buy-in you have invested in this vision you're trying to bring to life."

"I think we're going to have a good amount of vested interest," I say with a smirk. I finally have an ace up my sleeve. "Kutter the Poet confirmed a couple hours ago that he will perform at the community block party. He's actually going to take a break from his tour and be at the event. That alone will generate donations."

Just like that, Erica displays some emotion. She rolls her eyes and shakes her head in disgust. Without saying a word, she opens an article from Johns Hopkins about youth diagnosed with cancer, and the link to the total Trihalomethanes. Total Trihalomethanes is cancer-causing chemicals that have a relation to chlorination in water.

"I want you to understand what and who you're fighting for when you're fighting Titan Industries," Erica suggests, handing me the large iPad while standing up. "That's a gift from Titan Industries," Erica says, walking out the office leaving the iPad in my hands.

"Am I wrong?" I ask Kesha as she looks at me silently. I can't read her facial expression.

"I think you should think about the route you take with the 10th Bank," Kesha answers. "The Flamingo Club does a lot of community work, and their goal is truly to improve this city. The thing you need to think about is do their goals align with yours. The other thing you need to think about is if your goal is really being served the way you're going about things."

"Am I wrong for doing this fundraiser?" I ask Kesha, who shrugs her shoulders.

"No, but maybe you need to think this whole water crisis through," Kesha responds. "I want you to work with the mayor and with Titan to see where everyone can fit into this because people are dying. Mayor Hugo doesn't want that on his conscience; Erica Little doesn't want that on her conscience, and I don't believe you want that on yours."

Chapter 9

I'm walking through Leakin Park under a dark sky. Oddly, the light pollution from the rest of the city fails to break through tall trees. The park is filled with litter, a broken tricycle here, a beat-up bedroom dresser there. The smell of decay, and feces fill the air. Not just any air, an air that just sits, and dwells in the park.

Leakin Park was nicknamed Baltimore's Largest Outdoor Cemetery because of how many bodies have been found here throughout the years. More than 90 bodies have been found in this large public park. It is believed that more than 100 bodies are currently undiscovered in this park. In late 1999 a young Asian American high school student was found dead, and her classmate, an Islamic American football star, was charged with her murder. The facts surrounding the football player's incarceration led to the spark of the true crime and podcast craze. Since the COVID-19 pandemic, Baltimore has been plagued by the murders of the Charm City Strangler, who has discarded his victims in this very park.

"Why are we here?" Marshawn Bell asks, as he walks beside me. He's wearing a black suit, with a black buttoned up shirt and a black tie.

"What do you mean?" I answer with a question of my own as we walk past a body lying on the ground. It's not a victim of the Charm City Strangler, it's a victim of Marshawn Bell. His name was Milk. Marshawn killed him the night he kidnapped me in front of my home.

"You're helping with the water crisis. Why are you dealing with this strangler case?" Marshawn questions.

"I'm not," I respond as Marshawn shakes his head in disagreement.

"Look around," Marshawn demands as I notice my parents lying lifeless near a tree and a broken sink. "Everything is connected. In 2016 Tyrone Clinton and Kannard Lyles-Bey were murdered, causing a spike in drugs on the streets of Baltimore. It also gave me an opportunity to make enough money to get my mother in cancer treatment. In 2019 Commissioner Alex Tillman killed a series of people, including a city councilman, an interim police commissioner, a judge, a state prosecutor, a TV personality and the leader of the Alpha gang. The city pinned Alex Tillman's murders on Paul Douglass, Roland Wise and the Alphas. Alex Tillman disappeared. In 2020, the world was rocked by COVID-19. In 2021 the Charm City Strangler began claiming the lives of African American youth, that are either squeegee workers, drug dealers or dirt bike riders. The riots in 2019 brought light to the water crisis. Everything is connected."

"What you're saying is apples to oranges," I counter as Marshawn and I begin to walk through the produce section of a grocery store. It's not the small grocery store I created in the Old MarketPlace; this is a large grocery store. I can't make out any of the logos or details in the store, but I feel it is a Giant Food or a Safeway.

The store is chilly, and smells like gunpowder. A smell I've become accustomed to, thanks to Marshawn Bell shooting Milk in front of me, me killing my father, along with the gunfire between Alex Tillman and Paul Douglass at Hakeem's church. Why do I smell gunpowder at a grocery store? The aisles to my left are blurry, and it's difficult to make out what's in them. Why can't I make out the shelves around me, but I can see the fruit and veggies in front of me. How did I get here when I was just in Leakin Park? When did I go to Leakin Park?

"Tiffany," a voice says.

I look around to find Marshawn, but he's vanished.

"Tiffany," the voice repeats as I notice my five children and Duck walking through the electronic door of the grocery store.

"Mom!" Kenya yells with excitement and runs toward me. She's older than I remember. She's taller, and strongly resembles my cousin Tina.

"Tiffany!" I hear the voice again. Instantly, everything goes black before I open my eyes and see I'm seated on the couch, next to Hakeem. The news is playing on the TV, and they are talking about another body being found in Leakin Park.

"Your food is going to get cold," Hakeem says with concern in his voice.

"How long was I out?" I question as Hakeem shrugs his shoulders as if to say he's not sure.

"How was the bible study?" he asks, and I search for the words to say.

"I hated it," I blurt out. I don't know why, but I didn't even think of warmer words to say. Hakeem chuckles at my response, causing me to give half a smirk. "I swear your family's church is a cult. You know that, right?"

Hakeem and I walk to the kitchen to grab heavy black Styrofoam trays off the stove and walk back towards the living room. Hakeem is still smiling off my comment about the cult because he knows I'm right. I open my tray to find it packed with six fried chicken wings, mashed potatoes with gravy, string beans and a dinner roll. It all smells heavenly.

"Your cousin Raymond asked the members of the church to bring in their paycheck stubs next week to bible study," I say. Hakeem's eyes grow wide. He lets out a "tuh," then shakes his head slowly. We both know where Raymond is going with this. Hakeem smiles again before revealing his tray, which is filled with potato salad and BBQ ribs. We will definitely be sharing.

"Kesha just sat in the pulpit drifting off to Lala land or something," I continue as Hakeem chuckles again before he prays over his food and eats a few string beans from my tray. "It's like she hates running that church or something."

"She does hate it," Hakeem finally responds. "My father wanted me to run the church and have a seat at the table of the Flamingo Club. He wanted Kesha to handle the finances of the Flamingo Club. When I finally broke away from Andrews Memorial and my father, Kesha was thrust into a position she hated. It was smart for her to have Raymond handle the church's day-to-day ministry responsibilities."

"You know she's hoping that you take a place on the ministry staff at the church," I mention as he continues to chew. Finally a nod from Hakeem, before shaking his head no.

"Tiffany, I'm in no place to lead these people," Hakeem confesses after he finishes chewing the food in his mouth. "My brother died, New Hope Greater Love Church and your family's home was burned down in 2019. Three of my biggest failures. I couldn't protect my brother when we were trying to fix our issues. God punished me by burning down a church I had no business pastoring. He also punished me for not protecting you by burning up your home while you and your family were sleep; as a result, Trinity suffered severe injuries physically and mentally. I'm not a real pastor. I was playing church and I was punished for it."

"Do you really believe that?" I ask. Hakeem nods yes. "Do you really believe that God was punishing you for doing good in Ridgely Square?"

"Either God's punishing me or God's not real," Hakeem returns in a serious tone. The smile that was present has left. He's looking forward at the TV with a blank look on his face. The blank look turns to sadness and I notice the tears developing in his eyes. Hakeem has not had a good cry or a release of his emotions surrounding his brother's death; he has just been moving. Completing a task here, helping with a group there. He hasn't taken time for self-care, apart from our honeymoon earlier this year.

"Let's play a game," I suggest. Hakeem rolls his eyes and eats more string beans. "I'm serious. Let's do a pros and cons game. If God isn't real, what's the pros to the work you've done in the community, and what's the cons?"

"I'm not doing that," Hakeem grumpily counters with a mouth full of food.

"Why?" I ask as he slightly turns his head in my direction and shakes it no. "You were there to help the members of the church during the pandemic by dropping off food and even paying bills for members that lost their jobs as a result of the pandemic. You worked with Aleem to establish the Knights, and as a result, crime has gone down in the community."

"Stop," Hakeem requests as he drinks tea from a large Styrofoam cup. "Right now, kids are being murdered by the Charm City Strangler. Right now, we have a water crisis. Right now, we're living in a house too small for our family. Right now, I'm trying to bond with my sister without getting sucked into the cult of my family's church."

"Right, but—" I begin to rebut as Hakeem continues to speak.

"After my brother was murdered by Roland Wise or Paul Douglass, the police blamed it on the Action Figure Killer, then they named Paul Douglass and Roland Wise as AFK, to cover up Commissioner Alex Tillman's crimes. Did I speak up? No. Why? Because I'm a coward. A man of God has no business being a coward. A father and husband has no business being a coward. Jamar was never a coward. My dad, as much as I disagreed with him, was never a coward. Raymond isn't a coward. You're not a coward. Darrin isn't a coward. But me, I kept my mouth closed and let the City of Baltimore cover up a vigilante serial killer, just to keep bad people in prison."

"Yes, because there's a lot of bad people that would get out if the truth was made public," I elaborated. "Alex

Tillman's son was murdered by a freed criminal because of a scandal."

"So, two wrongs make a right? That's the math we're going with now?" Hakeem questions in a loud tone. "I don't agree with that. Maybe I'm not Pastor Donald Avery, who was a great man with outstanding integrity, but I'm not my father. My father's seat at the table of the Flamingo Club was murky and filled with ethical concerns I personally have with him. That being said, he was there for the sick. When the pandemic happened, do you know how many church members from New Hope Greater Love Church died from COVID-19? The last time I counted, it was 14 members. You know how many members I was able to go to the hospital to visit, and pray with? The answer is zero. Not a single one of the church members I preached to, taught, counseled, married, or eulogized had me visit them at the hospital to pray for them. Why? Because of hospital policies. You know what that means? I failed them, Tiffany. I failed God. I failed you. I failed Jamar. I'm a failure."

"You're not a failure. Right now, you're working with Aleem to catch the Charm City Strangler," I interject as Hakeem places his food down on the glass coffee table by his side.

"I'm the direct definition of a failure," Hakeem countered. "My city council run, failed. My pastorship, failed. My law practice, failed. My practice as a counselor failed. Being a stepfather to these kids, failed. Being a brother to Jamar and Kesha, failed. Being a husband—"

"Stop," I demand. "The self-loathing is getting old. You're not a damn failure. Because of you, my best friend Sasha received a settlement from the city for when she was kidnapped by Marshawn Bell. Because of you, the Lyles-Bey family received a settlement from the city for the murder of Kannard Lyles-Bey. Because of you, we received a settlement for being targeted by Marshawn Bell. Because of you my kids got out the house alive when Roland Wise set it on fire. You're not a failure. You're a hero. We need more men like you. But you're grieving the deaths of your brother and your parents. Eventually you're going to have to come to terms with the fact that you're isolating yourself from your God-given gift because you're hurting."

"What's my gift, Tiffany?" Hakeem inquires.

"Helping, serving, standing up and fighting for those that can't stand up and fight for themselves," I boldly answer. "The day I stood up to my father, I shot and killed him. His shadow left me. The day Roland Wise and Paul Douglass held me captive, I beat the dog shit out of Paul Douglass. I realized the day I pulled the trigger on my father, I don't need a savior; I need the tools to fight for myself. You're nobody's savior, Hakeem, you're the tool used to help people learn to fight for themselves. But, if people can't fight for themselves, you're there to fight for them."

I try to embrace Hakeem as he stands up with a stoic face and walks out the front door to sit on the stoop. This is a behavior Hakeem began to develop following the murder of Jamar. He would go outside and sit on the top stone step leading to the front door. He would stare out at the street, at cars and houses for a long period of time before coming back inside. Many times, I'd be sleep or working on paperwork from the bank. I've learned that he needs his space, and nothing that I can say or do will change this inward hurt and resentment he has for himself. But I still try to be there and encourage him.

On the TV the mayor and the current police commissioner are talking about the body most recently found at Leakin Park. It is another suspected victim of the Charm City Strangler. As I begin to panic thinking about Darrin, he walks through the front door with Duck laughing and talking loudly. The two childhood best friends grab the PlayStation remotes and change from the channel I was watching and play their basketball game. I smile for a moment, as I think of all the times Jamar and Hakeem would come over to my house to play the PlayStation together. I also smile thinking about all the times I would play against Sasha on gaming systems growing up.

I walk to the front door, watching Hakeem look at the houses across the street in silence. I say in a low tone, "Moments and memories are all we have. Good moments and memories may not happen all the time, but it's important to appreciate the good moments when we have them and pull from those memories when we need them. Come on upstairs, Hakeem, let's take advantage of the moment we have and make some fun memories."

"Is your mom talking about sex?" Duck loudly asks as Darrin gags in disgust. The two adolescents laugh among themselves, but Hakeem doesn't move or respond. He's sitting quietly, breathing, staring, and thinking.

Chapter 10

Two weeks have passed, and here we are at the end of June. It's a sunny Saturday afternoon at Harlem Park. The park is filled with vendors, tables, chairs, and people. The DJ is blasting music, people are laughing and eating crabs or fried fish at their tables. Individuals are taking pictures together, food trucks are parked along the streets that border Harlem Park from the community, and several tents are set up with various activities inside.

Mayor Hugo and the current police commissioner, Keith Mercer are walking through the park, talking and taking pictures with community members. I keep finding myself around Duck, Darrin, and Kutter the Poet. Kutter is a tall, skinny, light skin male with long locs. He's wearing a black t-shirt along with black jeans and black Nike Air Force 1s. He has a big infectious smile on his face, and constantly takes time to talk to everyone near him. His top and bottom teeth are covered in white gold and diamonds. He recently completed his performance and immediately started greeting the people in the park afterward. His DJ, Lor Deezil, and a local comedian are entertaining people on the microphone.

I'm trying to make my way to the booth for Nubian Media and my eye catches a burley Caucasian man with a bald head. This shouldn't come as a surprise, but this is no regular burley Caucasian male, this is the former police commissioner, Alex Tillman. The same police commissioner who was fired for an angry outburst during a press conference when Kannard Lyles-Bey, a young unarmed African American teenager, was murdered by the police for spray painting the side of a building. Alex Tillman was also involved in killing two members of the Alphas, who posed as protesters while attempting to kill Officer Edward Carter. In 2017 Alex Tillman also shot and killed Marshawn Bell, a crooked police detective that worked with the Alphas to control Baltimore City's drug trade.

Alex Tillman would later unleash a reign of terror upon the Alphas, donning the persona of the Action Figure Killer, also known as AFK. As AFK, Alex Tillman would kill members of the Alphas, crooked politicians and anybody else that was on the wrong side of the law. His deeds were covered up by the FBI because of the impact his incarceration would have on the City of Baltimore. Nobody has officially heard from Alex Tillman since 2019, but there have been a number of murders that many people theorized were related to the real AFK. Some of the murders included a young white male in South Carolina who killed seven black people at a church; and a person in Florida that was part of a neighborhood watch who killed an unarmed African American teenager coming home from football practice.

"You did a great job putting this together," a woman's voice says in my ear. I turn my eyes away from Alex Tillman to lock eyes with Erica Little. To my surprise she gave me a nice compliment.

"Thanks," I respond, not knowing what to expect next from this lady. She's only the CEO of Titan Industries, the same company trying to purchase every piece of land in West Baltimore and has used the water crisis to her company's advantage.

"Titan will be making a sizable donation to the 10th Bank with the goal of placing new sewage and freshwater pipes throughout the underserved areas of Baltimore City," Erica continues as I try to locate Alex Tillman, who has vanished out of sight.

"Thanks, but why?" I ask, still scanning the park for Alex Tillman.

"The 10th Bank is on the right side of history," Erica answers. "Look around this park. People are happy, enjoying themselves, donating money to an important cause, and bonding. That's something that I overlooked for years when we were purchasing property in Ridgely Square for the community redevelopment. We saw the violence, the addiction and poverty, but missed this. These same people live, sleep and eat in this community. Furthermore, we want you as a member of the Flamingo Club. We can still redevelop this city into something greater, and keep the good parts, like this event. Let's put down the new plumbing and gas lines together. Also let's stop the illegal dumping of toxic waste in the Inner Harbor."

"What's in it for you?" I ask as Erica chuckles.

"We build a better Baltimore City, while making a statement to the rest of the state. Hell, we'll make a bold statement to the rest of the country. Here's the headline: Baltimore City, the Los Angeles of the Atlantic. We can be a bigger marketplace than D.C., Atlanta, New York, or Boston. But it starts with baby steps. Let's fix the water problem. The mayor is doing his part by bringing in major businesses and tourist attractions."

"What's in it for me and the people of Baltimore I represent?" I ask as Erica looks around the park.

"That's easy. Continue building a better Baltimore," Erica mentions. "Titan Industries will continue doing business as usual, trying to improve the less than desirable areas of the city. The 10th Bank will continue to save the city the best way it knows how, growing businesses and reaching the people of Baltimore that are often overlooked.

As I cut my eyes towards Erica, clearly not trusting a word she's saying, DJ Lor Deezil calls me to the stage area. Surrounded by the stares of the attendees, I'm at a loss for words when Kutter the Poet walks over to hug me.

"This whole thing, this great occasion was one woman's idea," Kutter the Poet says into the microphone as many people begin to clap. "That woman is Tiffany Andrews. When my little cousin Duck told me about the water and lead problem in Baltimore, I was shocked. I asked him how could I help. When he told me about this fish fry and crab feast fund raiser, I instantly paused my tour and had to participate. My record label, Habeas Corpus Entertainment, agreed to assist with the challenges that Baltimore City is facing."

As Kutter the Poet continued to give his speech, two people with Habeas Corpus t-shirts walk to the stage holding large cardboard checks and head in my direction, revealing one check for $10,000,000 and another check for $4,000,000.

"Habeas Corpus has agreed to donate $10,000,000 to the 10th Bank with the goal of fixing the plumbing and lead problems in Ridgely Square, West Port, Mount Winans, Green Mount, Edmonson Ave and several other areas of the city. I will donate my recent tour earnings to the 10th Bank as well for the plumbing reconstruction," Kutter the Poet decrees, while giving me a hug.

To my surprise, Mayor Hugo and Erica Little walk on the stage holding a large cardboard check. My eyes dance around the crowd to locate Alex Tillman as Mayor Hugo begins talking to me about today's successful event. My heart begins to beat faster and faster as I think of the danger Alex Tillman poses to everybody here.

"It is with great pride," Mayor Hugo states calling my attention back to the stage, "I want to inform you that the mayor's office has dedicated $20,000,000 for repairs throughout the city. The repairs will start with Harlem Park, Ridgely Square, West Port, Cherry Hill, Edmondson Avenue and many underserved communities. This will be a multiple phase approach to make sure every area of the city is served. We are also in talks with the governor to request financial assistance."

As I look around for another cardboard check, a member of the mayor's office hands Hugo a black folder with Baltimore City's logo embossed in gold. "In my hand," Mayor Hugo continues, "is a copy of a decree that the City Council President, City Councilwoman Mya Rodriguez and myself drafted together to address the water crisis. This decree will take place immediately. While I would love to take credit for this event and the work that was put into making these changes, I cannot. I have to give total thanks and credit to Tiffany Andrews, the 10th Bank and the great people that supported her in these efforts, including Kutter the Poet."

"Are you freaking serious?" a woman's voice screams from the crowd surrounding the stage. "We have someone killing black boys and leaving them in Leakin Park, but here we are safe at Harlem Park, raising money for a water crisis. A whole generation is being killed off. Murdered in cold blood. What do you all do? You celebrate something you should have *been* doing."

As I glance closer at the person talking, I notice it's Ms. Jean Pugh. Her grandson, Miles was one of those confirmed as murdered by the Charm City Strangler. She's become a huge advocate for finding the Charm City Strangler.

"Ms. Pugh, I'm grateful to see you're here and fighting for justice for your grandson along with the other victims of the Charm City Strangler. This is something that is a top priority for my office along with the Baltimore City Police," Mayor Hugo returns as eyes from the crowd begin to surround Ms. Pugh.

"You're giving me nothing but lip service," Ms. Pugh counters. "You want to bring in big businesses to the city. You want to open another casino, an indoor water park, and create this major financial district. The problem with all that is we are suffering. I'm not talking about the people in Canton, Federal Hill, Harbor East or Ridgely's Delight. I'm talking about the blue collar hard working black folk that have lived here for generations. You don't give a shit about us. You wouldn't have moved a dime to fix the water pipes in the city, if it wasn't for the 10th Bank making as much noise as they have. I wish you would quit trying to act like some white savior and be the real son of a bitch that you're pretending not to be. If this was one of your kids, you'd bust your ass to fix this problem. You created the Paul Douglass Law but haven't implemented it yet. Why? Are you scared that one of your racist buddies from the Right Hand of God Fellowship Church will get caught?"

"Ms. Pugh, we're trying to catch and incarcerate the Charm City Strangler, and to our knowledge the Right Hand of God has nothing to do with the Charm City Strangler," Mayor Hugo quickly defends.

"Prove it," Ms. Pugh demands. "And seeing that your friend Tiffany Andrews seems to be the only person to get shit done in this city, I hold her accountable as well. Y'all work together and make a difference."

Before I can open my mouth to say anything, Ms. Pugh walks away from the crowd. I make slight eye contact with Hakeem standing in the rear of the crowd with an emotionless look on his face.

"You can't fix every problem," Hugo says to me with the microphone away from his mouth.

"We need to catch this guy," I suggest as Hugo nods in agreement.

"Let's take care of this water crisis, and the police commissioner will continue to investigate the

Charm City Strangler." Mayor Hugo says into the microphone as the crowd cheers in response.

Out of nowhere, Dr. Lor Deezil begins playing music as Kutter the Poet returns to the stage, giving me a hug. He's standing side by side with Duck and my son Darrin. The three of them begin singing Kutter the Poet's hit song, "A Vibe" as the crowd sings along.

Chapter 11

That evening I'm standing in the Legacy of Florence Marketplace with my aunt Gina and my best friend from childhood, Sasha. Sasha's skin has become clearer since she has reduced her drinking. Since the pandemic of 2020, she's run the grocery store and the restaurant. Since the water crisis, I've closed the restaurant and left the market in Sasha's full control.

"I heard the crab feast and fish fry was a success," Sasha says checking the temperature of the produce. She's very analytical with her checks, starting with the collard greens, kale, cucumbers and cabbage, then making her way to the fresh parsley, broccoli and asparagus.

"Yeah, wish you had been there," I remark to a slight smirk on Sasha's cheek. I can clearly see the dimple on the side of her face.

"Why, so I coulda got kidnapped?" Sasha says in a sarcastic tone. "I was where I was supposed to be."

"Sasha, your son was killed, and your voice could move mountains with these parents that are experiencing grief from this Charm City Strangler," I suggest as she does not stop moving throughout the produce department checking temperatures.

"My voice was used by you, your aunt and Anna Cartwright a few years ago," Sasha recounts as she picks up a wilting spring onion. "You remember when Hakeem was shot in front of the house? Do you remember when Milk held me at gunpoint? Do you remember when Marshawn Bell murdered Milk in front of me? Do you remember the Alphas making threats in front of our home? Gina was in witness protection for the shit she put us through. Here she is living her best life, working for Nubian Media. You run your bank, and I'm running your grocery store. I'm happy right here. I'm under the radar, and Gina being around means nothing but drama is coming in the near to short term."

"Me?" Gina asks as I try to stop her from getting involved.

"The whole FBI investigation was your fault," Sasha reminds Gina. "You went into witness protection up in Vermont or some shit. We had to fend for ourselves. AFK ran around this city killing anybody they could. Paul Douglass and Roland Wise tried to kill everybody attached to you. But you, Gina Simms, you were in Vermont on my tax dollars. You haven't done shit to contribute to society but get high and out some crooked police, but you were safe from all the drama. Then you come back like Jesus with holes in his hands, with a TV show and a podcast on Nubian Media. I don't feel safe around you."

"The Alphas and NAFA are doing federal time," Gina interjects. "There's nothing to worry about.

"Three hundred sixty-four," Sasha blurts out looking at oranges and lemons.

"What does 364 mean?" Gina asks.

"Last year, 364 people were killed in this city," Sasha answers. "Those might just be statistics to you, but to me, those are sons, daughters, mothers and fathers. The Alphas are still around, they just changed their name. We still have the Cabal, we still have the Glock Boys, the Garcia Family, the Delaney Crime Family and the Black Tie. Your work on the documentary didn't solve anything. It just put a target on hard working people's backs.

"Wait, who's the Black Tie?" Gina asks as the supermarket gets eerily quiet.

"It's an Asian Mafia," Sasha answers. "They date back to the 1920s. They protect all immigrants from Asian countries, including Chinese, Japanese, Indian, some Russians, Vietnamese and Koreans. They typically wear all white suits with black ties. All the Asian owned and operated companies in Baltimore City are affiliated with the Black Tie in some way. Of course their leader is a good friend of Tiffany's sister-in-law."

"What are you talking about," I inquire as Sasha finally turns to me making eye contact.

"You have to do better than this if you're going to be a leader," Sasha states. "Khin Lao, he's a prominent member of the Flamingo Club. He's probably the scariest member of the Flamingo Club because he has a whole army behind him that follows him like a cult leader."

"What am I supposed to do?" I ask as Sasha slightly looks at Gina then returns her gaze back to me.

"What do you do best, Tiffany," Sasha remarks. "You try to fix problems. I'm glad you've been busting your ass to deal with the water crisis, but the problems in Ridgely Square are a lot deeper than some lead-based water. The mayor is corrupt just like those police your aunt was trying to stop."

"He's legit trying to help," I dispute eagerly as Sasha shakes her head in disagreement.

"How much money did he put up before you got Kutter the Poet involved?" Sasha questions. "The answer is none. He don't care about this version of Baltimore. The 10th Bank gave you and so many others that look like you the power to stand up and not take no for an answer. Best believe if he didn't have to contend with the 10th Bank, he would have kept on about business as usual and destroyed each house in the community."

Before Gina or I could say another word, Duck and Darrin walk over to the produce section with a cart full of ramen noodles, 2-liter sodas, ice cream sandwiches and chips. "Aunt Sasha!" Darrin screams, running to her and giving her a hug.

"I heard y'all were the brains behind the concert," Sasha says as Darrin begins to laugh. "Honestly, Duck being cousins with Kutter the Poet was the thing that made everything a success. I'm glad everything worked out."

"When are they supposed to start the construction in Ridgely Square?" Gina asks as Sasha begins placing spoiled vegetables inside of a shopping cart.

"Hugo Titan stated that the construction will start next week," I answer as Hakeem walks over to me, giving me a tight embrace and kiss.

"Public displays of affection," Sasha utters in a disgusted tone before smiling and laughing.

"Who's buying all that," Hakeem questions pointing at Darrin's shopping cart.

"Pops, we need food at the home," Darrin responds. "You always talk about not eating fast food, so I'm getting slow food, or whatever this is supposed to be called."

Hakeem begins to laugh uncontrollably at Darrin's statements, looking around in the produce section. Hakeem and Darrin's relationship continues to grow into a great bond. "Where's the oatmeal pies?" Hakeem questions as Duck runs off to grab a box of oatmeal pies.

"Serious question," Sasha asks Hakeem, "do you have any concerns that the Alphas are going to return and cause more damage in Ridgely Square?"

"Here's the truth," Hakeem begins. His smile changes to a serious look, and his voice begins to deepen. "Baltimore is plagued by a lot of challenges, including gangs, drugs and poverty. Agencies like the 10th Bank, Justice 4 All and the Knights are doing everything they can to prevent the growing number of murders. We're working with the courts to implement harm reduction initiatives to prevent incarcerations. The mayor has been working nonstop to create programs for high school age youth to gain skills with the goal of obtaining blue collar careers upon graduation. This city is trying to head in the right direction. Will it happen overnight? No. Will it happen? It will."

"What about that Charm City Strangler?" Sasha questions.

"Without a shadow of doubt, he'll be caught," Hakeem answers as Sasha picks up an apple that appears to be spoiled.

"Will they handle it like they did the Action Figure Killer?" Sasha questions.

"What do you mean?" I ask.

Hakeem and I never shared the true story of AFK. As far as Sasha and Gina know, the real AFK is Paul Douglass, who killed himself. The true story is AFK was the former Baltimore City Police Commissioner Alex Tillman. Baltimore City Police and the FBI covered up his illegal activity with the goal of preventing violent offenders from winning appeals if the actual truth gets out.

"The Action Figure Killer, Paul Douglass, or Roland Wise depending on who you ask," Sasha begins. "He killed himself at Hakeem's church to make himself a martyr for the Alphas. At what point will the police arrest this Charm City Strangler before letting him go out on his own terms?"

"This is an active investigation, and it doesn't happen overnight," Hakeem mentions as Darrin walks away. "I have faith in the Baltimore City Police Department on this case."

"The same police that murdered my son?" Sasha yells as spit flies out her mouth. "The same police that the Narcotics and Firearms Taskforce was a part of? The same police that raided Cabal gang members' homes, took the drugs and sold them to the Alphas? This police department is just as corrupt as the politicians."

"I'm not trying to disagree with you, but I want to have faith in them on this," Hakeem returns.

"Was your brother's murder closed?" Sasha asks as Hakeem's eyes begin to narrow. I've seen this look from Hakeem before. He's gnashing his teeth together, trying to hide his anger. "I can read between lines; there's another coverup with the police involved, the public might not know, but the fact that nobody was officially convicted for Jamar's murder lets me know something went wrong with that investigation."

"Sasha, my brother was murdered by Paul Douglass and Roland Wise for refusing to allow their illegal money to go into the 10th Bank," Hakeem proclaims. "Detective Murphy narrowed the murderer down to Paul and Roland but couldn't say with 100% certainty which one killed him."

"Convenient," Sasha quips. "When they want to close a case, they can pinpoint who did it. Yet, when your brother is murdered in broad daylight they go back and forth. We had a serial killer, and they couldn't say with complete certainty who pulled the trigger."

"With all due respect, I would like to move past this subject," Hakeem says as Darrin and Duck return to the produce section with more junk food items in the cart.

"You're a good man, Hakeem," Sasha blurts out of nowhere. "My son, Tyrone, didn't have a lot of good male figures in his life. Coach Eddie Carter was probably his only real role model. Sometimes I think he was so good at football because he was so happy to be around his coach. I said that to say I see how the kids are with you, Hakeem. It's a beautiful thing."

"Thanks," Hakeem says with an embarrassed smile. In his defense, how do you respond to a compliment like that. Sasha's son was murdered by police back in 2016, and she's gone through hell and back emotionally. She picked up a drinking habit, was threatened and kidnaped by Marshawn Bell, went to treatment, was threatened to find Gina while she was in witness protection. She was publicly embarrassed by a TV personality named Anna Cartwright twice. The first time was after her son was murdered. The second time was when Sasha was invited to speak on Gina's documentary, and they surprised her by bringing in one of her son's killers just so he could tell his side of the story.

"Mr. Hakeem," Duck yells with pure excitement. "You got to see these burgers over in the meat department. It's like the butcher made the ground beef into patties. There's onions, bacon and cheese mixed in with the ground beef. I bet you could grill these up real good!"

"Can we have a cookout tomorrow?" Darrin asks as Hakeem smiles.

"Let's take a look at these burgers first," Hakeem responds with a smile that lit up the produce section brighter than it already was. Darrin and Duck begin doing silly dances as they walk towards the meat department. Hakeem briefly winks in my direction before walking with them to the rear of the store.

Chapter 12

The next day didn't go as planned. Hakeem, Darrin and I were supposed to go to Sunday morning church service at Andrews Memorial, but we got an early knock at the door from Duck, with eyes filled with tears. Duck had a difficult time getting the words out until Hakeem welcomed him into the house and brought him a cup filled with iced tea.

"What happened, Duck?" Hakeem asks as Darrin paces near him.

"Cam," Duck utters before wiping his eyes and mouth on his forearm. "They found Cam dead in Leakin Park under a white bed sheet."

"You're playing," Darrin responds as Duck shakes his head no. Darrin begins crying as well, thinking of the death of their friend Cam.

Cam was born Camron Barnes. His father died of a fentanyl overdose shortly before the 2020 pandemic. Cam's mother was active in her heroin addiction and was frequently in-and-out of jail for theft, prostitution, assault or some form of child neglect. Cam became a squeegee worker, cleaning the windows of vehicles at red lights, to make extra money to pay for items around the house. Cam would pay the light bill, or purchase food for his younger brother. Cam was younger than Duck and Darrin. He might have been 12 or 13, but he was always shorter than other kids his age. He was always outside with Darrin and Duck. Cam would find himself at the busy intersections on Fredrick Rd. and Hilton Parkway, or Patapsco Ave and Hollins Ferry Rd.

"I walked over to his house and knocked, but he wasn't home," Duck recounts. "I normally watch him work on the weekends to make sure nothing happens to him. The old head Von that came home from prison last year said that he saw him get into a car after he cleaned the person's window. The person offered him money or whatever to wash a car at their house."

"Did Von say what the person looked like?" I ask. Duck answers no. "Any idea of what kind of car, if the person was a male or female, anything?

"No," Duck answers. "Ms. T, please don't tell the police what Von said. He just got out of prison from that long bit, and he trying to do right."

"Ma, we don't need to be talking to the police about nothing," Darrin contributes. "We don't need this house burned down."

"Them niggas mess around and kill you this time, Ms. T," Duck points out.

"How did they find Camron?" Hakeem asks. Camron was a kid that played basketball at Hakeem's recreation center and would do his homework at Jamar's community center.

"I heard the janitor from Douglass High School was in the park getting high when he found the body under a sheet."

Before I can say another word, there's a knock at the front door that startles us. Hakeem walks over to open the door, as the sunny sky enters through the front door and exposes the face of my aunt, Gina.

"I guess y'all not going to church either?" Gina asks with a serious look on her face.

"No, Darrin's and Duck's friend was found dead at Leakin Park," I answer as Gina's eyes grow large.

"Y'all knew this kid?" she asks in surprise and excitement. "Do you think I can interview y'all for the podcast? I'm looking into the Charm City Strangler for Nubian Media."

"Absolutely not," I answer as Gina appears confused by my answer.

"Tiffany," Gina begins to plead. "We can catch this guy. A person is murdering youth. You were able to help with the water crisis. You and Hakeem can crack this case wide open. Especially with the work y'all have been doing with the Knights."

"No," I reiterate as Ms. Pugh walks to the bottom of my steps.

"You thought I was crazy for talking about this monster killing our youth while y'all was celebrating with crabs and fried fish," Ms. Pugh yells at me. "If you're going to serve this community, do it. If not, stop faking and allow real people to help."

"Ms. Pugh, the police are working this case, the 10th Bank was trying to fix the water crisis that's plaguing all of us," I explain as Ms. Pugh begins to walk up my steps.

"The Charm City Strangler might not mean much to you right now, but when he hits home with one of your kids, then you'll understand," Ms. Pugh utters in a serious and angry tone.

"Ms. Pugh, the kid that was found was a friend of my oldest son," I explain as she stares me down. "The 10th Bank isn't the police, we're a bank. Let the police do their job and solve this case."

"Funny how you can raise millions to solve a water crisis, but you haven't raised a dime for a reward for the capture of the Charm City Strangler," Ms. Pugh highlights while pointing in my face. Her head is shaking with rage she speaks. "Your grandmother would have been up the police commissioner's ass for these kids being killed."

"My wife and I are doing everything we can to help the city," Hakeem returns in a passive tone. I can't really call that a defense, but it's better than him just standing here quiet.

"You're going to let her talk to you like that?" Marshawn's voice asks in the back of my head as I stare down Ms. Pugh. "We can slap this old biddy."

"Shut up!" I yell out loud in response to Marshawn as Ms. Pugh looks on in anger.

"You don't talk to me like that, ever!" Ms. Pugh returns and I shake my head no.

"No, I wasn't talking to you," I attempt to explain as Gina stands between Ms. Pugh and me.

"Ms. Pugh, we're all concerned about the Charm City Strangler," Gina interjects. "Just as we're mourning the life of the young man they just found at the park, the City of Baltimore is dealing with a water crisis that is being resolved, thanks to my niece."

"I'm tired of lip service," Ms. Pugh yells in my face. "Y'all know that Carson Jessup, and his Right Hand of God Fellowship Church has something to do with this. They've been killing our black men for years, and you're standing by and doing nothing. I'm not going to stop until I get justice for these kids."

As Ms. Pugh turns around and walks down the steps, I can hear Duck and Darrin talk among themselves in the house. I slightly overhear Duck theorize the idea that the murder could have come at the hand of one of Carson Jessup's church members. A few seconds later Darrin and Hakeem yell for Gina and me to come in the house. Upon entering the house, we hear the TV playing a news report that Carson Jessup is filing an appeal for his murder case.

"Carson Jessup, the pastor of the Right Hand of God Fellowship Church has entered an appeal for his case, citing new evidence of his innocence," the young African American woman reporter says on the TV. "Guy Dulaney, the former state's attorney, and Baltimore City Mayor turned Maryland governor that was forced to step down from office in 2018 after questions about his involvement in the Dulaney Crime Family, has publicly stated that he's taking over Carson Jessup's case. Dulaney stated that he will be presenting new evidence that the recent child murders in Leakin Park are linked to the murders that Carson Jessup was charged with."

"Can you believe this?" Hakeem says with frustration, "Carson Jessup and Guy Dulaney are going to milk this Charm City Strangler situation. Did people forget he was just cooperating with law enforcement when he admitted to the murders?"

"There's no way this will work, right?" Duck asks as everyone in the living room quietly looks at him. Hakeem, Darrin and I, remember all too well the coverup of the Action Figure Killer. Gina was a part of the case that brought down the Narcotics and Firearms Taskforce. This household is very familiar with the mishandling of justice in the City of Baltimore.

"You never know," I finally answer, as the words "Breaking News" come across the screen with bright yellow letters.

"This just in," the female news anchor states. "Another body was found in Leakin Park. This body was identified as 16-year-old King Mercer, the son of the current Baltimore City Police Commissioner, Keith Mercer. We're about to go live with Mayor Hugo, and Police Commissioner Mercer."

"This isn't good," Gina announces, like she just discovered fire.

"Ms. Pugh is going to have a field day with this," Hakeem proclaims looking at the TV screen.

"I swear if she wasn't just here, she'd be there for this press conference," I add as I notice the sadness on Darrin's and Duck's faces.

"The mayor and the commissioner are going to make a big deal out of King Mercer's death, but didn't do anything about Cam," Duck mentions while crying and punching his thigh repeatedly in anger.

Mayor Hugo, dressed in a blue button up shirt and a tan colored suit stands in front of a cordoned off crime scene in the woods. To his right is Commissioner Keith

Mercer, wearing a white polo shirt with a Baltimore City Police Department badge stitched on the left breast.

"This has been a very emotional 24-hours," Mayor Hugo begins speaking in a solemn tone. "Yesterday, Kutter the Poet, the 10th Bank, Nubian Media, and Ridgely Square Medical Center put on an amazing fundraiser in Harlem Park, with music and great food. This was done to raise money to deal with the current water crisis in the city. Where this should have been a highlight for the city, it was short lived after a young child, Camron Barnes was found not too far from where we're standing. While detectives were combing Leakin Park for clues and collecting evidence, they found another body belonging to King Mercer, the son of our very own Police Commissioner, Keith Mercer. While no words I can say will bring back King Mercer, Camron Barnes, or any of the other youth that were murdered at the hands of the Charm City Strangler, I will make one promise to Baltimore City, to the families of the deceased and the murderer committing these acts of violence: We will catch you."

Mayor Hugo continues, "While all lives are important and matter, this recent murder strikes close to home for our police department and our city. This scumbag claimed the life of Commissioner Mercer's son. That being said, effective immediately the Paul Douglass Law is now in effect. All doorbell cameras, surveillance equipment, and digital electronics, such as phones, tablets and computers, will be monitored by our command center set up to catch the Charm City Strangler. We will also initiate a city-wide curfew that all youth 21 and younger must adhere to. The curfew will go into effect every evening at 7 pm. Anybody under 21 seen out on the street without a parent or guardian will be charged with violating curfew laws and obstruction of justice. I will now invite our great commissioner, Keith Mercer to say a few words."

"My son…" Commissioner Mercer begins but pauses as he sheds tears. His face is stoic like a statue, but sadness and heartbreak are clear in his eyes. "In my career, I've worked on countless homicide and violent sex crimes. You always want to find the words to say to the families and the victims involved. Sometimes you can say the right words, sometimes you hope you've said or done enough. To be honest, I don't want to say anything. I want to catch this monster and bring him to justice. This city has had enough challenges, including the water crisis, and now to add in another serial killer… Here's your only warning for your own safety. Turn yourself in now." Commissioner Mercer lifts his mouth in a slight smile before his face breaks down into pure sadness. "A few years ago I watched a previous police commissioner, Alex Tillman, give a highly charged press conference, while he was dealing with anger and grief. Having this position now, I understand his reaction and his rage when he delivered the press conference speech that led to his termination. That being said, I'm going to conclude my portion of this press conference and spend time with my family. Please respect my family's privacy as we grieve the death of my son."

"I'm going to call a community meeting at the Allen Bradley Funeral Home," Hakeem says out loud, shocking everyone in the room. He's been down in the dumps for several months, actually since the murder of his brother. This is the most I've seen him acting in his natural element as a community leader.

"Tell Aleem, Ms. Pugh, my aunt Monica, my sister Kesha, my cousin Raymond, and whoever else you want, I want to meet with everyone affected by these murders on Tuesday," Hakeem demands as Gina nods in agreement.

As Gina walks towards the doorway, I stop my aunt asking, "Where are you going now?"

"To the church," Gina answers nonchalantly. "I'm a part of the private bible study group. Today we're studying the movies Rambo and Saw."

"You guys are doing what?" Hakeem questions as I begin to laugh causing Hakeem to turn his look of disgust towards me.

"Raymond and Monica have us studying a series of movies and books," Gina explains. "His goal is for us to be faithful disciples to the ministry and to Christ."

Chapter 13

That Tuesday Hakeem and I find ourselves in the Allen Bradley Funeral Home leading a townhall meeting. We're in the newly built forum hall that has been used for family gatherings and community meetings. The funeral home's director, Allen Bradley, personally asked Hakeem to pastor his former church, New Hope Greater Love, inside of the forum hall, but Hakeem turned down the idea. The grief of Jamar's death, along with the mystery surrounding his parents' deaths, the burning of the original New Hope Greater Love Church and the constant problems in Baltimore City have taken a heavy toll on Hakeem's psyche.

The fellowship hall is spacious, seating more than 600 people with space to spare. Today there are close to 200 people present. In attendance is Mayor Hugo, Hakeem's sister Kesha Stokes, Ms. Pugh, Hakeem's aunt Monica, Aleem, Erica Little, several members from the media, a few neighbors and some police officers. The forum venue is frigid, but that's welcoming compared to the 97-degree heat and humidity outside.

"It seems like if it ain't one thing happening in Ridgely Square, it's another," Hakeem opens with, but the people in attendance have no reaction. The atmosphere is cold, not because of the blasting air conditioner, but because nobody is happy about being in this meeting. Nobody's in a joking mood. Baltimore has a water crisis, and someone has been murdering teenage boys in our community. If I threw a chair right now, it would probably set off a small riot.

Reading the room, Hakeem changes his tone from hopeful and energetic to serious and less relaxed. "We're in uncharted territory right now," Hakeem states as not one person responds. Historically Hakeem comes across well with the people from the community. In 2019 these are the same people that were more than happy to vote him in office for City Counselor after Councilman Dawson abruptly resigned from the position. If it wasn't for the murder of his brother, Jamar, Hakeem would have won by a landslide over Mya Rodriguez.

"There've been a lot of our children being murdered and discarded in Leakin Park by some monster," Hakeem firmly states to the room filled with glaring eyes. "Growing up we had a code, don't snitch. I'm not one to talk about going against a code, but as of today, our world has changed. A lot of us live off our phones, tablets, computers and the internet. That is now the medium being used to monitor what's going on around us, thanks to this Charm City Strangler. The surveillance plane is watching and recording our movements. Kids have a curfew during a hot and sunny summer here in Baltimore. Aleem and several other community leaders have done a lot of hard work to open recreation centers, but thanks to understandable laws, those hours are cut down to catch this child predator."

"What are you going to do about it?" Ms. Pugh yells at Hakeem as others cheer her on. "You called this meeting, invited these kids out here to talk about their feelings, but how are you going to stop this monster from killing our kids? I can't get my damn grandson back, but what are you going to do to stop it from happening to other kids? Does the mayor have to have his child murdered too in order to get some reasonable justice? We know who's doing the murdering. It's those damn whites that go to that Right Hand of God Fellowship Church. They been killing black people for years."

"Ms. Pugh," Hakeem begins to address Ms. Pugh's statements, "the police department has been investigating the hell out of this case. To date, they have found no correlation between the Right Hand of

God Fellowship Church and the Charm City Strangler."

"You're lying," Ms. Pugh retorts. "The kids that are murdered are black. The people that Carson Jessup and his members killed were black. Carson Jessup and that racist ass Guy Delaney are trying to pin this on somebody from our community."

"Where are you getting this information?" A woman from the audience asks as Ms. Pugh turns towards the brown skin woman who challenged her.

"The news," Ms. Pugh responds. "The internet. Anybody with a brain can look around and see someone with money, resources and a method to go undetected has been killing these youths. Commissioner Mercer and those crooked ass Baltimore City Police would have locked a nigga up weeks ago if it was truly a black person doing these murders."

"We're talking about street kids," Hakeem's aunt Monica chimes in. "Commissioner Mercer's son, King, was a known dirt bike rider. Camron Barnes was a known squeegee kid that harassed people at red lights for years. These are the people that we're mourning? Not kids going to school or work. We're talking street kids who need to have actual parents raise them."

"Excuse me," Ms. Pugh returns back to Monica. "My grandson did not deserve to be murdered and thrown under some sheet in the woods. If he rode a dirt bike or solicited money at a red light, that's still not a cause for murder."

"You must have never had to drive in this city," an older dark skin gentleman said sitting near Ms. Pugh. "I'm sick and tired of these dirt bike thugs riding round the city, not obeying traffic laws and damn near causing accidents. If one of them hits my car, who's covering the damages? If I hit one of these little niggas, I'm either going to get murdered by his gangster homies or I'm going to have to live the rest of my life with trauma because I hit one of these idiots with my car, by mistake of course. Let's not forget these other 'squeegee workers' won't leave you alone. I can say, 'I don't have it,' to these kids and they just call more of their friends over to my car until I give them $1 to $2 dollars to leave me alone. Or I can say, 'no thanks,' and they still clean my window, ask for money, and blow that funky ass weed smoke in my car. I don't want these kids to be murdered, but what is Mayor Hugo going to do about this problem once they catch the Charm City Strangler? 'Cause right now, the squeegee kids and the dirt bike riding has decreased. It's like the Charm City

Strangler is doing God's work, 'cause their parents ain't do shit but make excuses and more babies."

"I'm a whip yo' black ass!" a woman seated about three rows behind the older gentleman screams in anger, while holding a small baby.

"It's the truth," the older gentleman exclaims as he turns towards the woman holding the male infant. "I been telling kids for years, 'Hey, come by Mr. Wright's Auto Shop. I'll teach you how to repair vehicles. You'll have a trade and can always make money.' Those kids told me to kiss their ass, walked out my shop and stood on the corner across the street soliciting drivers for money. Who the hell wants to get their windows wiped when the rest of your car is dirty?"

"Nigga if you broke, say you broke," the angry mother screams back to the older gentleman we now know as Mr. Wright.

"Can we get back on subject?" Hakeem suggests in a forceful tone. Though he tries to hide his frustration, it's clear on his face. Hakeem takes a lot of pride in his presentations and public speaking. Interactions like what's going on between Mr. Wright and the mother holding the small child is something that makes Hakeem's blood boil. To be fair, a few years ago, these same people would be cheering and clapping for every word Hakeem would say. Following the incidents of Marshawn Bell, NAFA, the Action Figure Killer, Paul Douglass, Roland Wise, COVID-19, Titan Industries purchasing every piece of property, the murder rate, poisonous water and the Charm City Strangler, the tides have changed course in Baltimore.

"We've approached an impasse in the city," Hakeem continues as the eyes in the room lock onto my husband. "The mayor and the police commissioner are doing everything possible to catch this psychopath killing our children."

"Whoever it is, is a saint and doing the works of the Lord," Mr. Wright yells out as the mother of the young child attempts to get out of her seat and climb over others to get to him. She's restrained by several people seated near her.

"I'm going to whip yo' ass today, you old ass nigga," the woman yells at him.

Hakeem peers at Mr. Wright and the angry woman in the same manner I would Darrin, Desha, RJ or Trinity when they were younger. My youngest child, Kenya, never gave me problems. Kenya never acted out. Even though she died at a very young age, she was a good girl throughout her entire life.

"It's been a while since we actually sat back and thought about your youngest child," Marshawn says to me. His voice is almost a whisper in my mind.

"Let's not do this today," I say out loud as a male sitting to my left cuts his eyes towards me. Does he think I'm crazy? I'm not crazy, I just got stuff going on.

"You killed your dad," Marshawn points out. "Most normal people don't kill their father, and then gloat over their successes to their dying mother. Tiffany, your mother was dying in a hospital room, and you wanted to point out how she sucked as a mother."

"You forget; she enabled my father to rape me growing up. Then she denied it every chance she got," I explain out loud as the male sitting next to me turns in my direction. Almost as if I'm annoying him. Actually, I might be. I'm talking to a voice in my head during a community meeting.

"Tiffany, you won," Marshawn yells as everything goes black around me and I'm standing in front of Marshawn Bell in a large dark room.

"How did I win?" I ask. He leans against a chalkboard with several words written in white chalk and checkmarks next to the words.

"Let's walk you through your accomplishments," Marshawn states, pointing a yard stick at the board, imitating a teacher. "You freed yourself from the mental oppression of your father. You have made great accomplishments without the help or support of your mother. You graduated with a bachelor's and a master's degree in social work. You graduated with a master's in business. You've successfully raised four children. Trinity, who was severely burned in the house fire is receiving the best care money can buy to help with her trauma and night terrors. You run a bank along with owning a restaurant and grocery store. Your bank has helped address the water crisis. You're married to Hakeem Andrews. Y'all live in a nice home. Your old home is being rebuilt. Desha and RJ are doing great in art school. You and Sasha are back on speaking terms. You're actually bonding with your aunt Gina. You're not a victim, you're a winner."

"I'm glad you look at it that way; I'm a failure, though," I respond.

"No, you're not," Marshawn retorts. "You know how many women, or little girls have gone through what you've gone through? Do you not understand what your story would mean to them. You are an overcomer. You lost your daughter, Kenya to a hit and run. Unlike Erica Little, you didn't push away your surviving children. You went a little crazy, hearing voices, talking to dead family members in your grandmother's basement. Even letting me tell you to pull the trigger and kill your dear old dad. But you saved yourself. Even when you were kidnapped by the real Marshawn Bell, you didn't need Alex Tillman to save you. He chose to do that. When you were in the lawyer's office, you beat the dog piss out of Paul Douglass. You could have killed him yourself, but Alex Tillman got involved. You're your own hero. It's time other people recognize, you're not some woman that needs men to validate you. You're a woman that has pulled herself up and men can compliment you, but they don't make or mold you. Not even me."

Marshawn vanishes from the dark room I'm standing in, and my grandmother's face appears in front of me. It's as real as the times I used to go over to the house to eat Sunday dinner. She doesn't say a word. It's been so long since she died I've forgotten what her voice sounds like. She just watches me a while before winking her eye at me, then color and lights flood the dark room, bringing me back to the forum in the Allen Bradley Funeral Home.

"Instead of you and your wife acting like a power couple, we actually need you out here fighting for us," a middle age woman says to Hakeem. "You want to be Baltimore's hero, and your wife wants to be Baltimore's mother. Your wife fought against the water crisis, raised money, thanks to Kutter the Poet, and that's great. The problem is we have dead sons, and you're not helping. This meeting does nothing for any of us. Catch the Charm City Strangler. Hold people like Mya Rodriguez accountable for not being present and not meeting with us. We wanted you in office, not her. But you supported her, now she's in the Arts District working over there. She's not on the School Side, the Old Market Place or the Ridgely Homes side of Ridgely Square. Mya Rodriguez isn't even in the Duketown area."

"First, my wife and I don't believe we're some power couple. Second, I will reach out to Councilwoman Rodriguez about your concerns," Hakeem affirms. "Aleem and I will continue to work with the Knights to protect the Ridgely Square Community. I do plan to meet with the mayor later this week. I also plan to hold meetings in this very room for the rest of the week. In those meetings I plan on discussing grief, loss and feelings related to the Charm City Strangler murders. The kids need an outlet, and they need to know someone is out here for them. Years ago, we had Coach Edward Carter, a high school football coach and Baltimore City police officer who was gunned down by Alphas during the Kannard Lyles-Bey riots. I'm making it a point to stand in the gap and reach out to these youth that are hurting. I don't want to do this by myself. I'm inviting anyone in this room to help me with this effort. We still have two more months before summer break ends. Let's make it a point to reach out and help these kids."

Chapter 14

A few hours later, Hakeem and I go on a date to the DeLuca Bistro and Bakery. The current owner is James DeLuca, heir to the DeLuca Bakery fortune. His family moved to America from Sicily and started the bakery and oil press company that has become a major staple in Baltimore City. James DeLuca would later invest in Formula 1 racing, becoming a minority owner of the Baltimore Orioles and the Baltimore Ravens, and currently he's purchased a lot of land in the Sparrow's Point area to build a mega sports complex. His goal has been to bring a professional basketball and hockey team to Baltimore.

"How did it feel being up there speaking today?" I ask Hakeem and watch as his eyes light up.

"It felt great," Hakeem answers. He notices the tall thin-framed James DeLuca walking around the restaurant, speaking to guests and taking pictures with several of them. "We have to catch this Charm City Strangler guy. I don't think the city can survive another AFK situation."

"What do you mean?" I ask as Hakeem leans closer towards me.

"The copycats," he answers. "The reason the coverup worked so well for AFK was because Paul Douglass and Roland Wise attempted to carry out copycat killings. If you heard the guy Mr. Wright, the Charm City Strangler has been doing vigilante work in his opinion. AFK was looked at the same way until they pinned the murders on Paul Douglass."

"Why can't we let the police handle this?" I ask. Hakeem nods in agreement.

"We have to do something, though," he suggests. "All these kids are being murdered and left in Leakin Park. I get the park is big, but nobody has a clue, an idea or anything."

"I hear you, but let's let the police do their job," I restate as Hakeem makes a drum beat sound on the table before picking up the menu.

"If you could remake any movie, with any cast, what movie would it be and who would you cast?" Hakeem questions.

"We haven't played this game in a while," Marshawn says in the back of my mind.

"We haven't played this game in a while," I repeat out loud to Hakeem; he nods his agreement.

"Little Shop of Horrors," I answer, and Hakeem laughs loudly.

"You're weird," Marshawn says before finally shutting up for once.

"Who's your cast?" Hakeem asks while still laughing. James DeLuca makes brief eye contact with us as my husband continues to laugh.

"Hear me out," I plead attempting not to laugh at Hakeem's laughter. "Jim Carrey could play the dentist, the comedian from Baltimore, Monique, she could play the Audrey 2. Well, her or the other comedian from Baltimore, Manny the God."

"Who would play Seymour?" Hakeem asks as we both laugh uncontrollably.

"Don't laugh," I beg as Hakeem attempts to stop laughing before laughing and giggling some more. "Tom Holland or Jake Gyllenhaal."

Hakeem stops laughing and stares at me with the most inquisitive look in his eyes. "That actually is great casting. Who would you get to play Audrey?"

"Zendaya," I answer without any doubt in my mind. "Your turn."

"We live in a world of remakes and stuff," Hakeem replies before tapping on the table some more, making another drumbeat. Hakeem pauses for a few moments in silence, looking around the restaurant. The smell of fresh baked bread, oil, and spices fill the air.

"Ninja Turtles," Hakeem finally answers. "Not just any Ninja Turtles, the one from like the 90s, the Secret of the Ooze Ninja Turtles movie."

"That's hella specific," I answer as Hakeem begins laughing again.

"Michelangelo would be voiced by Kevin Hart," Hakeem expounds with his face turning red. He's trying to stop himself from laughing long enough to give me the cast. "Rafael would be voiced by Jason Matsoukis. Donatello would be voiced by Neil DeGrasse Tyson or Jesse Eisenberg. Leonardo would be voiced by 50 Cent."

We both burst out laughing louder as I ask, "Who would play Shredder, April O'Neal and Master Splinter?"

"Shedder can be played by Vincent D'Onofrio, or Hiroyuki Sinada," Hakeem suggests. "April can be played by Margot Robbie or Zazie Beets. Master

Splinter should be voiced by Morgan Freeman, Dewayne "The Rock" Johnson, or Ice-T."

"That is the craziest casting choice I've ever heard, and I want to see that movie," I contribute as James DeLuca walks to our table wearing a blue suit, with a white shirt and a multicolored tie. He's tall, appears to be in his mid-forties, with shoulder length slicked back brown hair. He has a clean-shaven face with a strong jawline.

"How are you two doing this evening?" James DeLuca asks. He talks with his hands moving and displays a lot of energy with his facial expressions. We both respond, "Good," as he leans forward to say, "Strength through elegance."

I've never heard that phrase before, and I'm unsure what James DeLuca is talking about as Hakeem shakes his head no towards James.

"My apologies, I figured that you both would have joined by now. You know, with Hakeem Andrews finally back at Andrews Memorial and all," James DeLuca mentions with a huge smile on his face, giving Hakeem strong eye contact."

"My sister follows more in my father's and grandfather's footsteps than I do," Hakeem informs DeLuca. "While the Flamingo Club has been a major part of the Andrews and DeLuca families, I'm not a member."

"What about your beautiful wife?" DeLuca asks. "The bank and grocery store owner. They call her the "Mom of Baltimore." The Flamingo Club needs your grace in our presence."

"Let's get the new water lines put in and catch this Charm City Strangler before I take on any more responsibilities," I joke, but I notice the happiness on Hakeem's face has dissipated.

"Well, either way I'm happy to have my friends in my restaurant," DeLuca exclaims, putting his hands together and bowing his head slightly. "Let me know if you all would like a bottle of wine. It's on me. Dr. Hakeem Andrews used to come here every year for his birthday. My father would make sure the best bakers were here every year to make Hakeem a fresh birthday cake. We used to buy newspapers and clip out all the accomplishments Hakeem, Kesha and Jamar made. Your parents raised three wonderful kids. I'm truly glad to call you my friends."

DeLuca shakes both of our hands and walks to the next table. I ask Hakeem, "What was that all about, that 'strength through elegance' line?"

"It's how the Flamingo Club members greet and say goodbye to each other," Hakeem answers. "Like their secret inside code amongst themselves. Outsiders aren't supposed to know about that. I watched my dad meet with James DeLuca's father and grandfather for years. They discussed all kinds of Flamingo Club business right here in this booth."

"Does it bother you?" I ask as Hakeem glances at DeLuca. "Like everything… being back at your father's church, being here, your sister pastoring, even the whole Flamingo Club inviting us in. Does any of that bother you?"

"All of it does," Hakeem admits. He glances at James DeLuca speaking to a couple at another table before looking back in my direction. "I never wanted to be a pastor. I left my father's church years ago because I knew it was a cult. I knew things weren't right with my parents, my aunt Monica, and the Flamingo Club. I was working as a social worker and getting my juris degree when Pastor Donald Avery first reached out to me. When I went to seminary school to get my doctorate in seminary, Donald Avery reached out to me again. Around that time, he knew he was dying from cancer. When Donald Avery died, Allen Bradley and I knew we had to do something, so we tried to revive and save the church. When we ran the church out of the funeral home, I tried to fix the financial problems Donald Avery and Florence Simms were dealing with all those years. Then Paul Douglass happened, and of course the fire that destroyed the church."

"None of that was your fault," I try to explain as Hakeem rejects my empathy.

"I should have never played church," Hakeem proclaims. "God has a way of showing himself to you and exposing you for being a fraud. I went to law school to expose the Maryland Board of Social Work for suppressing data and causing a shortage in licensed male mental health therapists due to their license exam. I was where I was supposed to be in those arenas. In the world of ministry, I was not in the right place."

"What are you talking about?" I question, in shock at Hakeem's reasoning. "Because of you, New Hope and Greater Love Church got out of debt and had money in their savings account. Because of you, New Hope and Greater Love Church was able to support several Baltimore communities and people in need. Because of you, several pastors and Islamic leaders joined together to create the 10th Bank. Because of you, Ridgely Square has its own patrol unit called the Knights, actually making a difference."

"You're saying because of me, not because of God," Hakeem points out. "God may have wanted me to advocate, organize and build. God did not want me to lead. The church was burned down because of me. Your grandmother's home was burned down because of me. Tiffany, it was a warning shot from God. It didn't matter if Milk, Marshawn Bell, or Alex Tillman pulled the trigger. The word of God has a scripture that reads, "Touch not my anointed." I was playing with the anointed people of God. I was acting in a role not meant for me. I was no better than my father or grandfather."

"Hakeem," I plead and he immediately cuts me off.

"You asked me a question, I just wanted to give you an honest answer," Hakeem explains. "I don't mind working in the community. I think this is what I'm supposed to do. But Kesha wants me to pastor Andrews Memorial so she can step down. I can't lead God's people. I don't even want to be in that church. Honestly, since Jamar was murdered, I don't know how I feel about God."

"Meaning?" I ask. Hakeem takes a sip of water out of the glass cup sitting on the table.

"If God is real, I have to be cursed," Hakeem elaborates. "I avoided Jamar for all those years just for him to get murdered when we bonded. I left my father's church, became a pastor and the freaking church burns down, with you and Darrin inside of it and shot. Trinity was burned up inside of your home, while we all were sleep, thanks to a home bombing. You got kidnapped and I got shot. Legit, everything bad that has happened in this city came because of my work as a pastor."

"All of that isn't your fault," I attempt to explain and provide reason, but Hakeem continues to reject my perspective.

"Tiffany, my existence is only to humor God," Hakeem says with a serious look on his face. "I figured that out a few years ago. Actually, it hit me in the hospital while the medical staff was doing scans and tests on Trinity after the house fire. As long as I keep God's name out my mouth, stay out of a pulpit and don't preach, my life will be ok. Sure, Jamar will still be dead, but nobody I know and love will have to suffer."

"Are you comfortable with your cousin, Raymond Nesmith, pastoring your family's church?" I ask. Hakeem shrugs his shoulders.

"I couldn't care less," Hakeem answers. "Those people at that church love the fact that it's a cult. They don't want me, they don't want the truth, they don't want to change."

"What happens if you have the opportunity to help them, and you don't because you have some unresolved grief over your brother's murder?" I question.

"My brother, my parents, the church members that died from the Coronavirus. All of it," Hakeem contextualizes. "I guess I'd be cursed. Who knows. That's on Kesha, not on me."

"But Kesha came to you with the idea of you pastoring the church, correct?" I ask as Hakeem nods yes. "Then trust the fact that God wants you to still do his work, just over here and not at New Hope and Greater Love Ministries."

As I finish my appeal to Hakeem's religious confliction, several appetizers arrive at the table. This catches me completely off guard because neither Hakeem nor I ordered anything. I turn towards James DeLuca who winks and smiles at my husband and me before he walks to the back of the restaurant.

"How do places like this restaurant stay open, even during the water crisis?" I ask Hakeem as he looks over the appetizers.

"Well water from a reserve near Ellicott City," Hakeem answers confidently. "Back in the 1970s my grandfather purchased a lot of land in Westminster. Baltimore Gas and Electric purchased that land paying millions to my father in the late 1990s. My father took a tiny portion of that profit and purchased several acres of land in the Woodstock area of Baltimore County. My father soon learned that under that land was a huge underwater bank of fresh water. The Flamingo Club wanted to start a water purifying company with the newfound fresh water, but my father said no. The Flamingo Club soon found an underground body of fresh water on the edge of Ellicott City. They worked with my father in the early 2000s to run fresh water from what they called The Titan Industry Reserve in Ellicott City to this restaurant, Andrews Memorial and a couple other places."

"What happened to your father's land in Woodstock?" I ask eagerly, anxious to hear the answer but also wanting to eat.

"My father built a large homeless shelter on the property for displaced families and women fleeing domestic violence," Hakeem answers, while reaching onto the table for shrimp scampi. "Kesha recently started building out there, too. They were trying to start a college."

"Are you going to say grace, or are we just diving into these free appetizers?" I ask as Hakeem partially smiles and agrees to pray over the food. Before he can get a word out, my cell phone begins to ring. Before I hit the Ignore button, I notice it's my son, Darrin, calling. Not sure what to expect, I answer the phone to an excited and animated Darrin. Darrin is not an animated teenager. I know he's been going through his own grief because of the recent murder of his friend Cam.

"Ma, are you still out on a date with Hakeem?" Darrin asks, as I confirm his suspicion. He's talking loudly and his words are coming at a rapid-fire pace. He sounds like he's in a panic. "Ma, it's bad. I been looking for Duck all day, that's why we weren't at the funeral home earlier when you and Hakeem were speaking. The police just found Duck dead in Leakin Park. He was under a sheet. It's all over the news. Can you come home?"

"We're on the way," I say as Hakeem looks on, confused by my statement.

Chapter 15

A little over an hour later, Hakeem and I were home. Darrin sat on the couch listening to music through his headphones. The wooden living room floor is swept and mopped, something I normally have to beg Darrin to do. The first-floor bathroom was completely spotless and smelled like Pine-Sol. The jackets, hoodies and shoes are inside the closet, instead of thrown about near the front door. There's an open brown Bible on the coffee stand near the long couch. I'm confused. Is this the same son I have to beg to wash dishes, that's doing his part tonight?

"Is this what grief does, makes children do chores? If that's the case, let me go kill some more of Darrin's friends," Marshawn jokes in the back of my mind, making me roll my eyes at his sordid sense of humor. I look over and notice the pure sense of sadness on Darrin's face.

Darrin sits between us, Hakeem on his right and I sit on his left. I touch his knee to get his attention. "I want to tell you I know the words to say, but I don't."

"I've lost so many good friends, Mama," Darrin utters as he takes the earphones off and places them on the coffee table. "Back in 2019 Moose got killed during the Incident. The dudes Antonio and Jeff that stayed in our building, they got killed for nothing. Then they killed Ms. Stone, the lady that used to let Desha and me use her internet for schoolwork. Why did they kill her? Why is murder the answer? Even with that whole AFK thing, did he have to kill all them niggas? If he was white, would he have gotten away with what he did?"

"Darrin," I begin, searching for the words to say. My oldest son is hurting because his best friend since childhood was found dead in the woods. I don't have the words. As Darrin looks at me with bated breath all I can think about is the look on his face when I told him and his twin sister Desha that their younger sister, Kenya, died in a hit and run car accident. I can't avoid this moment like I did in the past. Back in 2017 I would just hide in the basement and not talk about Grandma Florence's, Kenya's, Uncle Larry's or Tina's deaths. Even when the house was firebombed, I didn't know what to say. We were at the burn unit with Trinity for weeks, and I never knew what to say. Hakeem was grieving the death of his brother Jamar but spent more time dealing with my family drama instead of processing his own problems. Is that fair? Is that what a man is supposed to do? Is that what we project on men in society?

"Darrin," Hakeem chimes in, "when I was 16, 2 friends of mine were murdered for 2 different reasons. My friend Tyrell was murdered leaving a house party over at the West Port Homes. Back in the day, high school and middle school kids used to have basement parties. We'd play club music and the best R&B or hip hop tracks and dance for hours. Kids would hook up, kiss, all kinds of stuff. Anyway, Tyrell went to this party over there. For whatever reason, my dad wouldn't let Kesha, Jamar or me leave the house that day. We gave him every excuse why we should go. He forced us to play the keyboards and the guitars that evening. When Jamar and I started putting up the music equipment and started cleaning the kitchen my dad got a phone call from Tyrell's mother letting us know he was shot and killed leaving the house party."

"What about your other friend?" Darrin asks.

"That was this kid named Quintin," Hakeem answers. "He played football with Jamar and me. He used to come over all the time and play basketball around the corner from the house. Quintin got killed because one of his best friends liked his girlfriend."

"What did you and Jamar do to get him revenge?" Darrin questions. You can see the hopelessness in his face. He's looking for anything to make himself feel better, or maybe he just wants someone to connect with him. Lord knows I've sucked in that department. I didn't even know how to talk to him or Desha about their father being murdered in prison.

"We couldn't do anything," Hakeem answers looking down at the floor. "The guy who killed Tyrell was a dude name Swift. Tyrell used to hustle for Swift and owed him money for a long time. Swift got murdered a few months later, but it had nothing to do with Jamar or me."

"What about the Quintin nigga? What did y'all do about that?" Darrin explores.

"His best friend turned himself in a day or two after the funeral," Hakeem recalls. "I'm saying all of this for a reason. Sometimes bad people and murderers exist. They take and they hurt the living, forcing us to lean on old memories when we wish we could be making new memories with the people we miss. You and Duck have been best friends since y'all were like eight or nine months. Take the time to be angry, sad, cry, and ask questions. Don't bottle up the feelings you have right now. You and Duck were the best of friends. Y'all always had each other's back. You don't have nothing to regret."

"Do you have any regrets?" Darrin asks as the atmosphere in the room shifts. Darrin's eyes grow wide with hope, but Hakeem's facial expression breaks down to pure sadness. His eyes look weepy, his cheeks and lips rest into an expression I can only call broken.

"I do," Hakeem answers after taking a deep breath and exhaling. Hakeem takes a brief glance at the ceiling before turning towards Darrin. "I wish I went to Quintin's funeral. I lied to my parents and told them I had to go to work that day. I just didn't want to see Quintin lying in that casket and then watch him get buried. I wasn't there. I wanted to deny that he was dead. Like, maybe he moved or got locked up. But when I came home that night, there was Quintin's obituary on the table. I saw his picture on the cover of that obituary, and I lost it. I cried, Darrin. I wanted to kill Quintin's best friend after I found out it was him who did it. I wanted to buy a sniper rifle and shoot him while he was working out in the yard. Then I saw Quintin's mother, and my anger turned to something else."

"What?" Darrin asks, completely locked in on every word Hakeem is stating.

"Shame," Hakeem answers. "The funeral wasn't for me; it was for her. Quintin was her son, and that was the last time she was going to actually see his body. Quintin's classmates, friends and teammates were there, but his best friend wasn't. To this very day, I don't know what to say to her. I just see his face when I look in her face. She loves me like I'm Quintin now, and I respect that. She's proud of all the "things" I've accomplished, but I have shame for not being there for her when she needed me. That's not even the worst part."

Hakeem takes a deep breath, turns to me and then back to Darrin, "My biggest regret is all the years I didn't talk to Jamar. Jamar got me out of so many bad situations when we were younger. Then I let my dad and the church divide us. I acted like he killed Quintin or Tyrell when he got locked up for selling drugs. I should point out, a portion of the drugs he was caught with I was supposed to be selling. He never told on me. Not to the police, not to our parents. But I let time pass us by. If it wasn't for the Alphas and that crooked detective Marshawn Bell, I probably wouldn't have talked to him to this day. He may still be alive if I never got back in contact with him. Darrin, that's the point I'm trying to make. You were a real friend to Duck. You loved Duck, your brother RJ loved Duck, Trinity and Desha loved Duck. Duck loved all of y'all. You have nothing to regret as a friend. You can feel bad, sad or depressed, but don't walk around with the guilt or burden I have because of Jamar."

"I hope you're happy," a voice yells from outside. "Tiffany Andrews, bring your Mother of Baltimore ass outside!"

Caught off guard, Hakeem, Darrin and I look at each other before Hakeem hands me a dark gray handgun from under the couch cushion. Hakeem reaches between the armrest and the couch cushion and pulls out another handgun. As he and I walk armed to the door, we fan Darrin away in the hopes that he doesn't get hurt.

"Tiffany, come outside," the voice yells as we open the door to find Ms. Pugh standing on the sidewalk in front of our home.

"What can I help you with, Ms. Pugh?" I ask with my heart beating hard as hell. A group of young men are across the street leaning on a car, smoking weed and laughing at this whole scenario. And halfway down my block is a pile of stuffed black trash bags, boxes of bottles and trash-filled grocery bags. Draped on all of that is a middle-aged man lying faced down clutching a bottle of whisky, loudly singing the most unique version of "Oops" by Tweet I've ever heard. It sounds good, though.

"That kid Duck, that's on you!" Ms. Pugh yells at me.

"Ms. Pugh, you can blame me or whatever, but do you have to yell?" I ask as she begins to charge up the stone steps with her fist clenched.

"You don't want me to yell?" Ms. Pugh asks in an intimidating fashion.

"Sorry to butt in," Marshawn says in the back of my mind. "Why is she intimidating us when you and Hakeem are armed and dangerous? You can send her to her daughter and grandson, like right now. Is she not reading the room?"

"Shut up!" I yell at Marshawn and Ms. Pugh walks directly in my face.

"What did you say to me?" Ms. Pugh asks as I hold my gun-free hand up, trying to get her to calm down.

"No, that wasn't for you," I explain. The best part of that, I wasn't lying.

"Don't play with me, little girl," Ms. Pugh demands.

"Don't disrespect me calling me a little girl," I bark back.

"That boy Duck was murdered. The police chief's son was murdered. My grandson was murdered. You wanted to do a damn crab feast fund raiser for tap water," Ms. Pugh monologues. "Are you dumb, stupid or losing a terminal battle with common-sense cancer? We have black boys being murdered. We have a religious organization admitting to killing black working people. You two are the most influential people in Baltimore. You do a fundraiser in Harlem Park for the freaking water, but don't even mention the dead black kids in Leakin Park. You have yet to raise money for a reward. Your husband has his fake group of police called the Knights and they been letting this Charm City Strangler snatch kids right in front of their faces. I need y'all to do better. Protect these black boys like you was quick to protect this house with them two ugly ass guns."

"Goodnight, Ms. Pugh," I say as she begins to walk down the steps to the drunken singing of James Brown's *It's a Man's World.*

As I turn away from Ms. Pugh, I lock eyes with Hakeem, who leans in to kiss me. I mentally I feel liberated. For the first time in my life, a man defended me. He wraps his firmly toned arms around me, holding his 40 caliber handgun, as I wrap mine around him holding my 32 caliber. We pull each other closer, embracing and sucking each other's lips as the group of guys across the street provide play-by-play commentary for our moment of passion, which has now escalated to him grabbing my buttocks and pulling me into the house. We continue to kiss, grab and pull away at each other's clothes with the front door open. In this very moment, we're like two animals in heat. There's a magnetism between us that's unbreakable. Hakeem grabs my hair, pulling it back gently, but in a dominating fashion while sucking on my neck near my collarbone. As Hakeem begins to move his hands down my body and starts unbuttoning my jeans, there's a beeping sound in the background that pauses all of our adult festivities. What was that beeping sound? I've heard it a billion times. Suddenly, we hear the TV turn on. Darrin has the PlayStation remote in his hand, ignoring us.

"My bad, Darrin," Hakeem says as he and I giggle. It's like we got caught. Since our destination wedding in Jamaica, Hakeem and I have been sneaking around the house, hiding from the kids, just to make out or make love. Sometimes the lack of privacy leads to arguments, sometimes wordless frustrations. That being said, we still love each other. With everything that has been happening over the last few years, the two constants in my life are Hakeem and the children. It doesn't matter if the community loves me, or Ms. Pugh hates my guts, Hakeem is always in my corner. For decades Sasha has been my best friend, but Hakeem has started to secure her spot. It's not because I dislike Sasha, I love her, but the bond and partnership I have with Hakeem trumps the sisterhood I have with Sasha.

"Y'all going to go upstairs or should I?" Darrin asks, looking at Hakeem, and I stand frozen at the front door.

"Why you stop them niggas, dummy? We was 'bout to get a free show till this dickhead wanna go and break them two up." One of the guys across the street scream into the house as Hakeem closes the door. We all laugh for a moment until Hakeem grabs the other game controller and sits down next to Darrin. Hakeem's facial expression changes from pure bliss and tranquility to sadness. It's like a heavy burden just took him over as soon as he closed the door. I'm glad he's spending time with Darrin; he needs him more than ever thanks to Duck's murder. I just wish we could have had some adult time together tonight.

"Nothing ever goes right in this family," Marshawn jokes as a slight smirk appears on my face.

Chapter 16

A couple days later my aunt Gina, Darrin, Ms. Pugh and Duck's mother, WaKitta are sitting in the family meeting room at the Allen Bradley Funeral Home. Gina came to support WaKitta with the goal of having her as a guest on my aunt's podcast. Ms. Pugh has been active with all of the families whose loved ones were killed by the Charm City Strangler. Darrin wanted to be here to support WaKitta because Duck was his best friend since they were toddlers.

WaKitta is a short, chubby dark-skinned female with shoulder length hair pulled back with a rubber band into a ponytail. The whites in her eyes are completely yellow and she has puffed cheeks. Her lips are nearly black in color, and she has a dark line across her nasal bridge. Her bottom teeth are all gold, and she has a large tattoo of a star on her neck. She actually has several tattoos that are very hard to make out, on her fingers, and the back of her hand and wrist. WaKitta is a few years older than me, and we never had the best relationship when we lived across the hall from each other. She lost legal custody of her other two children in 2015. When Titan Industries purchased our apartment building, WaKitta and Duck moved into a room for rent near the Westside Shopping Center.

"Why are *you* here?" Ms. Pugh asks me in a raspy and challenging voice. She's slowly growing me to anger and I'm trying my best to chill. I respect my elders and all, but this lady is getting real disrespectful towards me.

"The 10th Bank is committed to doing work in the community," I answer as politely as possible. "We learned that Ms. WaKitta has a Go Fund Me page set up because she doesn't have life insurance in place for Duck. The 10th Bank is willing to cover all the expenses for Duck's services."

"I'm not some piece of charity," WaKitta sternly says with a sharp tone. She has a strong and loud voice. When she speaks, her facial expression changes as if she's seeking a confrontation or challenging someone to say something after her.

"No ma'am," I respond. "The 10th Bank wants to do right by anybody affected by violence in this community. Our mission is to serve our people to make a better Baltimore for all of us."

"Lying wench," Ms. Pugh spouts. "You was out doing crab feasts and fish fries when them white folks were killing our boys and dragging them into the woods. They even killed that police chief's boy. Now they done got her son. Why you didn't fundraise for that instead of them water pipes."

"Ms. Pugh, I don't want to go back and forth with you," I state as WaKitta shakes her hands for Ms. Pugh and me to stop talking.

"My nephew's going to pay for Duck's services," WaKitta reveals. "My nephew is Kutter the Poet. He'll be in this meeting in a few minutes."

"WaKitta, if there's anything the 10th Bank can do to help, please let me know." There's a knock on the door and Kutter the Poet enters the room. He immediately walks over to WaKitta and hugs her as the two talk and sob together.

"Hey y'all," Kutter the Poet greets in a deep and somber tone. "I'm going to take care of all the expenses for Duck's funeral. My Aunt WaKitta told me she wanted to do a service and a cremation."

"You don't want to bury him?" Ms. Pugh asks as WaKitta shakes her head no.

"I don't want to ride nobody's bus or get a ride to the cemetery and then have to ride all the way back home.

I heard people was getting robbed at the cemetery anyway. I can get him cremated right here and have him home with me all the time."

"Can we help at all?" I ask as I look at the angry expressions on both Ms. Pugh's and WaKitta's faces.

"You was out solving a water problem in the city when we had another serial killer terrorizing our black boys," WaKitta answers. "You have helped enough."

"We're putting a reward out for this Charm City Strangler," Kutter the Poet adds. "I'm putting $80,000 of my money on the table for anyone that can give me information on who this Charm City Strangler guy is."

"You, not the police?" Gina asks as Kutter the Poet, Ms. Pugh and WaKitta briefly chuckle.

"The Charm City Strangler killed the police chief's son. Did y'all forget?" WaKitta asks. "The best hands to handle our problems are our own. If you want to get the Knights involved that's cool, but I don't want Baltimore City's crooked police nowhere near this. We gonna find this nigga and deal with him ourselves."

"But—" I begin as WaKitta cuts me off instantly.

"If you want to help, tell your husband to preach at my son's funeral," WaKitta says, "also, I want his funeral service at Andrews Memorial. You do that, and we can call it even."

"They won't hold the funeral at Andrews Memorial," I state as WaKitta stares me in the face and Ms. Pugh looks on with a disgusted expression. "Andrews Memorial has a strict policy that non-members of the church aren't allowed to be married or have funeral services at the church."

"So, you're useless," Ms. Pugh proclaims.

"I'm not the pastor. It's out of my hands," I respond. I feel out of place and now I'm fearful that I'm going to have to fight my way out this room.

"What if I give them some money?" Kutter the Poet asks. I shake my head no.

"We'll have the service here at Allen Bradley's Funeral Home then," WaKitta states firmly. "I still want your husband to give the message."

My mind begins to race as I think about Hakeem and the changes in his mood since his brother died. Hakeem went from a man who loved doing community service and doing ministry work, to being a shell of his former self.

"He'll do it," Darrin answers. Darrin and Hakeem have a great relationship, and my husband would do anything for the kids. If anybody can haul Hakeem into a pulpit to give a 45-minute sermon, it's Darrin.

"What are you talking about," Marshawn says in the back of my mind as everything turns black and all I can see is him wearing a black t-shirt that says, "Staff," in white letters.

"What do you mean?" I ask Marshawn as he points at a theater screen behind him. The movie screen magically appears out of nowhere as a black and white film of Marshawn and me starts to play.

The film is from 2019, days after my mother died from organ failure. Hakeem is sitting quietly on the couch at home as I walk into the house with my twins Darrin and Desha. I remember this day. Hakeem and I were engaged, Trinity was in the burn unit at the hospital and RJ was in the basement practicing on the piano. Allen Bradley came to the house that day and wanted to offer to hold my mother's funeral service for free. This was a few days after the church burned down. Allen wanted Hakeem to move New Hope Greater Love Church back into the funeral home until the church was rebuilt. Hakeem said no to bringing the church back to the funeral home because he was having a conflict of faith after Jamar was gunned down by Roland Wise and Paul Douglass.

"Things didn't get better after this day, did it?" Marshawn Bell asks as I respond no. "This was around the time when Hakeem started to really detach from the world. Do you remember the breakfast on the yacht in Jamaica, the morning before the wedding?"

That was a weird day, Hakeem would only talk to Darrin or RJ. Allen Bradley, who owns and operates the funeral home we're at right now, tried to talk to Hakeem the whole trip but was unsuccessful. There was a couple staying at the resort that was arguing the whole time, and when things got physical between the two, Hakeem tried to fight the guy. The resort staff broke up the altercation. Then there was the fight at the poolside bar. Hakeem and some random guest got into it about who knows what. The whole trip on the yacht was weird cause of that fight. I remember he got heated when someone asked him about Jamar.

"That's not exactly what happened," Marshawn continues. "Allen asked Hakeem if anyone from Andrews Memorial would be joining us. As you and I both know, only Raymond and your aunt Monica were in attendance. When Allen asked about what happened to Hakeem's parents in Africa, that's when Hakeem snapped."

What did happen to his parents? I wonder as a large bulletin board appears with pictures and phrases thumbtacked to it. There are red and black strings running from one picture to the next picture and then to phrases. In the center of the bulletin board is a picture of Hakeem's sister, Kesha with her head circled with a red marker.

"What happened to Pastor Andrews and his wife?" Marshawn asks. "We know what happened to Jamar, sadly. All we know about Hakeem's parents is they died on a mission trip in Africa around the same time Jamar died."

"We need to focus on this funeral planning," I say, trying to redirect the conversation as the board begins to change. Kesha's face is large in the center. A small red yarn string stretches across the board as a picture of Mayor Hugo's picture appears in the lower left corner of the board. A small red string stretches across to the bottom of the board as a picture of Erica Little appears in the right corner circled in black marker. The red string runs up the board to a picture of Alex Tillman at the top right-hand side. Another red string runs across the top of the board to the top left corner as a picture of a silhouette with a red question mark in the center appears.

"What is this?" I ask in a panic. I don't like blacking out and talking to Marshawn, especially when I'm conducting business. It's like the basement at my grandmother's house but worse. At least when I talked to the voices in the basement, nobody was around. Nobody in the outside world thought I was crazy. These blackout spells happen without warning, and it's always Marshawn Bell. It's never my father, my mother, my grandmother, my cousin Tina or my daughter Kenya.

"You've healed from your parents, your daughter and Tina," Marshawn answers without my permission. He's always giving unsolicited advice. "The problem with healing from grief is the world keeps turning, so more problems arise. When you inherited the home from your grandmother, Florence Simms, you would have never guessed that you'd be dealing with the Alphas, the Cabal and the Narcotics and Firearms Taskforce. You would have never thought you'd be in a collision course with Paul Douglass. You would have never thought that you'd be in the path of the Action Figure Killer, yet all those things happened."

"Ok, but what's your point?" I ask as Marshawn points at Kesha's picture on the board and other pictures appear with skull and bones crossed on the chest areas of the pictures. The pictures include Roland Wise, Jamar Andrews, Paul Douglass, Marshawn Bell, Junior Dawson, City Councilman Dawson, State's Attorney Jada Austin, and Duck and Anna Cartwright.

"In 2016 Erica Little and her then husband Sedrick Little were in the process of starting the community redevelopment project in Ridgely Square with Hugo's adult twin children, Chanel and Chandler Titan. During that time, Erica and Sedrick's child Silk was murdered in the Old Marketplace Area of Ridgely Square by your father. Those events would set in motion several catastrophic events that included the rise of the real Sgt. Marshawn Bell and the partnership he created with the Alphas. It would also set the Action Figure Killer in motion to terrorize the people in Ridgely Square. Jamar would be killed as a byproduct of the insanity that was going on."

"What does that have to do with anything?" I ask as Marshawn points back at Kesha's picture.

"New Hope Greater Love Church was burned down," Marshawn explains. "You and Hakeem went back to Andrews Memorial with the goal of bonding with

Kesha and the rest of Hakeem's family. The problem is Hakeem's parents were killed and his sister has never given a clear answer as to why. Kesha also wants Hakeem to take over the church. Hakeem is adamantly against it but won't give any further context other than the church being a cult. So, I leave you with this question, why?"

"Why what?" I question.

"Why would Kesha want Hakeem to run the church when Raymond Nesmith is right there doing the work?" Marshawn ponders this as a picture of Raymond Nesmith appears next to Kesha. "We need some truths. We need to know what happened to Hakeem's and Kesha's parents in Africa. We need to know why Kesha wants Hakeem to run the church so badly. We need to know what Kesha is really up to."

"How are we supposed to get those answers," I question as everything turns bright around me and Ms. Pugh looks on at me disgusted.

"Are you with us, Mrs. Andrews?" Ms. Pugh questions as I nod to provide an answer. "I thank you for your time. Please let me know what your husband says about preaching at Duck's service."

I feel embarrassed. I don't know how much of the conversation I had with Marshawn Bell was said out loud. I need to get some help. These blackout spells are happening too frequently.

Chapter 17

That evening our home is awkwardly quiet. Hakeem is in the basement lifting weights and punching his heavy boxing bag. Darrin is in his room listening to music through his headphones. I am able to video chat with Desha, RJ and Trinity, which is always a plus. Darrin now keeps all conversations to hi, bye, thank you and no thanks. Since I left the Allen Bradley Funeral Home, I've gone back and forth on how to talk to Hakeem about his parents' deaths.

This conversation is easier said than done because I know Hakeem doesn't have the answers, but I'm not sure if he's asked any of the questions.

"What are the questions?" Marshawn asks me as I walk into the kitchen to grab lunch meat and cheese out the refrigerator. As I close the silver door to the fridge back, I notice pictures of Hakeem and me, along with pictures of the children that are stuck to the fridge by way of magnets.

"What happened in Africa?" I say out loud. "Who was with them on the mission trip? Did your parents have any problems with any of the people on the outreach trip?"

"Do you want me to answer those questions, or are you just thinking out loud?" Hakeem questions walking up the basement steps, drenched in sweat with a black towel draped over his head. There's a visible smile on his face that gives me calm based on his up and down mood as of late.

"I don't know how to ask you the questions, and I don't know if you have the answers," I respond.

"With the water crisis being resolved, and Duck's funeral being put together, we can talk about my parents and the church," Hakeem answers. "I want to give you all the answers on what I know, but I think we should call my sister to get the full picture of what happened."

"Are you sure you're ready for that?" I ask as Hakeem dries the sweat off his face and shoulders.

An hour later, Hakeem has showered, and the two of us are sitting on the couch, Kesha walks into the living room wearing jeans and a t-shirt that reads, "Andrews Memorial." My mind is racing because this conversation can go brutally bad. We're dealing with trauma and family secrets. To be fair, I was raised up with trauma and family secrets. It's shocking that

Hakeem's family is so much different from mine but so similar at the same time.

"Hey Kesha," I begin. I had this whole speech in my mind. I've been rehearsing in my head how to talk to Kesha about this whole situation, but now that she's here, the words won't come out. If it was my flesh and blood, I couldn't care less, I'd just ask the questions. But with Hakeem, his family has been a staple of greatness in the Baltimore black community for decades. How do I, a person from Ridgely Square, approach a Kesha Stokes. The same person that made the 10th Bank successful. The same Kesha Stokes that handles the finances of so many athletes and celebrities. The Kesha Stokes that handles the finances of the Flamingo Club. I think I bit off more than I could chew. This could potentially be a mistake.

"Kesha," I begin again, "In 2019 Jamar was taken from us all by the Action Figure Killer."

"Not the real AFK, but I understand why you're keeping up with the story the FBI and the police want told around me," Kesha blurts out, surprising me that she knows that the real AFK didn't kill Jamar.

"In 2019 Jamar was taken from us by who the police have identified as the Action Figure Killer," I restart as Kesha begins to drink out of her bottle of water.

"I'm going to tell you all the facts before you go any further," Kesha assures as she takes a large gulp of water. "In 2019, our father, Pastor Hakeem Jonah Andrews and his wife, Grace Andrews, our aunt and uncle, Monica and Kelly Nesmith, and our cousin Raymond went on a mission trip to Burkina Faso. During that time the FBI were investigating the Alphas because of NAFA, and your aunt, Gina Simms. That being said, Paul Douglass, and other members of the Flamingo Club were using our private jets, provided by Erica and Sedrick Little, to move synthetic opioids developed by the West Baltimore Medical Center all over the globe."

"Why was my father allowing that?" Hakeem questions as Kesha stops him.

"Our father was against it," Kesha explains. "Our father and Paul Douglass would have several conflicts of interest during our Flamingo Club meetings. Dad was not a fan of Paul Douglass, and he hated the heat that Paul had on him from the FBI. Paul had gained favor with other members of the Flamingo Club that included Neil Goldberg, that owns the West Baltimore

Hospital, Khin from the Black Tie, and James DeLuca. The synthetic opioid also kept the Dulaney Crime Family in debt to us, which made them easier to control. The Dulaney Crime Family has been a rival of the Flamingo Club for decades, but we have always kept it professional."

"They're a bunch of racists," Hakeem exclaimed, and I agreed with him.

"Of course the former governor, Guy Dulaney, is a part of them," Kesha agreed. "The Right Hand of God Fellowship Church is also affiliated with them. Mayor Hugo didn't want anything to do with the Dulaney Crime Family, nor did he want anything to do with Paul Douglass."

"What happened to our parents?" Hakeem questions.

"Paul knew that Mayor Hugo couldn't stand him," Kesha continues to explain. "When the Club decided it would be best to have Hugo run for mayor and correct the course of the city, we had to figure out what to do with Paul Douglass. In every sense of the word, Paul was dangerous. He was connected with the Alphas. He knew our workings as a shadow mafia. He knew how we controlled the whole city at every level. So the initial goal was to have him killed by the FBI. But there was a huge deal with a person known as General Midnight in Burkina Faso.”

“Who the hell is General Midnight?” I ask as Hakeem and Kesha look at me.

“Born Franklin John, General Midnight was known to traffic women, boys and girls all over the world.” Then Kesha provides further insight, “General Midnight, Paul Douglass, Khin and Neil Goldburg got really close and started planning the mission trips with our father. To make better sense of things, when our father would go to Brazil, Chile, different parts of Asia or Africa, General Midnight and Paul Douglass were smuggling drugs, people and organs in the church’s private jets. In the end, our father stood up to the Flamingo Club and tried to get everybody back to what we stood for.”

“How did he die?” Hakeem questions as a slight expression of concern shoots across Kesha’s perfect face.

“Midnight and his people killed our parents and Uncle Kelly,” Kesha answers. “They made me promise to handle the Flamingo Club’s finances and keep what they were doing off the books. Hugo was against what General Midnight and Paul Douglass were doing. Neil

Goldberg and Khin continued to work with General Midnight. DeLuca, who made a small fortune moving cocaine all over the world and washing the money through his Formula 1 race car team was against General Midnight and Paul Douglass."

"Can you get to the damn point," I ask as Kesha peers in my direction in annoyance.

"When the Action Figure Killer, the real one, the Alex Tillman version killed Paul Douglass and Roland Wise, it put things in perspective. A few weeks before Jamar was murdered, our parents were killed. We kept it hush hush with the goal of figuring out how to spin it to the church and the rest of the Flamingo Club. By now, you've figured out the Flamingo Club was involved in their murder, or I should say a fraction of the Flamingo Club was involved in their murder. My mission was course correction and getting out of the Flamingo Club," Kesha explains. "The first step in getting out was finding the replacements necessary to make a clean exit. With the success of the 10th Bank, bringing Tiffany into the fold made great sense. The money from the Club is already in the 10th Bank, and the 10th Bank is already doing great work in the community. Hakeem returning back to the church was great, because we could install him as pastor, and I could step down and run my side project."

"Is that what this is all about?" Hakeem questions. "You want to get out and throw me back into this mess I escaped from?"

"No," Kesha answers. "I want the church out of the Flamingo Club completely. I can't trust Raymond with the title of pastor. He's enamored with the thought of being a part of the Flamingo Club. He loves the church, but he really wants to be like our father and our grandfather. He's fixated on the power that Andrews Memorial has in Baltimore City. Hakeem, I see you as the person that can break the tradition. You will run Andrews Memorial and guide the church into the future. Tiffany and I will figure out how to get the Flamingo Club away from the 10th Bank."

"You just said they killed your father; you really want them to have a chance with me because I don't want to play ball with them?" I ask in fear. This silent mafia is dangerous. "Where is General Midnight?"

"He was killed in an off books mission," Kesha explains. "The details are sketchy. Some people said that the real AFK killed him."

"What?" I ask as a smile finally shoots across Kesha's face.

"Somebody with talents like Alex Tillman. It would be right up his alley to do something like that," Kesha explains. "Alex Tillman, the real AFK, already took out several members of the Alphas and the Cabal. He also took out several crooked politicians and big names in the city. When he was going on the run, I had a friend of mine from the FBI reach out to him. We gave the AFK a laundry list of targets that we both agreed were appropriate. Some of the names included a racist from Florida who shot and killed an unarmed African American child walking home from football practice in 2013, and a racist piece of garbage who shot up a black church in South Carolina. He's also took out a racist police officer in Michigan who killed a black college student walking to his dorm room, and another police officer who shot and killed her black neighbor in his apartment while he was watching TV."

"So you turned AFK into a weapon for the Flamingo Club?" Hakeem questions.

"No," Kesha responds quickly. The smile on her face vanishes as quickly as it appeared. "He's working with me and an FBI agent to take out the criminals that the law let slip by. That's not what's important. What's important is Andrews Memorial is doing something it has never done. Not be attached to the Flamingo Club. We can all accomplish that if we work together."

"I'm not pastoring that church," Hakeem expresses while pounding harshly on his chest.

"Why?" Kesha asks.

"It's a cult," Hakeem answers. "That church is all about status, presentation and is a joke. I'm not Dad. I can't do the work needed as pastor, knowing all the secrets that church has. I don't want any ties to the Flamingo Club either. You've been pastoring that church; you keep doing it."

"No," Kesha responds. "It has to be blood, our father's blood that runs that church. Jamar is dead. As far as everyone knows, I'm you're adopted sister."

"Again, another family secret," Hakeem blurts out.

"You're not wrong," Kesha agrees.

"No, don't do that," Hakeem continues. "Dad used to agree with people to get his point across and things would work out for him. Don't do that with me. We have the same parents. Our father covered it up because his wife couldn't have children. Jamar and I were looked on as blessed and you were looked on as the adopted sister who had a whore mother; in reality all three of us had the same father and mother. When your mother died, they sat in the pulpit and trashed her legacy and memory every Sunday. I didn't forget any of that. Now you want me to come back and lead that church with the secrets and lies that church was built on? Nope. Not going to do it."

"Hakeem, hear me out," Kesha pleads. "Andrews Memorial needs to go in a new direction. You are the perfect person to do it. Look at what you did at New Hope Greater Love Church. In a funeral home, you were packing it out week in and week out. When you all went back into that church building, you were packing that small church out every Sunday. Imagine what you can and will do at Andrews Memorial."

"I'm not interested," Hakeem exclaims. "I'm only there now to spend time with you. I don't want to be near Aunt Monica, I don't want to be around the drama of that church. I don't even want to preach."

"But you are asked to preach at Duck's funeral." I interject.

"Yes, and Duck's family would like for his funeral service to be at Andrews Memorial," Hakeem adds.

"Neither Duck nor his mother were members at Andrews Memorial; it won't happen," Kesha says with a stern tone.

"They will need to find a church for their funeral, and you will need to find a pastor for your church. I guess we even," Hakeem jokes, but Kesha does not find it funny.

As the three of us look at each other in silence for a few moments, the only sounds that can be heard are the air conditioner, the motor from the fish tank, and the ice machine in the refrigerator. Suddenly there's a loud boom outside, followed by several more explosions. I instantly start to think about the house fire in 2019 as Darrin runs down the stairs with his phone in hand.

"What is going on?" Kesha screams out loud in panic.

"Gas and water main explosions in Edmonson Village, Walbrook, parts of Sandtown, Gwyns Falls and Smallwood, Dukeland, Bentalou, Harlem Park and Ridgely Square," Darrin explains, pointing at a news report on his phone. "What should we do?"

"We just worked our asses off getting the money to repair and update the water and sewage lines in the city, and now they're exploding when the city starts the repairs," I say in a solemn tone. I feel so defeated.

"I can set up a meeting with Mayor Hugo in the morning," Kesha suggests.

"What about tonight?" Hakeem questions.

"There are people in Pigtown trapped inside their houses," Darrin adds. "People up and down Edmonson Ave, Hilton Ave, and Monastery trapped in their houses because of the explosions."

"Andrews Memorial has a campus in the county," Hakeem ponders out loud. "If we can get a couple church vans on the road now, we can help the people that are displaced and move them into the campus in the county."

"We can't do that," Kesha refutes. "That's for our college and our shelter and other programs we don't even have in place yet."

"We have a person named the Charm City Strangler," Hakeem explains. "We are about to have a lot of displaced people that we can help right now. I'm not playing politics with the resources our church has. Tell Raymond to get the bus drivers together and meet me by Fredrick and Athol street. We're going to ride to all the areas affected and try to help every single person we can. I don't want that Charm City Strangler to think he's going to have easy access to his next victim because of a situation like tonight."

"So, you're leading Andrews Memorial now?" Kesha asks. Hakeem answers no.

"The moment you let Duck's family have the funeral service at the church is the moment I take that offer seriously," Hakeem dictates as Kesha rolls her eyes.

"I'll meet with Aunt Monica and the inner circle of deacons and elders tomorrow. I'll work out the details for Duck's funeral and get them back to you," Kesha reluctantly states as Darrin runs over to her and gives her a warm embrace with tears in his eyes.

"Darrin was Duck's best friend," I explain as Kesha looks on, confused by the hug.

Chapter 18

The next day, Hakeem, Monica, Kesha and I are at the Woodstock Campus, walking through the packed soup kitchen. More than 500 people are currently eating or in line waiting to receive their food. They are all victims of last night's explosions. My husband's decision to place these people out here might have saved several lives. The growing number of gas explosions, water main breaks and power outages over the last 20 hours has to be a record. Mayor Hugo attempted to place several displaced residents in hotels, but the number of victims continues to rise.

The Woodstock Campus is a large multiple acre piece of property owned by Andrews Memorial. The property has fresh well water, along with solar and turbine generators to provide clean energy. The campus has several large buildings that resemble a college campus. The property also has quite a few nice sized single-family homes. The campus has a few dorm buildings on the north side of the campus. Near the south side of the campus are large barracks used to house the homeless. Andrews Memorial has housed the homeless population from Baltimore City and Baltimore County in the barracks for the last few years.

Raymond Nesmith began arranging for church vans to patrol the city and parts of the county to pick up people that were homeless and take them there. Raymond will see to it they are fed, bathed and clothed. The only thing Raymond wants in return is for the homeless guests to attend his church services on Sundays. Some of the people join the church, begin working, obtain housing and become members of Raymond's private bible study group, Inner Circle.

"Crazy how the biggest problem you had before was the fundraising dollars going to the water crisis," Marshawn says in the back of my mind. "It went from the water crisis to the Charm City Strangler, then Kesha coming clean about Hakeem's family, and now here we are at a shelter helping residents displaced because of the gas and water main explosions."

"Not the time." I watch as Erica Little walks toward me. The sight of her makes my skin crawl.

"These people are lucky you care so much," Erica says to me as I try to ignore her. "My goal was to continue building the planned community. You wanted to fix the water problem and save the black homeowners. The irony is, several homes are now gone in the explosions, and I can't build nothing because of the water crisis, and the lead levels in Ridgely Square are high, thanks to the explosions."

"Why are the lead levels high because of the explosion?" I ask as Erica looks on at the people standing in line. The room is well lit and clean. The floors are freshly waxed. The food smells great; in the air is the aroma of fresh garlic, basil, and charcoal. Some of the men from Aleem's mosque, Masjid Allahu, went out to the campus a couple hours ago and began grilling food for the displaced.

"Lead travels," Erica explains. "That's the thing that makes explosions like this one so bad. The lead travels, and you can't use the contaminated water to keep the levels down. I'm sure your sister-in-law, Kesha told you that the mayor will be here shortly to survey the conditions in the area, and he wants to meet with you and Hakeem."

"Are you here to help or talk shop? There are more than 500 people here that need our help right now," I say to Erica who chuckles to herself and walks off

"Hey, we need to talk," Kesha says to me, almost appearing out of thin air. "Let's keep the exit strategy from the Flamingo Club to ourselves."

"Sure, we never had the conversation," I concur as Kesha walks me into a large office with the Flamingo Club's logo on several items throughout. The Flamingo Club's logo is a flamingo standing inside a golden circle with one leg bent. There are marble statues with the logo, as well as awards, insignias, and cigar cases.

"I'm glad that we're on the same page, because we're about to have a meeting with them right now," Kesha says. My heart rate immediately begins to rise. Why would the Flamingo Club be coming to meet me right now? What do they want with me? All of a sudden Kesha places an arm around me and says, "Breathe. It's not that big of a deal. We're just doing some strategic planning, thanks to the explosions last night. It's going to be with the church's inner circle, not the Flamingo Club. That meeting is after this one."

As I try to wrap my mind around what Kesha just sprang on me, there's a knock at the large wooden door with the Flamingo Club's insignia carved on the left side and Andrews Memorial's logo, a large shield with two swords crossed behind the shield, on the right side. You can see the handles of the swords and the tips of the blades. On the shield is a large A and M. There's also a dove, a flame and a cross drawn into the logo. The more I look at the Andrews Memorial logo, the more I notice other details. I like the version on this wooden door because it was carved by hand, just like the Flamingo Club's logo.

Walking into the meeting room are Monica and Raymond Nesmith, and Hakeem. I thought more people would be present, seeing this is an inner circle meeting. This church has thousands of people in the sanctuary every Sunday, but the inner circle is only 3 people: Kesha, Monica and Raymond.

"I think you're reading this situation wrong," Marshawn points out. "I think you and Hakeem are now a part of this small group of people."

"I don't want to hold any of you long, we have a lot going on right now," Kesha starts. "Last night there were several explosions throughout the city. I called Deacon Smith and Elder Sanders and told them to get as many church buses as they could on the road. I asked Sister Pittman and her nursing team to get 1 to 2 responders in each van and save as many lives as possible. Anybody that was displaced I want them here."

"By bringing these people onto our Woodstock campus, you've set us back by 6 months for phase 2," Raymond says. I'm confused by his statement.

"What's phase 2?" Hakeem asks before I can open my mouth.

"In phase 2 we move our elite members onto the campus," Kesha explains. "Our goal is to have the college fully functional and ready to take residents by September. We are also training our paramilitary staff to keep the campus clean."

"Training them how?" I ask as Raymond reveals a gun in a holster on his side.

"We have fully stocked armories throughout this campus," Raymond answers. "We have pistols, assault rifles, shotguns, vests, gas grenades, riot gear and handheld radios. The whole idea was to keep our students and residents safe. As we continue to work on our expansion, we want 100% of the church's membership to live here. That being said, we have to make some adjustments still with phase 1."

"What adjustments would that be?" Hakeem questions as Monica opens up one of the thick wooden blinds and points at a large building.

"The homeless dorms," Monica adds. "The homeless dormitory is too close to the school campus, and the school dorms. I want to cut down on the interaction between the homeless guests and the students. I also want to cut down on the cross contamination between the homeless and our valued church members.”

“Contamination?” I ask out loud and that famous stank expression appears on Monica’s face as she turns in my direction.

“The homeless people we serve are guests,” Raymond contextualizes. “That being said, we are God’s chosen people. We don’t need the sinful poor to put their dirty fingers on our pure students and church members. If we can convert these damned souls, great. If we can’t, they can go back to Baltimore. Speaking of which, why are these dirty city folk staying on our campus right now?”

“Haven’t you heard?” Hakeem questions Raymond, “there were a ton of explosions that displaced many Baltimore City residents last night.”

“Why is that Andrews Memorial’s problem?” Raymond counters. “These people never set foot in our church. These people never tried to better themselves, but sin caught up to them. They were unprepared like the five foolish virgins and now they want to reap the rewards and hard work of our ministry. I want them all out, immediately.”

“We’re not going to do that,” Kesha denies in an authoritative tone. “They’re going to stay here, and we're going to treat these people with dignity. The Flamingo Club will meet and discuss these challenges."

"But Bishop, each moment these people are here, phase 2 loses momentum," Raymond explains as Kesha rejects his statements. "Also, our social media minister is telling me that J'won "Duck" Foote will have his funeral services at Andrews Memorial. How? Neither he nor his mother were ever members of our church. Duck's mother, WaKitta, doesn't even have a real career. We can't lower our standards for people like that."

"I agree with my son," Monica contributes. "We've spent decades building this church up to be better than every other church in the city. We don't need to make a decision like that just because Hakeem's bastard stepson was friends with the street trash that was killed for being a sinner."

"I've made my decision," Kesha confesses. "I want to make sure that the hospitality and the outreach ministries are available all week."

"What happens when school starts back and the water problem still exists?" Monica asks. "Are you still housing these sinners at this location?"

"I'm going to do the right thing," Kesha answers. "We have the opportunity to help, and that's what we're going to do. I don't want to hear anything about money, status or power. I want to see every member of this ministry pulling their weight and helping our guests. That's it for right now. We'll reconvene tomorrow the same exact time in this office to see what new developments we have."

As Monica and Raymond walk out the office, Kesha reaches her hand out and touches my hand gently to stop Hakeem and me from leaving. "The Club is coming here next," Kesha says moments before Mayor Hugo, Erica Little, and Commissioner Keith Mercer enter the office.

"How bad are the damages?" I ask as Hugo slams his right hand on the large boardroom wooden table.

"We might be fixing all of these damages going into the Christmas break," Hugo answers. "All the money Tiffany raised, on top of the money I set aside don't mean nothing now. I have places like Canton, Fed Hill and Charles Village breathing down my neck asking about their repairs. Johns Hopkins University and their hospital were impacted by the water and gas explosions. I'm going to move some money over from the mayor's office to Andrews Memorial for you all to keep these people housed."

"I'm not sure how long I'll be able to keep them here," Kesha inform Hugo as he stands up and begins to pace the room.

"Kesha, I need these people to stay here until I can call a meeting with City Hall and then with the governor," Hugo pleads. "I'm right at the cusp of changing this city into something meaningful. This hiccup happened, but it's not the end of the world."

"The timing of it was perfect," Erica blurts out as everyone turns in her direction. "Andrews Memorial is able to play hero and help with the people displaced. Titan Industries and the 10th Bank are working together to deal with the water crisis. The police commissioner is working tirelessly to catch the Charm City Strangler. This whole incident spins a narrative that we are a united city, and that we are tirelessly working together to solve every problem the city faces."

"Even General Midnight?" Hakeem asks as the room grows eerily quiet. "Cause the way I see it, the Flamingo Club can work together on community issues, but y'all ain't help my parents at all with General Midnight."

"This isn't the place, son," Hugo attempts to calm my husband as Hakeem pounds the table with his fist.

"I'm not your damn son," Hakeem screams as spit flies out his mouth and lands across the room. "I had a father and he died believing in the crap y'all are doing right now. I don't want to be here as a member of this church, or as a member of the Flamingo Club. I'm here as a professional courtesy to the Ridgely Square Community. Tiffany, you and Erica should meet with the mayor to discuss the next steps in reconstruction of the city. Commissioner Mercer, you, Aleem Muhammad and I should meet to see how we can work together to catch the Charm City Strangler."

"He's a natural leader like his father Bishop Andrews," Mayor Hugo says, pulling a cigar out of his sports coat pocket. "Dr. Andrews, I have a few stops to make today. I had to close all the pools for the rest of the summer, thanks to this water crisis, and the explosions made things worse. I have community leaders that want to blame the explosions on the Right Hand of God Fellowship Church. I have a former governor, who was also a former state prosecutor, by the name of Guy Dulaney, trying to get that racist piece of garbage,

Carson Jessup, out of prison for crimes he admitted to. I have companies in Baltimore County, Carroll County, Howard County and Anne Arundel County dumping toxic chemicals in Baltimore City's water. I have a police commissioner whose son was murdered by our latest serial killer, the Charm City Strangler. I have a woman named Ms. Pugh breathing down my neck about said Charm City Strangler. I have major companies trying to back out of contracts they already signed because of the water crisis. I have a growing homeless population because of people that were displaced by the explosions last night. I have companies suing the City of Baltimore because of the water crisis. I have dead children as a result of the water crisis and the Charm City Strangler. I have dead elderly people as a result of the water crisis and the explosions last night. Please forgive me, Dr. Andrews, if I don't jump and run when you or your wife want me to. I actually take this job of mayor very seriously."

"Mayor Hugo—" Hakeem attempts to state his case, but the mayor stops him.

"You mean well, Dr. Andrews," Mayor Hugo continues. "If you or your wife would like more access to me, or would like to make serious changes, take our invitation and join the Flamingo Club. When you're ready, Kesha will let us know. In the meantime, I'm expecting Tiffany Andrews and Erica Little to work together with the redevelopment process. The displaced will continue to stay at this campus, and Kesha will send my office a bill for how much it costs to house all of your guests."

As Mayor Hugo, Erica Little and Commissioner Mercer leave out of the boardroom, Hakeem and I sit quietly looking at the wooden table. Something we did a few years ago when the house was on fire, and we sat in the burn unit waiting for the medical staff to tell us the status of Trinity. That freaking house fire may have scared Trinity, but it damaged my whole family. RJ and Desha buried themselves in their music and art. Darrin became more protective, Hakeem feels like a complete failure and the house is gone. What the fire didn't destroy, the fire fighters did. In addition to that, the insurance company took forever with the payouts because of Erica Little's lawyers trying to take the house from me. Then, of course, COVID happened, so I couldn't get a construction crew to come out and repair the damages. The lead stories started to spread, then the water crisis, and my grandmother's house is barely holding on, thanks to some wooden support poles holding the siding up.

Chapter 19

A few days later, many Baltimore City residents, community leaders, politicians, members of Andrews Memorial and media personalities piled into the large Andrews Memorial cathedral. Hakeem was sitting in the pulpit area with his sister Kesha, cousin Raymond, his aunt Monica, police commissioner Keith Mercer and Mayor Hugo. The large pulpit stage is about 6 to 9 feet above the floor level of the church where the congregation seats are. There are steps leading to the pulpit area from the left and right sides of the stage. On the congregation floor are several decorative flower arrangements in tall, ornate containers given in remembrance of Duck, along with a few pictures of him. The first picture, positioned near the drums, keyboards and organs, is from when Duck was in the JROTC. The second picture of Duck is from when he went to the junior prom.

The days leading to the funeral were filled with a lot of drama and several meetings. Kesha, Erica and I had several meetings with the mayor and different planning committees about the restoration of the water and gas lines. There were meetings with different county executives about toxic waste being dumped in the city.

We had a few press conferences about the next steps with the new water and gas lines. Of course, Hakeem and Aleem met with the mayor and police commissioner about the Charm City Strangler. Then there was the big blow-up fight between Monica, Hakeem, Erica, Raymond and me about the usage of the church.

The altercation between Monica, Kesha, Hakeem, Erica, Raymond and me all started when Kesha explained that the funeral service will take place at Andrews Memorial. Monica and Raymond lost their collective minds at the thought of the funeral of a non-church member, Duck, being held at the church. Monica and Raymond were already up in arms about the Woodstock Campus being used to house displaced Baltimore City residents that were victims of the explosions. The Woodstock Campus had to welcome more displaced citizens on Thursday following another group of explosions that impacted the Mount Clair, Carlton Ridge, Preston and Appleton communities.

Monica and Raymond believed that the people should have been placed in emergency shelters, or the City of Baltimore should have paid for the residents to stay in hotels. Monica even volunteered for the residents to stay at the motel she owns if the home insurance or the City of Baltimore agreed to pay the bill. Raymond expressed his concerns about having "street kids" at the Woodstock Campus.

One of the biggest points of concern was raised by Monica, which was the Charm City Strangler's desire to kill young African American males. Monica questioned what would stop him from coming to the Woodstock Campus and having a field day with the youth. This was met with the same energy as when Ms. Pugh held a townhall at the Cross Street Market Place, stating that the Charm City Strangler was already at the Woodstock Campus. Kesha, Monica, Hakeem and Raymond had several discussions about Ms. Pugh's statements and how to beef up security on the campus. The solution included bringing in members from the Knights to patrol the campus. Kesha made the final decision to hold the funeral at Andrews Memorial. I agreed to have a few pallets of water brought to the church for the funeral, which was a great idea because the heat is in the high 90s today.

The viewing for Duck was yesterday, which was a lot of drama all by itself. There were fights between his family members and members of the press. The Allen Bradley Funeral Home cremated Duck yesterday following the open viewing. The media took up a lot of space in the funeral home, which says a lot because the viewing was held in the largest viewing room at the funeral home. Members from different news outlets didn't give members of the family the opportunity to grieve, instead they asked questions about the Charm City Strangler and "How is your family handling this sad event?"

Commissioner Mercer and Detective Murphy have been in frequent contact with WaKitta. I think it helped a lot that Mercer is also grieving after the murder of his son by the Charm City Strangler, so there's a sense of authenticity when he talks about his grief and his quest to catch the serial killer. Gina has been very respectful of WaKitta, and everybody involved. Working on the Charm City Strangler documentary has not been an easy task for my aunt. Add in the recent drama with the water and gas problems, and her documentary will be packed with information.

The Neo-Soul choir and the performance jazz band from Duck and Darrin's school has been singing and performing for the last half hour. I had the honor of reading Duck's obituary with Darrin, which was not easy. Darrin was trying to fight back the tears reading the first page of the obituary, and I was trying to console him while reading to the people in attendance. The church is fairly cool, which is an escape from the normal freezing temperatures of Andrews Memorial in the summertime. It's weird, you don't realize how much you miss a casket in the front of the church at a funeral until there's no casket in the front of the church at a funeral. I get the expense of transporting and freezing a body, but I kinda wish Duck's body was laying in the front of the church, instead of everybody being gathered to mourn him, but he's not here.

Two of the ushers bring the podium to the front of the pulpit as the Neo-Soul choir continues to sing. One of the ushers returns with a large bottle of water. The song they're singing is coming to a close as the band continues to perform at the highest level I've ever seen. In complete fairness, I think the Neo-Soul band at Darrin's school is better than the performance band at Desha's and RJ's school. Here's why that comparison is weird, Desha and RJ attend an arts school; Darrin goes to a regular zone school. As the music continues to play, and I ponder why this band is playing so well, my husband walks towards the podium with a Bible in one hand and an iPad in the other. As he places his Bible and iPad on the podium, then he steps away for a moment to let the choir and the band continue to play. After a few moments, and the band begins to play their music lightly, Hakeem walks back towards the podium, picking up his black cordless microphone with a gold sticker that has the number 1 on the bottom of it. Every microphone in the church has numbered stickers. The preacher, normally Raymond, has microphone number 1. Kesha keeps number 2 near her chair, and Monica keeps her microphone on her lap throughout every church service.

"Can we give a round of applause to the choir and the Neo-Soul band?" Hakeem says into the microphone as the church begins to applaud. This is Hakeem's first time preaching since New Hope Greater Love Church was burned down. "I was asked to deliver a message of comfort to the family and friends of Mr. J'won Foote, a young man we fondly called Duck. As I thought, prayed, meditated and wrestled with the idea of preaching a eulogy, I landed on a word, and that word was accountability."

Hakeem pauses for a moment to drink water from out the bottle before returning back to the microphone. "Bear with me, I haven't preached since 2019, but Duck was a good friend of the family. I would dare to call Duck family if that is ok with WaKitta." The tearful mother nods her head in approval to Hakeem as a male family member places his arms around WaKitta to console her. "It's good to have someone to hold you accountable. Earlier this year my wife Tiffany and I were married, and we made a vow to God to hold each other accountable for everything. Prior to getting married, I had a brother, Jamar, who held me accountable."

Hakeem chuckles to himself for a brief moment before regaining his composure. "Jamar held me accountable for everything I did. When we were younger, like Duck's age, I used to hang out with the corner boys and Jamar held me accountable for my actions and he protected me. As we got older and I went to college, earned degrees, purchased my home and attempted to serve the people of Baltimore, Jamar held me accountable. When youth like Tyrone Clinton and Kannard Lyles-Bey were murdered, Jamar held me accountable. 'Am I my brother's keeper?' A simple question Cain asked God after he murdered Abel. What does that truly mean? For years I watched Duck and his best friend Darrin hang together, play together, play sports together, joke together and because of the Charm City Strangler, protect each other."

As a few people clap, Hakeem takes another sip of his water. "Duck wasn't just like that with Darrin, he was like that with his own mother, WaKitta. He would bring her groceries in the house, fix items around the home, and even bring food that my wife cooked to his house to make sure his mother had something to eat. Duck was the heart and soul of his family, not because I said so, but because of his actions. Now listen, I don't have a heaven or hell to put J'won 'Duck' Foote in, but I can say that his words, actions and deeds were a direct reflection of what God was looking for. In the Bible, there's a scripture that talks about love being patient, love being kind. That verse goes on to talk about love never boasting and love protects and preserves. Here's the part that gets me every time: love never fails."

Hakeem pauses for a moment to walk around the large pulpit with the microphone in his hand and then stops, standing right in front of a large picture of Duck, on a stand next to several large decorative flowers. "Duck's love and compassion for everyone never failed. Duck took accountability daily, because he felt a sense of ownership and responsibility towards others. Since 2019, Baltimore has faced challenges, such as the Action Figure Killer, the Alphas, the Cabal, the Narcotics and Firearms Taskforce, and gentrification. One of the biggest challenges that we have all experienced in this city is the water crisis. My wife, Tiffany, wanted to combat the water crisis and went to the mayor, who is sitting behind me, to advocate for improvements. She didn't stop there, she set up a fundraiser with the help of her aunt, Gina Simms and Duck. You may be wondering, how did a teenage boy help with the water crisis? Well, here's how.

"Duck networked. He reached out to Kutter the Poet, who's sitting in the front row of our church. Duck asked him to perform at the crab feast and fish fry, which was a total success, and Kutter the Poet said yes. Not only did Kutter the Poet agree, but he also left his tour, performed for free and made a large donation to address the water crisis. Along with Kutter the Poet making a donation, the mayor's office also donated, and Titan Industries did as well. We had no idea at the time that the pipes would explode, displacing several residents and resulting in blocks of destroyed homes and flooded streets. If Duck was alive right now, he'd be trying to help the Knights and everyone he could that has faced the recent challenges, thanks to the water, lead and now gas crisis.

As people clap for a moment, remembering Duck's heart and hard work, Hakeem continues to look at Duck's picture in front of the pulpit. "Accountability. When Jamar was murdered, Duck and Darrin came to my house with chicken covered in hot sauce and ketchup, to cheer me up. When Tiffany's family home was burned down, Duck brought us blankets, food from his fridge and the little money he saved to put us in a motel." Hakeem pauses again to laugh before looking back at the congregation that are looking on. "Accountability. Duck knew he was his brother's keeper, but he never limited who his brother was. At a moment's notice he would have tried to keep Darrin, me, Tiffany, his mother or anybody safe. If Duck would have had more time on this earth, I guarantee Duck would have found out who the Charm City Strangler was and brought him to justice. Duck was a man with integrity, with a purpose, he was an angel wrapped in the flesh WaKitta birthed him in."

"Even in death, Duck is doing God's work," Hakeem continues walking up the stairs back to the pulpit and towards the podium. "I gave up on this. Preaching. Honestly, I gave up on God at one point. My brother's death rocked me hard. Then my parents' and uncle's death hit me hard. My father and I weren't that close because he wanted me to preach here, but I went elsewhere. When that church was burned down in 2019, and nobody from this building came to my brother's funeral, I developed a resentment towards God. I questioned if he was real. I questioned if I was failing God. I questioned if I was on the wrong path. I even questioned if there *was* a right path. You're born, you live, then you die. It could be for 17 years, like Duck, or it could be 117 years like the lady from Owings Mills that was on the news the other night. What's important is what you do with that time you're here.

"Ms. Pugh has dedicated her time to trying to bring down the Charm City Strangler," Hakeem explains. "The Charm City Strangler killed her grandson, and from what we know, her grandson was one of his first victims. Tiffany has dedicated her life to making this city a better place to live with the 10th Bank and the Legacy of Florence Grocery Store and restaurant. The question I want to leave with you all is, what are you going to do to leave a lasting mark on this world? Who will hold you accountable to make sure you do your best work. There's another story in the Bible about accountability. Jesus was fasting for 40 days and 40 nights. During that time he had some of his disciples with him, and they were sleep while Jesus was praying and talking to God. Jesus asked if it's possible, let this cup pass. The people that were supposed to be praying with him, the ones that he held accountable, were sleep. The lady at the well came to Jesus when she was going to be stoned for having sex with married men. Jesus took accountability and defended her, yet, when his own people were met by Roman soldiers, he was denied three times."

Hakeem pauses again, walks down from the pulpit and looks at Duck's picture. Hakeem then walks over to WaKitta and the two embrace with a long hug. The two then walk with locked arms to the front of the church, standing below the podium on the carpeted area of the church floor, slightly in front of the large wooden communion table.

"Family, friends, loved ones, today I want to hold each and every one of you accountable. Not to me, but to this mother. WaKitta Foote. Her son was murdered, and while we don't know who the Charm City Strangler is yet, we do know this woman. This is our sister, our daughter, our aunt, our mother, our friend. WaKitta Foote. She has to live with the hardest burden of them all, living after the death of her son. There are questions that exist that I don't have the answers to, like who is the Charm City Strangler, how has he gotten away, when will he get caught, and is he a part of the Right Hand of God Fellowship Church? What I do know is that each one of us should answer this call to responsibility. Each one of us should and need to be accountable to WaKitta Foote. Not just today, but tomorrow, next week, next month and next year. I promise you all this, eventually death will knock at your door and people you love will have to answer, then one day it will be your turn. Until that day, I hold you accountable to be there for WaKitta Foote. Be there for the people sitting next to you in this church. Be there for the people that live in your community. Be there for the people that work at your job. Be there for the people at your doctor's office. Be ready to be accountable."

As the church members begin to clap and music from the church's band starts to play, Hakeem hugs WaKitta one more time before walking her to her chair, and then he ascends the pulpit stairs back to the podium. "Friends, I'm closing with this statement. Be accountable to those you are charged to be accountable to, but don't do it because it's what you want to do. Don't do it for fame, don't do it for a payback, don't even do it because you think it's the right thing to do. Do it because it's your mandate, do it because you are your brother's and your sister's keeper. Do it because you were led by the spirit of Christ to do the right thing. If you're doing it for yourself, you're doing it wrong. Do it with love, because 'love is patient, love is kind. It does not envy, and it does not boast. It is not self-seeking, it is not easily angered, it keeps no record of wrongs. Love does not delight in evil but rejoices with the truth. It always protects, always trusts, always hopes, always preserves. Love never fails.' That's the end of my message, family. Duck, I love you and we will see you on the other side one day. WaKitta, we are all here mourning with you, my sister, and we will continue to be there for you. God bless you all, heaven smile upon you."

As Hakeem attempts to walk away from the podium, Darrin rushes the pulpit and hugs my husband with a full embrace with tears in his eyes and mucus running from his nose. A short moment later Hakeem begins to cry as the two embrace each other. WaKitta, and Kutter the Poet walk onto the pulpit to join in the tearful hug. Shortly afterwards, almost every member of the church is embracing each other and sobbing. Music is faintly heard as one of the students begins singing in a microphone. The words I can make out from the song are "it may look like I'm surrounded, but I'm surrounded by you."

I notice Kesha sobbing and covering her eyes with a handkerchief. Raymond and Monica are seated with stern looks on their faces as four men dressed in black suits block the steps to the pulpit. The four men are the church's armed security; they're trusted members of Raymond's private bible study group. Normally they follow Raymond all over the church or the Woodstock location. The four men also go with Raymond when he speaks at other churches. As more people continue to embrace and share this tearful moment, I look to my right and see a young girl no older than an eight years old with long braids staring at me. The child is brown skinned and has a smile on her face with her arms extended towards me. As I hug her, she says, "It's ok, Mommy."

It's ok, Mommy? I think to myself as she holds me closer. The child says, "It's ok to let me go, Mom." For a moment I try to place the voice as tears begin to run down my face, and I try to look at the beautiful young child with the chubby cheeks and braids. Then it hits me as everything around me goes black. "Kenya?" I say aloud. She stands back and nods. Kenya was my five-year-old daughter that died in a hit-and-run accident with my ex-boyfriend Keyon back in 2016.

"It's ok to grieve now, Mommy," Kenya says to me before embracing me again. "You've been going and doing for everyone else since I died. Take the time now to be sad for yourself, Mom." As Kenya says the words I never knew I needed to hear, warm tears run down my face. Since Kenya died, I have attempted to numb the pain by burying myself in school, work, the bank, the restaurant and the market. There was a point where the kids suffered because of my grief. I was hiding in my grandmother's basement talking to the voices in my head as counsel. I didn't even realize I was carrying around this grief. It's heavy. I lost so many people, my grandmother, my uncle Larry, my cousin Tina, Pastor Donald Avery, Jamar and now Duck. I've gotten so used to going and doing for everyone, I forgot what it was like to actually be in the moment and grieve my own pain.

"It's ok, Mom," Kenya says as she begins to fade into the blackness of the room I've mentally placed myself in. I fall to my knees, reaching out to her as everything around me turns bright again, and I find myself back in the packed church, on my knees and sobbing. There's an arm around me consoling me as I think of Kenya and all the things she could be accomplishing right now if she were still alive. The heat from my tears fades away and now it feels like cool streams of water running down my cheeks and towards my lips. I don't know who this is that's holding me, but I'm grateful I'm not going through this moment alone.

I faintly hear my grandmother say in my ear, "You're never alone." As I attempt to wipe the tears from my eyes, I notice Kesha, Gina and Sasha are standing over me holding used tissues from wiping my face. Sasha helps me up from the floor as Kesha and Gina embrace me.

Chapter 20

Following church service the next day, Kesha offers to take Gina, Erica, Sasha, Monica, WaKitta and me out to eat for brunch in Silver Springs. Monica declines to join us after she learns that WaKitta will be present. Monica expresses her desire to "stay away from the impure that God has chosen to punish for being a failure as a mother." Sasha declines to join us for the brunch, expressing the importance of being at the market because of the water and gas crisis.

The brunch location is an exclusive five-star restaurant called Winecastle that has a two-year waiting list for reservations and Kesha was able to get us in without a problem. What kind of power does my sister-in-law really have? Do the Flamingo Club members really have this much clout? The all-you-can-eat brunch bar is stuff you can only dream of. To name a few items I can see there's sea bass, smoked and blackened salmon, butterfish, Alaskan red king crab legs, filet mignon, New York strip steak, bone-in ribeye steak, gourmet omelets, caramelized bacon, lamb chops, cream of crab soup, fresh fruit, waffles, Bananas Foster French toast, and crispy edged pancakes. The best part of this meal was Kesha paid for everything.

As time rolled by, we discussed different subjects, such as dating as an adult, raising children, home ownership, and even guilty pleasure movies. About 30 minutes into our expensive bonding experience, WaKitta asked the difficult and most uncomfortable question no mother wants to answer, "At what point does the hurting stop? I can't stop thinking about Duck. I don't want to stop thinking about him, but I feel stuck."

"You don't ever stop hurting, you just start coping and keep moving," Erica answers before I can stop chewing. "When my daughter, Sabrina, was killed in a hit and run accident, my whole world stopped. I buried myself in my work; my husband did the same. My son, Simon, suffered as a result. I didn't realize the psychological impact his sister's death had on him."

"You're talking about Silk?" I ask while chewing. I was being a smart ass, but Erica Little is far from a friend. Erica Little is the reason why people like WaKitta and I were displaced in 2016. I was blessed to have a grandmother to will me a home after her death. WaKitta and Duck rented a room in a basement.

"Yes. Silk, as you call my son Simon," Erica replies, cutting her eyes at me for a brief moment before turning her attention back to WaKitta. "Silk's mental health started to get the best of him; I wasn't well versed with mental illness. I didn't realize that trauma at Silk's age would create multiple personalities. Honestly, I thought that was something white people said and acted out to get attention from their parents. When Simon started calling himself Silk, I figured it was a phase he was going through. When he was staying at the homeless shelter and told me my daughter, Sabrina, was living in his head, I realized I'd screwed him up by not getting him all the help he needed as a child."

"Silk was the person that used to be on the radio, right?" WaKitta asks as Erica and I nod in agreement. "I always thought Silk was cool. I never thought of her as mentally ill."

"Silk was mentally ill and was grieving the wrong way," Erica spouts. "Sadly, Silk was murdered in the Old Market Place area and never received the help he truly needed."

"You ever think that the help she needed was having parents that supported her, instead of having her live in shelters and kept calling her Simon even though she legally changed her name to Silk?" I ask.

"I don't agree with delusional behavior," Erica answers. "If I would have done more than what I attempted, I would still be married to Sedrick Little and Silk would still be alive.

To be honest with you all," Erica continues in a relaxed tone, then pauses. Her appearance shifts. Erica always looks professional, always guarded but attacking. Her appearance has suddenly shifted to vulnerable. Erica points to a barely-drinking-age brown haired white male server walking past and signals for some wine in her empty glass on the table.

"To be honest with you all," Erica repeats after the server fills her wine glass. Before the server can walk off, Erica takes the bottle of wine from him and takes a large gulp from the bottle. Erica now clenching the neck of the bottle forcefully says, "I'm divorced and rich. I was born rich, thanks to my parents who founded and owned Psalms Airline. With all the money I have, I'm alone. My kids are dead, and my husband left me because we didn't process Silk's death the right way. You know what bothers me? I didn't take the time to learn about what was going on with Silk as an adult. I wanted Silk to be the little boy I birthed. I wanted Silk to be more like my ex-husband Sedrick."

Erica takes another large gulp from the wine bottle before slouching back in her chair. "Gina, you were close with Silk, what was he like when you two were friends?"

My aunt Gina, caught off guard by this inclusion into the conversation, wiped her mouth with the black cloth napkin before placing it on the table. She was chewing on her catfish, shrimp and grits platter. Before this conversation started the catfish, shrimp and grits was all she could talk to me about.

"Silk was a sweet person," Gina answers. "She was complex because there were two Silks. The first Silk was the young person I met when I was working between the Old Market Place area, Patapsco Ave., and near Morrell Park. That Silk was down on her luck after losing her job at the radio station and becoming homeless. Silk was trying to survive and was on her own. Being a trans person in the Patapsco area isn't easy, especially back in 2016. I would wear a skirt, switch while walking and twerk to get customers. Silk had a different build and would face a lot of insults from people. Several times she was assaulted when a customer learned she was a trans woman. She had a busted lip here, a black eye there, needed stitches on her right index finger because a customer tried to stab her to death, and she blocked it. Anyway, that Silk didn't know what she was doing."

My aunt stops for a second to take another bite off her plate as we all sit silently waiting for her to continue. "Silk needed protection, so I tried to introduce her to some of the people in our community. A couple of like-minded women, and a few men to keep us safe from the really bad predators. I got Silk a room for rent near the Westside Shopping Center. Around that time, she wanted to go to church. She got down really bad. She was dabbling in stuff here and there, like crack cocaine and different types of pills. She was depressed. Mainly because she didn't have a relationship with you and your husband," Gina explains, pointing at Erica.

"Silk asked me about going to church," Gina states moving her hand towards the glass of orange juice in front of her. "I told her about Pastor Avery's church, and she said you and your husband used to go there back in the day."

"We visited once," Erica responds. "We were always members of Andrews Memorial."

"Ok," Gina chimes back in. "Silk landed a job at UPS or FedEx or something, thanks to one of the church members there. That was the happiest I ever saw her. She was off the corner, and out of danger. She was in a shelter getting counseling and case management. I was proud of Silk. Then she got into an altercation with you,

Erica, on the way to the new job, and that sent her into a downward spiral. She was doing a lot of crack and heroin pills. I thought she was trying to kill herself. She was taking risks, sleeping with customers we don't deal with normally. Then she got killed by Cube."

"Did the pain of her murder ever go away?" WaKitta asks as Erica replies yes and Gina replies no.

"If it wasn't for the hurt I had because of Silk's murder, I would have never tried to get back to my actual daughter Tina," Gina expresses. "It was too late for me; Tina killed herself by overdosing on pills in a bathroom. I'm such a failure as a mother."

"Do you think I'm a failure for how Duck was killed?" WaKitta asks as I shake my head no.

"I didn't know Silk. I know you, WaKitta. You're not a failure," I respectfully insert. "You loved Duck and did what you could with the hand you were dealt. The Charm City Strangler killed Duck. Silk was murdered by trying to survive on a dangerous career path. Duck was murdered by an evil person because Duck was doing teenage boy stuff.

"How did you get over Kenya's murder?" WaKitta questions me.

"I didn't," I answer truthfully. "I lied to everyone. I went to counseling, but I half assed it. I went to church, but really, I was too angry at God to actually appreciate the fact I was still blessed with Darrin, Desha, RJ and Trinity. I just kept going. I put together the Legacy of Florence restaurant and market. I worked with Hakeem, Kesha and Jamar to create the 10th Bank. I raised my kids, I took care of the house and I just kept moving on to the next task, even getting married. I basically blocked out the grief by trying to build something."

"Do you think that helped?" WaKitta questions, as I notice Kenya and Marshawn standing behind them shaking their heads no. I know they're not real, but they look so real.

"No, it hurt me," I admit. I don't know if I should come clean and tell the truth here or stop talking. Gina is my aunt, and I'm glad we're bonding. Kesha is my sister-in-law and I'm still learning about who she is as a person. WaKitta and I have never been friends, and I really can't stand Erica Little. I'm going to eat some of my French toast.

"All of my sons' deaths still hurt me," Erica blurts out, catching everyone off guard. I only know of Erica having one son; I didn't realize she had others. "My son

Asa was six years old when he died from cancer. Why would God bless me with such a blessing just to take him from me? I always think about what or who he would have become. Not too long after Asa died, I gave birth to Atlas, who died of child incidental death syndrome, also known as CIDS. I never talk about it. Actually, Andrews Memorial policy forbids me to talk about it because it comes off as a weakness and God only wants us to prosper."

"You ever think about addressing that policy or some of the policies like that?" I ask.

"An Andrews male has to make the policy changes at Andrews Memorial; those are in the bylaws my grandfather created," Kesha explains.

"How did the death of Atlas come across to the church?" WaKitta asks, beating me to the question.

"It didn't," Kesha answers, looking down at the table. Her voice is low, deep, sad. There's regret in her tone. "My father, Bishop Andrews, disciplined anybody who asked how the baby was or where Asa was."

"How did he do that?" I ask.

"You don't want to know," Erica says, sipping out the bottle.

"Yes I do," I answer and WaKitta seconds.

Kesha takes a deep breath. Still looking down she says, "My father would order the deacons to bring any member who had a question to the front of the church, strip their clothes off their back and publicly whip them in front of the communion table. That's what he called keeping order.

"How did you process it?" WaKitta asks.

"You don't," Erica explains. "You suck it up, give it to God and know your role. I'm a member of Andrews Memorial and this is what that looks like. You suppress what hurts you and you build on what helps you. That's what Bishop Andrews taught me."

"We're going to catch him, you know," Kesha blurts out of nowhere after there was silence for a few moments. We all look on, questioning what Erica is talking about. "The Charm City Strangler. We're going to catch him. The mayor has made it his top priority to catch him."

"The streets will get him before the police do," WaKitta counters. "My nephew, Kutter the Poet, put up his own money, just like he did for the water problem. Now you have athletes putting up money to catch him. I actually heard that Guy Dulaney was putting up a reward to catch this guy too, but he just wants to prove that Carson Jessup is innocent."

"He's still a racist murderer," Gina contributes. "He admitted to his crimes and gave details. It's amazing how his Right Hand of God Fellowship Church was able to operate out in the open, killing African American men and we're just now catching him."

"By mistake," WaKitta jokes. "They only caught Carson Jessup and his church members because of that Paul Douglass Law. They were looking for AFK and members of the Alphas and found Carson Jessup along with his followers were hunting down black men."

"People do strange things in the name of religion," Gina adds as Kesha cuts her eyes towards her, almost as if my aunt said something offensive to her.

"See that's why I don't be going to church; all that cult stuff be killing me," WaKitta utters in a sassy tone towards Gina.

"Girl bye," I quip back. "You don't go to church because you don't go to church. The Right Hand of God Fellowship Church has nothing to do with why you don't go to church. You just don't want to go to church. That's fine, you have the right to make your own decisions, but don't sit here and lie about Carson

Jessup's church being the reason why you don't go to nobody church unless it's a funeral or a wedding."

The table grows silent as I think about what I just said. She did go to church yesterday because of her son's funeral and I just threw it in her face. I'm not lying, though. Even when we lived in the same apartment building, I never have so much as seen her in dress clothes on a Sunday. Honestly, other than buying weed or drinks, I ain't seen her move from her apartment on most days.

"You ain't have to put me out there like that," WaKitta says, clearly annoyed by my statement. "It do be weird stuff happening at church, but that's not why I don't go. If I work, and I'm struggling, I still got to pay offering? My son hungry and you talking about 10% of my paycheck. The pastor sleeping with me and my best friend. His wife does my sister hair, but all that is fine 'cause it's not a cult."

"What church is that?" Gina asks.

"It's a hypothetical situation," WaKitta explains as Gina gives an uncomfortable chuckle.

"So this situation hasn't really happened, but that's your excuse for not going to church?" I ask as Erica calls the waiter over to ask for another bottle of wine.

"I just don't believe in God," WaKitta admits. "It don't make no sense. You know everything. You make a world, put two people in Africa and tell them not to eat the apple. The snake tells them to eat the apple, they do, then they get cursed, but the woman has to have a period. Then you flood the world because of sin. You burn down two towns cause of sin. Then there's the whole 'obey your master thing.' I'm sorry, if sin is so bad, and the devil is the reason for it, why not kill the devil instead of damning our souls. It says we're born in sin. If the devil is killed, are we still born in sin or is everything a wash? 'Cause I don't understand murdering your son, but not the devil, who's your literal enemy."

"It's an oversimplification, but I understand your point," Erica jokes while taking a large chug from her new bottle of wine.

"I don't mean to pry in your business, I just want to know why you don't believe in God?" Kesha says as WaKitta scoffs.

"Slavery, white Christ, racism, dead children, starving people in Africa, poverty and now my dead son Duck," WaKitta lists before eating food off her plate. "If God is so real, why do black people suffer so much? If God is so real, why is it whenever a black person points out their oppression by other groups, they're shut down or forced to apologize? I could talk about my reasons all day, but it doesn't change what you believe and what I don't."

"I didn't want to debate, I just asked out of curiosity," Kesha admits.

As almost everyone at the table continues to eat in silence, Erica Little continues to down wine bottle after wine bottle. A part of me hopes that she will make herself sick from drinking, another part of me wonders why she is drinking like this.

"You good, hun?" Gina breaks the silence and asks after several minutes.

"Just thinking about everything that's coming this week," Erica answers, taking a sip from the wine bottle. Currently there's eight empty bottles of wine sitting in front of Erica, and she's gripping a half-filled bottle. "Titan Industries has partnered with the City of Baltimore to fix these destroyed water and gas lines. Thanks to Tiffany we have the money to do it. The mayor is angry about the multiple explosions, and the people that are staying at Andrews Memorial's Woodstock Campus, because he has to pay for that service. In addition, we have a psychopath killing teenagers and dumping them in Leakin Park. The part that pisses me off the most is I was trying to avoid shit like this from happening, but Tiffany and Hakeem have fought me for years."

"The Charm City Strangler would have existed in Baltimore City, Baltimore County, Ann Arundel County, Prince Georges County or Carroll County," Kesha rebuts. "Baltimore City has a larger African American population, and Carson Jessup, Paul Douglass, and NAFA just added more eyes nationally to the problems that plague the city."

"The killer didn't choose any other park, he chose Leakin Park," Erica continues. "The same park where so many human remains have been found. The same park where the podcast and the true crime craze was started, thanks to the murder of Hae Min Lee back in the late 1990s."

Hae Min Lee was an 18-year-old high school student that was murdered, and her remains were found in Leakin Park. The case would spark controversy and start the true crime obsession because of the events surrounding the murder case, the ex-boyfriend being convicted, and the handling of the case. In the past, previous police chiefs would tell officers going into Leakin Park to only find the body of the crime they are working, leave any other corpse wherever they found it. Many of the discarded bodies date back to the early 1900s. It is suspected that more than 200 bodies are in Leakin Park, which is an eerie place to walk through because of the discarded trash and the feeling the park gives. It has been said that bodies would be dumped in broad daylight, and within days the park would absorb the body, hiding it from the world forever. So for a person like the Charm City Strangler to constantly dump several bodies there and leave them under white sheets as a calling card is kind of outlandish. Almost like this person wants the public to know it was him, and to gloat about the work he's done. The bodies aren't dumped deep in the park, but right near the road where the sheet covering the body is visible.

"I just want to catch my son's murderer," WaKitta angrily states. "No mother should have to go through what I've gone through… what all the mothers at this table have gone through."

"I agree, and the mayor along with the police commissioner are making it a point to catch him," Erica states while looking at WaKitta and Gina. "I know y'all don't like hearing this, but the planned community we have been proposing for years would have prevented this from happening."

"The Charm City Strangler would have done the same things, just elsewhere," I scream as Gina nods in agreement. "If it would have happened in any other county, the seriousness of the murders would have fallen on deaf ears, those who wouldn't care about one Charm City Strangler victim, let alone 40 plus. Even the police commissioner's son was murdered by this bastard."

"You don't know that," Erica refutes as everyone at the table shakes their head no in disapproval. "I don't know what y'all's problem is, but this guy is going to get caught, it's just a matter of time."

"Who else has to die before he gets caught?" I ask as WaKitta and Kesha glance in my direction. "He killed the police commissioner's son. You would think they would have him in custody right now."

"In due time they will," Erica says with confidence.

Chapter 21

That afternoon, Kesha, Hakeem and I sit in the living room of our home. Kesha has several folders and yellow notepads spread across the glass coffee table in front of our couch. Hakeem and I sit together on the couch, but Kesha uses a chair from the dining room, which is odd because we have loveseats and recliners in the living room.

"Hakeem, I need you to take over Andrews Memorial," Kesha bluntly states in a deep voice. This deep voice is one I've never heard from her.

"No," Hakeem answers without thought or hesitation.

"You have to," Kesha pleads.

"No," Hakeem repeats.

"I'm not supposed to be the leader of Andrews Memorial. I'm not supposed to be a pastor, elder, bishop, none of that. This position was for you since the day you were born," Kesha exclaims.

"I said no," Hakeem returns back.

"Hakeem, you've seen what this church was and continues to become. How our father and grandfather used the church to wash the money of the Flamingo Club," Kesha voices. "Then the partnership our father made with Psalms Airline to get private jets to travel the globe, doing his mission and ministerial work."

"What's your point?" Hakeem snaps. His face is annoyed. There's no mistaking the frown on his face. Hakeem has stated several times he doesn't want to preach or lead a church after the Incident of Ridgely Square claimed New Hope Greater Love Church in a fire.

"I can't lead this cult no more," Kesha admits. "Our parents were killed by that General Midnight. The Flamingo Club used our private planes to smuggle drugs and people. The Alphas got the majority of their product flown here in our private planes. I want to walk away and wash my hands."

"I'm sorry, I won't do it," Hakeem dismisses the idea.

"I'll handle the financial books for the Flamingo Club, we'll get all of the Flamingo Club's dirty money off our accounts. Hakeem. Think about it. You, Jamar and I all had the same parents, but they covered up our dad's arrangements and his affairs like it was some secret. Our real mother hung herself, Hakeem, and our father covered it up. We need leadership. Someone who cares and loves God. Someone who isn't corrupt."

"It can't be me; ask Raymond," Hakeem suggests.

"Raymond has a problem all by hisself," Kesha laughingly states. "He wants to be famous; he wants to be great, but he wants to be pastor to continue the cult-like behavior. The arranged marriages, the public whippings, the giving of money, titles and deeds for co-ownership. Raymond wants to do more than that once the compound gets up and running. I need you to take my role, sit Raymond down and lead."

"Even if I did, Aunt Monica…" Hakeem ponders and Kesha agrees.

"Aunt Monica is a problem as well. She and Raymond want to run and control Andrews Memorial. The only difference is Raymond wants a seat at the Flamingo Club table. You would make sure the church is out the Flamingo Club, and I will stay in with Tiffany to make sure we have a seat at the table to fix Baltimore."

"You know I know you better than that," Hakeem chuckles.

"What do you mean?" Kesha asks.

"What's the next step in your exit plan. Like when you leave the church what will you be doing?" Hakeem asks as Kesha smiles.

"Come take a ride with me, I want to show you something," Kesha suggests as we both agree to go with her.

The three of us climb into Kesha's white BMW Alpina, leaving from the city, heading towards Baltimore County. I notice highway signs that say Security Boulevard, Lochern, Owings Mills and 795 until we pull up to a large glass office building that oddly looks familiar.

"This is the Ginger Hill Research Center," Kesha states as we park in the front of the building in a spot that reads, Reserved for the CEO. "Ginger Hill was the name of Jamar's, Hakeem's and my actual mother. Her conception of Hakeem and Jamar was covered up by Andrews Memorial. My conception was considered a curse because our father continued the affair after the arrangements between Bishop Andrews and our "real mother" was complete. When Ginger Hill died of cancer, our father adopted me, and they considered the adoption a blessing to me and God extending grace to my life. This is my second research facility. Tiffany, you visited the other Ginger Hill Research Center in Newport News, Virginia back in 2017.”

“No, I didn’t,” I respond as Hakeem and I follow Kesha to the front glass door.

“The medical center where you were kidnapped by Sgt. Marshawn Bell and forced to bring his mother to. That was the other Ginger Hill Research Center,” Kesha educates as we walk through the huge glass door and into the expansive facility with marble floors. The walls are made of glass, with large screen televisions that display running videos of the work the research center is doing. There’s soft piano music playing in the background. In the middle of the vestibule are two Parisian marble statues, the first is of Henrietta Lacks, an African American woman from Baltimore City who died from cervical cancer, but her cells have been used for multiple generations to treat different illnesses and for other modern-day breakthroughs. The second statue is of a thin-framed woman with long hair wearing a dress. As I attempt to study it, I notice a nameplate that reads, Ginger Hill.

We follow Kesha into a massive glass office with a small putting green, a glass chess set on a round glass table, and several pieces of art hang behind the sizable glass desk. "It's normally busy in here, but it's a Sunday, so everybody's off."

"What is this place?" Hakeem asks, looking around the building through the glass wall.

"This is the Ginger Hill Research Center," Kesha says in a relaxed tone. Her voice isn't deep like she makes it when we're around Mayor Hugo or Erica Little. "It's a research center I've had off the books for the past 12 years. We've been researching cures for cancer, HIV and other illnesses. Our lead researcher, Dr. Myron Smalls developed something ground-breaking, and we used it originally as an experiment to treat pancreatic cancer, and it worked. Out of 80 test subjects back in 2017, 78 of the participants lived and their stage 4 pancreatic cancer went into full remission."

"How?" Hakeem and I ask as an average-height, heavy set African American male enters the room. His hair is braided, and he's wearing a white lab coat with a white shirt and black dress pants underneath.

"CH18," the person says, entering the room with a jolly smile on his face, reaching out to shake Hakeem's hand and mine. "My name is Dr. Myron Smalls. Years ago, I started developing CH18. It's a mixture between stem and nano cells that can morph into dangerous cells attacking the human body and then destroying them. The cells then morph into white blood cells and proteins to help improve the immune system, preventing the dangerous cells from returning, and giving the patient a longer and more meaningful life."

"Why have I not heard about this," Hakeem questions.

"When we completed our clinical trials for pancreatic cancer back in February 2020, the U.S. government wanted everyone to prepare for the spread of COVID-19," Myron explains. "Funding started going crazy to save the lives of people dying from the coronavirus, and there was a decrease in funding for experimental research like this. Thankfully, Kesha used her money to continue the research and allowed us to see how far we could go with this type of treatment. As a result, we have two fully functional research labs that have had some groundbreaking results."

"But everybody doesn't know I'm tied to this," Kesha explains. "For example, I've kept this hidden from the Flamingo Club and Andrews Memorial folks. The Flamingo Club will try to attach this treatment to the West Baltimore Hospital and Neil Goldberg, which will just corrupt the good we're trying to do. I don't want the church involved, because this has nothing to do with Andrews Memorial."

"The same church that covered up your mother giving birth to you, Hakeem and Jamar," I add as Kesha nods in agreement. "That makes sense. They tried to turn your mother's name to mud, and you used your mother's name to save lives."

"Exactly," Kesha affirms. "That's another reason why I need to step down as bishop and pastor of Andrews Memorial. It's time to take this public and save lives. After we're done with the water crisis, I want to walk away from the Flamingo Club altogether."

"I'll help," Hakeem says. "How do we handle Aunt Monica and Raymond?"

"I don't know," Kesha replies in desperation.

"If I do this, then there's going to be a lot of changes," Hakeem proclaims as Dr. Myron leaves the office and closes the door behind himself.

"I brought the back office files for Andrews Memorial to your house just for this conversation," Kesha confesses.

"No, there will be no more Andrews Memorial," Hakeem states. "We're changing the name of the church. All the affiliated churches, we're cutting off. The mission trips will be effectively canceled. The partnership with Psalms Airline, done. The inner circle, done. The private bible study groups, done. Whatever was going on with Woodstock Campus is on pause and will be re-evaluated after the water crisis is over."

"We can work through some of those details," Kesha attempts to negotiate as the bass returns to her voice.

"Those are my terms, Kesha," Hakeem demands as Kesha presses her two index fingers together in almost a triangle shape, placing the tips at the bridge of her nose.

"We'll lose members, money and clout," Kesha exclaims.

"Andrews Memorial will lose members, money and clout," Hakeem corrects. "The New Hope Greater Love Church will have a new church building, and we can start rebuilding from where we left off following the Ridgely Square Incident."

"But Hakeem—" Kesha starts as I make a suggestion.

"Why not just give the church to Raymond?" I ask as Kesha rolls her eyes.

"Raymond wants the church, he wants to be at the table with the Flamingo Club, he wants to be important,"

Kesha explains. "Giving him the title of bishop and pastor of Andrews Memorial would be the worst thing I could do and might lead to bigger challenges down the line."

"Like what?" I ask.

"Have you met our aunt Monica?" Kesha asks in a facetious way. "Monica controls Raymond. I can't speak for what goes on at her motel on Washington Boulevard, but at the church and everywhere else, she's power hungry and aggressive. More aggressive than Erica Little. The last thing the Flamingo Club needs is for Raymond or Monica to have a seat at the table, running the city. As both of you stated before, Andrews Memorial is a cult, and would you want a cult leader that's manipulated by his mother to run a secret society that pulls all the strings of the city?"

"When you put it like that, no," I answer as Hakeem laughs to himself.

"Things have to go my way," Hakeem demands. "I'm willing to talk about the details later, but if you're going to part ways from the ministry and we're going to correct the ship, let's do things the right way. What you're doing here is major, and I'm all for it."

"What about the money the Flamingo Club has tied up in the 10th Bank?" I ask as Kesha pulls out a file from her top drawer and plops it on the table.

"I'll continue handling the financial books for the Flamingo Club, and you will hold their money in the different accounts," Kesha answers. "The church will be completely in the clear. I'll reinvest the Flamingo Club's money into other ventures. By the time they learn we're cutting them off, their money will be in foreign accounts that Tiffany and I will control for our safety."

"What happens when they get their money from those accounts?" I ask, in fear that my family will get killed by a secret society.

"By that time, we'll work out all the details. All parties will be happy," Kesha says in a very confident tone. "But I want to point out, neither the Flamingo Club, nor Andrews Memorial can know about the Ginger Hill Medical Research Centers being owned by or affiliated with me. They like controlling every financial asset. That, and Neil Goldberg will find a way to use this treatment center to make himself richer and absorb it into the West Baltimore Hospital or Sinai Hospital."

Hakeem and I look at each other as Kesha looks on, patiently waiting for an answer. I see this as a benefit. If Kesha can continue to grow this research center, there are a lot of lives that will be saved from cancer, HIV and other diseases. Yet, if the Flamingo Club learns of this treachery that Kesha is planning on doing, we could all be in danger.

"I say let's do it," I blurt out. "We survived NAFA, Sgt. Marshawn Bell, Paul Douglass, Roland Wise and AFK. We will survive the Flamingo Club."

"Tiffany, you will have to become an official member of the Flamingo Club, for the next phase of this plan to work," Kesha states. I nod in agreement while Hakeem sits quietly.

"I don't want to turn into the monster our father was," Hakeem whispers in a loud enough tone that we both hear. "Power corrupts, absolute power corrupts absolutely. I just want to make a positive difference in the city. I don't even want to be in a pulpit anymore."

"Why did you preach Duck's funeral, then?" Kesha questions.

"Duck was family," Hakeem answers. "He was Darrin's best friend since they were in diapers. It was the right thing to do, especially when his freakin' mother asked me to do it."

"How did it feel preaching his eulogy?" Kesha asks. Hakeem smiles.

"It felt good, to be honest," Hakeem answers. "I haven't stood in a pulpit to preach in so long. I felt like I was supposed to be up there."

"Then why run from it?" Kesha asks.

"Because I don't want to become our father or grandfather," Hakeem answers.

"Create parameters to protect yourself," Kesha suggests. "You and Allen Bradley are such great friends, make him your assistant pastor and fire Raymond Nesmith. Cut everyone off that's part of the inner circle. Make the church a blank canvas and paint it how you see fit."

"When would this take place?" I ask as Kesha smirks.

"I'll schedule a meeting with the inner circle first, and then we will have a church meeting and tell the members," Kesha explains. "Not a word to anybody outside of this room until we meet with the church's inner circle."

"Maybe we should hold off on making these changes until we get the residents out of the Woodstock Campus," I advise. "We have a lot of Baltimore City residents staying in those buildings, and we don't know what kind of backlash there will be from the members of Andrews Memorial. Let's not have innocent visitors get hurt. They've been displaced once because of the city's negligence. Let's not have them get displaced again because of our own."

"Agreed," Kesha voices as she pulls out two lanyards from her desk's drawer. "Let's take a tour of the facility.

Chapter 22

I'm hiding behind an overturned church pew as a machine gun keeps firing, striking down fleeing members of Andrews Memorial. The church is filled with smoke, fire, broken glass and screams. The smell of gunpowder is thick in the air, as a male voice screams, "Where's the pastor's wife?"

As big as this church building is, I can't find a clear way to escape. I'm not sure how many armed gunmen there are. My heart is beating out my chest and I can barely catch my breath. As quick as I can inhale, I exhale faster. I'm on my knees and hands in the balcony area of the sanctuary. I can hear Monica bark orders from the pulpit to capture me and Hakeem, but I can't see exactly where she's standing. Can she see me? If she can, how stupid do I look hiding from this lady.

Suddenly I hear several shotgun blasts behind me and notice a green army man toy by my right hand. As I pick it up, there's a man wearing riot gear and a black ski mask holding a shotgun and winking at me. He has loaded clips, grenades and zip ties attached to his vest. He's attacked from behind by several members of

Andrews Memorial and dragged to the pulpit area, where Raymond and Monica are standing side-by-side. They pull the mask off the person, revealing that the masked man is the former police commissioner Alex Tillman. Behind Monica and Raymond, Mayor Hugo walks in holding a handgun and firing a fatal shot directly between the former police commissioner's eyes. As Alex Tillman falls lifeless on the pulpit, Monica orders Raymond to locate Hakeem.

"We have to get out of here!" Marshawn says to me, pointing at the exit. He's wearing the same outfit that Alex Tillman is wearing, except he doesn't have a face mask on. "We can get out that exit if I can cause a diversion."

"You won't be causing any diversions, pig," a familiar voice declares before shooting Marshawn several times. As Marshawn's last ditch effort, he pushes me away from the gun blast coming from the person who I now realize is Paul Douglass. "Last time I checked we were tied one and one in our fight. This time I won't make it as easy for you."

"Tiffany!" a voice shouts. "Tiffany!" the voice screams again as Paul Douglass disappears. The smell of smoke and gun powder dissipate and everything turns black.

"Tiffany, wake up. I thought you wanted to talk about what Kesha said before we went to bed."

As my eyes open, I look around trying to figure out where I'm at. I can feel the cold breeze from the air conditioning, and the rainwater beating against the window. We're currently getting some residual rain and wind from a hurricane down in Virginia. I must have fallen asleep on the recliner after the Baltimore Orioles game. I'm glad the rain waited until the evening before it started to pour down.

"How long was I out?" I ask as Hakeem gives a boyish smile.

"About two hours," he answers before reading through more charts from the files and folders Kesha left at the house earlier today.

"Are you seriously going to do this?" I ask, not sure of what his answer will be; Hakeem hates Andrews Memorial. He loves his sister, and I'm glad he's trying to bond with her, but he's avoided preaching or anything ministry related since 2019. I was shocked he agreed to preach the funeral, but I figured that was a one-off event because of how close Duck was to the family."

"What if I can make things right?" Hakeem ponders as I look on with a puzzled expression. "We don't know how to time travel, but what if God gave us a second chance at the right time. Through death comes life. There's always a payoff to death. Someone grows closer to God, families become closer, release of a stressful situation like abuse, or financial help. What if in Duck's death, he allowed me to have my second chance. Maybe Duck was my Jonah moment."

"Your what?" I question, trying to follow Hakeem's line of thinking. He's talking rapidly, excitedly. I'm trying to understand what he's talking about, but I also just woke up and I'm trying to make sense of that dream I just had.

"My Jonah moment!" Hakeem exclaims. He's animated, moving his hands around while he's emphasizing every word. "In the Bible Jonah was ordered to preach to some people he didn't want nothing to do with, but God was going to curse and destroy them for their sins. Jonah preferred for God to destroy them, so he set sail to another land, just knowing God was going to destroy the people he didn't like."

"Basically his *oops*," I jokingly add.

"Yeah," Hakeem agrees, then laughs. "God was going to destroy Jonah's oops, but he would spare them if Jonah would prophesy to them. Jonah dipped out on a boat. The boat was on bad waters and people knew the waters were angry because someone was cursed. Jonah admitted he was the cursed person and got thrown overboard. A big fish swallowed Jonah…"

"Oh, this is Jonah and the whale!" I shriek with excitement, cuddling up to Hakeem.

"Yeah, but no. The Bible said a big fish, everybody else says a whale," Hakeem corrects me but blushing 'cuz I'm hugged up on his arm. "He stayed in the belly of the fish for three days and three nights. Then Jonah was spit out. Jonah ran to the town in abnormally fast time to preach the message and God spared the people."

"Ok, but how does this have anything to do with you?" I ask, hoping he will explain this long, drawn-out scenario more clearly.

"My goal has always been to uplift, advocate and help the people of Baltimore," Hakeem says with pride. "I became a social worker and a civil rights lawyer because of that goal. I founded Justice 4 All because of that goal. I even used ministry as a way to keep up with my goal. I went to Pastor Avery because he had a similar goal and I admired him. When he died, I took over his church and we grew that goal with the help of God and Allen Bradley. Then the fires happened. Your grandmother's home was destroyed because of the fire, and New Hope Greater Love Church was destroyed because of the fires. I ran from God. Considered myself a failure. I became a shell of my former self. What's worse is I turned my back on what my goal was. Preaching at Duck's funeral made me realize something… that wasn't my goal all along, that was the calling God had for me. I was walking away from what God wanted me to do. When I spoke to the people at the church, I realized my voice is needed because it's my calling to uplift, advocate and help others. We're helping the people whose homes were destroyed, because my calling and your calling is the same. We serve in different arenas, but my calling and your calling became a ministry the day we said I do."

"We unionized," I joke as he kisses me gently on my lips.

"That's true," he acknowledges with a nod and a half smile. "And in that ministry, I still have to go in the direction God chose for me. In that direction you were already going with the 10th Bank and with the Legacy of Florence. But as the head of the house, am I supposed to lead? We take the church back, we help the people of Baltimore. We free the city of the secret rule of the Flamingo Club, and we destroy the false teaching my family has spoon fed to the people of the church for years. Right now, you've solved the water crisis. Right now, we can solve the string of youth murders committed by the Charm City Strangler, if we want to."

"Why did you tell your sister no so many times if this is what you're going to do?" I ask, wanting to call him out in a lie.

"Because I knew she wasn't just walking away," he answers. *Damn, he's good.* "I knew she was either invested or involved in something and she wanted to dump Andrews Memorial on me. Yet, I do like what she's trying to do with saving lives from horrible diseases."

"So just like that you're back in ministry?" I question as he places a bunch of papers on the table and begins to look at a digital chart on his iPad.

"No." Hakeem pauses to think, then says, "There's a lot at stake with the transition of power, thanks to my aunt and Raymond, so we're going to have to smooth over that process. That, and we have house guests at the Woodstock Campus that Monica and Raymond really don't want there. So we play this slowly, and we make ourselves look like assets to Andrews Memorial."

"I love this excitement you're showing about getting back into ministry," I admit as Hakeem leans back on the couch.

"I feel free!" Hakeem exclaims, "I've been under so much pressure and feeling like a failure because of what happened during the Ridgely Square Incident. It was something freeing when I studied and preached that eulogy for Duck. It was like God wanted me to deliver those words of comfort to those people. It was therapeutic. I felt healed. The hurt from my brother, gone. The hurt from my parents, gone. My feelings of failure after your house and the church burned down, gone. It's like this is the path God truly wants me on. I have a purpose."

"The Jonah moment!" I scream with excitement and he agrees. We start to cuddle and kiss as Darrin walks into the living room, pauses and then walks back upstairs to his bedroom.

Chapter 23

The next morning, I am in my office at the 10th Bank with the news playing in the background. I sit behind my desk drinking my cucumber and lemon water, while reading reports from the weekend. "The police commissioner and the mayor have stated that the Paul Douglass Law is still in effect," the male voice says on the television. I barely have it high enough to hear, but I need the background noise. I've come to learn that silence in empty rooms triggers the voices I'm trying to drown out. "The mayor has signed off on 3 surveillance planes to fly over and take pictures of Baltimore continuously for the next 21 days, or until the Charm City Strangler is caught and brought to justice."

One of the benefits to the Charm City Strangler, is that crimes initiated by youth have gone down 80% in Baltimore City. I don't think people living in fear should be the right payoff for crime reduction. "Hypocrite," a child's voice says in my head. I'm confused because normally it's Marshawn that talks bluntly to me.

Before my eyes, I see the young girl appear with the braids I hugged at church during Duck's funeral. "A few years ago, you and everybody else praised AFK for killing the bad people of Baltimore City. It's funny how now, this guy is public enemy number one," the little girl says before she cocks her head to the side and places her hand on her waist, as if she is posing. Before my eyes, she ages to about 13 or 14 years old and I realize, that's no normal little girl, that's my daughter Kenya. She died in the hit-and-run back in 2016. Great, now I'm back to hallucinating her again.

"Ma, you got to get this shit together," Kenya says, shaking her head as she talks. "You're handling this water crisis, Hakeem is handling the church, who's handling Darrin?"

"What?" I ask out loud as Kenya frowns to the point where I can see the dimples in her cheeks.

"*Darrin*," she repeats. "His best friend was just killed. I'm still dead. Tina is still dead. Your mother Linda, still dead; Jamar, still dead, all his Cabal friends, still dead, and there's a Charm City Strangler still on the loose. Also, thanks for thinking of me instead of our cousin Tina," Kenya says before vanishing.

"In other news, in Dayton, Ohio, a police officer, Gerald McGuine, was murdered last night. Dayton police are reporting that this murder may be linked to the recent copycat AFK killings. The name Gerald McGuine may seem familiar to many of you, as he was at the center of a murder trial in 2019, for shooting an unarmed black man, Terry Lester, who was smoking a cigarette on the doorstep of his new home. For those who don't remember the controversy, McGuine responded to a call where neighbors thought Lester was trespassing or attempting to rob, not knowing that Mr. Lester had purchased the home a few days earlier. McGuine responded to the call and reported that he thought the Newport cigarette that Lester was holding was a smoking gun, so he shot and killed Mr. Lester, fearing for his life. The judge, Evan Daily, threw out McGuine's case, and allowed the controversial officer to return to work with back pay and an undisclosed settlement for slander and defamation of character.

"You know it's him, right?" Marshawn asks wearing a black three-piece suit. The suit has slight purple tones on the jacket and vest.

"Who?" I ask.

Marshawn responds, "The Action Figure Killer, the real Action Figure Killer. Alex Tillman."

"How do you know that?" I ask as Marshawn rolls his eyes and vanishes.

There's a knock at the door to my office and Monica and Raymond Nesmith enter the office without giving me a chance to give permission to enter.

"We need to talk about savings funds the church needs to sever," Monica demands.

"We have staff that can help with that," I reply as the two invite themselves to a seat in front of my desk.

"You don't want this to get out," Monica explains. "That Narcotics and Firearms Taskforce Case that included the Alphas trafficking people all over the world, they funneled that money through Andrews Memorial under the name *General Midnight*. We want to distance ourselves from that as soon as possible."

"I think that's a meeting you should have with Bishop Kesha Stokes before demanding a meeting with the owner of the bank," I sarcastically reply as Raymond stands up, attempting to posture above me as I stand up as well.

"You don't understand, we need to sever that relationship now," Raymond demands. "We have innocent people staying at the Woodstock Campus.

What happens when people associated to General Midnight want to get those people and start moving them around like he did years ago with the Alphas."

"I have no idea what you're talking about, but you should take that up with Bishop Stokes," I dismissively say before I pick up a file off the table, ignoring the two.

"If General Midnight's people have a problem with Andrews Memorial, then they have a problem with the Flamingo Club and the 10th Bank," Raymond states in a deep voice.

"Let's say I know who General Midnight is," I entertain. "Isn't he already dead?" I ask as Monica and Raymond look at each other.

"His mission is not dead, his people have been working in Maryland," Monica states, placing a picture of a tall African man wearing jeans and a brown t-shirt, standing amongst James DeLuca, Erica Little, and Hugo Titan. "They might not have the muscle of the Alphas, but their mission is still the same, waging war against the people that occupied his country. The funding for that crusade with sex trafficking, black market organ sales, and the sales of the synthetic opioid that the West Baltimore Hospital created."

"Not my problem right now," I express with complete disregard to Monica's appeal to my humanity. "We're trying to solve this water crisis, and that's the only reason why you have those 'innocent' people staying at the Woodstock Campus."

"You're going to have more blood on your hands if you don't do anything," Monica declares.

"I don't have blood on my hands now," I dismiss as the two stand up and walk towards the door.

Marshawn laughs in the back of my mind saying, "Yes you do have blood on your hands, and I helped you. Let me ring a bell, sing along to the jingle if you know the words. "Your father, who art not being in heaven, hollow tips froze his veins. Blown to kingdom come, for his will that was done. Cremated and thrown on earth, may he burn and not see heaven."

"Quiet!" I whisper to myself, hastily turning to my side so that Monica will not notice.

"Before I go," Monica states while pausing mid-stride to the door. I'm not sure if she heard me talking to myself or not. "How did you find out who General Midnight is?"

"That's not the important question," I answer with a smug look on my face. "What will happen when he finds out you came here and tried to cut him out of Andrews Memorial?" Monica and Raymond leave out the office slamming the door, as I release a large exhale.

"Somebody's lying," Kenya says, appearing before me again as I sit down in my leather office chair.

"The quicker we get away from Andrews Memorial, the better," Marshawn adds, standing next to my daughter.

"No, we need to take over the church and help those cult-following idiots," Kenya refutes Marshawn's claim.

"It's not their fault," Marshawn defends. "Them church folk didn't ask to be part of a cult. For all they know, they're just worshiping God the best way they know how. Hakeem will be the pastor of that church soon enough, and the church will head in the right direction."

"You're just as insufferable as a dead figment of my mother's imagination as you were when you were alive," Kenya snaps back.

"We've never met, when you were alive, missy?" Marshawn jokes as Kenya looks at her cell phone and starts chewing gum.

"What the hell is going on?" I scream as the two begin laughing.

"That's the right question to ask," Marshawn states as he sits in the chair where Raymond previously sat moments ago. "If General Midnight is still alive, what affiliation does he have with the Flamingo Club right now, and how can we get him away from the church's affairs?"

"That's none of your business; leave that man where he is," Kenya barks back at Marshawn. "When Kesha hands the keys to Andrews Memorial over to Hakeem, best believe he will right all the wrongs that church has made over the years.

"What happens when the members of Andrews Memorial fight back against Hakeem?" Marshawn ponders. "What happens when the Flamingo Club doesn't like the exit that Andrews Memorial makes from that secret society? Can this family really withstand being in the crosshairs of another beef? First it was the Alphas with NAFA, then it was the Alphas with Paul Douglass and Roland Wise. Are we really going to be fighting the Flamingo Club and Andrews Memorial? Especially now that they're helping us with housing these displaced residents. We actually have an audience with the Flamingo Club, which includes the mayor. Are you sure it's wise to spit in their faces when we're getting some important shit done?"

"Important shit like what?" Kenya asks. I cut my eyes at my daughter for cursing in front of me. "You know I'm not real, Mom," she jokes while blowing a large bubble and sitting next to Marshawn.

"The water crisis," I explain to Kenya, returning to her question. "We are getting the water crisis handled, thanks to the Flamingo Club. Mayor Hugo is paying for the lodging of the residents staying at the Woodstock Campus right now. The streets are being repaired, and the 10th Bank has been granted a contract by the city to assist with the rebuilding. Mayor Hugo and Erica Little have seen to it that my grandmother's home will be rebuilt by the end of the summer."

"What about the Charm City Strangler?" Kenya questions. "What are you doing about that? Have you even put up any money for a reward for his capture?"

"What if the Charm City Strangler is General Midnight?" Marshawn questions and I laugh out loud.

"The real you was a detective, I can't live with a fake detective in my head," I state as Marshawn smiles and sits quietly. "You do have a point, though. Duck was my son's best friend; it is only right that I put money towards his murderer's capture."

"I think you better think of something fast," Kenya says as the news continues in the background about Kutter the Poet, Ms. Pugh, WaKitta and others walking through Leakin Park searching for more victims.

"It has been several days since the last claimed victim of the Charm City Strangler," the female news reporter states. "The last victim was J'won Foote, also known as Duck. His mother, WaKitta and others desperately search for clues that will end this reign of terror. The current police commissioner, Keith Mercer, has encouraged residents not to get involved with the investigation, but tensions are running high as the former disgraced governor, Guy Delaney, has called for a new trial in the conviction of his client, Carlson Jessup. Guy Delaney has stated that there are too many similarities between the victims of the Charm City Strangler and the alleged victims of the Right Hand of God Fellowship Church. Guy Delaney has claimed that Jessup was coerced into making a confession about the murders he admitted to. A group of appeal judges have agreed to review the case later in July."

"Something doesn't add up," Kenya says while looking at her cell phone and inhaling from a silver vape pen. "Why is all this happening now? This didn't happen during the pandemic when the world was shut down. There was never a mention of General Midnight. The closest we had to a mention of the Right Hand of God Fellowship Church was when your friend Detective Murphy alluded to them back in 2019 at your restaurant. Why is all this happening right now, when the city is having water problems? The Flamingo Club is winning, in theory. They have the mayor as a member of the club, Erica Little has the contracts to do the community redevelopment, they have accounts in your bank, why is Kesha trying to break away? Why is Kesha trying to throw the keys to the church at your husband? Why would she open up about the Ginger Hill Medical Research Center now?"

"You need an outsider's point of view," Marshawn adds, leaning back in the chair. "Not Hakeem, not Allen Bradley, not Kesha, definitely not Monica or Raymond."

"Then who?" I ask as Kenya and Marshawn stare at me in silence. "No. I'm not going to contact him," I declare as the two nod in agreement.

"You have to," Kenya explains before the two start to evaporate before my eyes. "The way it looks, he will make his way back to Baltimore before we know it."

"That nigga is scary, tho," I say as I realize I'm in the room all by myself looking at a small green army man toy sitting next to my wooden hourglass. In 2019, Alex Tillman left three of these on my desk before he vanished. I keep one in this office, one at Legacy of Florence and one in my purse as a constant reminder that he's out there. What's worse is nobody knows how dangerous he is because all of his crimes were covered up by the police and the FBI. They pinned all his murders on Paul Douglass and Roland Wise.

As I try to think of anything else, Marshawn reappears and stands by the door to my office. "You're doing a lot of great work for the city; maybe it's time you become more hands on with the Charm City Strangler case. AFK might be the person to help you with that."

Chapter 24

Later that evening, a press conference is called in the lobby of the 10th Bank. Standing behind me are Hakeem, Darrin, Aleem, Allen Bradley, Mayor Hugo, Erica Little, Commissioner Mercer, Ms. Pugh, and WaKitta. I made a quick announcement on social media that I would be calling a press conference, and the next thing I know, everybody wants to get involved.

I'm glad the air conditioning is pumping, because it's a very hot early July day. "Good afternoon, everyone," I begin. There are cameras pointing in my face as I stand in front of a podium with the 10th Bank's logo on the front. "Since 2019 the 10th Bank has been dedicated to doing the hard work our communities need to thrive. This hard work has included helping struggling families keep their homes, investing in companies, and most recently, addressing Baltimore City's water crisis. Thanks to Mayor Hugo, Erica Little, the good folks at Titan Industries, Kutter the Poet and Andrews Memorial, the water crisis is being handled, and by August, every Baltimore City resident will have access to clean, uncontaminated tap water."

A group of people watching begin to clap half enthusiastically as I continue. "With that being said, the outreach mission for the 10th Bank has to change to a problem plaguing the city right now. The problem has a name but no face. The problem has impacted so many families and has placed a dark cloud over the great efforts Mayor Hugo, Titan Industries, the Knights and the 10th Bank have attempted. That problem's name is the Charm City Strangler. Effective immediately, our outreach department will look at innovative ways to help the residents of Baltimore City, along with the Baltimore City Police Department to bring down this psychopath who's caused so much damage to our residents. Effective immediately, the 10th Bank has agreed to put up $200,000 to any man, woman or child that can provide law enforcement with definitive details that will bring a conviction to this horrible person."

As the people in attendance begin to clap, I point at Commissioner Mercer, WaKitta and Ms. Pugh. "Up here with me are individuals impacted by the Charm City Strangler. As a mother who's lost a child to senseless violence in this city and has another child in treatment for the trauma she's endured, this is important to me and the 10th Bank. I think I can speak for my husband, Dr. Hakeem Andrews, when I say that we're going to utilize every resource we can while working in concert with the police department to catch this madman."

A short thin-framed Asian woman asks, "How do you know for sure the Charm City Strangler is a man?"

"I don't," I quickly answer. "I'm not the police, I'm not the FBI and I'm not the mayor. What I am is a mother. I have four living children, 2 boys and 2 girls. My heart breaks for people like Commissioner Mercer, Ms. Pugh and WaKitta. There have been 40 plus confirmed victims of the Charm City Strangler found in Leakin Park, and while there were no new bodies discovered since the body of J'won Foote was found, we're not going to wait for him to strike again. This is Baltimore City, the place where we take care of our own, and it's always us versus you whores. And by whores, I mean predators like the Charm City Strangler."

Darrin walks to the front of the podium, holding a large cardboard check that reads $200,000. "This check is a symbol of our commitment to fight for justice for each victim, the deceased and surviving family members of the Charm City Strangler. The 10th Bank and Allen Bradley Funeral Home have also agreed to financially support any family member facing difficulty burying their loved one who is a confirmed victim of the Charm City Strangler."

As the people in attendance begin to clap, and some of the media reporters attempt to raise their hands to ask questions I add, "I would also like to announce that effective immediately the 10th Bank, in conjunction with Justice 4 All, will be launching our life insurance service. This life insurance service will be available for all Baltimore City residents at an affordable rate. In this insurance policy, there is a built-in checking and savings account for the applicant to use while they are living. The policy allows the applicant to choose what they would like done with the money in their savings and checking during the time of their death in addition to the policy amount. The life insurance policy will also provide investment options for the policy holder. Meaning, if the policy holder would like to open a money market, a mutual fund or any retirement investment account, it is attached to your policy, and you can contribute today after a brief screening by our team. This insurance policy, like the $200,000 we're putting towards the capture of the Charm City Strangler is a part of our dedication to the people of Ridgely Square and all of Baltimore City. Any questions?"

"Does this insurance cover, or help with family members that had a loved one claimed by the Charm City Strangler?" A female reporter asks.

"If they're insured, yes," I answer, thinking that this should be a no brainer. "The Allen Bradley Funeral Home and the 10th Bank have agreed to a $500 grant for funeral expenses at the Allen Bradley Funeral Home, for victims that will need financial support for their final arrangements. This grant will be awarded on a case-by-case basis. One of the requirements for the grant is the victim must qualify for the Maryland Criminal Injuries Compensation Board."

"What about the citizens that don't have insurance but need to bury their loved ones?" the reporter continues. I'm actually annoyed by this question. I just created an affordable insurance policy and a savings account for the citizens of Baltimore City, and all we can focus on are people with no insurance. I just want to point out how dumb this is.

"Sadly, this is a life insurance policy, along with savings and checking accounts," I answer, trying not to show my frustration with the stupidity of the question. "Every person, not just the citizens of Baltimore, should have a savings account, a checking account and life insurance. We should not have to rely on borrowing money when a loved one dies, especially when there are options to take care of end-of-life services. If a person can buy a bottle of alcohol, weed, go on vacation, or eat crabs, they can make affordable monthly payments to an insurance policy. We need to break away from the custom of begging and borrowing money to bury our loved ones and make investments to insure there are no hold ups with their end-of-life services. Mothers, fathers, sisters and brothers, don't be a burden on those who love you. Get an insurance policy, get a will, get an advance directive. We're trying to help, but we can't force you to take the help."

"How is this helping with my grandson's murder?" Ms. Pugh yells, causing several faces to turn in her direction before they roll their eyes noticing who just made the scene.

"Where is this money coming from?" a man screams from the back, where the catered food is set up.

"We have made a lot of positive strides to take these steps," I add, trying to make out the face of the person who asked the question. As more questions come in, I notice that it was Raymond Nesmith that asked the question.

<h1 style="text-align:center">Chapter 25</h1>

The next morning, Darrin and I are serving food at the dining hall at the Woodstock Campus. It's crowded as a mixture of homeless people that receive shelter at the Woodstock Campus and displaced individuals from the gas and waterline explosions are eating breakfast together. Kesha has made it a point to greet everyone and take time to speak with each person.

Darrin has found his calling, serving the people of Baltimore City at the Woodstock Campus. Mayor Hugo and the Baltimore County Executive Cleo Rodgers have both made their presence known today. The bane of my existence, Monica Nesmith, has requested to meet with me today. I have attempted to ignore her, and dismiss her requests, but there she is, standing by the kitchen exit, waiting for me to turn around.

"Tiffany!" Monica loudly calls from behind me. I don't care for her tone, as it is very demanding and demeaning. "Tiffany, I need to speak with you now!"

I turn around, wearing my white apron and latex gloves, gesturing to her that I'm working. Monica signals for me to follow her as a church member to my right slides over to the tray of eggs and bacon I've been serving.

As I throw the gloves in the gray trash can and walk to the exit, Monica says, "We really need to talk, right now."

The two of us walk to a door that reads Chef's Office. As we walk into the bright room, Raymond walks in behind us. "Take a seat, Tiffany," Raymond demands, wearing a red polo shirt that says R. Nesmith Brand in cursive black letters on the left side of the shirt. "We need to talk about the Rules of Engagement."

"I don't feel comfortable having this conversation with you all without my husband, or your bishop," I respond as Monica slams the door behind me.

"You don't have negotiating power on this," Monica says. She sits on the desk with her feet barely touching the white tile floor. "How long will your guests be staying at our campus?" Monica questions.

"That's between Bishop Kesha Stokes, Mayor Hugo and—"

"Bullshit," Monica returns. "You and my nephew, Hakeem, are planning something and you have Kesha involved in it."

"Kesha Stokes is the bishop of this whole operation; if you have a problem, I encourage you to take it up with her," I state as Monica cocks her head to the side and Raymond walks in front of my face in an intimidating fashion.

"We're not here to play with you, Tiffany," Raymond says with his fist clenched as Monica moves from behind him.

"Where is the money coming from for that insurance policy?" Raymond questions.

"Funny thing happened when I was auditing files," I say, unfazed by Raymond's posturing. Clearly, he doesn't know I shot and killed my own father, and I held my own against Paul Douglass. One thing I'm not is a victim or someone's punk.

"What did you find?" Raymond questions.

"You're not my boss, Elder Raymond," I point out in a sassy tone. "Yet, I'll humor you. There was an account labeled Midnight Fund. That account had more than $50 million in it. The names connected to that account are Paul Douglass, who's dead, a Franklin John, Monica Nesmith and Raymond Nesmith. What's odd about this is Kesha Stokes's name was not attached to it. Also, the dates of the deposits line up with mission trips to Africa, Asia, and South America. When I dug a little deeper, I noticed that several incarcerated Alphas have opened accounts with the 10th Bank and wired money into the Midnight Fund. Would you care to talk about that?"

"I don't know who you think you are, but you do not question anything this ministry does," Raymond demands. I stand up and get close to his face, daring him to fight me.

"Franklin John is dead," I add, not missing a beat and with no fear. I add bass in my voice for the next revelation, "Franklin John was known as General Midnight. He was found dead from asphyxiation and was lying in a shallow water-filled bathtub. Here's where things get really weird, his dead body was found less than 24 hours after the murders of Bishop Andrews, Grace Andrews, Kelly Nesmith and Patrick Stokes."

"If you have something to say, then say it," Monica demands, and I laugh in her face.

"The money that y'all put in my bank was from your drug deals and human trafficking," I point out. "I can go about this one of two ways. The first way, I can report this to the FBI. The second way is I use this money the right way, and all your other business dealings go on as planned.”

“Do you think the Flamingo Club will allow this?” Raymond questions.

“I have a better chance of finding out than you,” I quickly respond. “You see, I actually add value to the Flamingo Club, and I will be a member of the club very soon. You, Raymond and Monica, are replaceable. You’re not the pastors of Andrews Memorial. You don’t handle the finances of the Flamingo Club. You know what that means? You’re just two people who go to this church and have a title.”

“And you’re in our house, with some unwanted house guests,” Monica reminds me.

“Monica Nesmith, trustee of Andrews Memorial. Are you telling me that you’re not interested in the missionary work that Andrews Memorial has taken pride in for decades? Are you not interested in growing the church? That seems sacrilegious, and one thing I’ve learned about this family, y’all love y’all’s religion.”

“Who do you think you are?” Raymond questions as I place my right index finger in his face.

"Your worst nightmare if you try to pull some bullying tactics like this again," I declare, jumping in Raymond's face as if I were going to punch him, just to watch him flinch. My smile has just grown larger now that I've seen that small piece of fear on Raymond's face. Before I can say another word, Monica places her hand on my shoulder and forces me down to the brown leather cushioned chair with the metal legs.

"Do you really want to play with that money?" Monica questions, walking around to face me, pushing Raymond out the way. "The church has washed the money for the Flamingo Club's illegal business dealings for years. That is one of many accounts we have, and it serves a purpose."

"I don't care," I dismiss her reasoning. "My bank. If you have a problem with how I handled your illegal activity, I can contact my friend at the FBI, Agent Parker..." Monica gives a small smile and wink causing me to pause my monologue.

"You don't know how to read the room, do you?" Monica questions. "Agent Parker has been paid off by the Flamingo Club, dating back to the Action Figure Killer investigation. Why do you think we've been able to operate without any penalty. Why do you think your bank has been so successful?"

"What?" I question.

"Your bank," Monica repeats. "Do you understand the money that helped your bank to get started, is money from this church, money from the Flamingo Club, money from different connections we have, just like the Black Tie. Not money that you had. We gave you power, and now you want to spit in our faces. You're a fraud, and we can expose you at any time. Keep thinking that you're fighting for the greater good; in all honesty, your hands are just as dirty as ours."

"Are we going to fight, talk or hug?" I ask, quickly growing annoyed with this conversation. I would rather walk across the campus to wait for my husband to pick me up. Yup, walking across this campus, all the way out in the boonies, with nasty disgusting frogs just hopping along the sidewalks.

"Your son, Darrin," Raymond interjects, "he's been helping out here at the campus a lot. I want him in our vacation bible school with the other kids around his age."

"No, he stays with me," I reject the proposal to Raymond's dismay. "He feels like serving the displaced and the homeless people of Baltimore is his ministry, as you'd call it."

"Well, can I get him to work with my mother at the motel?" Raymond counters. "He can make some money in the process, and it will keep him safe from the street kids that keep getting hurt in Baltimore."

"That's a creepy request, especially after you just tried to threaten me," I point out as the two roll their eyes. The tension in the room has oddly relaxed me.

"We're on edge, Tiffany," Monica admits in a more relaxed and chill tone. There's still something about the way she's talking that appears like she's talking down to me. "Kesha has been distant since her parents and brother died. Raymond has had to carry a lot of the load of the church since the mission trip in Africa that claimed her husband, my husband and her parents. Then learning of Jamar's death did a number on her and Raymond. It may not seem like it, but we are glad that Hakeem came back to Andrews Memorial. We just want to make sure things continue to move forward like they have been. Hakeem does his Justice 4 All work, along with the work he does with the Knights. Andrews Memorial has a lot of moving pieces, so I don't want him getting involved in stuff that will set him up for failure or slow the church down."

"So you think my husband wants to take over Andrews Memorial?" I ask in a genuinely interested tone.

"No, I hope not," Raymond abruptly states before pausing and looking at Monica. "This campus is going to be a fully operational college, with a high-end prep school attached. People who go to this college that want to work in education can get firsthand work experience. People who want to work in ministry can get trained here. The homeless can receive shelter, food and vocational services on the south side of the campus. We have single family homes on this campus, along with residential buildings for students and apartments. That's a portion of what we've been doing with this campus. We also have the convention center at the north end of the campus, where we plan on holding a large event at the end of July. Music, workshops and motivational speaking. The county executive has already agreed to sponsor a job fair at the convention hall.

"With all of those things we have going on at this location, we don't want Hakeem to get lost trying to find his place," Monica points out. "It seems like we may have gotten off to a bad start, Tiffany, but I really want what's best for Andrews Memorial. This is my family's legacy, and I truly don't know what Hakeem was poisoned with when he worked with that cuckoo Pastor Donald Avery."

"Maybe we should all sit down and talk about these feelings," I suggest as Monica agrees.

"My apologies for how everything came across earlier," Raymond says. "There's a lot riding on our church, and this campus. As a token of good faith, can I interest you in having Darrin join my private bible study group?"

"No," I say emphatically. Raymond raises both his hands.

"Tiffany," Monica calls out to me, "don't make any other decisions on how to handle the money I deposit for this church."

"The illegal money has to go somewhere, and I'm not going to turn a blind eye to it. I wasn't going to let Paul Douglass do it, and I'm not going to let this church do it," I voice.

"Paul Douglass and the Alphas moved money through the church and in your bank before you ever knew it," Monica recounts. "Paul's locked up homies, his big name suppliers, all that was tied up in your bank. General Midnight—oh my God—do you know what he was tied up in? He trafficked little kids across the globe, using the church's mission trips as his cover. The prostitution ring the Alphas were involved in, General Midnight basically ran that operation up until 2019. The drug smuggling, General Midnight. The black-market organs, that was also General Midnight. Why am I telling you this? Because that money is tied up in several of your accounts. We haven't even gotten started on Neil Goldberg, Khin Lao or the Black Tie. Unless you close that precious bank, your hands are dirty. Problem with that is, The Flamingo Club would kill and replace you before you could finish your resignation press conference. We may not get along, but *they* are your true enemies, not Raymond and me."

I feel a chill go up my spine as she finishes her statements. Raymond politely walks over to the door to open it for Monica and me. He's so tall and massive, but he has this boyish look on his face. "Please think about what I asked. I really do want to build a bond with your son."

"I will." I surprisingly didn't choke on that lie. I walk out of the office and back to the kitchen area where my husband is now standing next to Darrin serving food to the growing number of people entering the dining hall.

Chapter 26

That Wednesday, Hakeem and I are seated together next to my aunt Gina at Andrews Memorial. Raymond is leading the open bible study, in the half-packed church. Monica is seated on the far right side of the pulpit, but noticeably absent is Kesha Stokes. Several ushers are passing around a clipboard to the members in the audience, as Raymond continues his lecture on prosperity through loyalty.

"When we think about loyalty, we have to think back to the beginning of time," Raymond says as he watches the ushers walk up and down the aisles with the clipboards. "God made man in his own image to have someone to worship him willingly. Before anybody points out the angels, let me remind you, Lucifer was the only angel that had free will in all the heavens. God wanted beings that would worship him without hesitation, without excuse, without rhyme or reason. He created Adam and then Eve. God placed them in the garden of Eden, giving them all they could ask for or want, *for free*. He just had one rule: Don't eat the fruit from the tree of knowledge. Then the serpent came to Eve, convinced her to eat the fruit from the tree of knowledge and then she turned and gave it to Adam.

Even though Adam was loyal and trusting toward Eve, when he ate the fruit, he was not loyal to God. From that point, we have had wars, famine, racism, poverty and illnesses. God does not want us to complain, or make excuses, he wants us to willingly serve him, without a second thought."

An usher walks to the row that Hakeem, Gina and I are sitting in, and hands us a wooden backed clipboard. The clipboard has a form with space for us to fill out our full name, date of birth, social security number, credit score, home address, banking information and employment history.

"You should fill that out," Gina suggests. I cackle loudly as if she has said the funniest thing I've ever heard in my life.

Before I can get Hakeem's attention to make a joke about the form attached to the clipboard, the usher asks me to walk to the rear of the church where 10 other people are standing. While I look on in confusion, Monica walks down to Hakeem and asks him to join her in the pulpit seating area.

Deacon Jordan, a tall, skinny brown skin man with bushy hair that dresses very flashy escorts us out into the hallway filled with pictures of Hakeem's parents and grandparents. We walk past group photos of the deacon and evangelist boards. All the members of the deacon, evangelist, and elder boards are very young and attractive looking people. Even the missionary and outreach ministry members are young and attractive. It's like the church wants to flaunt sex appeal before your eyes. In the pictures they're all wearing trendy and revealing outfits. There are framed pictures of the young adults at the beach, at concerts dancing, even washing cars. As I try to make sense of what I'm looking at in the eggshell white hallway, Deacon Jordan leads our small ensemble into the mini chapel area. Deacon Jordan appears to be no older than 25 years old, with an inviting face. Evangelist Nelly walks into the mini chapel with 4 other people. Evangelist Nelly is an early 20-year-old dark skin woman that is heavy busted. She's wearing a tight short yellow and orange dress that is hugging her like a boy that grew up in foster care and he's just been reunited with his biological mother on Christmas morning.

"Why are we here?" a man wearing blue jeans and a faded purple Baltimore Ravens jersey asks.

"To answer any questions and help with doubts," Deacon Jordan answers with a smile. "Everyone in this room either hesitated to answer the questionnaire or thought it was funny. Elder Raymond Nesmith wanted us to pull everyone together that showed signs of doubt to hold a private discussion."

"Is this like his private bible study?" I ask as Deacon Jordan denies this meeting has any relation to the private bible study. "I'm not comfortable with being here, can I leave?"

As I finish my sentence, a tall, large muscular man wearing a brown suit, walks in the room. I've seen him at the church before, his name is Deacon Harris. He was an offensive lineman in college and had a career-ending injury his rookie season when he was drafted to the National Football League. He then became a competitive body builder and had the goal of doing movies or professional wrestling. He won a few body builder competitions and was in a few movies.

"We're just here to talk for a little bit," Deacon Harris reassures, blocking the door out the mini chapel.

"What are we going to talk about?" I ask as Deacon Harris points at the pews, silently ordering us to take a seat. I feel really uncomfortable in this situation. I wish I had my gun, or Hakeem or Darrin. Oh crap, Darrin is at home by himself, and that Charm City Strangler might be prowling around, looking for his next victim.

There hasn't been another victim of his found since Duck.

"Membership," Evangelist Nelly answers with a large smile. "A lot of y'all have been attending this church for the last few months but haven't joined the ministry. We understand that we're not like most churches, which is true, we're *better* than most churches. Did you know right now, in Baltimore County, we're housing the homeless and the Baltimore City residents that lost their homes because of the explosions?"

As several of the people sitting in the pews talk amongst themselves, I can't help but wonder how my son is doing. I'm so glad that Desha and RJ are at the art camp.

"What about Trinity," Marshawn questions in the back of my mind. "Are you happy that she's in the residential program? You know how she got there, right? The house fire! She's in a residential program because of the trauma from the house fire. Do you think that's better than being home and avoiding a serial killer?"

"I…" I begin to say aloud. All eyes appear to be on me. I stop for a moment, feeling embarrassed that I just brought attention to myself. I pull out my cell phone to open the screen and look at pictures of my children, but Deacon Harris walks up to me asking me to put my phone away, and I listen. I mean seriously, this guy looks like he punches open doors to sealed pyramids, and you think I'm going to challenge this dude? Hell no to the naw naw. He said put the phone away; the phone is in my pocket.

"We wanted to show everyone why Andrews Memorial is more than just a church, it's an experience," Deacon Jordan says with a bright smile on his face as a slim built light skin woman walks into the room wearing tight leggings and a shirt that I can only imagine was made to be lingerie. Who wears this kind of stuff?

"Evangelist NoLesha, glad you made it before we left," Deacon Jordan says, his eyes gleaming at who we should presume is Evangelist NoLesha. Deacon Jordan's eyes are clearly centered towards this young woman's perfectly shaped bosoms. What the hell is going on, and why am I involved? I'm out.

"Elder Nesmith wanted us to show you all a great time, and we're about to do that," Evangelist NoLesha says in a shrieky voice. It's like too happy and overexcited for no reason. Who gave this woman coffee laced crack during bible study? I swear, if this high yellow diva has a stroke, I'm going to make a documentary about this church.

The four clergy lead me and my fellow strangers to a black Cadillac Escalade limousine outside the church doors. "I can't leave my husband, he's my ride home," I scream as Deacon Harris steps in front of me.

"There's no need to worry, Mrs. Andrews," Deacon Harris says in a deep, but intimidating voice. He towers over me as I look up to make eye contact. "Elder Nesmith has made provisions to contact anyone you all came with and will ensure everyone gets home completely safe tonight. Things will be better when you return home than they were when you came to bible study tonight."

"What do you mean?" A bald man, possibly in his mid-forties, says. He's in decent shape, possibly 6 feet tall.

"Mr. Douglas Peoples," Deacon Harris calls out, walking over to the man like a drill sargent approaching new soldiers in basic training, "You've been coming to Andrews Memorial for the last 9 months. You work as a house cleaner and do roadside assistance on interstates 695 and 83. You lost your home and your savings due to a data breach. You're currently 3 months behind in rent on your apartment, your car is about to be repossessed, and you can't afford to pay for the classes you need to graduate for your bachelor's degree in education."

"I figure if I get a career, I can get my life back on track," Douglas murmurs, looking down in shame.

"Elder Nesmith paid it all off," Deacon Harris says, but Douglas has not processed his words yet. "Every single debt, everything that was corrupted from the data breach, fixed. He even paid your rent up for the rest of the year. Check it on your phone."

As Douglas opens his smart phone and accesses different apps, his eyes begin to water, his arms shake and he falls into Deacon Harris's arms, crying uncontrollably. Evangelist Nelly walks in front of us as Deacon Harris holds the crying Douglas and says, "God has blessed Andrews Memorial with an abundance of great things. Let's go out, celebrate and enjoy all of God's riches and glories. And guess what, all of you, all of your financial burdens are gone. Check your phones."

As everyone piles into the limousine, we begin to ride through the city of Baltimore. We see several of the neighborhoods destroyed by the explosions, and others that were not impacted. We notice a handful of people standing outside, some homeless, some panhandling to wash windshields, some getting high and others selling narcotics. We find ourselves in front of the Nesmith Motel. The motel has four long buildings that have two floors for its residents. In the front of the motel is a large lounge area that serves as a restaurant, bar and dance floor. The music is pumping from out of the dimly lit lounge area, and we see the flickering lights moving to the rhythm of the bass coming out the walls. With smiles on almost everyone's faces, we enter.

I'm still confused about the purpose of all of this. Why are you taking us to party when we were just in bible study? How does this look, bank owner and community activist out partying while the rest of the city fears for its life because of the Charm City Strangler, along with water and gas explosions. Oh yeah, don't forget about my teenage son being left alone at home while that child killing psychopath preys on the youth.

I walk into the lounge, impressed by how clean it looks. The lighting is perfect, as well as the space, and from what Deacon Harris said, all the food and drinks are free tonight. I make my way to a booth and sit down to look at the menu. I think I might do the crab cakes, or the shrimp alfredo. I wonder if I can get a to-go tray for Hakeem and Darrin.

"What's up with all of this?" Marshawn says, sitting across from me. Next to him is Kenya, looking at her phone. Wait. Why does hallucination Kenya have a cell phone? Why is she even appearing as if she doesn't want to talk to me.

"What's up with what?" I ask as Marshawn points around the lounge.

"The church took a group of potential members out to the lounge, while everybody else stayed at Bible study?" Marshawn questions in a sarcastic tone. "All the people that didn't sign that clipboard were brought here and shown a good time. He also paid off their debt. Something seems off."

"Yeah," Kenya adds looking at me. "You. You keep hallucinating people for no reason. It's stupid. At one point it was Grandma Florence, Tina and me. Then there were times you were talking to your parents, of course this was while they were living, which makes it even weirder. I have no idea why you keep having Marshawn come to you for advice, or for comfort."

"I live in her head, rent free," Marshawn jokingly blabs. "I mean she got to listen to me talk, and talk, and talk for hours as I drove her to the Ginger Hill Medical Research Center the night I was murdered by the real

AFK. So we kind of have a bond. She got to know me, the real me, right before I was murdered in front of her. And I pushed her out the way of the gun fire. So I saved your mother's life."

"She ain't save mine," Kenya snaps. "Just let me go right through that windshield. Hey Ma, how come you don't have a driver's license?"

"I get anxiety getting behind the wheel of a car," I answer.

"Anxiety about what, not having enough gas?" Kenya continues to interrogate me in an antagonizing tone.

"No," I answer. "My grandfather was murdered during a carjacking."

"What does that have to do with you?" Kenya continues to probe as I feel a rush of warmth run over me. I'm uncomfortable.

"It was all my fault!" I yell. "I had stolen some makeup from the mall. I was trying to look pretty for my dad. The prettier I used to look for him, the nicer the sweet he would buy for me from the bakery as a treat. Anyway, I stole from that damn Macy's in Security Square Mall and got caught. My grandfather was taking me home, he was still on duty as a police officer. We were by Park Heights and Keyworth when some guy flagged my grandfather down asking for help. While my grandfather's head was turned to listen to the man, someone else walked up to the window and shot him several times. The guy who was talking to my grandfather threw him out the car, and the two men drove the police car around for like two days."

"Where were you?" Kenya asks as I begin to shake.

"With them. They kidnapped me," I admit with my head down. "When they finally let me go, my father thought I had cheated on him."

"I'm sorry," Marshawn expresses in a solemn tone.

"Don't be," I say boldly. "I'm nobody's victim. I've learned to save myself from the dangers that are in the world. When my dad broke in my home, I killed him. When you had me in the back of your car with your dying mother, I could have grabbed my own gun or yours and pulled the trigger. When Paul Douglass had me in that lawyer's office, I was going to drown and stab him to death. Bad things may have happened to me in life, but I'm no victim."

"Then what's our play here?" Marshawn questions as we look around at the people dancing and laughing.

"We stay to ourselves. Let's see if they'll let me go for a walk outside," I say to Marshawn and Kenya as I walk up to Deacon Jordan talking to Evangelist NoLesha, as they share drinks. "Hey, can I walk around outside for a second? I promise not to go too far; I'll stay in the hotel parking lot," I say with a smile on my face as NoLesha says, "Yeah," with a giant grin and a thumbs up for extra animation.

As I walk outside, I feel the cool breeze of the night air, but I smell the musk from the tractor trailers that are parked or driving near the motel. This area is filled with industrial parks, warehouses and freight yards. I walk down the sidewalk, pass several rooms as a person in a white van parks and three people get out of it, grabbing someone wrapped in a sheet, struggling to get away. I freeze in fear, determined to not say anything as one of the people barks orders at the others, "We have to hurry up and stage it." I have no idea what that means. Then a tall older dark skin man opens the door to a motel room wearing overalls and smoking a brown colored cigarette. He states, "These people come here all the time with their weird sex fetishes. I can't wait to get off the waiting list so I can move into the senior housing in the county."

I slowly back away from the creepy old guy as I see the three men bring their bondage sex partner hostage into the motel room. I turn around to find Evangelist Nelly outside flirting with a truck driver and trying to get him to join everyone in the lounge. I think I'm going to order that crab cake now.

As I walk back into the lounge area, I go back to the table where I was previously seated as the waiter asks if I would like something to drink. To his surprise I ask for water with lemon. As the waiter explains that everything at the bar is free, I point out to him I don't drink. Since I was a little girl, I was always scared to drink or get high because of my aunt Gina's addiction. Not to say I haven't had wine, or a mixed drink from time to time, but I always had a voice in the back of my head telling me I was going to be just like her, so I never really enjoyed drinking. Then, of course, when Sasha had her drinking problem, the idea of sipping something with alcohol in it made me sick. As I order the crab cakes and the steamed shrimp, Kenya appears before me.

"Do you love Sasha or feel bad for her because her son was killed?" Kenya asks as the waiter walks off with my order.

"What are you talking about?" I respond out loud.

"When Titan Industries purchased the apartment building, they made everyone there homeless," Kenya says. "You inherited your grandmother's home and moved Sasha in. Sasha started drinking a lot and became a shell of the woman that used to babysit me. Even after she got out of rehab, you gave her the manager position at Legacy of Florence. Right now, you're thinking about having her move back into your grandmother's house now that it's rebuilt. Why?"

"She's my best friend," I admit. "And she blew her settlement money she got from the city."

"I'm your daughter, you ain't doing nothing for me," Kenya returns as she begins to age in the face again, looking like a grown woman, and not the little girl I normally remember her as.

"What is your problem with me?" I ask Kenya as she takes a deep inhale from her vape pen before blowing smoke everywhere.

"I was killed in a hit and run," Kenya says standing up as she begins to look like a woman in her early 20s. "You never blamed my dad for it; the car crash was not his fault. But you never really blamed the person who did it."

"I don't know who did it!" I scream back at her.

"That's the problem!" Kenya slams her hands down on the table and gets directly in my face. She looks just like the girl she was the day she got in the back seat of her father's car for the final time. "You never pushed the envelope to find out who did it. You and Aunt Gina brought down NAFA, Marshawn Bell, Roland Wise and Paul Douglass. You're helping with the water crisis. You're putting up reward money for information on Duck's murderer. I'm dead, too. I was birthed by you. What are you going to do in remembrance of me? Last time you kind of tried to remember me and have a moment with my brothers and sisters, and you killed my grandfather in the basement. Maybe this time you'll actually kill the persons who killed me. But who am I kidding, you'll probably just open another restaurant, grocery store, or another bank. You're a failure. Of all the things you've accomplished and done, the things you're supposed to basically do, you destroy, or watch fall apart. You failed me. You failed Tina and you're failing Darrin, Desha, RJ and Trinity. But great job with the 10th Bank and Legacy of Florence."

"I'm not a failure," I utter, trying to convince myself as I think about the house fire, with several of the pictures and memorabilia that were destroyed in the house bombing.

"You can't lie to yourself, Mom," Kenya says as the waiter returns with a plate filled with steamed shrimp and another plate with two large crab cakes. The food looks and smells delicious, and it sounds like the music has gotten louder as more people enter the lounge and get on the dance floor. These Andrews Memorial people know how to party.

Chapter 27

The next morning, Darrin, Hakeem and I are at the Woodstock Campus serving food to the guests as a young man asks about attending the church this coming Sunday. The truck driver that was talking to Evangelist Nelly last night is standing next to Hakeem serving food with us. His name is Mark, and he's actually a nice guy. We got a chance to bond earlier this morning before the crowd came into the dining area. His wife recently left him because of financial challenges the two shared, and their daughter died from COVID-19. Mark has been trying to find a meaning to life since those events, and feels he has a genuine connection to Nelly.

"Hey, Tiffany, can I speak to you for a moment?" a pleasant sounding voice yells from the back. As I turn around, I notice it's Monica. This has to be the nicest she has spoken to me. Hakeem and I share a brief glance that silently symbolizes, *What the hell is that about?* before I walk towards Monica, taking off my hair net, serving gloves and apron. The two of us walk into the chef's office.

"Hi, Ms. Monica, what's going on?" I begin, puzzled by this meeting. I'm always confused about whether to call her Ms. Monica, Aunt Monica, or just Monica.

"You can call me Aunt Monica or just Monica," she responds, easing the tension I came into the room with, then we both sit down. The atmosphere is relaxed. I don't feel on guard today, maybe it's her mood, maybe it was being able to hang out with the people from the church last night at the hotel. Not sure, but today feels like such a good day. Even the people that were in the dining hall were in a positive mood, which is uncommon because everyone there is displaced, whether being street homeless or being displaced by the explosions a few weeks ago.

"Thanks," I return with a smile, noticing the warmth in Monica's face.

"The mayor, the city council president, Erica Little, the county executive and a few state delegates came by earlier," Monica informs me with a relaxed look on her face. "It seems like the water and gas lines are being put in ahead of schedule, thanks to your hard work at the 10th Bank. The chair of the Maryland House of Delegates' finance committee also provided Kesha and Raymond with a very accommodating compensation check for all of the work we've done for these residents."

"That's great," I exclaim as Monica hands me an iPad with a picture of a large hotel on the screen.

"A few years ago, my husband purchased this old hotel in southwest Baltimore, near the Baltimore County line," Monica explains. "We did a lot of renovations on it. We were turned down by several banks for loans that would allow us to reconstruct this hotel to our liking. My goal was to have a high-end version of the Nesmith Motel. Thankfully, over the years we were able to get the property to our liking, but we still had some challenges financially."

"Would you like to apply for a loan through the 10th Bank to complete the construction, or are you going to use the money you received from the House of Delegates?" I ask in a serious tone. "I would encourage you to speak with Kesha before making a decision about using that money from the House of Delegates given to the church for your hotel."

"No, that won't be unnecessary," Monica quickly dismisses. "One of the teachings of Andrews Memorial is to not accrue debt. We proudly boast in being the lender not the borrower. That being said, my son's R.

Nesmith Brand has helped with the reconstruction of the new Nesmith Suites, which are now fully functional. Of course, that credit does not rest alone with my son, Erica Little and Mayor Titan also made financial contributions with the goal of moving the residents displaced because of the explosions to the hotel by Monday. I planned on having a celebratory dinner and party here at the campus following church on Sunday before we start moving the displaced Baltimore City residents. We will keep the homeless clients we serve on the south side of the Woodstock Campus and reopen the soup kitchen. We will also deep clean all the other facilities with the goal of being classroom ready for the upcoming school year with our college."

"That's great. I'm truly happy for you." I indulge this conversation, not knowing where it's going. It's not like Monica and I are friends.

"I need to come clean with you about something, Tiffany," Monica says as her voice drops to a serious tone, her face stoic. "The Midnight account you found, I withdrew $29 million from it last year to make the renovations I needed for the Nesmith Suites. Now that old hotel is 23 floors of something to be proud of in Halethorpe and Arbutus."

"I have a question," I begin to inquire, "Kesha's an accountant and handles the books for the Flamingo Club. You're the head trustee at Andrews Memorial. How does that work? Like how is she so hands-off with the church money but hands-on with the Flamingo Club's money? It's weird because the Flamingo Club washes their dirty money through the church."

Monica chuckles, now knowing I know intricate details about the church. "Accountability," Monica continues to light-heartedly laugh. "Kesha can always deny any knowledge about the illegal money in the church, and nothing is traced back to any member of the Flamingo Club. The money just looks like family members of incarcerated loved ones made donations to the church. Some accounts aren't that easy to explain away, so in situations like that I take the charges outright. As the matriarch of the Andrews family, it's my number one priority to preserve the legacy of the Andrews Family, and that legacy starts with Andrews Memorial.

"That being said," Monica continues, "I would like to hire your son to work for me at the hotel," she subtly throws out. Before I can say no, she continues, "He's been at this campus every day. He's actually the first person here. He treats these people with love and respect. He has a true calling for working with the less fortunate and people that need support. He has the soul of a missionary and a loving heart. If other street kids can see him work at the Nesmith Suites, then that might make them want to work there or at the Nesmith Inn."

"I don't know…," I ponder out loud as Monica continues to try to sell me on the idea.

"It's a great idea," she tries to convince me. "He's about to graduate high school. He can make money, buy a car, go on dates, and do things kids his age should be doing. There are so many street kids selling drugs, riding dirt bikes all through the city and bothering hard working folks by asking to clean their windshields at every red light. Darrin could be the leader to change the culture of the city. He's a good kid, and I think you know that."

"I'm his mother, I think I should know that," I fire back as Monica begins to show me pictures of the inside of the newly renovated hotel. The artwork, and the decor are stunning.

"I really wish he would join the vacation bible school," Monica adds as I look at the pictures of the large rooms. Each room has a jacuzzi in it. "Wait until you see the honeymoon suites and the penthouse rooms. Also, we have a rooftop lounge area with a heated infinity pool.”

“Will all this be available for the people here at the campus?” I question as Monica nods yes.

“Every person that was displaced by the explosion will be eligible to stay here,” Monica answers. “Titan Industries agreed to pay for their room and board until each house has been rebuilt and all the gas and new water lines are installed.”

“But you want my son to work here?” I ask.

“I need your son to work here,” she answers. “I’m not saying he should make this his future, but he could be an ambassador for Andrews Memorial in the community by doing something he naturally does, serve and love people.”

“I’ll talk to him,” I give in and say as my mouth opens wide in amazement at how the rooftop looks. “I just don’t want him exposed to what I saw last night.”

Monica’s expression changes to shock and confusion following my statement. “What did you see last night?”

“From what one of the residents at the Inn said, there was a group of guys carrying a lady into one of the rooms for some kind of bondage sex fetish. Is that normal over there?" I ask as Monica nervously looks around the office.

"Tiffany, the Halethorpe and Arbutus communities are known to truckers, and sex workers," Monica explains. "I don't have too many problems with the guests, but from time to time you have the wild and freaky groups of people that rent rooms for a night. I've also had people who shoot porn rent rooms for multiple weeks. A couple days ago I had a rapper and a sound engineer rent a hotel room for a few days to record music. I'm not going to turn away those customers at the Inn, but at Nesmith Suites, the population will be different. The cost is dramatically higher, and it's designed to grab the tourist crowd that wants to attend the baseball or football games. The mayor is also opening tourist attractions and bringing in major companies to the city; those people will want somewhere nice, yet fairly affordable to stay. That's where the Nesmith Suites will come in handy. I have already received approval to hold card tables and electronic slot machines for gambling in the hotel. We are even allowed to use the same liquor license from the motel at the Nesmith Suites."

"What's the catch?" I ask, waiting for Monica to say something suspect to anger me.

"You really don't trust me," Monica counters with a serious look on her face. "There's no catch, this is business. I even want to open the new hotel's business and day-to-day accounts at the 10th Bank. Every employee of the Nesmith Suites can get their life insurance and 401k benefits through the 10th Bank. Yes, I did enjoy the presentation you made the other day about the new services the 10th Bank will offer.

"Fair enough," I surrender. "Let's get my son's opinion."

As I walk out the office to get my son and walk back into the office, Monica is now seated behind the desk, with three chairs set in front of the desk; two of the chairs are empty. In the third chair is a young lady close to Darrin's age, wearing shorts and a revealing top that barely covers her breasts. Seriously, the top and bottom parts of this young woman's boobs are out, it's a tiny bit of material covering her boobs.

"Hi Darrin, this is Nevaeh," Monica says as the teenage girl gets up and gives Darrin a full body hug, before returning to her chair. Darrin, blushing from ear-to-ear, sits in the chair next to her. "Nevaeh works at my hotel, the Nesmith Suites, and she attends Andrews Memorial. She's also a member of our vacation bible school that I wish you could attend. Anyway, I wanted to know how you would feel about working with Nevaeh at the hotel?"

I'm at a loss for words. When did this little huzzy get in this office? Where did she appear from? Who are her parents? What part of this child's body doesn't have a tattoo on it? I need to get Hakeem.

"Yes, ma'am, I'd love to work there," Darrin exclaims, with his eyes bursting with joy looking at Nevaeh. Darrin has not made any eye contact with Monica or me. She done made my son horny. This can't be right.

"Great," Monica says, but Darrin doesn't turn his gaze away from Nevaeh, who is now staring Darrin in the face. It's like these two fell in love at first sight. "I will have you start next week. The people who you've been feeding here will be moving to the Nesmith Suites on Monday. I can't wait for you to join us."

"Yes, ma'am. Thank you so much," Darrin graciously responds as Nevaeh grabs Darrin by the hand and looks in his eyes.

"Mrs. Nesmith, is it ok if I set Darrin up on the computer tomorrow so that he can start on his orientation?" Nevaeh says with a soft voice.

"Darrin comes in here every day to volunteer and feed the people—" I begin, but Darrin cuts me off.

"Should I catch the bus there or do you think Hakeem will drop me off?" Darrin asks as Monica smiles, looking at me with an, *I got one up on you,* look on her face.

"I can pick you up," Nevaeh says, flashing her car keys at Darrin. "Hey, do you want to come to vacation bible school with me tonight?"

"Yeah, if that's ok with you, Mom?" Darrin questions as I'm completely lost on what to say or do.

"The Paul Douglass Law!" I yell out in desperation. "There's still a curfew in effect because of the martial law and the Paul Douglass Law."

"I'll be extra careful bringing him home, Mrs. Andrews," Nevaeh suggests in her soft voice.

"I don't have a problem with you taking him to work or to the church, Nevaeh," I answer. "My husband will pick him up from the church, though. I don't want to take any chances with the Charm City Strangler getting to my son."

"Well, who's going to protect me from the Charm City Strangler?" Nevaeh asks in such a sweet tone. Which I find odd, because the Charm City Strangler has yet to kill any women or teenage girls. Also, if this child needs so much protection, why is she riding by herself to vacation bible school to begin with?

"I'll allow him to ride with you, but I will need Darrin home immediately after vacation bible school. No extra stops," I demand as they both agree, smiling at each other.

Chapter 28

Later that afternoon, Mayor Hugo calls a press conference with Commissioner Keith Mercer present. Several members of the police department, the Baltimore City Council and Maryland State Delegates and Senators are standing by the mayor. Instead of going to City Hall for the press conference, I go to my office at the 10th Bank to look through other accounts from Andrews Memorial. I have the TV playing the press conference in the background.

"We've had an interesting summer to say the least," Mayor Hugo begins. "We went from having another record low of murders recorded in the City of Baltimore, to having a serial killer called the Charm City Strangler targeting African American teenagers. As a result of this public crisis, we had to activate the Paul Douglass Law, and create a 9 pm curfew throughout the city for all citizens under 18 years old. I don't want to jinx anything, and I do believe in superstitions, but since the murder of J'won Foote, no new murder cases have been linked to the Charm City Strangler. For that reason, we are pulling several officers from the Leakin Park staged post that was created a couple weeks ago. We will continue to have the surveillance planes, and detectives working this case. The FBI has agreed to assist with resources in this case as well. I was debating with my fellow legislators about pausing or cancelling events like the National African American Caucus, also known as AFRAM and Artscape for this year. We have agreed that cancelling those events would do more harm to the city and would allow individuals who rain terror on Baltimore, like the Charm City Strangler, to win. That being said, AFRAM and Artscape will go on as planned this year.

"We are keeping the Paul Douglass Law in effect, but we are concentrating the surveillance in certain areas, as we get closer to apprehending this person that has done so much damage to the citizens of Baltimore," the mayor states in a sad tone. "I want the Charm City Strangler to know this: We will catch you. I'm shocked by Ms. Pugh's absence from this press conference, as she has been a huge advocate and voice for the capture of this psychopathic monster, but my promise to her is the same to all of you, he *will* be captured. We will bring him to justice. We will protect your children. I would like to thank Kutter the Poet and the 10th Bank for their impacts in this case, including putting up reward money. I would also like to thank everyone that has provided information to our tip line.

"I would also like to announce that we will be doing what no other mayor or police commissioner has thought to do in the past," Mayor Titan says with a serious look in his eyes, "We are going to comb the entire Leakin Park, digging in several areas and searching for any and every person that was buried at that park, also known as "Maryland's Largest Open Air Cemetery." Will that mean more homicide cases? Yes! Will that mean that the homicide detectives will be working more cold cases? Yes! Will that mean that bad people will be brought to justice? Yes! As Ms. Pugh stated before, we need justice. I don't care if the Charm City Strangler or Al Capone killed and buried people in that park, I want justice for each one of those discarded people. Those brothers, sisters, mothers, fathers, husbands and wives deserve justice, and we have the ability to accomplish that."

"When will the digs happen?" A male reporter asks as several other members from the media get closer holding their recorders, cell phones and cameras closer to the mayor.

"My goal is for the exhuming to start in late August or early September," the mayor answers then continues, "We are dealing with a water crisis, that is being resolved, thanks to Titan Industries and the 10th Bank. I'm very proud of the work that is being done to restore several of the homes in many of the impacted communities. I'm also glad to announce that the West Baltimore Hospital and the University of Maryland have acquired property in Edmonson Village and Edmonson Square, with the goal of building high-end homes and redeveloping the shopping center. For those in the Westgate Community, this plan should not come as a surprise because of the Jewish College that was being built near Woodridge Rd. and Walnut Ave. With that being said, I would like for our police commissioner to update us on the latest details in the search for the Charm City Strangler, and how the police department will be working with the community to help with the current water crisis."

As I turn off the TV in my office, my husband enters the room with two large containers of food in a plastic bag. I can smell the curry and jerk seasoning coming from the yellow-colored bag. "I brought your favorite!" Hakeem says with excitement, knowing my love for oxtails and rice from the Jamaican restaurant from the Randallstown area of Baltimore County.

"Thanks, that place by Cold Spring and Reisterstown Road made me sick the last time," I respond sarcastically, with a smirk to match. To be fair, the last time he went to the Jamaican restaurant on Cold Spring and Reisterstown Road was before we learned about the water crisis in the city.

"Where's Darrin?" Hakeem questions as he glances at the clutter that has consumed my desk. We both walk to my circular table that has served as my lunch area for the last year or so. It's perfectly out of sight for people that want to look in my office to find me, and quaint enough to have a quick intimate moment with my husband, and we have had intimate moments on this desk in the past.

"I went by the house to grab him before I went to ride out to Coco's Jamaican Quizine, and he wasn't home," Hakeem continues.

"He's at vacation bible school with his new girlfriend, Nevaeh," I answer as Hakeem's eyes grow large with surprise.

"They're still following the same playbook," Hakeem says, shaking his head with frustration. I look on and question what he means as I open the clear plastic lid to the circular container that is packed with rice, beans, oxtails, and plantains. "My father had this "vision" to bring in young members of the church, and that idea was to use sex appeal. He would encourage the young women to wear revealing clothing and show interest in good looking guys in their schools, colleges and jobs. The idea was to bring them in and have them give their money and other resources to the church. He would also do that with the good looking young men in the church."

"That's just flat out wrong." I gasp and put down my steaming fork filled with food.

"My father knew how to grow Andrews Memorial into what it is today," Hakeem shamefully reflects. "Between the companies he brought under Andrews Memorial and the people he brought in, he turned Andrews Memorial into an international ministry worth millions. His efforts got the attention of famous musicians, actors, and political figures. As you know, he even had private planes to do his mission work. Who wouldn't want to be part of a church if all the young people are attractive, into you, and the members are successful. Even how the church is set up is by my father's design. The VIP members sit in a section in the front, the attractive members sit not too far behind the VIP members, and the unattractive members sit further back, in the overflow rooms or in the balcony."

"Why would Kesha allow this to continue?" I question as Hakeem opens his container that reveals jerk chicken and shrimp.

"Our aunt Monica refuses to let any of my father's or grandfather's traditions die," Hakeem elaborates. "She basically uses Raymond to ensure everything stays the course and doesn't deviate from what has worked for decades. As you know, Kesha's done with the church altogether, and wants out."

"Which leaves you and Raymond," I point out as I pick up a steaming forkful of rice and beans, before blowing on it.

"Facts," Hakeem returns with a slight pause. "I'm not going to follow my father's or grandfather's way. Raymond and Aunt Monica will probably give me the biggest problem, but Kesha has made the call to make me the pastor and she's stepping aside to run her research facility. When Kesha finally calls the meeting with Aunt Monica, Raymond and me, maybe I should put all the cards on the table then. We're getting away from the name Andrews Memorial, and if they want to stay as part of the ministry, they will have to follow in the direction I'm leading."

"What direction is that?" I ask. Hakeem appears confused by my question. "The Woodstock Campus will start classes this coming semester for the college students, along with the private grade school. The Woodstock Campus also has the shelter for the homeless. What do you do with that if you plan on making Andrews Memorial into New Hope Greater Love Church 2.0?"

"We keep the shelter, the inpatient addiction clinic and the schools," Hakeem answers as he takes a bite of chicken.

"What about the planes, the different ministries, and the bank accounts? Many of those bank accounts have a lot of money in them," I interrogate.

"And a lot of that money is tied up in illegal business," Hakeem contributes. "We're talking big time kingpins who have washed their money through a prison ministry here, illegal activities of the Flamingo Club there, and tons of question marks everywhere. We need to be on the up and up. For too long the Andrews name has been tied to the Flamingo Club, and we've helped them operate their dark deeds in the daylight."

"Hakeem, the Flamingo Club's money is tied up in this bank," I point out. "If we cut them completely off, like even out this bank, we could get killed. This bank won't stay afloat without the financial backing of the Flamingo Club. People will lose their homes, companies they own, life insurance and retirement benefits. At this point we have to find a middle ground."

"Then we keep one hand on the wheel, the 10th Bank stays involved with the Flamingo Club, but the church is out," Hakeem suggests as I turn my head towards him, caught off guard by the idea.

"Tiffany," Hakeem starts with his pleading voice. "I'm not saying we do this long-term, but until we can figure a way out of this. We're fighting two battles that are connected. Andrews Memorial must fall in order for us to defeat the Flamingo Club. Kesha has given us an out by stepping down from leadership and going her own way with the research clinic."

"What happens when they find out what she's doing?" I ask as Hakeem turns towards the window in silence. "You know like I know, this will not end pretty. Even if we win, we will have some losses."

"I can't afford another loss!" Hakeem bangs his right hand on the table and yells. "I lost my brother, I lost my parents, but I'm not going to lose myself or my morals because of this church. The legacy of Andrews Memorial will stop with me, no matter the cost."

"No matter the cost?" I yell back with tears in my eyes, hurt by the thought of what could happen. "You could get killed playing chess with the Flamingo Club. My kids could get killed. We're talking about powerful people, not some Alpha gang members. We're talking about a silent mafia that operates in the daylight, and brags about what they've done while looking like champions or heroes."

"In the 1940s a group of philanthropists donated land, cages with lions, bears, and flamingos to Baltimore's Druid Hill Zoo. The city called them the Flamingo Club. From that point on the Flamingo Club would go on to invest and open up hospital buildings, rebuild the Inner Harbor, invest in colleges, schools, highways, bridges, science centers and everything else you can think of," Hakeem blabs. "I know exactly what I'm up against. People like my father were happy to be along for the ride as it gave him riches and a life he felt was owed to him. Monica is the exact same way. I'm going to see to it that we stop the Flamingo Club as a whole unit, starting with Andrews Memorial and we cut the head off of them with the 10th Bank. They made their biggest mistake placing all of their money in this location."

"Because they trust your sister, who handles their finances, like your father and grandfather used to do," I point out. "Do you think they won't try to kill her if we really go up against them?"

"That's why we have to be strategic about this," Hakeem says with a charming look in his eyes, but I'm not caving in to his thought process.

"Hakeem, my daughter Kenya died in a hit and run. That death still hurts. I don't think I can psychologically handle another child's death, especially if it's because of me, and if it's because of you, I'm going to have serious resentment towards the man I love."

"Are you saying we keep things how they are?" Hakeem questions. "They use sex as a way to bring in young people. They manipulate people into signing over companies, paychecks, mortgages and any other financial capital in the name of Christ and ministry. What are we supposed to do when we have an opportunity to stop them?"

"We plan," I answer.

"Let me tell you a story," Hakeem says. "I used to have a girlfriend named Michelle. We were together from 6th grade until I was a sophomore in college. We broke up because she was raped by a member of the church named Aaron Horton Jr. Aaron Horton Sr., was an elder in the church. Every year the youth would take a trip to a beach or somewhere nice. We'd take pictures during the trip that the church would put in newspapers, magazines, on billboards and across the church building. Some are framed and hanging up in the church right now. Andrews Memorial has a certain kind of justice for undesirable behavior and offenses. Sometimes it's public whippings, public water spraying, being punched and kicked by the deacons and elders, it all depends on the inner circle of clergy and the pastor's decision.

"Aaron Jr. broke into Michelle's hotel room while we were at a beach in Delaware and raped her. Aaron Jr. was privately paddled by my father, Aaron Sr., Michelle's father and a few other elders. Then they were asked to keep the situation quiet. Michelle's family left the church but were discredited and made a mockery of by Andrews Memorial clergy. I stood up for Michelle, wanting to make the cover up public, but this led to me being called a liar and became one of the major reasons I left Andrews Memorial. Michelle went on and got married, has children; she lives somewhere in the county. Aaron Jr. recently married a church member at Andrews Memorial named Kamilah. This is the type of ministry Andrews Memorial is. They hurt people and they cover things up. Michelle wasn't Aaron Jr.'s only victim; there was a teenage girl named Shakira, who Aaron raped in the janitor's closet at the old church building during a bible study. Aaron Sr. and the clergy staff had a private meeting, heard her case and deemed Shakira as a liar. Shakira killed herself by overdosing on medication. She left a note blaming the church for her decision to take her life. This is personal for me, Tiffany. With or without you, I'm going to take down Andrews Memorial. I love you and I'm hoping it's with you."

"I love you too, but what happened to Elder Aaron Sr.?" I ask as Hakeem's eyes drift back towards the window, then to the table, then back to me.

"After Shakira took her own life, I tried to kill Aaron Jr.," Hakeem admits. "I tried to get a gun from Jamar, who was running with Paul Douglass's crew at that time. Jamar told me I wasn't built to take a life, and he attempted to kill Aaron Jr. Aaron Sr., I don't know how, but he knew Jamar was coming for his son, so he informed the police, and Jamar was locked up for violating his probation by carrying a loaded handgun. My father worked something out with the judge where Jamar didn't have to do a long stent in prison for the violation. Aaron Sr. was allowed to pastor my father's church in New Orleans. A few months later Aaron Sr. had surgery on his hip and back, leaving him bedridden, then came Hurricane Katrina. Aaron Sr. was unable to get out the house and drowned."

I notice the heavy emotions on Hakeem's face as he recounts his past at Andrews Memorial and say to him, "We're in this together. I should tell you that Darrin and his girlfriend are working for your aunt's hotel, and I'm not talking about the motel in Halethorpe. She purchased the old hotel in Arbutus and renovated it into a high-end luxury hotel, using Flamingo Club money that was hidden in a church outreach account called Midnight. The displaced residents from the explosion are being moved from the Woodstock Campus to that hotel on Monday."

"I'm going to take that down too," Hakeem proclaims before looking down with sadness.

"We're going to take that down too," I second, as Hakeem looks back at me. We pause for a brief moment looking at each other before we start eating in silence.

Chapter 29

After Sunday morning church service, Hakeem, Monica, Kesha, Raymond and I go out to eat at DeLuca's Bistro and Bakery. Darrin and Nevaeh decide to go paint balling with the teenagers from the church. The owner of the restaurant, James DeLuca, places us in a private dining room with our own personal server.

"Today's service was really good," I say, attempting to get a dinner conversation started.

Not missing a moment to respond to any word I say, Monica replies, "It's always a great church service at Andrews Memorial." Monica's tone wasn't as curt or snappy as it normally is. "I'm glad to see Hakeem's name is now placed on the roll with the other elders of Andrews Memorial. Tiffany, I would love to see you join me in the trustee's room."

"I don't think that would be a good idea," I refute to Monica's surprise.

"Why is that?" Raymond inserts himself.

"Andrews Memorial has a bank account with the 10th Bank. I don't think it would be ethical, or appropriate for the church or the bank for me to serve in the role of trustee while holding the church's bank accounts. It leaves the door open to temptation if and when something arises," I attempt to explain and surprisingly, Monica agrees with me.

"She's right," Kesha adds, placing her cell phone on the table. "I'm just glad we can all enjoy this moment as a family. It's so easy to get lost in the day-to-day work of the church; we lose who we are as a family."

"That's what our family is," Raymond points out. "We're people of God. The church is what binds us, and what brings us together."

"Are you saying that Andrews Memorial is your whole identity as a family?" I question as Raymond looks confused. He takes his large-framed eyeglasses off and cleans them on his button-up shirt before reapplying them.

"We're a God-fearing family," Raymond answers. "We grew up learning how to run the church from Hakeem's father and grandfather. We had to learn how to play the piano, the organ, the drums, and the guitar before we could do our times tables. As a family,

Hakeem, Kesha, Jamar and I had to usher, collect the offerings, greet visitors and even count the money. Kesha was balancing the church's checkbook with my mom before she was in 4th grade."

"What did y'all do for fun growing up?" I question, now really invested in the history of this family as the server brings several bottles of wine to the table.

"Tons of stuff," Hakeem blurts out as he and Monica make awkward eye contact, almost as if she dared him to say something negative about the family or the church.

"Hakeem and Jamar's dad was our football coach growing up," Raymond chimes in with a smile on his face. It's so easy to forget how tall and massive he is because he can make himself appear so small and harmless in settings like this. "He would do stuff like take us fishing or have cookouts, or take us to Six Flags, or even go-cart racing at the professional track, always with the other kids from the church."

"That was a super-fast track!" Hakeem remembers with a fond smile on his face. "I think that speedway is still open. Them tires were slick. It was like a real racetrack. You had to sign a waiver and all that."

"We also would go on trips every year," Raymond continues but stopping mid-thought. "Well, my dad stayed home during those trips. He would have Elder Aaron take us. But it would be Hakeem, me and the rest of the teenagers. This was like high school age," Raymond clarifies with a Cheshire cat grin. "We'd all have our own hotel room at some beach or resort or something. My bishop would have some account set up so we could get any room service we wanted. If we wanted steak at 2 am and the hotel didn't serve it, the staff would find us that steak, have it cooked right and delivered. We had a great life."

"Yes, you did," Monica says patting Raymond on his back. It's weird how she babies him. Raymond is in his early 40s like Hakeem. Why does she treat him like some child that's making strides but needs heavy praise and reassurance.

"I don't always remember it that way," Hakeem says as Kesha shakes her head no at Hakeem. My husband notices Kesha's desperate plea with her head movements for him to stop talking about what it was like for him and her as children. "I remember us dominating all them kids at sports," Hakeem adjusts with a joyful look on his face that comes with a wide grin, big eyes and those damn dimples.

"You right about that, cuz," Raymond gloats. "Remember when we used to have the 3 on 3 basketball tournaments? We'd be winning every year, but we'd get cheated by refs and rules in the finals. They only did that because of who my uncle was, Jamar and Hakeem's dad, and it wouldn't look good if the Andrews boys won every year. But we were great. Think about it, when we had the football league, who could stop us? Hakeem was so fast on the field and could juke anybody. You should have went pro, cuz."

Raymond's face is pure cheer as he brags on Hakeem, and their times growing up. Monica is eyeballing Kesha who has checked out from the sports talk and has been spacing out looking at the bottle of wine in front of her.

"What about you?" Monica sounds off at Kesha in the midst of Raymond's laughter and Hakeem's comedic storytelling of their youth. A lot of the stories Hakeem was reflecting on didn't go exactly as he narrated to everyone at the table. On countless occasions, Hakeem has reflected on how tumultuous it was growing up in his father's shadow, and how his father was more of a bishop to the church than a father to him, Jamar and Kesha.

"You know how it was, Aunt Mo," Kesha answers without making any facial expressions, still staring at the bottle of wine on the table. This kind of reminds me of the brunch we had with Erica Little when Erica decided to start drinking from the bottle and opened up.

"No," Marshawn rebuts in the back of my mind, "Kesha's hiding something and doesn't want to talk about it."

"Tell me about it," Monica demands as Raymond looks on with glee, anticipating a fun-filled story.

"My father believed in me," Kesha voices as Monica leans back in the chair with a smile. "He saw I had potential when I was working in the trustee's office with you, Aunt Mo. As you know, he had me balancing the books for the church, and then working closely with the Flamingo Club. So close with them, I was offered a seat at the table."

"Your father was very proud of you and knew you had a major calling in Andrews Memorial," Monica contributes, not realizing that Kesha was not happy about her life. "Now that Hakeem is on the roll as an elder at Andrews Memorial, what's the chances that he's going to have his rightful place at the table of the Flamingo Club?"

"I don't want a seat at that table," Hakeem points out in a passive tone. "I want to find my place at Andrews Memorial and hopefully be useful to the ministry."

"You're an Andrews," Monica counters. "Your grandfather and father were both members of the Flamingo Club. The pastor of Andrews Memorial is supposed to have a seat at the table."

"And she does," Hakeem agrees, pointing to Kesha.

"Andrews Memorial is supposed to have a male pastor, an Andrews," Raymond states as his boyish smile fades and a grim look starts to overtake his eyes, cheeks and jawline. The fairly high-pitched voice fades slowly to a deep baritone as he continues to speak, "I'm not an Andrews, I was adopted. In theory, Kesha isn't an Andrews either, she was adopted by your father. You should be the pastor of this church. You should be at the table."

"Can we stop with the lies and coverups," Kesha shouts slamming both hands on the table, shaking the appetizers, candles and lightly filled glasses. "Let's set some things straight, my father is the same man that is Hakeem and Jamar's father. My mother is the same woman that was Hakeem and Jamar's mother. We had the same parents, and it has been the biggest coverup in the church's history because of how things would have looked."

"What are you talking about?" Raymond questions as his facial expressions tense in confusion.

"Grace Andrews couldn't have children," Kesha blurts out as Monica grows frustrated and attempts to cut Kesha off, but she continues talking, "My mother, Ginger Hill, agreed to have Hakeem and Jamar for our father and Grace Andrews. The problem was our father continued the affair after the arrangement was over and got her pregnant with me. Of course, our mother died, and our father adopted me, but saved face as a pastor. He said some lie about 'Ginger Hill was cursed for being an adulteress, but I've blessed this cursed baby by bringing her into my house and raising her as my own.' That was all a lie. Any blood test will prove it."

"*Liar*," Monica yells out. Kesha quickly opens up her purse and pulls out four different sheets of paper, slamming them on the table.

"I'm the pastor, not you, Aunt Mo," Kesha yells. "Know your role when you talk to me. I ain't got no reason to lie. Those are four different blood tests that prove that Hakeem, Jamar and I are all 100% blood related. Look at it!" Kesha screams pointing at the papers. "I have a seat at the table of the Flamingo Club because I was raised to have one, and I'm best suited for the role. I'm the bishop of the church because of the bylaws created by our grandfather. That being said, I don't want the title of pastor of Andrews Memorial anymore."

"What are you talking about, you're the bishop?" Raymond questions in concern. "Who's going to pastor the church, me?"

"No, you're not blood-related," Monica answers in Kesha's place but turns her attention towards Hakeem. "That's the reason Hakeem accepted the elder's role. He wants to take over the church and poison us just like he did the people at New Hope Greater Love Church. I'm not going to let that happen to this family."

"You don't speak for me or this church," Kesha explains. "If I say Hakeem will be the pastor of the church if and when I step down, he'll be the damn pastor. You don't have a say in my decision making, Aunt Mo."

"Yes, I do!" Monica yells back. "You will not make this church go to hell in a hand basket. We have too many successful operations going on for you to throw them away with Hakeem running the church. It's a reason why your father gave up on him."

"Because I didn't give in to the cult stuff going on at the church," Hakeem sarcastically adds.

"Stop calling Andrews Memorial a cult. We are a staple in the Black Community," Monica continues to yell and starts to stand up.

"Andrews Memorial isn't a cult?" Hakeem questions out loud then laughs. "Let's pull up the church's bylaws and start from there. Oh, you don't want to do that, right? How about the cover ups, like Elder Aaron and Aaron Jr. with the whole Michelle rape? What about the kid from 2015 y'all publicly paddled with his bare butt out, in front of the whole congregation because he didn't fall down when my father was laying hands on him while praying for him? What about the woman that didn't speak in tongues after she was baptized by my father, so y'all baptized her over and over again until she faked it. That woman was scared for her life, thinking Deacon Harris was going to drown her because of how he was slammin' and holding her in the baptismal pool."

"You're out of line," Monica screams, pointing at Hakeem and standing up.

"The whole church is out of line," Hakeem counters. "Let's talk about Psalms Airline donating private planes to the church and how we used those donated planes to smuggle drugs and people for the Flamingo Club."

"Shut your damn mouth, boy," Monica demands as Raymond stands up.

"I ain't shutting shit," Hakeem dismisses. That's my first time ever hearing him curse. Shit just got real. "If I was to take over the pastoralship of this sham of a church, the first thing I would do is change the name of it and get y'all out the building immediately."

"Don't play with me," Monica barks as Raymond attempts to approach Hakeem.

"Can we please have dinner, and let this whole thing go?" I plead as everyone says "*No!*" collectively.

"God has closed every door in your life, Hakeem, for you to be here," Raymond professes. "You're spitting in the face of the Lord going into ministry for yourself and ruining this great thing that God has allowed us to have."

"The Flamingo Club and greed have allowed us to reach the success we have reached as a family,"

Hakeem points out. "I just want y'all to remember, not a single one of y'all came to my brother's funeral. Why? Because of some fake ass country bumkin religious cult my grandfather created that has ruined lives for generation. If I'm pastor, the story of Andrews Memorial will end with me."

"Of course it would," Raymond agrees with his deep intimidating voice booming across the room. "You don't have any children of your own. That wife of yours birthed 5 children that have no relation to you, and you married that heffa in Jamaica. Now you want to lead this church. You couldn't even lead a church in a low-rate ass funeral home. You're a joke, and your father was right. I should have been his son, not you. You're basically a person with leprosy in God's eye. You're unclean, just like your wife and your bastard step-children."

"Leave my children the fu—" I begin to scream as Hakeem punches Raymond, knocking him out on the dinner table.

"You disrespect my wife or any of my kids, I will bury you next to your adopted father, are we clear?" Hakeem screams as he picks up a napkin, cleans his hands and mouth with it and throws it in Monica's face.

Monica glances over in disgust at Raymond as he attempts to collect himself on the broken wooden table with the black tablecloth and food covering him. Kesha and I are both seated with food, water and wine covering our outfits. We glare at each other silently, processing what just happened. Monica and Hakeem are standing opposite each other, and she glares as she utters, "You will regret this, nephew."

"Regret what, standing up for my wife? Protecting a black woman? She's a mother of 5 and her youngest daughter died. You don't know what she's overcome to sit here at this table, the Flamingo Club's table, or any other table God has for her," Hakeem proudly shouts.

"You're going to need an heir," Monica casually states, unfazed by Hakeem's words or Raymond who is still trying to get up from the floor. "Andrews Memorial will need to be run by an Andrews, and it has to be from our bloodline."

"If Kesha was to make me pastor, we would do away with a lot of the traditions at Andrews Memorial," Hakeem says with bass in his voice and leaning his head forward towards Monica.

"I have no problem with you being the pastor," Monica responds, "but you will not break tradition. This wife of yours is not clean enough to be a mother to an Andrews baby. Maybe you should do like your father and have an arrangement to have a real Andrews son. One that will actually be anointed, because something went wrong with you and Jamar."

"Keep my brother's name out your mouth," Hakeem says with spit flying out of his mouth.

"He sealed his fate when he turned his back on the family. Don't you be just as dumb," Monica says as Raymond rolls to his knees and attempts to gain balance by holding onto a chair. The chair falls over, causing him to fall back down face first into the shrimp scampi and the crab meat filled mushroom caps.

"You have no idea what I've sacrificed and what I have done with my bare hands just to preserve this family," Monica says as she signals for a server to come in the room. As the young woman enters the room, Monica states in an authoritative voice, "Clean this mess up and reset the table just like it was before my son was knocked out. And bring new bottles of wine. I know those bottles didn't break, but they touched the floor. That's unacceptable."

As she barks her orders, additional servers come into the room to clean up the mess and bring in new tables. I glance at Hakeem, questioning if we're still about to have dinner and he nods yes, while whispering, "Family tradition, when we have family dinner, we don't leave until everyone is full. Even if there's a fight, we just re-start."

A few moments go by as the table is reset and we are all seated. Monica says in a chipper voice, "Who's looking forward to the going away celebration at the Woodstock Campus tomorrow?" When nobody answers, she continues, "They're moving into the new Nesmith Suites. Erica Little is calling for a special meeting for all the residents on Tuesday."

Chapter 30

That Tuesday, over 200 adults find themselves seated in the forum room at the new Nesmith Suites. In the rear of the room are gold and stainless-steel chafers with lit sternos and servers standing behind the tables. Erica Little and Mayor Hugo Titan are standing behind a wooden podium with the Nesmith Suites logo prominently placed front and center. The adults in the hotel's forum recently moved here from the Woodstock Campus. These are the same people that have lost their homes throughout Baltimore City as a result of the gas and water main explosions a few weeks ago.

"I'm glad everyone was able to make it to this impromptu meeting," Erica greets with a smile as some of the people in attendance talk amongst themselves. "In the rear of the room, we have a nice brunch prepared for everyone. We have a lot to cover, and I don't want to waste too much of your time. Sadly, several homes throughout Baltimore City were destroyed due to the gas explosion and complications with the outdated plumbing. Some of the houses were insured and will be rebuilt upon the city's redevelopment plans. A lot of the homes and businesses were not insured. While our great mayor has offered to pay for hotel stays here at the Nesmith Suites during the renovation, the stays will be looked at on a case-by-case basis starting next week because many of the homeowners didn't have home insurance and others were behind on their taxes."

"What are you saying?" a middle-aged brown skin male wearing a purple polo shirt and a baseball cap questions.

"Without going through legal litigation with the city of Baltimore, those uninsured homes will be lost," Erica bluntly says. "What Titan Industries is willing to do right now is pay $250,000 to each resident today that is willing to sell their property and start over. It doesn't matter if your property isn't insured or you're behind in your taxes, we will hand you a check from Titan Industries today. I also want to point out, many of the homes that were destroyed were valued at less than $30,000 upon last appraisal. The lead and asbestos problems didn't do you all any favors. Sprinkle in the spikes in crime over the last few years with the Alphas, NAFA, AFK and now the Charm City Strangler, and the place that many called home was nothing more than a title and not worth the hassle of being rebuilt. The option we're providing is a fresh start. We will purchase what remains of your destroyed property, the

City of Baltimore will absorb your past due property tax and water bill, and each of you can have a fresh start."

"Why can't you just let us keep our homes? I own my house outright," an elderly woman screams.

"I'm not saying you can't," Erica assures her. "With the growing murder rate, the shrinking property values, the decline in the education system, lack of fresh food markets, lead in the air and in the water, on top of companies dumping toxins into the city, this is a great start, or restart for many. Like I said, we have the checks for $250,000 available right now. The only thing we'll ask for is a name, date of birth and social security number. We have staff members that can pull up the title of your home and your tax status with the city. The money will be yours and you can start over. Move into a home in Bethesda, or Glen Burnie, or White Marsh, or Prince George's County. Send your children to a better school. The only string attached is we can start our reconstruction of several neighborhoods long forgotten by people who should have remembered you. I'm trying to make right what is wrong with this city. I lost two children to this city as you all know. One child died in a hit and run crossing the street, the other was murdered in the Old Market

Place before Tiffany Gibbons, I mean Tiffany Andrews started redeveloping that area."

"What about my restaurant?" a balding Asian man, possibly Korean, yells. "I had a restaurant up in the Edmonson junction, it's gone now thanks to the explosion. What can you do for me?"

"Was your place insured?" Erica asks, relaxed and confidently.

"No, none of our stores had insurance," the man answers with frustration. "They say they're building a college now on the property. My livelihood is wrapped up in that restaurant. My kids are in college; how am I supposed to pay for that now? The guy next door, he sold furniture, all of that is gone in the explosion. The person on the other side of me ran a dry cleaners, that's gone. Nothing is left standing in the shopping centers; do we get anything?"

"Did you own the property or were you renting it?" Erica questions, but looking at the smug look on her face, I think she knows the answer.

"No, didn't you hear what I was saying?" the man continues in frustration. "The person who owns the property is selling it to some people trying to build a college. What happens to us? Everything that we had is gone thanks to the explosion. How are we supposed to live?”

“Did you lose your home as well?” Erica asks as the man nods yes. “Legally, we don’t have to give you anything, because you didn’t own the property your restaurant was on. That is a matter you are supposed to take up with the insurance company, and because your business was operating without insurance, you were breaking a Baltimore City law by operating a restaurant without insurance. That being said, you did lose your home. Did you own or rent the home.”

“I owned it,” The man responds with a calmer, humbler tone. “My wife, children and some other family live with me there.”

“If you sign the paperwork today, I’ll see to it you get the $250,000. I can’t make any promises about what I can do to help with your restaurant, but I have some resources I can connect you to that will help you get on your feet. How does that sound?” The man nods and begins to walk to the front of the room where there’s a table set up on the side by a large black speaker. The table is operated by people with blue polo shirts that say, Baltimore City Public Safety and Titan Industries. As the man walks up, nearly everybody else in the room walks towards the same direction, forming a very long line.

My phone begins to buzz, and I see my aunt Gina has forwarded me a text saying, They found Ms. Pugh. Before I can write her back, she's calling me. I hate when people text you and then call. Just text message me, I could be busy like I am now.

"Tiffany!" Gina yells, "Tiffany, you there?"

"Yes, Aunt Gina," I respond, annoyed because I'm trying to listen to what Erica Little is talking about in the microphone as more people make their way to the line.

"For those of you that have signed up, the mayor's office has agreed to pay for your hotel suite here at the Nesmith Suites for 90 days with emergency funds for food. In that 90 days we hope you find a home to your liking," Erica says as others walk to the front. "For those that have not signed, the moving process may change again. We understand how difficult it was to find shelter after the explosion, then staying in Woodstock, Maryland, and now staying in this hotel. Our goal is to make your next stop a permanent location that you will be proud to call home."

"Tiffany, I need you to listen," Gina screams, regaining my attention from the meeting I'm actually at.

"Yeah, Aunt Gina, they found Ms. Pugh. I didn't know she was lost," I add in an annoyed tone. "I know she and Kutter the Poet wanted to start a nonprofit to help the families that have suffered grief at the hands of the Charm City Strangler but—"

"She's dead," Gina blurts out, stopping me in my tracks. "They found Ms. Pugh at Leakin Park, covered with a sheet. Commissioner Mercer has confirmed that Ms. Pugh is the first female and adult victim of the Charm City Strangler. They're being tight-lipped about the details surrounding her body and how they are able to confirm it's actually related to the Charm City Strangler."

"Oh my God," I gasp. "The mayor is here at this function."

"I'm sure he's going to get briefed about it soon as he leaves," Gina says as I notice a young African American male dressed in a black suit whisper in the mayor's ear and the two walk out the side door.

As I attempt to walk towards the back door, I notice my son smiling ear to ear looking at Nevaeh. Before I can greet or congratulate him on his work here at the hotel,

Erica walks up from behind me placing her arm on my shoulder as if we're good friends. I can't stand this woman.

"This went great!" Erica says with excitement. She smells of alcohol and cigars. "We're about to house the people that were impacted by the explosion, new water lines are being put down, your bank has made a huge difference because the checks that my name is signed to have your company's logo on it. We are all winning in this."

"I didn't realize we were going this route. I thought we were going to work together in the rebuilding of this city," I voice with frustration.

"We did," Erica tries to convince me. "Look around this room. We're the two most powerful people here. You have the most successful bank in the city. I have a company that can save this city by improving property values, inviting business and changing the perception of this dying metropolis. The mayor can't fulfil his mission without the two of us. The Flamingo Club needs us more than we need them. Once you join, you'll understand. Speaking of joining, you'll be getting your invitation soon to sign your name on the ledger of members of the Flamingo Club."

"Thanks," I snarl, attempting to leave.

"What's wrong with you?" Erica asks as I wave at Darrin and Nevaeh.

"The Charm City Strangler may have killed another person, this time an adult woman," I answer Erica as she freezes in her tracks. She looks around the crowded room and back to me.

"Like in her 20s?"

"She was a grandmother. Ms. Pugh! He killed Ms. Pugh," I yell as anger overcomes me. I think about all of the times Ms. Pugh has hassled me, pushed my buttons and called me out when I was trying to do good in the community. In the end, if I would have walked away from this water crisis and focused on the Charm City Strangler, she might be alive. So would Duck.

"You don't know that," Marshawn tries to convince me in a comforting tone.

My daughter Kenya, now looking like a woman in her early 20s appears before me. "You know the truth. Her death is your fault, Mom. It took Kutter the Poet and Ms. Pugh to put out a reward for the 10th Bank to lift a finger towards catching the Charm City Strangler. Now that lady is dead. All she wanted was justice for her grandson. I wish you wanted justice for me." Kenya vanishes for a moment before I see her face on Nevaeh's face. Nevaeh looks towards me confused as Darrin says something to make her laugh and the two begin serving food to the guests.

"One is the loneliest number," Kenya says, now standing in front of me looking like a 14 year old with locs. I look at her, confused by what she's saying. "You did so much to get to the top, just to be at the top by yourself. You won so much for yourself you created losses for everyone around you. You wanted to fix the water crisis, then the homes exploded when you raised the money to fix the problem. You saw so many people die, you wanted to create an insurance fund, but you messed with money that was tied up in Hakeem's parents' murder. Now Duck is dead. You see Darrin? He's buried himself in a relationship just to grieve the loss of his best friend. You damn sure wasn't there to help him grieve. Desha and RJ are in band camp, not with you. Trinity is in a residential program because you're not there for her. Your best friend Sasha is running a grocery store that you just had to open. You keep winning in life, with your millions of illegal dollars in gift cards hidden from everybody. You keep winning with your bank. What are you losing in the middle of your wins? Don't mind me, though, I'm not real. You lost me long ago."

Chapter 31

Nearly an hour later, I found my way to Leakin Park with Hakeem. Several police and news crews had the entrance from North Avenue blocked off. Hakeem parked his royal blue Buick Lacrosse in front of Mike's Carry Out, which is not too far from the fire station. As we walked over to the park, we heard several people out and about stating, "What if it's the copy-cat AFK," or "What if it's the Bunny Man."

Earlier when I heard one of the guys make the Bunny Man comment, I laughed to myself, but now, Baltimore has had a lot of Bunny Man style serial killers. The weird thing about the Bunny Man, nobody ever knew who it was, and at one time, they said the killings never happened. That's basically what the police and FBI did with the real Action Figure Killer once they found out it was the former police commissioner, Alex Tillman.

"But let's get something clear, this isn't Alex Tillman," Marshawn says as an apparition walks next to Hakeem as we make our way through the crowd of people gathered in Leakin Park.

"How do you know?" I whisper, hoping Hakeem doesn't hear me.

"The real AFK only killed people that were in connection to Paul Douglass, Roland Wise and the real me. You were there like I was. He really did the AFK killings just to get his hands on that fraud of a state's attorney turned TV personality, Anna Cartwright. I mean yeah, he killed Paul Douglass, and he killed a lot of Alpha members. If the police and FBI didn't lump all his murders into the attempted murder Paul Douglass was trying to commit with his Rico case, Alex Tillman might have been heralded as a hero. At one point people were wearing shirts with AFK on it until they realized it was just a gang member trying to cover his ass."

"So who do you think is killing these kids… the Right Hand of God?" I continue to whisper as Hakeem shoots an eye towards me, and then back towards the crowd we're trying to get through.

"No, they're laying low," Marshawn continues as he mimics how Hakeem is walking. My husband's chest is all puffed out and trying to look so serious as he goes through the crowd. "Any of the Right Hand of God Fellowship Church members that weren't locked up because of Guy Dulaney's participation with the investigators, definitely aren't doing anything because of the new trial Guy Dulaney's trying to have, thanks to these Charm City stranglings."

"They not gonna let that man and his church members go free. He admitted to hella bodies," I say out loud not even believing the words I said.

"Carson Jessup?" Hakeem questions, catching me off guard that he heard me. The apparition of Marshawn walks in front of us, turns and then looks at us as if this is entertainment for him. It's torture for me because Marshawn isn't real, and I can't help but notice him. I'm around all these people and I'm seeing people that aren't there. I can't do this. I'm handling all these people's money and I'm losing my mind one day at a time. I can't do this. I'm a fraud. A crazy, broke, baby momma, who murdered her father, should not be in the position I'm in.

"Yeah," I shamefully answer Hakeem because he has no idea of the conversation I was having with someone not even here.

"I honestly don't know how this will play out," Hakeem, at a loss for ideas, answers. "I mean, his church admitted killing black working people and taking trophies. The detective that was working the AFK case before the COVID-19 pandemic, Murphy, said that the church was active for a while before the governor made Murphy destroy all the evidence."

"And guess who the governor was," Marshawn and I say at the same time.

"The governor was Guy Dulaney who is now Carson Jessup's defense attorney who's requesting a new trial," Hakeem answers as we are at a standstill in the massive crowd going into the park. Nobody is allowed to walk the grassy area because of the ongoing investigation. All of the trees near the blacktop are covered with yellow police tape.

"Want to hear a weird fact?" Hakeem asks, turning to me but lowering his voice and leaning in. I nod yes and Hakeem whispers in my ear, "Guy Dulaney used to be a member of the Flamingo Club. He and some of the heads of the table got into a major dispute when Guy Dulaney wanted to focus primarily on the drug trade. We're talking cocaine from Columbia and opium from all over Asia. He wanted to be the single person in control of that market and then would make decisions behind my father's, or Hugo's father's back. Eventually he split with some of the Flamingo Club members and founded the Dulaney Crime Family. The two parties have had their problems off and on but no full-on battle. With Hugo Titan as the mayor, I wouldn't put it past Guy Dulaney to have started the Charm City Murders, and the gas explosions just to hurt Hugo's public image."

"That's some devious stuff if that's true," I respond as a grin shoots across Hakeem's face.

"Want to know something even weirder?" Hakeem questions as I shrug my shoulders. "Sgt. Marshawn Bell, the head of the Narcotics and Firearms Taskforce, the guy who kidnapped you, he took down the Dulaney Crime Family years ago. He had a major bust over by an old parking lot by Harbor Hospital. The parking lot basically sits between Brooklyn and Cherry Hill. People used to go there and learn how to drive. I think it used to be an old bus stop or something. Anyway, the drop off happened in that parking lot; a lot of the Dulaney family members went down. Like mothers, aunts, uncles, cousins, even a priest. Guy Dulaney was the governor at the time. He took a deal with the General Assembly, the State Central Committee and the State's Attorney to step down from office and he would avoid all prosecution. Of course he could still practice law because he was the former state's attorney before he was governor."

"That's weird," Marshawn whispers with intrigue, rubbing his chin.

"So you think this Charm City Strangler could be connected to some sick shadow mafia family battle between the Flamingo Club and the Dulaney Crime Family?" I question in a confused tone.

"I can't be 100% certain, but if Guy Dulaney gets Carson Jessup out of prison, that means the other members of the Right Hand of God Fellowship Church will get out," Hakeem explains. "Members of the Right Hand of God Fellowship Church were actually killing black people in Baltimore for hunting sport. The idea of setting those people back on the street and cleared of their records sounds like a major problem to have in our community."

"So what do you hope, it's just one of the Right Hand of God people, so the idea of a new trial will go away?" I ask as a few people nearby start to move in closer to listen in.

"Honestly, that would be the best-case scenario," my husband theorizes. "Of course the worst-case scenario is these Charm City Strangler killings were AFK murders, then the Right Hand of God, and the bad guys that can appeal Tillman's cases will both be on the street."

We arrive at the front where Mayor Hugo and Commissioner Mercer are standing with their backs to crime scene investigators and officers using equipment to search the woods.

"This is a somber moment for Baltimore City," Mayor Hugo begins. "Like damn, who else has to die for this to stop? This grandmother, Ms. Pugh had to bury her daughter a few years ago, and then her grandson. She spent the rest of her life being a voice for the children that were murdered and discarded here in these woods. For what? What are we accomplishing with these murders? You have taken Commissioner Mercer's son, Ms. Pugh's grandson, and 68 other confirmed children. I'm not attending another funeral for one of these children that you've killed. I'm going to see to it personally your ass is brought in. This city has gone through enough. If we can see the light at the end of the tunnel for our water problem, we can definitely shut the door on this Charm City Strangler fiasco. Your days are numbered, sir, that is a promise from your mayor. That's not just a promise from the mayor, that is a promise from Baltimore City!"

Chapter 32

Later that evening, Hakeem and I went to Andrews Memorial for the open Bible Study session. Not present but definitely missed, Kesha Stokes did not show up to Andrews Memorial tonight. To be fair, she told me she was going to be working late at the Ginger Hill Research Center. An hour ago Raymond and Monica had a meeting with the Inner Circle Bible Study group. Aunt Gina, who recently became one of the newest members of that bible study group has been trying to get my attention to talk. The church is abuzz because this is the week the teenagers and young adults go to the beach, and this year Andrews Memorial has paid for them to go to Miami, Florida. Food, travel, and lodging will be covered completely by Andrews Memorial.

There's a group of young women dressed very sexy, singing songs in the pulpit. This part of the service they call praise and worship. They have different groups of singers that perform backup and lead some songs. The reason they don't lead every song is because Andrews Memorial provides a residency to music industry performers to lead the praise and worship team. The resident performer signs a contract for 3 months to perform at every open bible study and Sunday church service. The resident performer leading the praise and worship right now is the four-time Grammy-nominated India Joy. I wish Darrin was here to hear her sing, but he and Nevaeh are at home watching movies. Sitting to my left at the pew's end is my husband and scooting into the empty seat directly next to me is Aunt Gina.

"Tiffany," Gina whispers loudly. "That private bible study is a trip. They cover all kinds of topics. But mainly it's all about loyalty to Elder Nesmith and Monica Nesmith. They want the people in the private bible study to be the direct guard and loyal servants to Raymond."

"That's weird," I respond in a whisper. "You sure you're not overthinking what they're talking about?"

"I'm sure," Gina answers as an usher walks by our row and requests that we stop speaking. The usher returns shortly after with a basket filled with cell phones and tablets demanding that we place our electronics in the box. I turn to my right and notice other ushers are doing the same with the other members throughout the sanctuary.

A few minutes later Raymond has the microphone and is standing in the front of the church. He's wearing a red suit, with a white shirt unbuttoned at the collar. I guess he didn't feel like wearing a tie this week.

"There are some things that have been brought to my attention over the last few days," Raymond begins. "No, I'm not talking about the street kids that have been killed. No, it's not about the poisoned water in the city, or even a new parasite found in the city's water supply. No, this is closer to home. It hurts me to my core, because it's not at all what we stand for at Andrews Memorial."

I have a slight concern, because I'm beginning to think he's about to do something disrespectful to Hakeem. If Kesha is planning to make Hakeem the pastor here, what might Raymond do to drive a wedge between the church and Hakeem? My heart beats faster as I await the next words from Raymond Nesmith.

"You know, I was raised with loving parents who adopted me when I was young," Raymond confesses as he walks along the stage, taking time to pause at each part as members in attendance take pictures of him with their cell phones. "My parents even argued from time to time, but they never wanted to harm each other. Sometimes people have a difference of opinion. Jesus and the Pharisees stood at odds. As a child, I stood at odds with my parents because they told me I would never be pastor of this church because I was not a blood Andrews. Yet, through God's grace I'm allowed to serve as an elder. Here's the thing, when rules are made, and the people understand them, don't break them. Especially when it makes us all look bad. I would like to ask my private bible study group, my disciples to come to the front of the church and stand below the pulpit facing the congregation."

As Raymond instructed, Deacon Jordan, Deacon Harris, Evangelist Nelly, Evangelist NoLesha, my aunt Gina, and the truck driver from the other night, Mark, approach the pulpit and turn and look at the congregation. "I would like for Brother Aaron and Sister Kamilah to approach the pulpit," Raymond states in a deep and serious tone as an usher hands Sister Kamilah a microphone.

"I would like our sister to address by disciples and the church," Raymond orders. "It is important that we see and know corporately."

"Hi, I um," Kamilah says, shaking and stuttering over her words. "I have been beaten by my husband, Brother Aaron, for the last few weeks. He punches me in the stomach, slaps me in the face, he even raped me at knife point a few nights ago. I'm in constant fear that I'm going to do something that displeases him, and he will beat me again."

"Thank you, Sister Kamilah, go take a seat. You will be free from this behavior from this point forward," Raymond declares as Deacon Jordan hands Raymond a thick brown leather bag. Raymond unzips the bag revealing several brown leather knotted cat o' 9 tails. Raymond walks to the group he deems disciples and hands them each, except Gina, a cat o' 9 tails whip.

"Sister Gina, I know you said you feel uncomfortable with this, so you can go back to your seat with Elder Andrews and his wife," Raymond orders as Gina walks back to us, but repeatedly looks back at the group standing in the front of the church with whips. Raymond then walks to the center aisle and towards the middle, and then he faces the pulpit area.

"Aaron Jr., we have a long history, don't we?" Raymond continues as he walks from the middle of the aisle to the back of the church, and then back to the middle of the aisle. "Years ago, I guess we were teenagers then, you raped a girl that went on a church trip with us. You were punished by the deacons and elders, as the bylaws state. Today you stand before us a woman abuser and a rapist again. Disciples, after hearing the testimony of Sister Kamilah, how do you find him?"

"Guilty," the members scream.

"To spare the rod is to spoil the child," Raymond quotes as he continues to pace back and forth. "Brother Aaron, and I use the term brother out of respect of this ministry, not as to what I think of you, we don't hit our women. May he sin no more," Raymond says, turning his back and walking to the rear of the church as the group of disciples begin to whip Aaron.

Aaron falls to the floor in his black slacks and light blue button up shirt and loud cracks and spacks hit him repeatedly. Parts of Aaron's shirt and pants are ripped away by the whips. His face, towards me, is crying and clenched with fear and pain. His eyes close and he bites his bottom lip. Even his cheeks appear to be clenched in pain as his arms clutch his legs.

Raymond then walks over to a balled up and beaten Aaron, who has tears and mucus falling from his face. The disciple group stops hitting Aaron and Raymond says slowly, filled with rage, head shaking and clapping after every word, "We don't hit our women." Raymond repeats the words again, but this time the group of disciples begin whipping Aaron again. "We don't hit our women."

"Have you learned your lesson?" Raymond asks as Aaron attempts to get the word, "Yes," out, but the group continues to hit him.

"Sister Kamilah, by the laws of this church, do you forgive him?" Raymond asks.

"Yes," she yells back to Raymond as the group stops whipping Aaron.

"Sister Kamilah, do you accept this as an appropriate sacrifice for Aaron Jr's sins and transgressions against you?" Raymond asks, walking up the aisle and away from the group.

"Yes," Kamilah responds back to Raymond.

"Sister Kamilah, will you take him back and his past deeds be forgiven?" Raymond asks. Kamilah has fear and confusion on her face. She's silent, lost in thought, and her eyes begin to water.

"Sister Kamilah, as stated in the bylaws of this church, after having a suitable sacrifice, does this satisfy you for you to take him back forgiven for his past actions and deeds against you?" Raymond asks again, but

Sister Kamilah still doesn't answer. Instead, she's shaking and crying.

"Sister Kamilah, as the bylaws of this church state, if a sacrifice is done and the deed is not forgiven by the accuser, the accuser is then held liable for punishment for breaking the ordinance with the church. Is that what you're doing?" Raymond asks as Kamilah shakes her head no, quickly and in panic.

"Sister Kamilah, do you forgive Aaron Jr., and will you take him back, without these events or his sins against you ever coming back up? Has his blood purified your marriage?" Raymond asks as Kamilah says, "Yes."

"With great pride I say Sister Kamilah come to the front of the church and be a helpmate to Aaron Jr. Please take him to the infirmary so you can be instructed on how to properly care for your husband."

Less than a minute later Hakeem, Gina and I are inside a daycare room, painted purple with several bible figures and animals on the walls. The room is very organized and clean, with toys and tables placed in the corner. The custodial staff appear to have vacuumed the room earlier today.

"What the hell was that?" I scream at Hakeem and Gina. I'm fearful of what will come next. The ushers have our phones and this group of "disciples" just beat a man half to death."

"To be fair, he's a rapist and a woman beater," Marshawn jokes in my ear. "What's the difference between that guy and your father? You shot your father; the church didn't do anything to stop his behavior. At least justice was served by the church in this situation. Didn't Hakeem say his ex-girlfriend Michelle was raped by that asshole on a church trip when he was a teenager? I think everything has worked itself out. Amen, my sister!"

"This is why I didn't want to come back," Hakeem vents, scratching his head and pacing.

"You knew this place was nuts?" Gina questions in an elevated and panicked tone as I try to quiet her.

"That's why I was happy to leave and do work with Pastor Donald Avery a few years ago," Hakeem answers, still pacing.

"Is he going to die?" I ask, out of true concern for Aaron Jr. I can picture the blood and the ripped clothes from the beating.

"Only two people have died because of Andrews Memorial's disciplinary practices, and that's because their deaths were planned," Hakeem confesses. "There's a lower-level basement where the inner circle used to take the most difficult members that broke bylaws, and they would whip them with coax cables and hardened ropes, until the member would bleed out. The elders and deacons would then take the bodies out to decompose in an undisclosed location."

"Like Leakin Park?" Gina questions. Her mind is racing a mile a minute, and I'm starting to think she suspects the church is the Charm City Strangler.

"No," Hakeem quickly answers. "They're not serial killers, they're misguided. They think this is a form of punishment ordained by God."

"How do we know those children that the Charm City Strangler killed weren't victims of the disciples or as you call it the inner circle?" Gina asks. "What if the Action Figure Killer is behind this and he's actually a member of the inner circle? What if they pinned all those murders of the Action Figure Killer on the wrong person. Oh my God, the Action Figure Killer and the Charm City Strangler are the same person! I have to get to the studio and record this for the podcast."

"Stop," I scream, blocking Gina from exiting the door. What should I say next? Gina can't keep a secret. If I tell her the truth about the Action Figure Killer being the former police commissioner, Alex Tillman, it could lead to a lot of overturned cases and bad people returning to the streets. What do I tell her?

"Gina, the Action Figure Killer was—" Hakeem starts as there is a knock on the door and we all are startled. Hakeem and I jump for a moment until my husband pulls out a small 40 caliber handgun out of his pocket. That's the Torus I purchased him for his birthday. He carries that around like I carried the .38 that Jamar gave me back in 2017.

"The same gun you killed my grandfather with," Kenya says appearing before me. As the door to the daycare room opens, Hakeem points the gun down towards the floor and postures so that the person walking through can't see it.

"Elder Andrews, I have you and your wife's phones," the young male usher says. He's maybe 10 or 11 years old and wearing a black suit with a white shirt and black tie and he's holding a basket with several cell phones in it. The usher notices Gina and hands her her phone as well. "Y'all have a blessed night," the usher says as he closes the door and walks away.

"Let's leave," I demand, not allowing Hakeem to finish his statement, nor allowing Gina time to process this conversation any further.

"Ok," Hakeem agrees. I'm unsure if he's catching my hints to stop talking to Gina about AFK. Gina is the reason why the Narcotics and Firearms Taskforce coverup became public. I don't think she would be able to stand up against a former police chief taking the law into his own hands and it being covered up by Baltimore City Police Department and the FBI.

"Funny how you know the details on all of that, but you don't know who hit me and my dad that day we died," Kenya flaunts in my face as her apparition appears before the door to the room. "Go do the right thing. 'Cause you didn't do that when you had the chance to protect Tina from your father. But we don't talk about that no more, right? You outgrew that trauma the day you pulled the trigger on him in the basement. You're Ms. Untouchable now. What you gonna do, fight the church cult, kill the Charm City Strangler and then kill AFK? You do know if you kill the former police chief, America will find a way to publicly execute you."

"Let's go home," Hakeem says looking at me and Gina. "Aunt Gina, please don't talk about my church on the podcast. There's a lot of stuff wrapped up in this, and we don't need any more drama in this family."

"Drama like having the Flamingo Club kill everybody?" Kenya mocks. "It'll be another fire bombing. At least my brothers and sisters won't have to be home this time. Speaking of which, the curfew law is still on, you better make sure Darrin is home."

"Trust me, Hakeem," Gina starts with a grin, "all I'm allowed to talk about this week on air and on the podcast is the murder of Ms. Pugh."

Chapter 33

The next day I catch a ride to the Ginger Hill Research Center in Owings Mills to speak to Kesha. Darrin and the youth from the church went to Miami for the annual vacation trip. My mind is still racing from last night. I keep having flashbacks of the whipping that Aaron Jr. received at the hands of Raymond's disciples. Hakeem and I had a deep conversation at home last night about what happened, and the history behind the public disciplines. Hakeem explained that the inner circle was in charge of the church's discipline, and that Raymond has been using his private bible study group as a way to build his own inner circle at the church.

Hakeem made a lot of sense in his explanation last night as he explained that Kesha has stepped back in all leadership functions, other than the title of bishop, and Raymond has been dedicated to the mission of Andrews Memorial from the time he was adopted by Monica and Kelly Nesmith.

It's busy at the Ginger Hill Research Center. There are plenty of people in scrubs, and white lab coats walking the hallways of the first floor, taking elevators to various destinations, and frequent conversations between the staff members as they come and go. The security staff has escorted a few representatives from local area pharmacies to one of the lecture halls set up for a demonstration of the CH18, and different breakthroughs the Ginger Hill Research Center has made to treat different forms of cancer and HIV. I'm thinking about joining the group in the lecture hall to hear Dr. Myron Smalls' presentation on CH18, and where they are with the clinical trials. The president of the Ridgely Square Medical Center, Lori Reed, is walking around the first floor with Kesha as I look on from the office.

This is such a huge positive for medicine and could be a game changer for employment opportunities if we can capitalize on it. Mayor Hugo has invested money into Baltimore City schools to learn radiology, with the goal of high school seniors being able to graduate with certifications in X-ray, ultrasound, MRI and CT-Scan. If Kesha could somehow talk Hugo into partnering with the schools to create jobs here for the Baltimore City youth, we could possibly stimulate the city's economy with lucrative job options and rebuild the industry that Hakeem and I were hoping to build when we started the 10th Bank. The problem is this whole research center is off the books. The Flamingo Club has no knowledge that this has any relation to Kesha

Stokes. Kesha has purposely avoided involving Neil Goldberg and the West Baltimore Hospital. I find it odd because Neil Goldberg, the CEO of the West Baltimore Hospital, is a long-time member of the Flamingo Club and has been a leader in different forms of research and treatment, primarily around substance abuse and cancers.

As Kesha finally walks into the office wearing a dark blue turtleneck, black slacks and high heels, she cleans her hands with sanitizer from the mounted dispenser by the front door. She makes little eye contact with me as she sits at her large glass desk filled with glass awards the research center has won over the last few years. Many of the awards mention the research center in Newport News, Virginia.

"I'm glad you could make it," Kesha greets with her deep voice, sitting upright in her leather office chair. "There's a lot of moving pieces going on today. A few people from the National Cancer Institute will be here soon for the demonstration. I was hoping you'd stay to watch."

"Sure," I respond quickly, not realizing that Kesha was still talking, and was not expecting me to chime in.

"I plan on calling a meeting with Andrews Memorial next week to announce my stepping down as bishop and pastor," Kesha continues. "I'm going to name Hakeem as the successor. It's only right. His name is Andrews and he's a man, fitting the bylaws of the church perfectly."

"Why do the bylaws of the church make it so only a man can lead that church? Why couldn't a woman, like Monica or you really lead the church? I've noticed Raymond doing the day-to-day functions of the church while you just—" I begin, but Kesha stops me.

"Andrews Memorial was my grandfather's legacy, and my father believed in it. I fell into the title of pastor and then bishop because of situations like Hakeem leaving the church and my parents being murdered on the mission trip. I'll be more than happy to finally step away from that role. Hakeem's work with the New Hope Greater Love Church was amazing. Andrews Memorial needs to go in a new direction, and my brother has shown with his work at New Hope Greater Love, he's the perfect person for the job."

"What about the Woodstock Campus, the college, the shelter and everything else that was being developed out there?" I question. "Do you think Hakeem will continue with that if he takes over?"

"I don't plan on it. Hakeem wants to do away with the traditions of Andrews Memorial, and I don't blame him. Monica is the matriarch of the family and wants to keep the traditions as they are," Kesha admits. "I think that college and the prep school on the Woodstock Campus could be great. It could be among the names of Coppin State University, Morgan State University or even the University of Maryland. I have money set aside in the mission fund for salaries to bring in the best leaders in collegiate educators. That's a conversation I'd love to have with you and Hakeem, and possibly with Raymond. The biggest hurdle will be my aunt Monica. She believes that she will lose control of the church after Hakeem is named pastor, and she's right. I want her out of the trustee room, and I want the church away from the Flamingo Club."

"That's the reason why you don't have them involved in this research center?" I question, knowing the answer is yes.

"The Flamingo Club serves a purpose, but it doesn't mean I agree with the methods they have used for the last few decades," Kesha continues. "I've made millions as the accountant for the Flamingo Club, along with handling the finances of several well-known local celebrities. I'm not proud of how every dollar was earned and moved around to hide the source of where it came from. Hakeem gives the church a clean slate, this research center gives me a clean slate."

"And the Flamingo Club?" I ask.

"The Flamingo Club has its own problems," Kesha expresses in an exhausted tone. "Neil Goldberg's greed to control all of Baltimore's medical treatment centers, Erica Little's desire to redesign the whole city and force out all the low, middle class and people in poverty will hurt the City of Baltimore. Hugo Titan really wants to help the city, but he's fighting an uphill battle against the day-to-day drama with the city. You know all about the water crisis, complications with the cost of living and rising murder rate. Hugo wants to bring in major companies to impact the city's economy, but there's too many hurdles for him to jump. You have Khin Lao and the Black Tie who believe that the Asian community hasn't received fair treatment in Maryland since the 1940s and have thought about separating from the Flamingo Club. If Khin Lao leaves, that's guaranteeing a conflict between the Flamingo Club and the Dulaney Crime Family. The Delaney Crime Family doesn't have nearly the amount of muscle they used to have back in the day, but if Khin Lao decides to go his own way, that would leave the Flamingo Club vulnerable enough for a takeover."

"Well, aren't they busy enough with the whole Right Hand of God Fellowship Church investigation?" I ask.

"Not really," Kesha dismisses, tapping her finger on the desk as if she were playing a piano. "The Charm City Strangler is a situation of circumstances. What the Right Hand of God has done for decades is well documented. The judges are in the pockets of the Flamingo Club. Even if Carson Jessup gets a new trial, he and his followers will go back to prison for the crimes they actually committed. The issue is, there may be other players involved in the Dulaney Crime Family, and this whole push for a new trial is a public distraction for something going on behind the scenes."

"Where does that leave me?" I ask, confused as to why I have to join the Flamingo Club.

"You own the bank," Kesha points out. "Take your seat at the table of the Flamingo Club. Use the power of the Flamingo Club for your own good. Just like you did with the Midnight account." Kesha pauses and notices the shocked expression on my face. I had no idea she knew about what I did with the Midnight account.

"I um…" I attempt to defend myself as Kesha just looks through me.

"I'm not upset about it. Monica was pissed, but it is what it is," Kesha explains. "You created an opportunity for so many Baltimore citizens to have life insurance and investment accounts. You're earning that title, "Mom of Baltimore." With Ms. Pugh's recent death, I think it would be wise for Hakeem and the Knights to work closely with the mayor's office to catch the Charm City Strangler. Before we leave the Flamingo Club, we're going to help the people of Baltimore thrive. We're going to keep the Ginger Hill Research Center as our little secret, and once we have positioned ourselves, we'll walk away from the Flamingo Club. Trust me, you don't want to hang around the drama for too long, because eventually the Dulaney Crime Family will come after Hugo Titan, Erica Little, Neil Goldberg and James Deluca."

"Why?"

"The Delaney Crime family were once members of the Flamingo Club but were kicked out because of their involvement in the drug trade and racially motivated attacks on the Black and Latino communities," Kesha explains with no expression on her face.

As we sit silently for a moment. Kesha's cell phone begins to ring, and she points to Raymond's name and picture on the screen. "Hey Ray," Kesha answers as there's yelling in the background.

"Where did they take her?" Kesha questions in a loud tone. She then throws the cell phone across the office before taking several deep breaths. Kesha's eyes dart from where the phone landed, to me, to the staff walking outside of the office, and then back to me. Kesha then pushes a button that causes the clear glass walls to frost over making it impossible for anyone to look in the office or look out.

"Four things need to happen very fast," Kesha quickly says to me. "I have to schedule a meeting with Raymond and Hakeem, then I need to schedule a meeting with the church members."

"What about Monica being at the meeting with Raymond and Hakeem?" I ask, cutting Kesha off as she continues talking, as if I never opened my mouth.

"I need you to take over as trustee of the church, removing my aunt from all of the official books of the church, at least until I can visit her," Kesha continues as I'm trying to follow what she's saying. I think my confused expression has registered on Kesha's face as she elaborates. "The police locked up my aunt Monica at the motel about an hour ago. They sent a swat unit to the Nesmith Inn and the Nesmith Suites. Allegedly they've found several dead bodies with ropes tied around their arms and legs in shallow-filled bathtubs at the Nesmith Inn. Nothing was found at the Nesmith Suites."

"What?" I respond, even more confused. "Are they sure she did it and not Raymond?" I question. "I mean he did have his inner circle of disciples beat a person half to death."

"Aaron Jr. is not a person, he's a demon, a rapist and a woman beater. He's a wolf in a poor excuse for sheep's clothing, but for some reason everyone forgets he's a wolf," Kesha describes, irritated. "My cousin Raymond is not a murderer. He loves the church and this family with his whole heart."

"What about Monica? I didn't take her for a killer," I admit as Kesha demands I call Hakeem. "That's the fourth thing we need to do. Actually, the first thing we need to do now. We need your husband to act as her legal counsel. They're holding her at the detention center in Towson. The quicker we get there the better."

Chapter 34

About two hours later, Hakeem, Kesha, Raymond and I find ourselves in Towson, Maryland at a large office building that has the Baltimore County logo on it that reads, Major Crimes and Investigation Unit. In the building are several floors, some marked for homicides, sex offenses, and cold cases. Following the explosions in Baltimore City a few weeks ago, the mayor and the governor agreed that all inmates, both pre-trial, misdemeanor, pre-release or felony will be moved from out of the Baltimore located facilities. The concerns about the water crisis and the parasites found in Baltimore City's water supply have raised a lot of civil rights concerns in relation to Monica, concerning how to properly house inmates.

Outside of the interrogation room, the Baltimore City Police Commissioner, Keith Mercer, Mayor Hugo Titan, and the state's attorney George Rude, a blonde haired early 40-year-old Caucasian male, clean-cut with a thin frame stands looking on. George Rude was a public defender turned lawyer for the police union and then ran for the District Attorney's office following the NAFA case and the murder of the former District Attorney, Jada Austin.

Hakeem, who is a bar-approved lawyer, was able to ask for a face-to-face meeting with Monica, who was being interviewed by several detectives and a member of the FBI named Agent Parker. The room is bigger than I would have expected, very cold, with several metal chairs and a small white table that is uneven and often makes a clinking sound when someone leans on it.

"I hear you're taking a deal with State's Attorney Rude," Hakeem begins as Monica nods yes. "Why? Are you being set up by the Right Hand of God or something? There's no way you killed all those kids and dumped them in the woods."

"That's exactly what happened, Hakeem, and I'm going to take my punishment," Monica retorts.

"Ok, let's say you're telling the complete truth," Hakeem continues. "How do we, the state or the FBI know you didn't have anything to do with the murders linked to the Right Hand of God Fellowship Church?"

"All of my victims were bound with a thin rope, at their feet and their hands. All of their victims had their hands tied behind their backs," Monica elaborates. "I never cut off a body part for a trophy like the Right Hand of God Fellowship Church did. All of my victims, except

Ms. Pugh were between 9 and 17 years old. They were all street kids."

"Why did you do it?" I ask, as Hakeem requests that I keep my voice low while talking to Monica. In all fairness, there are a lot of cameras filming us in the room.

"Because of the mission trip in Africa," Monica answers in a frank tone. "General Midnight killed your parents, my husband and Kesha's husband. He cleaned me up and kept me scantily clad, with the goal that I would have sex with his soldiers. All of his soldiers were young boys, between 9 and 17 years old. When the first kid came in my tent, a skinny dark-skin kid with bushy hair, I choked him as hard as I could. I thought he was dead, but a few minutes later he began gasping for air and moving. I began choking him again and put his face in the bucket of water that General Midnight had fetched for me earlier that day. After that kid was dead, I went through his pockets and found a beaded rope. One by one, that night I strangled every single one of General Midnight's soldiers, making them think I was going to have sex with them in their tents. Finally, I got hold of an assault rifle and killed General Midnight."

"Why didn't you tell this to any of us?" Raymond asks as Hakeem shoots his eyes towards his cousin, as if to say shut up.

"Because the battle never stopped in my mind," Monica deduces. "I kept seeing the flashbacks of my husband's lifeless body, Kesha's husband's corpse, along with my brother, Bishop Andrews and his wife. When I would drive to the motel from church or from home, I would see these street kids and all I could think was they were working for General Midnight. They were coming for vengeance. So I killed them the same way I killed the soldiers in Africa. I strangled them after offering them sex. I would take them to the motel, dressed in a sexy outfit and give them a sense of false confidence before taking their lives. I would run the bathwater in the motel room and place the bound bodies in the tub to see if any bubbles came out of their mouth or nose areas. If nothing came out, I would leave them in the room for a day or two before taking them to Leakin Park wrapped in the sheet from the room they were in. If bubbles did come out their mouth, I would choke them until no air would escape their body."

"And you had no help?" Hakeem questions.

"None except for Ms. Pugh," Monica reflects. "She came to me drunk asking me questions one night following bible study. I asked a few people from the discipleship bible study group to bring her to the motel in my work van. I told them I was going to pray the alcoholic demon out of her. That night I choked her to death. It was the hardest of the killings because that was the only murder I did that wasn't a flashback, but me covering my tracks."

"You murdered Duck?" I ask as Monica nods yes.

"He was a street kid," Monica expresses. There's no remorse in her face. "All of the street kids, the dirt bike riders, the squeegee boys on the corner, the drug dealers, the kids cutting school. All of them I had to kill. It was a rage, an impulse. I couldn't control it. I had to feed the rage. If they talked ghetto, dressed like thugs, played ungodly music, asked for money. All of that would trigger a rage, a wild energy I couldn't control."

"Were you going to kill my son?" I ask as Monica turns her face up in my direction like an animal ready to strike its prey.

"Yes," she says, scratching and salivating at the mouth. "That street demon needed to be killed. I tried to fight it. I wanted him in the church. He wouldn't come to the church or the vacation bible school. When I killed his best friend, I thought it would stop the craving, but I had to have him. Then I thought, *How can I kill this child?* I'll hire him on at my hotel. Then I remembered he was family and decided that if I brought him into Andrews Memorial by using Nevaeh as a guide, then he wouldn't be a street kid, and possibly a suitable Andrews to take over the ministry."

"And you've never killed an adult male, or any other adult females aside from Ms. Pugh?" Hakeem asks.

"No," Monica responds. "I will admit to every child I murdered. Please bring the state's attorney in so I can waive my right to a speedy trial. I'm ready to live out my days in prison."

"But we could make a case for your mental illness having an impact on what you did," Hakeem pleads, but Monica denies his suggestion. A detective opens the door asking us to leave the interrogation room.

In the hallway Mayor Hugo and Commissioner Mercer swarm over to Hakeem and me. "Did you know that she was doing that?"

"No," we both respond.

"Is this some sick thing y'all do in your church?" Commissioner Mercer asks as Hakeem and I shake our heads no.

Mayor Hugo asks Kesha and me to step over to the side with him, as he walks us near a vending machine. He's not happy, and his facial expression makes it clear he's annoyed. I can understand why. For several months the city has tried to catch the Charm City Strangler, and come to find out, the serial killer was Kesha's aunt. Kesha, who's a member of the Flamingo Club and the bishop of Andrews Memorial. In a way, it must feel like the murders happened right under the mayor's nose and he was none the wiser.

"I'm calling an emergency meeting with the Flamingo Club," Mayor Hugo says to Kesha but not looking at me. "I only want the heads of the table present until we can fix this situation. I'm sorry, Tiffany, but your invitation to the Flamingo Club has been revoked. We need to make sure that the city is back on track. These murders have gone on for too long and we need to regain the trust of the public. Tiffany, you were in front of the water crisis and then got involved in this, and the murders were committed at the hands of your aunt. You will need to do damage control on your end, and quickly because your bank along with that supermarket and restaurant may take a financial hit in the community."

"How did we lose the trust of the public?" Kesha questions in an authoritative tone.

"Your aunt murdered dozens of children and dumped their bodies in Leakin Park," Mayor Hugo yells at Kesha. "Andrews Memorial is the church that she went to, am I correct? That's the church that owns the Woodstock Campus, the same campus that housed the displaced people from the explosions. She also owns the motel and the suites. The same suites that housed the people that were displaced from the explosion. The same place that my office paid for temporary shelter for the people that were displaced. I have a confessed serial killer and cult leader, Carson Jessup, begging for a new trial, and your aunt just made his case stronger."

"She didn't commit the murders that the Right Hand of God members were involved in," I counter as Mayor Hugo raises his index finger in my face, as if to shush me. I grow angry at the notion that any man would try to quiet me.

"The fact is these events happened, and there are consequences behind all of this," Mayor Hugo voices in an irate tone. "How am I supposed to rebuild and fix this city if the public doesn't trust me? Your aunt has ruined almost everything I've tried to do since 2020." The mayor pauses for a moment as we all hear loud chanting and muffled screaming through a megaphone.

As Mayor Hugo, State's Attorney Rude, Police Commissioner Mercer, Hakeem, Raymond and I make our way out to the front of the office building, we find Minister Aleem Muhammad standing in front of a crowd of protesters with a microphone. Members of the media begin to make their way to the protesters as Hakeem and I are caught off guard by this attention.

"Now they want to pin the murders of these African American teenage boys on a black woman!" Aleem yells in the megaphone as members of the crowd groan and yell back. "How did that woman drop the bodies of all those children in Leakin Park? They're saying she killed Ms. Pugh. The woman that was fighting *for* these victims, the mayor and his cronies are trying to dump the blame on a black woman. To think about that, you have to think of what a black woman is. The black woman is the birther of life. Historically the black woman has gone from being worshipped to being trampled, run over, run through and silenced. We all know these murders were at the hand of Carson Jessup and his racist white counterparts. Our mayor, the white man that wants us to trust him, wants to close this case out so he can get reelected. They're planning on railroading the same queen that opened the doors to her brand-new hotel for the citizens of Baltimore that lost their homes due to the explosions. That's the woman they want to say killed all of those black boys. I ask you, *how*? I ask you, *when*? This woman has helped alongside a person I thought was my friend at his church. Any person who can turn their back on his culture, or his people, is no friend of mine. We will not let this go on quietly. We will not be silent. My sister Monica Nesmith, we stand with you in this fight."

As I attempt to approach Aleem, I'm flanked and blocked by Kutter the Poet and Duck's mother, WaKitta. Before I can say anything to her, she spits in my face, instantly causing me to punch her. The two of us trade blows, haymaker after haymaker until she kicks me hard as hell in my pelvis and strikes the left side of my jaw with a hook. As I fall, she attempts to kick me, but before she can connect with her foot, I pull her left leg, causing her to lose her balance and fall. Before I can jump on top of her to punch her, Kutter the Poet pulls me up, yelling in my face as Hakeem moves me out of the way, yelling back at the megastar rap artist.

"Y'all knew!" WaKitta screams towards me as Hakeem tries to pull me to safety. "Y'all knew your aunt was a murderer and you played me. You set up them life insurance policies so you could get paid for her murders."

"We didn't know!" I scream at WaKitta as she attempts to come towards Hakeem and me.

"Why she ain't kill *your* son, then?" WaKitta barks, fighting her way through the people that are separating us. "You got all them kids, but she ain't kill none of them lil niggas."

"She ain't kill them people," another woman screams at WaKitta and me. "It's all a set up. That lady put me and my kids in her brand-new hotel for free. She ain't have to do that. They trying to set her up so that Carson Jessup can get out of jail. This that Delaney Crime Family shit."

"Stop!" Mayor Hugo yells as a person from the crowd screams back, "Shut yo' white ass up. Fake ass mayor."

"You shut yo' ass up!" Commissioner Mercer returns back to the person yelling as the crowd yells at Mayor Hugo and Commissioner Mercer. "Did y'all forget my son was murdered by the Charm City Strangler?"

"Shut up, 12!" Another person screams as someone throws a shoe at Commissioner Mercer.

"This is an ongoing investigation," Commissioner Mercer attempts to yell as others begin throwing batteries, cell phone cases, shoes and rocks at the mayor and the police commissioner.

"Do your damn job and get them racist ass white folk off the streets!" Aleem yells in the megaphone as Hakeem and I attempt to retreat back into the building. As I look back, I notice Raymond is now standing with the crowd yelling at the mayor and police commissioner.

"I'll bail Monica Nesmith out right now! What's her bail set at?" Kutter the Poet screams as the crowd cheers.

"She confessed and gave details to every murder," the state's attorney yells back to Kutter the Poet, now being greeted by boo's from the crowd. "The fibers found on all of the victims match the fabric and fibers from the Nesmith Inn. We even have DNA matching Monica Nesmith, along with drone and overhead airplane surveillance footage placing Monica Nesmith at the scene during the time she discarded the remains of Ms. Pugh at Leakin Park."

"She ain't do that shit!" another person screams as Hakeem closes the door behind me, and overcome with the emotions from the crowd, he balls up his fist and slowly shakes his head.

"She needs to go to court," Hakeem says in a low tone. "These people won't believe anything unless they hear her on the witness stand."

"No," I respond with my head throbbing from the punches I received from WaKitta. "Gina needs to get an interview with her."

Chapter 35

The following day, my aunt Gina landed an exclusive interview with Monica Nesmith from the Towson Detention Center. The correctional officers set up the visiting room area for her to have the cameras and Nubian Media staff on hand to record the interview. Monica is dressed in an orange prison jumpsuit, with a badge snapped at the top with her face and inmate ID number visible, #1234. The prison ID number catches my attention as I watch from my iPad in my office at the 10th Bank. The number 1234 is significant to me, because my grandmother, Florence Simms died at 12:34 am. Ever since the day she died, that number has haunted me, and come up in various periods of my life.

"Some of you may require an introduction to my guest today, but what she is charged with is known to almost everybody in Baltimore City," Gina begins her introduction, dressed in a beautiful blue and black dress that has the R. Nesmith logo going downward on the left side. "My guest's name is Monica Nesmith. To many people she's the owner of the Nesmith Inn and the recently opened Nesmith Suites. Monica Nesmith was also a trustee at the Andrews Memorial church. She's the mother of the Andrews Memorial reverend, and local clothing label owner, Raymond Nesmith. Why is she here on my live daytime show and my podcast? you may ask. It's because Monica Nesmith is said to be the Charm City Strangler, and she admitted to the murders of more than 67 young boys and 1 woman. Today we will interview Monica Nesmith, with the goal of learning who is the person behind the title The Charm City Strangler. I'd like to welcome everyone to my show *The Court of Public Opinion with Gina Simms*."

"Welcome to my show, Mrs. Nesmith," Gina continues. "I want to ask you, would you prefer to be called Monica, or Mrs. Nesmith?"

"Monica is perfectly fine," Hakeem's aunt answers. "Lately all I get called is by my department of correction's number, so it's nice to hear my actual name."

"This has to be a rough transition," Gina says in a comforting tone. "I want to jump into the tough questions that everybody wants to know, if that's ok."

"Sure," Monica agrees, sitting upright in the light red colored plastic chair in the visiting room.

"Can you explain to the viewers how a hotel owner, matriarch of the Andrews family and church trustee at

Andrews Memorial is getting blamed for being a serial killer?" Gina questions.

"Because I did some horrible things," Monica answers very bluntly. "For years I've watched my family and Andrews Memorial become compromised by people like Paul Douglass and General Midnight."

"Paul Douglass, for those not familiar with the name, was the leader of the Alpha Gang, later found to be the Action Figure Killer. He was known for running the drug market in Baltimore City, along with trafficking young girls throughout the United States," Gina educates the viewers.

"Paul didn't work alone," Monica explains. I wonder how far Monica will go with this interview. Will she out the Flamingo Club? "Paul maneuvered himself into our outreach ministry and started working with a person known as General Midnight from Africa. His legal name was John Franklin. General Midnight had an army of child soldiers doing acts of terrorism throughout different parts of Africa. General Midnight was also involved in the black market, selling the organs of young boys and girls that he took from different parts of Europe, Asia and the United States. They used Andrews Memorial's private planes that we used for mission and outreach trips to smuggle drugs and bodies all over the world. When Bishop Andrews, my brother, and Hakeem and Kesha's father attempted to confront him about his illegal activity, my brother was murdered by General Midnight. The problem is, we were on a mission trip during this incident. General Midnight's young army killed my husband, Kesha Stokes's husband, and several other church members. His soldiers were going to rape and kill me, but I managed to escape, killing as many as I could with my bare hands, including General Midnight."

"Oh my God," Gina gasps.

"When I came back to the United States, I was unsure how to process what I'd done," Monica continues. "I couldn't talk about this to anybody. Not my son, Raymond. Not my nephew, Hakeem, and not my niece Kesha. All I knew was the church was free from the grasp of General Midnight and finally the last of the Alphas was destroyed. But when I saw the kids standing on the corners selling drugs, being thugs, riding dirt bikes and cleaning windshields at red lights with squeegees, all I could think about was those child soldiers in Africa. I lost all control. I would seduce some of the children and offer jobs to others. I would lure them to the Nesmith Inn, tie up their arms and legs. Choke them to death and place them in bathtubs with enough water to tell if they were still breathing."

"Did you ever try to get help?" Gina questions.

"A part of my mind thought I was helping the people of Baltimore," Monica responds sharply. "I thought I was doing God's work. There's a scripture in the bible that goes, 'The thought of my suffering and homelessness is bitter beyond words. I will never forget this awful time, as I grieve over my loss. Yet I still dare to hope when I remember this. The faithful love of the Lord never ends. His mercies never cease. Great is his faithfulness; his mercies begin afresh each morning.' What I was doing was providing mercy to these street kids. These hopeless street children that their parents didn't love. The city didn't love. What I did was send them to a creator to love them. It's not their fault that they've become minions for satan. Their parents and grandparents failed them. Doing drugs, having sex, listening to music that talks nothing about the love of Christ. My crusade was to help the city of Baltimore. These are the same people that killed young people, went to court, and came out to do the same behavior all over again. I stopped them because of God. Suffer the little children to come unto me. I gave them refuge. I gave them hope."

"There's a lot of people that are saying you're being set up to take the fall for a group of racist extremists that kill in the name of religion—" Gina starts as Monica stops her.

"The Right Hand of God Fellowship Church had nothing to do with the murders I committed," Monica points out. "They were killing black people in Baltimore and taking trophies. They were doing modern day lynching. I was killing because I couldn't help but see the kids that murdered my family in Africa. The people that were selling organs on the black market. The kids that assaulted and tried to rape me. I was in a war zone, trying to do the work of Christ. Even now, Baltimore is a war zone with no God in it. This city is filled with poverty, crooked politicians and agendas that don't benefit anybody. I opened the doors to my brand-new high-end Nesmith Suites for the people that lost their homes during the explosions. Those same people took a deal to sell their property and move out into the county. How many of those people paid an offering or tithes to Andrews Memorial? I was the trustee of that church; the number is 0. When we placed the people at the Woodstock Campus, do you know how many of them gave a donation when Titan Industries gave them money? Nobody. The love of money is the root of all evil, and I didn't let that consume me. I pity the greedy who will take handouts but never give back."

"Do you think you were justified in what you were doing?" Gina questions as Monica looks off for a moment. The sound of clanging steel and inmates talking and laughing can be heard in the background.

"A few years ago, your family was targeted by the Alphas," Monica points out. "You had to go into witness protection because of the very people I killed with my bare hands. The people who helped the Alphas became what they were, the General Midnights and his army of teenagers, I took out. I didn't see the mayor going after these kids in the streets. I didn't see my nephews Hakeem or Jamar Andrews getting these kids off the corner. I don't see Aleem Muhammad or the Knights getting these kids off the streets. God helps those who help themselves. The bible says let's not get tired of doing what is good. At just the right time, we will reap a harvest of blessings if we don't give up. Baltimore City has given up. The incident of Ridgely Square, the water crisis, the gang wars, NAFA, food deserts, poverty, AIDS, homelessness. Andrews Memorial did not give up. I didn't give up on God. I was overcome with rage and an intensity that had to be satisfied when I saw those street kids destroying the city of Baltimore. I did what had to be done. I put them in a place where the city could and should have forgotten about them. At Leakin Park. How many other bodies are at that park that nobody has tried to look for. How many of those kids died at my hands and nobody cared. But you attach the Charm City Strangler to the deaths of any of those children, then it's front-page news. You all don't care about the sin; you care about the sinner. The problem is I'm not a sinner, I'm doing the will of God. I'm in the trenches, fighting a holy war."

"Is there anything you'd like to say to your son, or any of your family members?" Gina asks, recognizing Monica has lost her sanity.

"I'm proud of my son Raymond," Monica answers. "I adopted him when he was a young boy. His younger sibling died of CIDS while his mother was shooting up drugs and died from an overdose in the same house. Raymond lived in that home with rotting corpses for several days before the police and the Department of Social Services found him. I gave him the best life he could ask for, and because of my dedication to the Gospel of Christ, and his commitment to the ministry, Raymond will enter the kingdom of heaven. He should be pastoring Andrews Memorial, but he's not a blood born Andrews, so I wouldn't be surprised if my niece, Kesha Stokes promotes Hakeem to the title of pastor."

"Did Bishop Kesha Stokes, Tiffany Andrews or Dr. Hakeem Andrews have anything to do with the murders you're being accused of?" Gina inquires.

"No," Monica firmly rejects the idea. "These sins are mine and mine alone. I had no real help from anyone during this process. I've admitted to my murders and I'm glad to accept my prison time. They may capture this clay that my soul rests in, and lock me behind these stone walls, steel fences, and treat me like an animal, but my hope is built on one thing. Jesus will return one day, and he will find my works and deeds suitable to enter his kingdom upon his time of judgment."

"What are your thoughts on people saying that you are using religion as an excuse for what you've done?"

"I don't say nothing to them," Monica answers with a flat expression. "I didn't have a choice. You may have a choice on how you deal with life. God has given me dominion and power over all things, not fear. I'm not going to fear some gang member at a red light shooting a child driving a rental car to his prom. I will take that murderous heathen of a child off the corner and send him to my Lord and savior for his final judgment. I see a group of children on Washington Blvd. and Martin Luther King Blvd., selling drugs, smoking weed and forcing themselves on drivers to clean their windshields, I have to take them out. They are disrupting what God wants for all of us. That is to have life and have it more abundantly. When Jesus went into the temple and threw tables, whipped the people and was angry, do you think he was thought of as crazy? Yes. Because he was correcting what was wrong for so long. When God burned down Sodom and Gamora, do you think people thought that was insane? Yes. It was necessary though, because sin got out of hand. Baltimore City is burning and dying with the water and financial problems because sin has become too great. I'm doing my part. I'm following my assignment. I'm a vessel used by God himself to correct the problems that have languished in this city for so long. My mission may have come to a close, but God's will is not done. I can promise you that."

"Is there anything you'd like to say in closing?" Gina asks, clearly at a loss for words with this interview.

"Let the words of my mouth, and the mediations of my heart, be acceptable in God's sight. My Lord, my savior and my redeemer. Amen," Monica says looking directly into the camera.

Chapter 36

The following day Kesha called Hakeem, Raymond and me to the Woodstock Campus for a meeting. We figured the Andrews Memorial Church may not be the safest place for a meeting. Many of the public still believe that Hakeem's aunt was a scapegoat for the Charm City Strangler, and believe that a racist from the Right Hand of God is the person really killing the young. The fact that Hakeem is Monica's nephew has created tension with other citizens because they think he and I knew what she was doing. Kesha has somehow avoided this whole controversy over the last few hours. The interview my aunt Gina had with Monica was one of the most watched true crime events in the last 10 years. People started creating reaction videos and podcasts just to get in on the attention the latest episode of Court of Public Opinion has received.

The mayor and Erica Little have avoided me since Monica was caught. Kesha explained to me that they still are considering me a member of the Flamingo Club, but they need to distance themselves from me and the 10th Bank until we can regain the trust of the community. In the past I would feel so alone and would seek refuge in my mind and listen to the voices that follow me. Over the recent years those voices have ranged from my grandmother, Florence Simms, to my father Daryl 'Cube' Gibbons, to my cousin Tina Simms, to my youngest daughter Kenya and of course Marshawn Bell. I don't understand why, but I feel like the whole city is against me, and I'm not retreating into myself. I feel like this is a place where we can prove to everybody what we're trying to do.

Sadly, there's another battle Hakeem and I lost over the last two weeks. It's the fight against Erica and Titan Industries acquiring a lot of the homes and black owned properties for the community reconstruction project. When Erica met the displaced residents who lost their homes due to the gas explosions, she offered them more money than their homes were worth. More than 200 people took the deal that day, only 2 abstained. The silver lining in that is those people staying at the suites didn't have to panic when Monica was indicted. Erica was more than happy to place all the people who signed a contract with Titan Industries into the high end 5-star hotels owned by her ex-husband.

Hakeem has tried to show me the positives in everything, for example our work to solve the water crisis was a success. The whole city will have fresh drinking water with brand new pipes by early September. The Charm City Strangler was caught and brought to justice. Also, the incarceration didn't cost the taxpayers much because she confessed and was offered a plea deal by the district attorney, George Rude. With things going the way they're going, I want Kesha to do what she really wants to do, run her research center and get away from Andrews Memorial and the Flamingo Club.

"I wanted to call this private meeting before the annual corporate meeting on Saturday," Kesha starts as she pulls out a yellow pad and begins jotting down some words. Kesha's Woodstock office has a lot of space, but it feels tight and uncomfortable because Hakeem and Raymond both have very serious looks on their faces. Raymond is a bit more fueled with anger because of his mother's incarceration, people destroying the motel, and the new internet movement to boycott his clothing.

"Is this about the pastoralship of Andrews Memorial or my mother?" Raymond questions as I turn towards Hakeem's cousin who has not broken his gaze from Kesha.

"Your mother is in prison," Kesha answers with her deep voice, wearing a black turtleneck in the freaking summertime. "This is about the pastoralship of the church. It's no secret my heart has not been in this ministry for years. Actually, since I was a child, I hated this church. If it wasn't for my father giving me the attention he didn't give Jamar or Hakeem, I probably would have burned this place down when I was in undergrad. I had to balance doing the taxes for this church and laundering money for the Flamingo Club. It's gotten old. I can't do it anymore."

"You're making Hakeem the pastor, I already know, he's your brother and he's a born Andrews," Raymond blurts out.

"If you want to be cut and dried, yes," Kesha admits. "But I want you to co-pastor the church with him."

"I grew up believing the church's mission," Raymond expresses. "I knew, being adopted by my parents, I wouldn't be pastor, but then you, Kesha, you gave me hope. You gave me an opportunity to lead bible study, preach services, have my own private bible study that I was able to turn into my own inner circle."

"We don't have to change what has worked," Kesha suggests as Hakeem denies her statement by shaking his head.

"Listen to Raymond, what he's saying is right," Hakeem points out. "Raymond has worked and acted as the pastor of this church for years. For years you've

worked on the Flamingo Club and recently with your
la—"

"Don't talk about that in this building," Kesha stops
Hakeem.

"What was he about to say?" Raymond questions.

"Nothing," Kesha answers.

"Fine, y'all keeping secrets," Raymond exclaims with
frustration. "I know I'm not y'all sibling, but it's not
fair. I was raised with you two and Jamar. I loved y'all
like my own…" Raymond stops for a second and
pauses in thought. "My sister."

"Your sister that died in the bed from CIDS when you
were young. When they found your mother overdosed
in the home," I mention with compassion as Raymond
barely looks at me. "You should have never gone
through that."

"It gave me a second chance," Raymond dismisses my
attempt to develop rapport with him. "It gave me a
family of successful people. It gave me real parents. A
real home, a relationship with God. I have a successful
clothing brand because of the Andrews family. I've
preached all over the world because of this family. I've
led this church in the direction that your father would

have been proud of. You hid in your office, hung out with that secret society known as the Flamingo Club, and have been doing God knows what. I've been faithful to this church, to this family and to you. Your brother, this nigga Hakeem, left us. Just like Jamar did. I knew how the game would end; Hakeem would come back, and you'd hand the keys to the church over to him, but it's not right. The church needs my leadership. Not some birthright politics."

"You're not wrong," Hakeem affirms as Raymond cocks his head sideways towards my husband in annoyance that he spoke.

"What's my role? Do the same thing I've been doing while this Andrews child gets the credit for the hard work I've done?" Raymond questions as he stands up. "You're going to parade Hakeem and me out there during the church meeting, mention that Hakeem is the pastor, and then call me the co-pastor. Guess what, these members know me, do they know him? He may have your father's name, but he doesn't stand for what your father stood for. He doesn't stand for what my mother stood for. He is a clone of Pastor Donald Avery. That's his claim to fame. The freaking New Hope Greater Love Ministries and the Justice 4 All not-for-profit. I would say the Knights, but it seems like Aleem has distanced himself from you, thanks to the Charm City Strangler business."

"How can we make this work?" I ask as Raymond leans against the wall next to Kesha's desk. "I want both of y'all to go away. We have missions all over the world, in prisons, housing homeless, providing inpatient and outpatient substance abuse treatment and now opening schools and colleges. We have thousands upon thousands of members, prominent musicians that attend this church week in and week out. You think you can handle any of that? Your father groomed me to be a leader when you left. Your father and my mother groomed Kesha to handle the day-to-day business of the church on the front and back end. Where were you? Fighting for some kid that was shot robbing a pizza carryout. We have wealthy people that want to hear about prosperity. We have members that are trying to become rich, dying to hear messages about prosperity. You are not that leader. You're the homie pastor. You're the "turn to your neighbor, high five that nigga and pray God will make it happen" pastor. You're not the leader that knows how to lead members who live in the Promised Land."

"What about the people trying to get into the Promised Land?" I ask as Raymond glances back at me, rolling his eyes before looking back at Hakeem and Kesha. I stop myself before making Jamar's quote, 'You can't move into the Promised Land before you kill the natives.'

"Y'all think this is a joke," Raymond says, pacing back and forth in the office. "We are the most successful ministry in the Mason Dixon. There's not a better ministry in Maryland, D.C., Virginia, North Carolina, South Carolina, Tennessee, Delaware, New Jersey or New York. We are revered for how great we are. We have television channels begging us to stream our church services on their platforms. There's music artists begging to sing in our pulpit. You think a failed store front pastor can truly lead these people into the future? How?"

"We can work together," Hakeem answers in a calm tone. The tension in the room grows, as the office begins to feel like it's shrinking. The air begins to grow heavy as the look of anger grows on Raymond's face.

"Work together? How?" Raymond questions. "I'm willing to bet the Nesmith Suites that you wouldn't hesitate to turn Andrews Memorial into that sorry excuse of a church you watched burn down in 2019. I'm not going to let you do it. Kesha should be the pastor if the leader must be an Andrews. If y'all are going to change the bylaws, I'll lead, but I refuse to work under you, Hakeem. You are not for us, you think you're better than us, but in reality, you failed without us which is why you're back."

"Dude, I'm trying to do this with you," Hakeem explains. "Yes, some things will have to change."

"Like what?" Raymond yells.

"The VIP seating and the seating based on attractiveness—" Hakeem rattles off. He attempts to continue the list, but Raymond cuts in.

"Those things make us successful," Raymond explains. "People come here knowing there's something greater to strive for. You don't understand that? People see my private bible study group, and they want to join. People see the business owners that go to this church, and they get inspired to become millionaires. You think the 10th Bank is the only thing making a difference in the Black Community? This church was doing it before you met your whore wife."

I instantly stand up and attempt to swing on Raymond as Hakeem pulls my arm, stopping me. "Don't disrespect my wife or her children ever again," Hakeem instructs as Raymond walks over to Hakeem, causing my husband to stand up. "You were never the athletic one. I'd knock you out three times before you'd hit the floor from the first punch. Step back before you hurt yourself."

"That's all you know," Raymond professes. "Violence. That's why you defended them kids that were murdered back in 2016 by the police. You know why we're here as a church? Tiffany Gibbons' aunt. And I will call your wife Tiffany Gibbons because she doesn't deserve the name Andrews. I deserve it more than her. But what I said was right, Gina Simms is the cause of all of our problems. If it wasn't for her going to Anna Cartwright and talking on live TV about the Alphas, NAFA and Sgt Marshawn Bell, I would have stayed happy, and business would have continued as usual. Gina Simms caused the disintegration of a beautiful partnership between the church and the Flamingo Club."

"Stop, this isn't going anywhere," Kesha pleads.

"No," Raymond rejects her words. "Jamar would still be alive if Gina would have stayed out of everything. Our parents would have still been alive. Hakeem, your little storefront church wouldn't have been burned down if it wasn't for Gina Simms."

"My aunt had to go into witness protection because she spoke out against the bad people that were tearing down our community," I respond, really frustrated with Raymond and his behavior. I can't believe this tall negro really made me defend my aunt.

"Your aunt's actions had causes, and those causes impacted our family," Raymond screams pointing at a picture on the wall of Hakeem's parents along with Monica and Kelly Nesmith posing together in front of the church wearing their Sunday best. "Kesha, am I lying?"

"No," Kesha answers after hesitating for a brief moment. "It's not like she didn't know that her good intentions would have such a major impact on our family."

"Our family had challenges before Gina Simms opened her mouth on live TV, and exposed the Narcotics and Firearms Taskforce, or the Alphas," Hakeem points out as Raymond begins to shake his pointer finger in disapproval.

"No!" Raymond screams. "You don't get to do that. We had a scheduled interview during the day Gina Simms spoke openly about NAFA and the Alphas. We had your father call Ms. Clair directly to convince her to stop the documentary from airing when we got word of what was spoken, but Anna Cartwright and Ms. Clair went through with everything. As a result, the relationships we had with Paul Douglass and with General Midnight were severed. People died because of Gina Simms and her big mouth."

"Then why did you have her join your discipleship bible study group?" I ask as Raymond reveals a small revolver.

"Because I wanted to kill her myself for what she did to our family. What she did to this church. What she did to the great legacy of the Andrews family," Raymond admits before putting the gun away. In the past, I would have been fearful that he or anybody would have a gun in a setting like this. I came here today with my small 40 caliber handgun that I won't hesitate to use on that tall, overly dramatic negro.

"What's the middle ground here?" Kesha asks, attempting to make peace between Hakeem and Raymond.

"Keep Hakeem as an elder," Raymond answers. "Let him relearn our ways, and after some time, then you step down and he can lead. I honor the bylaws of this church and the traditions of our family. An Andrews should lead this church. If it isn't you, it should be Hakeem, but it shouldn't be Hakeem right now. If you install him as pastor of this church now, I'll leave tonight."

"What's the difference between now and a few months from now?" Kesha asks as Raymond continues to pace the office floor.

"He's been out in the world, doing things that are not pleasing in the sight of God and our family's tradition. He just came back through these doors, and you want to hand him the church keys. We'll lose more than half the members of this church if we promote him to pastor now," Raymond pleads to Kesha.

"Raymond, if I make the decision today to make Hakeem the pastor of the church, will you co-pastor and assist him in his duties?" Kesha questions as Raymond leans up against the wall. It's like Kesha didn't hear Raymond just say he would leave a few moments ago.

"Since you're in a place of authority and that's your instruction as the bishop, yes," Raymond responds in a calm tone. "But, if you're stepping back from this ministry altogether and leaving everything in his hands, I'm gone, and so will many of the members that keep the doors open and lights on at the church and the Woodstock Campus. I know you want to have the church meeting on Saturday prior to the youth returning from their trip, but I think you need to think about your decision a little more."

"The meeting with all the church members will happen this Saturday, that's tradition," Kesha exclaims, slamming her hands on the desk. The forced deep voice she tries to put on has vanished, and a beautiful yet agitated sound escapes her mouth into the words, "If we don't stand on the traditions set before us in the bylaws, we're worse than sinners."

"Let's meet again on Friday night," Hakeem suggests as Kesha and Raymond nod in disagreement.

"I bet you want to do it at your house, Hakeem," Raymond contributes with a smile. "I'll grab pizza from DeLuca's Bistro and Bakery, I guess."

"If a meeting was to happen on Friday, maybe we should grab it from somewhere else," Kesha interjects with her deep voice returning. "We're not on the best terms with the Flamingo Club, you know, with your mom being the Charm City Strangler and all."

"I could grab the pizza from off Route 40. There's a spot called Santoni's, and they have pretty good pizza," I add, hoping to contribute something to the conversation as we all agree.

"No, we'll have the open meeting with the membership on Saturday at the church." Kesha reassures. "If the meeting doesn't go well, we can have a private meeting among ourselves at Hakeem's or my house."

"Nobody wants to meet at my house?" Raymond questions in almost a joking tone.

"We need to stay as far away from your house as possible," Kesha explains. "Even though your mother's incarcerated, there's still an ongoing investigation surrounding her murders."

Chapter 37

Walking through a lush, beautiful forest, I head to a large lake. It's a bright sunny day, but I cannot make out the blue sky, a cloud or a sunray. The color of the sky is uncanny, like it's not even real, but I can feel the radiation from the sunlight and the warmth of the beautiful day. It feels like early spring, with a cool breeze greeting my face. Around me are beautiful tall trees and a cabin several hundred feet behind me. Standing next to me in an all black suit with a black button up shirt and a black tie is Marshawn.

"You ever been fishing?" Marshawn asks as I try to figure out where this place is. "I went out to a place like this the day my uncle and mother dumped my dad in the water. Experiencing stuff like that changes you. You know that, you killed your father, although you didn't have to get rid of his body. They called your murder justifiable homicide. The murders my mom was involved in were family secrets."

"You did the right thing," a male voice says on my left side. I turn and notice a man that is another Marshawn, dressed in the same clothes. "Your father got away with child molestation, murder and he trafficked young girls for the Alphas. You took matters into your own hands, and you put him down.”

“Is that what you did?” Kenya questions, standing between me and the lake. She appears as a late teenage girl, smoking out of a black vape pen. “You don’t know what he was going to do. Yeah, he broke in the house, but he was on the run.”

“On the run for what, Kenya?” Marshawn questions as my daughter rolls her eyes. “He was a rapist. Tiffany’s mother protected him and covered everything up for years,” Marshawn explains.

“What’s the difference between what your mother did and what Andrews Memorial does?” Marshawn questions looking on at the lake. The water from the lake is still, almost lifeless. “Andrews Memorial covers up illegal activities from the Flamingo Club. They covered up the rape incident with Hakeem’s high school girlfriend, Michelle. When Raymond took matters into his own hands with his inner circle, shit got done. Why didn’t Bishop Andrews, Hakeem’s father, do it? You know what the city calls you?”

“The Mom of Baltimore,” Kenya answers in a sarcastic tone. “What a joke. She’s not even the mom to her own children. Trinity’s in treatment, Desha and RJ are away at some art camp, and Darrin is away on a trip with his new girlfriend from Andrews Memorial. How you the Mom of Baltimore and you not even the mom of home. Was you even my mom? Do you even remember what my voice actually sounds like?"

"Ignore her," the other Marshawn insists. "They call you the Mom of Baltimore. You have the power to be the leader and the voice many of these people need."

"I failed," I utter in almost a whisper. "I tried to stop Titan from taking over Ridgely Square and taking the homes away from the black homeowners. I tried to stop the water crisis. What I did was allow Titan to purchase almost every home in West Baltimore after the explosion."

"They still will need to rebuild and sell the homes," Marshawn reminds me. "You can provide the bank loans. We can still have an opportunity to provide homes for the black people of Baltimore."

"What happens when they're priced out of reach for the people I'm supposed to help?" I question as Kenya laughs and walks towards the still-watered lake.

"Do exactly what Kesha asked you to do," Kenya responds before falling backwards into the lake with her arms spread wide apart. "Join the Flamingo Club, get a seat at the table."

My daughter lands in the still body of water, then vanishes before my eyes. I turn towards Marshawn who points back at the log cabin, and says, "It's time we get to work. The city needs us, but your husband and that church need us first. Let's get Andrews Memorial away from the Flamingo Club, and then we can dictate how business will be run from now on. Remember what Erica said a few days ago, 'We're the two most powerful people in the room.' You run the bank they hide their money in. They need you. Kesha handles their money. This Raymond situation may not be pretty but endure. Remember what you said you wanted for your family when you and Hakeem had premarital counseling?"

"I said I want us to win as a family," I answer, thinking about how many losses my family has had over the past few years. Starting with my loser parents. My father always in and out of prison and being a molester. My mother an enabler, and so addicted to unhealthy food she sent herself to an early grave. My grandmother dying from Alzheimer's and being the person that held the whole family together. My grandfather being murdered because of my bad behavior as a child.

"Your grandfather's death was not your fault," Marshawn points out. "Neither was Kenya's death. It's time you become the boss you were born to be. If people don't want to follow in the direction you're headed, cut them off. Some people are only in your life for a season, Tiffany."

"Tiffany," a voice says as everything goes white.

"Tiffany," the voice repeats as everything goes black.

"Tiffany," Hakeem says in a gentle tone as the TV is playing low in the background.

"Hey, what's up babe?" I answer as I try to collect my thoughts. How long was I sleep?

"I grabbed food from HoodFellas Bistro," he answers with a smile on his face, knowing I love their crab cake egg rolls and their steaks.

"Oh bae!" I scream with excitement, hugging my husband. The news has been going nonstop about the Charm City Strangler, and the three cases they have officially charged Monica Nesmith with. They're grouping the other cases together due to inconsistencies with some of the evidence. The news reporter, Ebony, is saying that Ms. Pugh, Duck and the police commissioner's son are officially tied to Monica in her plea deal.

"I don't think I can co-pastor the church with Raymond," Hakeem states, which does not surprise me. "I've given it a lot of thought, and to me he's too tied to the old traditions of Andrews Memorial. If God really wants me to pastor again, then it has to be in a way that he'll be pleased with. That way is not what Andrews Memorial has stood for and still continues to even today."

"What are you going to do?" I ask. My stomach rumbles as the aromas flow in from the kitchen.

"When we meet tomorrow, I'm going to come clean with him and my sister about everything," Hakeem answers, offering me his hand as I pull up from the couch and follow him to the kitchen area. The kitchen is smaller than the one at my grandmother's house, but it's home and I'm comfortable here.

The home is colder than an igloo today, because the window unit air conditioners have been pumping nonstop. One of the best parts of this summer has been the one-on-one time Hakeem and I have had because of the kids being gone with the arts camp and Trinity being in her treatment program. Our alone time will end soon, because when the arts camp summer session ends Desha and RJ will return. We've been waiting to hear back from Trinity's mental health therapist at the inpatient program, but the communication paused when the staff stopped returning my calls. At first I blamed myself for calling so late because of my schedule, but with the recent resolves of the water crisis, the Charm City Strangler and the residents deciding to sell their properties, my schedule has started to open up.

Even traffic at the 10th Bank has slowed down, partially because of the public perception that my husband's aunt is the Charm City Strangler. The work I was doing to provide savings accounts, life insurance and help aid the residents of Baltimore City has pretty much stopped.

"If you could make a mixtape with your top 10 songs, what would they be?" Hakeem asks, breaking the silence in the kitchen and forcing me to get out of my own head.

"That's a good one," I quickly respond, searching for the answers and I take a bite of the macaroni and cheese on my plate. I'm so grateful that Chef Ben at Hoodfellas Bistro didn't let my sides and entre dish touch each other. That stuff drives me crazy, except when I'm eating Jamaican. Let those juices run together, baby!

"Ok, I'll go first. I'll give my first five songs, then you give your first five, then I'll give my final five and you'll do the same," Hakeem says with cheer as he notices me pondering and thinking. "Don't judge me for this either, 'cause the songs are covering a lot of genres." I nod affirming his request, trying to hold back a huge smile bursting through my cheeks.

"The first song would be, "Words I Never Said" by Lupe Fiasco, the second, "One More Road to Cross" by DMX, the third would be, "Fate" by H.E.R., number four would be, "Air Forces" by Jeezy and the fifth would be, "Roc Boys" by Jay-Z," Hakeem states, now waiting for me to give my first five.

"I like your choices so far. I'm weird when it comes to music," I admit. "Like it puts me in different places and some songs fit certain points in my life and different moods I was in depending on what I was going through."

"Completely understandable. You've gone through so much," Hakeem acknowledges as I smile back, feeling seen by the one man in my life that has truly taken the time to get to know me, inside and out. I take a deep breath and exhale. "I'll start with "Tired" by Kelly Price as the first song on my mix tape. "Best Friend" by 50 Cent would be number two. When you started bringing food over to the house back when my grandmother died, I used to sing that song when you would leave. I wasn't sure if you were hitting on me or just being nice," I told Hakeem.

"I was genuinely trying to be there for you and the kids, but it was something about the way we locked eyes the first time, I knew there was something more meant for the two of us. I didn't want to take advantage of trying to court you while you were going through the grief of so many family members, but I felt like there was something real. Something we could build towards," Hakeem admits with a blush on his brown skin face.

"Then you realized I was crazy," I joke, but seriously, *does he think I'm crazy?*

"You're not crazy," Hakeem rebuts. "You've endured more than most, and you've come out stronger each time life has punched you in the gut. You still have three more songs to name, though."

"Goodbye" by Slaughterhouse," I blurt out. That song has gotten me through the deaths of Kenya, Tina and my grandmother. I used to play that in my headphones all the time and cry when I sat on the toilet with that song on repeat. Trinity used to bang on the bathroom door and ask if I was ok. Sasha knew what was going on, but we never talked about it. Sasha's son was murdered by Baltimore Police during a botched robbery, and she lived with me for close to a year, but the NAFA and Alpha drama became too much for her, on top of the alcohol addiction she developed while grieving. Damn… I could have been a better friend to her.

"How?" Marshawn questions in the back of my mind. "She was living in your house rent free. You even gave her a job at the Legacy of Florence."

"You're right," I respond out loud. Hakeem looks up at me knowing something is off about my comment. "I have two more songs to go." Cool, I played that off. "Slipping" by DMX, and "U Don't Know Me" by T.I."

"Good choices," Hakeem admits, impressed with the choices I've made so far. "Number six for me would be "Human" by Rag'n'Bone Man; number seven would be "Realist in the Game" by Jadakiss; number eight would be "Who You Were" by Travis Green; number nine would be "In" by William McDowell and the last song is "You're Nobody" by the Notorious B.I.G."

"Ugh," I exclaimed. "I used to play that song on repeat every night growing up. I would lay in bed on the nights my father would be running the streets or locked up, and I'd play that song, crying myself to sleep."

"I never knew that about you, but I used to play that song on repeat until the CD would scratch, then I'd buy the double album, *Life After Death* all over again just to play that song on repeat," Hakeem admits, looking down at his plate. "Since Jamar was murdered, I've heard that song on repeat in my mind, but I've always been scared to actually listen to it because I know it would stir up too much emotion."

"Numbers six and seven are by this group from Colorado called the Flobots. Number six is called "Loneliness" and number seven is "The Rose and the Thistle." I like the two songs for the same reason you love "You're Nobody." I admit, I have always hidden the fact that I liked the two songs by Flobots from everybody, but this bonding moment with Hakeem has shown me that we're closer than we thought we were.

"I'm going to check them out… you said Flobots?" Hakeem questions as I answer yes while chewing on more food.

"I think you'd like them," I say feeling safe and confident with Hakeem. I love these moments where we can learn about each other by these random conversations. "The next song reflects our relationship big time, so don't judge me, ok?" I say as Hakeem's expression changes to a more serious one. "It's a song by Mary J. Blige called, "Father in You." It really defines me a lot, and sometimes where I see myself when I'm with you. Don't judge me when you listen to it."

"Safe zone," Hakeem says with a smile that hugs my heart. "Everything between us is safe and sacred."

I swear I love this man. He's not perfect, but he knows what words to say and how to be there for me when I need him most. I constantly find myself being stripped of the shackles that have weighed me down for years and comforted by him. It means so much to be seen by someone that views you in the way you never thought you were worthy to be viewed.

"What number am I on?" I ask while looking at the warm smile still resting on my husband's face.

"You have two more to go," Hakeem says holding up three fingers in a playful manner.

"Last two, here we go," I say, trying to pump myself up. "Number 9 would be "Press in Your Presence" by Shana Wilson. I got to see her live in Orlando once. I went on a road trip with a friend of mine that used to dance, and she was at the convention center performing. It was an amazing experience. I can't even put it into words. I was crying but I wasn't sad. I felt something that day I never felt before. I have two songs I'm going back and forth with for number 10."

"Say both of them," Hakeem encourages as I get excited.

"The Chain" by Fleetwood Mac and "Seven Days" by Mary J. Blige. Another Mary J. song that reminds me of our relationship," I admit as Hakeem smiles and states, "Seeing that we're doing a bonus track, mine would be "Like a River" by Joyner Lucas."

As we sit silently eating, Hakeem pulls out his iPhone, pushes buttons and then plays the song, "Father in You" by Mary J. Blige. "I put all the songs you and I named into a playlist. I figure we have the house to ourselves tonight, let's listen to the soundtracks to our lives and enjoy the night together." Before I can say yes or no, Hakeem goes into the cabinet above the sink and pulls out a large bouquet of roses that are burgundy, green, purple, red, light pink, peach and lavender in color. "While you were sleeping, I also took time to light some candles upstairs and put rose petals on the bed and in your bath water."

"My bath water?" I question, confused and surprised by his words.

"If we have the whole city against us because of my aunt's vile decisions, the least we can do is enjoy each other to the fullest while we have the house to ourselves tonight. We have brand new water pipes in the neighborhood, so it's not like you're going to get sick from the water," Hakeem mentions as I walk over to him and hug him. I begin to cry uncontrollably. Finally, something I've held on to for years has been released. Not having to be the person that has to do everything. I finally feel completely secure. "Well don't let the bath water get cold," Hakeem jokes as we both run out the kitchen taking off our clothes and race up the stairs.

Chapter 38

On Saturday Hakeem, Kesha and Raymond are seated in the center of the pulpit area of Andrews Memorial. The church is packed, and I'm sitting in the balcony in my normal spot, far in the back away from everyone but near one of the exits that leads down a back stairway to the outside. Hakeem, Kesha and Raymond are spread apart with large containers of flowers between them. There are also circular glass tables to their right side with bottles of water and a microphone placed there for each of them to use. The members of the bible study group that Raymond considers his inner circle are sitting in the choir loft, behind the top right side of the pulpit.

"I'm glad to call our 2022 annual church membership meeting to order," Kesha says into the microphone with her deep voice. She's wearing a black turtleneck sweater and a long colorful skirt. "I want to start out by saying this has been a very lucrative year for Andrews Memorial. While we have cut down on our foreign mission trips, we have been able to serve the homeless and the displaced people from the city's explosions a few weeks ago. In our efforts to serve the people of Baltimore City, we've grown in membership. That was an unforeseen blessing that nobody in this pulpit saw coming. As your bishop, I'm beyond proud of the effort the members of this congregation have made to ensure that the displaced residents felt at home while they stayed at the Woodstock Campus."

"I would like to take a moment to celebrate you all, and I ask everyone in this temple to celebrate each other for a moment," Kesha requests as everyone begins to clap. As I scan the room, looking at the members' faces, all I see are smiles on everyone's faces. "We've also had several members start companies, grow businesses, purchase homes and vehicles over the last year, and they cosigned the church on the titles," Kesha continues. "It's a blessing to know we are part of a ministry that puts God first in every walk of life. Even the newer members that work 9-to-5 jobs have bought into our dedication to God, by cosigning their bank accounts over to the church, with the goal of making sure we properly manage their finances. Bills are now paid on time, tithes are paid without struggle, and members aren't living paycheck to paycheck. Why? Because they have bought into a system that was theorized by my grandfather, put into practice by my father and is still reinforced by my cousin Elder Raymond Nesmith and me."

Kesha pauses for a moment to allow the members to clap and cheer and I notice several local celebrities sitting in the front near the VIP section. "I know many of you are happy and excited about new prep school and college, but I want to make sure this weekend is about giving back. That's always the purpose of these meetings. Transparency and knowing your work and efforts are not in vain," Kesha exclaims, in an almost animated tone. She's speaking charismatically, moving her hands as she speaks and there's excitement in her tone of voice.

"For the parents that had their kids go away for the annual youth trip, they will be back here by 4 pm," Kesha continues. "At 5 pm, we plan on having our annual cookout, but not here at Andrews Memorial, like we have in previous years. No, this year we will have the annual cookout at the Woodstock Campus. This will include multiple bushels of jumbo crabs, steaks, Italian sausages, hotdogs, hamburgers, lamb, macaroni and cheese, slow smoked collard greens and fried fish. We also plan on having activities out there tonight, including flag football, basketball, fishing, corn hole, spades, scrabble and fireworks. The best part about this is, everything is completely free for all the members in attendance today, the participants of vacation bible study, and the youth returning from the annual trip."

As the members continue to clap and praise Kesha, Hakeem and Raymond look on at the members of the church silently. Hakeem looks visibly nervous, and Raymond's face looks confrontational. He looks like a man ready to attack anyone that approaches him.

"Of course, there are some serious things to go over," Kesha notes, as the happy members stop their applause and listen closely. "First things first, Woodstock's college and the prep school will be starting late August. We have reached capacity with both, and have waiting lists for the prep school, at every grade level. We are fully staffed for the Bishop Hakeem Andrews Prep School. I would also like to announce that the satellite church we've named, Andrews Memorial 2, will be fully operational next week. This evening, I would love to provide a tour for all the members of Andrews Memorial."

I notice a brief moment of eye contact between Raymond and Hakeem as Kesha continues to talk about the Andrews Memorial 2 church. Kesha reviews the bylaws of the church, and the importance of following the rules that were set in place by their father, Bishop Andrews.

"Before starting the annual members only church meeting, I met with Elder Hakeem and Elder Raymond to review the bylaws, for a number of reasons. The first reason is to discuss how we as a church should move forward following the actions of my aunt and our former trustee, Monica Nesmith." Kesha pauses for a moment as the smiles change to more serious expressions. People in the balcony area lean forward. I'm caught off guard by this as well, because I just learned right before the start of this meeting that Hakeem, Kesha and Raymond met this morning.

"Sadly, I had to remove my aunt from the church's roster, and from everything she was attached to in the church. This has placed the ministry in an awkward situation." Kesha stands up and begins to walk around the large stage while addressing the members. "I looked at the other members of the trustee department, and I looked at the damage my aunt Monica did to the community, and I said to myself, "Kesha, what are we going to do?" I said it to myself several times. I had no answers. I prayed to God, and an opportunity presented itself. My brother on one side and my cousin on the other. You all know both of them. My cousin, Raymond, has been a very productive leader, teacher, preacher and friend to everyone in this room. Hakeem, my brother, was born to lead this ministry. Hakeem was born to pastor this church. He was born to step into our father's place of leadership once he died. Little did any of us know our father would be murdered while on a mission trip in Africa. Little did any of us know that our father, the great Bishop Hakeem Andrews would leave us with such solid footing as a ministry but shaky ground as a church family, and a family that all we know is church."

As the whole church sits listening quietly, Kesha continues, "Our family has a history of secrets, and those secrets have impacted this ministry and our family for decades. There's a reason why I wanted to go over our bylaws before I started having this candid conversation. A lot of people believed that my parents, Bishop Andrews and Grace Andrews, adopted me and raised me to be a sister to Hakeem and Jamar Andrews. In fact, that is not true. My biological mother is also the mother of Hakeem and Jamar Andrews," Kesha admits as the church gasps collectively and many members begin to boo and yell toward the pulpit at Kesha's revelation. "You don't have to believe me," Kesha continues while pointing at one of the large stadium size screens that normally shows the service for people that can't get a clear view of the pulpit. There's an image of a DNA test result that shows Kesha, Hakeem and Raymond as 100% DNA matches. The screen then changes to a picture of Grace Andrews, and a form that says 0% match.

A member in the congregation screams "Blasphemy!" As Kesha nods in agreement.

"This may come as a surprise to many of you, especially because this was a point of contention many years ago when my father stood in front of the congregation at the old church building and said my biological mother, 'died during childbirth because of her adulterous behavior.' What he didn't mention is that my biological mother, our father and Grace Andrews had an agreement to conceive Hakeem and Jamar Andrews, but keep the arrangement a secret from Andrews Memorial, because of rules set in place by the bylaws. The bylaws clearly state that the pastor of Andrews Memorial must not have an affair, and if the wife of the pastor cannot bear children, then she is to be banished from the ministry, and punished for attempted damnation of the church. Bishop Andrews and Grace loved each other, make no mistake about that. But our father continued to have an affair with our biological mother until I was conceived, and my mother died at her own hand. Yes, she committed suicide. Our father publicly insulted and demeaned her for having a baby out of wedlock, because their affair had to be kept secret for the greater good of this ministry."

"*Liar!*" a member yells as others continue to scream.

"I respect your opinions," Kesha responds to the member that yelled at her. In the past in bible study meeting or any church service, no member was allowed to voice their opinion. It's in the bylaws that every member must be in complete agreement with the pastor of Andrews Memorial. Asking questions or challenging the pastor or any of the elders would lead to punishment, including but not limited to paddling or public whipping. The fear of having an independent idea, one opposed to that of the leadership of Andrews Memorial, has led many of the members to not own their own bibles and only purchase books that were written and published by the clergy of Andrews Memorial.

"You're a liar!" Another member screams as Kesha takes a few steps back towards her seat, that is between Hakeem and Jamar.

Still holding the microphone in her hand, Kesha says, "I say all of this to say that it's time that we look at tradition, the bylaws and this ministry to ask, what can we do better? I thought about my Trustee department and pondered this. That is why I've elected to install Raymond Nesmith as the pastor of Andrews Memorial 2, and my brother, Dr. Hakeem Andrews will pastor this building."

"What about you?" an older lady yells from the rear of the church.

"I will oversee the transfer of leadership, and soon retire from ministry," Kesha explains. "My decision has nothing to do with Monica Nesmith, but her actions did impact the timing."

"I remember Hakeem and his brother Jamar," an older gentleman yells as he walks to the center aisle of the church. He's moving slowly. "Jamar was a thug and wanted to run the streets with them gang members from Ridgely Homes. Hakeem left this ministry to work with that crackhead false prophet that had a drug addicted wife. Why do we have to follow Dr. Andrews when God has already shown he doesn't want him to be a leader? Didn't Dr. Andrews's church burn down during the Incident of Ridgely Square?"

"Per the bylaws, none of what was acceptable throughout the years should have happened," Hakeem says into the microphone as the church begins to yell at him for talking. "My brother, sister and I were born out of adultery, that was kept silent to keep up with some cockamamie bylaws that weren't from God, not from Jesus, not from the holy ghost. They were from men with agendas of control. My goal as pastor of this building is to create a bible believing atmosphere. We will work in the community; we will win souls for Christ, and we will have a place of worship that God will be pleased with."

"As pastor of Andrews Memorial 2, we will keep up with the old ways set in place by my uncle Bishop Andrews and my grandfather Pastor Andrews," Raymond confesses as he stands up. "As the pastor of Andrews Memorial 2, we will not change tradition. We will not accept the lies that have come through the mouths of these two Judas's today. All of the members of Andrews Memorial 2 will wear R. Nesmith Brand clothing every day, to be seen and viewed as the real Christians we are. We will continue to pave a path forward, with the vision that the great Bishop Andrews started us on several years ago. Next Sunday, I personally invite each member of Andrews Memorial to Andrews Memorial 2 for a real church service. In fact, I would like to go on record today and call Andrews Memorial 2, the Real Andrews Memorial at Woodstock."

"That's fine with me, cousin," Hakeem returns as he looks directly in Raymond's eyes. "Effective immediately this church building will be called the New Hope Greater Love Church."

As members begin to throw items, such as hymn books, trash, cups and pens towards Hakeem and Kesha, Raymond's inner circle joins him in the pulpit. Raymond then lifts his right hand as a way of telling everyone to stop, he then slowly lowers his hand as everyone quiets down and sits down. "My beloved church family, today marks the beginning of the end of an era in this building. I encourage the real bible believers to join me next Sunday at the Real Andrews Memorial Church. We won't be catering to the likes of street kids, drug addicts, prostitutes and women that can't keep their legs closed long enough for God to bless them with their husband as the Word of God instructed. If you want to high five your neighbor, dance and enjoy poverty, go to my cousin's church. If you want to enjoy God as my grandfather and uncle saw fit, come join me at the Real Andrews Memorial Woodstock. As for this evening, let's enjoy the festivities at the campus of my church."

Raymond drops the microphone and walks off the stage with the members of his inner circle. Gina was not among them. I warned her about the gun Raymond had and his desire to kill her, which she initially thought was a joke, but has since kept her distance from Raymond and the Inner Circle bible study group.

"Go to the back door," Marshawn demands as I walk towards the exit. The members of the church begin to yell at Kesha and Hakeem. Some of the members even begin breaking items, like the pew chairs, the cameras and the sound boards in the audio booths. A handful of members begin throwing stuff at the large screens that project the pulpit area for everyone in attendance.

As I walk out the back door, Hakeem and I make brief eye contact before I break his gaze by looking down and escaping down the stairs.

Chapter 39

That evening Kesha, Hakeem and I enjoy crabs in the kitchen of our home. Kesha was able to obtain several jumbo crabs, a couple gallons of fresh brewed sweet tea, and some of the grilled food from the cookout. We had hoped to celebrate Trinity returning home for the weekend from her inpatient program. She took her medication and went to bed sometime around 3 pm. It's amazing that the sun is still out at 8 pm. Maybe Trinity will be able to enjoy a little bit of daylight when she wakes up. While in mid thought my son Darrin walks into the kitchen with a sad look on his face.

"What's wrong with you?" I ask as he shakes his head, not wanting to talk. "Would you like some crabs?" I ask, and he shakes his head no. He silently walks over to the stove where a gallon of iced tea is sitting next to the large wooden crate with crabs in it.

"I know that look," Hakeem says as he rubs the Old Bay left on his fingers onto his white t-shirt. "Y'all broke up?"

My son silently nods yes as his face breaks down into what I can only describe as heartbroken. No tears on his face, but just heartbroken. Finally, Darrin takes off his gray hoodie and sits down at the crab-filled newspaper-covered table with Kesha, Hakeem and me.

"I'm sorry about that," Hakeem consoles as Darrin pulls a large crab towards him and begins to open it.

"It's not what you think," Darrin finally voices. "We were away on the church trip. We all had our own rooms, and Nevaeh kept trying to stay in my room every night. Finally, I let her stay, but she kept trying to have sex with me. I just wasn't feeling it at the time. I'm still a virgin or whatever, so I didn't want to do it. Plus, I didn't have a condom. She told me I didn't need one, and I told her I didn't want to get her pregnant. She started yelling at me, talking about, 'Why, do you think you're better than me?' She then told me I wasn't good enough to be her child's father and told me she was pregnant with Brother Aaron's baby, but her mom and Brother Aaron and his wife thought it would be a good idea to have sex with me, say I was the father, and the baby would have been taken care of by our family."

"Oh my God! I'm sorry you went through that," Kesha exclaims. "I will address this with Brother Aaron tomorrow. This is his third violation and per the bylaws…" Hakeem coughs in a fake way as Kesha pauses. "We're not doing things the old way anymore. We can report this to the police. Nevaeh is an underaged girl, and that falls under the category of rape. It's time that Brother Aaron is brought to justice."

"Talk to Nevaeh about it; I'm done with the whole thing and don't want to think about it anymore," my son says as we all nod in agreement and eat crabs silently for a brief moment.

"What happened at the church today?" Darrin questions as we all slap our hands on the table and exclaim with random noises. "The church bus dropped everybody off at the cookout, but the driver told me to stay on the bus and brought me here. He said it would be better and safer if I didn't get out and join the members."

"Kesha's stepping down as Bishop, Hakeem will be pastoring the Andrews Memorial building in the city, and Raymond will be pastoring the one at the Woodstock Campus," I say in response to Darrin's earlier question.

"Yeah, it didn't go over well with the church," Hakeem contributes in a joking tone.

Kesha laughs, then says, "That's putting it mildly. There's no way I would have thought things would have gone this bad."

"Andrews Memorial is a cult," Hakeem responds to his sister then chuckles. "How did you not see this coming? I saw it coming from a mile away, and I'm still surprised we got out of the cathedral alive."

"After tomorrow's church service, we can work on the whole transfer of power and how that paperwork will look," Kesha states as her voice grows deep for a brief moment before returning to light and pleasant. "That's a next-week problem. We should just enjoy this moment. We've had some good wins in the month of June. The water lines are being put down, we were able to house people displaced by the explosions and the Charm City Strangler was caught."

"I heard it was Aunt Monica," Darrin blurts out as the table falls quiet for a moment.

"It was," I confirm to my son as Kesha and Hakeem look at each other. The room falls silent again as I hear the music from the playlist Hakeem and I created play in the background. "Titan Industries finally won in the battle for us to save the homes owned by the black homeowners. They offered a quarter million dollars to all the homeowners impacted by the gas line explosions. Legit, every person that was staying in the Nesmith Suites agreed to sell their homes to Titan."

"Wait, do I have a job to return to now that Aunt Monica is locked up for them murders?" Darrin questions as we all shrug our shoulders.

"Raymond now owns the hotels," Kesha adds as Hakeem and I release a large exhale out our noses.

"I'll give you a job at the grocery store, or at the restaurant now that the water crisis has been resolved," I answer. "The Legacy of Florence should be back at 100% operation in a week or so. I just have to reach out to Sasha to see how the grocery part is on staff. Depending on how well you do, I might make you the manager at the restaurant part of Legacy of Florence."

As my son barely nods yes, he says, "She killed Duck." We all look at Darrin as he looks at the large crab, still sitting in front of him untouched. "I can't believe she killed Duck. I mean she killed a lot of people, but she killed *Duck*. She just left him in Leakin Park and didn't care. The people on the internet was saying she did it all by herself."

"We honestly don't have the words for what she did," Hakeem admits. "This is one of the saddest things we've ever had to endure as a family."

"Yeah, and we've been groomed to run a cult since childhood," Kesha jokes. This woman actually jokes.

As I find myself impressed by Kesha's ability to open up, almost reminiscent of how Erica opened up at the brunch we had a couple of weeks ago, there's a knock at the front door.

I get up and wash my hands, clean them with a paper towel and walk to the front door as everyone in the room is enjoying the fellowship. As I open the front door I see my aunt Gina. "Hey, I got the message to come over," she says as I look on confused.

"What are you talking about?" I ask. I'm more than happy for her to join us and eat crabs, but I didn't ask her to come over.

Gina shows me a text message saying to come over, sent from my phone number.

"I didn't send that, but you're more than welcome," I respond as I walk Gina into the kitchen area, and she's greeted warmly by the family. My mind goes back and forth about who sent that text message before I hear Marshawn state, "They have apps on these cell phones that can use somebody else's cell phone number. It's probably a practical joke played by one of them church members."

"Or it could be worse," Kenya yells at me standing near the entrance of the kitchen. "Didn't you say that

Raymond was going to kill your aunt? Didn't Aunt Gina rat on a whole gang of crooked police? Wasn't that gang washing money through the church and the Flamingo Club?"

"Yeah, but the church is on the outs with the Flamingo Club, and they don't want nothing to do with Tiffany or the 10th Bank until the whole Charm City Strangler investigation blows over," Marshawn responds as there's a knock on both the front and back doors of the house. I open the back door and I'm met by the muscular Deacon Harris, and he's accompanied by Evangelist Nelly, Evangelist NoLesha, Mark the truck driver, Brother Aaron and Sister Kamilah.

"What is going on?" Kesha questions as Deacon Harris places his large hands on her shoulders, keeping her seated, but making eye contact with Darrin and Hakeem, daring them to do something.

There's another knock at the front door as Deacon Harris walks past me to open it revealing Raymond Nesmith and Deacon Jordan. Deacon Harris then walks outside for a moment and returns with two large black duffle bags and places them on the floor.

I notice a look of horror on the faces of Brother Aaron and Sister Kamilah, as Deacon Jordan unzips the duffle bags revealing several whips and cords. Oh God, not like this, I begin to think. My mind is racing because I never would have thought our night would end like this. I don't want to get beat to death. I don't want anything to happen to Darrin or Trinity. Oh no, what if Trinity wakes up, comes down here and sees this?

Raymond slams the front door closed and walks into the kitchen where Gina, Kesha, Hakeem, Darrin and I are seated. "Them crabs are property of Andrews Memorial and should be on the grounds of the Real Andrews Memorial. This is an abuse of power, and a direct infraction of the bylaws set in place by our grandfather," Raymond says as he drags a chair to the table and demands that Brother Aaron take a seat with us.

As we all sit quietly in the kitchen, Raymond and Brother Harris walk into the living room area, accompanied by Evangelist NoLesha, Evangelist Nelly and Sister Kamilah. The group is talking amongst themselves as Mark the truck driver stands guard at the back door of the kitchen. I really wish I was at my grandmother's house. Since we moved into Hakeem's home this was a safe place, a new beginning for my family and I, but tonight has really soured that feeling of security I once had for this place. I was really thinking about giving Kesha my grandmother's house, or turning it into a shelter, but after this is over, we're moving into my grandmother's house.

"You act like things will be different over there than they are here," Kenya yaps at me. "Didn't you kill your father after he broke into your grandmother's house? Didn't the Alphas try to stash drugs at your grandmother's home? Didn't Marshawn kidnap you in front of your grandmother's home? Didn't the fire-bombing happen at your grandmother's home. What's your logic in returning to your grandmother's home? Here's what makes sense, moving to Baltimore County. Take the money from Erica, sell your grandmother's home and this one. Get the hell out of Baltimore City. Operate the bank and the Legacy of Florence. It don't make no sense to keep living in danger like we have been. Wait, hold that thought. It don't make no sense living in danger like y'all have been. I actually died in this damn city."

"Kenya!" I scream out loud at her, as she vanishes. I was caught off guard by her using foul language, and briefly believed she was real. I look around at Hakeem, Kesha, brother Aaron and Gina looking at me.

"Who's Kenya?" Brother Aaron questions and Gina answers, "Her daughter. She was killed in a hit and run back in 2016."

"Why did you say her name?" Brother Aaron questions.

"It's tradition for black mothers to call on the ancestors and dead loved ones in a time of trouble," Gina blabs, covering for me. We have a moment of eye contact as she winks her eye at me.

A brief moment of silence passes as Sister Kamilah walks into the kitchen with a black whip, and hands it to Hakeem. Raymond follows Kamilah into the kitchen with a smile on his face, holding a blue steel revolver.

"Hey cousin, per the bylaws, Brother Aaron's behavior is punishable by death," Raymond says looking at my husband but with his gun pointed downward to the ground.

"What did I do since I was punished the last time," Brother Aaron panics as Mark the truck driver holds Brother Aaron down in the chair by his shoulders.

"You had sex with the young lady Nevaeh," Raymond answers. "She's an underaged girl. We have a growing problem with you at the church. You keep breaking the bylaws, but you clearly understand them. It's like a sickness you have. No matter the praying, and the work we do, you continue to disobey God and the ordinance set in place by this ministry. So, we're going to help you."

"How… how are you going to help me?" Brother Aaron responds in a panic.

"Well, that young lady Nevaeh is pregnant by you," Raymond answers as Darrin glances up at Raymond and is met by a quick eye wink, before Raymond continues to address Brother Aaron. "Your wife is sick of your cheating, and I'm sick of you having sex with underaged women and embarrassing this ministry. So I want us to go back to the original sin, and address that."

"What was my original sin? I'm sorry. Please don't do this," Brother Aaron pleads with tears and snot running down his face. Gina and I have not stopped looking at each other in pure fear of what will happen next. Hakeem is barely looking at Raymond and his facial expression turns to anger.

"Do you remember Michelle?" Raymond questions as Brother Aaron looks confused. "Many, many years ago we went away on the annual church trip. You and I were teenagers. You raped Sister Michelle."

"I don't know who that is," Brother Aaron screams in fear.

"At the time that was Hakeem's girlfriend. You were paddled by the church elders and her parents for what you did. That was your original sin. Today we will extinguish your heathen behavior, once and for all. Dr. Hakeem Andrews, would you mind taking this reprobate piece of garbage to the living room and whip him until he can't move anymore."

"No," Hakeem responds.

"Excuse me, Elder? Or should I say Doctor? I know y'all educated folks take that title seriously," Raymond returns. "Per the church's bylaws I'm well within my rights. His wife has affirmed his behavior and agrees with this discipline as appropriate, as ordained by God and Andrews Memorial."

"I'm not going to do it," Hakeem reaffirms.

"Fine," Raymond says, rolling his eyes before pulling the gun upwards and pointing it at Brother Aaron. "Brother Aaron, would you like to say a prayer or repent for your deeds and transgressions against God, your wife, the church and Sister Nevaeh?"

"Yes, please," Brother Aaron pleads. As he begins to say, "Our Father, who art in heaven—" Three loud bangs are heard as Brother Aaron's face falls lifelessly to his chest. Raymond shot him three times in the chest area and blood begins to drain from his chest cavity.

"May my works be pleasing to you, heavenly Father," Raymond says, holding the smoking revolver with his eyes closed, as if he were praying.

"I didn't come here for this," Mark the truck driver says before opening the back door to walk outside. Before he can take a step outside a loud bang is heard and he falls onto the wooden steps outside the door. A person outside can be heard yelling, "They shootin' in Rev's house." People in the community have often called Hakeem by the nickname "Rev," and even though he hates it, he's started to embrace the name.

Raymond then makes eye contact with my aunt Gina as Sister Kamilah, Evangelist NoLesha and Evangelist Nelly run out the front door in fear, leaving it wide open. "Deacon Harris, can you please take Brother Aaron's body to the church van?" Raymond asks as Deacon Harris walks over to Aaron's lifeless body, still seated on the chair, and throws the corpse on his shoulders, as if Deacon Harris were a fireman rescuing someone from a burning building. Deacon Harris then begins walking Brother Aaron's lifeless body from the kitchen to the living room area, down the front steps and into the white church van. After dumping the body,

Deacon Harris returns to the house as Raymond instructs him to pick up Mark the truck driver and take him to the van as well.

Deacon Harris made several attempts to lift Mark, before he gave up and just drags Mark by his feet from the outside of the home back through the kitchen, into the living room, down the stairs and yanks him aggressively into the church van. Deacon Harris returns to the home, slamming the front and rear doors shut.

"Deacon Harris, can you do me another favor," Raymond questions as Deacon Harris agrees. "Can you take the two of them and dump them at Leakin Park. I have some sheets from the Nesmith Suites you can throw over their bodies once you get there. After you do that, can you come back here? We still have some more ministry work to do tonight."

Deacon Harris agrees as I see the look of panic on Gina's face. Hakeem, Kesha, Darrin and I all look forward at each other in silence. A few years ago, I would have been scared out of my mind, but right now, I just want to make sure that Darrin and Trinity are ok. If I could some kind of way make it to the couch, I could grab one of the guns we have hidden and take Raymond out myself.

Raymond turns his attention towards my son and says, "Brother Darrin, life hasn't been kind to you, has it?" Darrin does not respond or flinch. My son continues to look towards Gina, me and Hakeem as Raymond says, "It's a shame what street kids like you have had to endure just to live. You poor cursed sons of Ham have no idea what iniquities you're born into. When your friend Duck was targeted, my mother thought it would make you run to the church and would have helped convert you to be a soldier for Christ. It took the beauty of Nevaeh and the displaced people from the gas explosions, to get you to buy into this ministry. Now here you are, in the counsel of the ungodly, standing in the way of sinners and sitting in the seat of the scornful. It's not your fault, you didn't ask to be the sinner you are. I didn't either. Thank God my mother adopted me after the woman who birthed me overdosed and left me in that home. God could have spared my little sister and had me die, but he saw an anointing, a purpose on me. A purpose my parents, Monica and Kelly Nesmith molded. A purpose that Bishop Andrews guided. A purpose that I embrace, and I will show you."

"Leave him alone," Gina yells, but didn't get out of the seat at the kitchen table. The smell of crabs has dissipated and has been drowned out by the smell of gunpowder and blood.

"Ah yes, the other original sin," Raymond voices, turning his attention to my aunt. He walks to the living room to grab another black duffle bag, pulling out a shotgun with a wooden stock. "Gina Simms, your sins go back longer than I've been in ministry. Where do we begin… your drug abuse, adulterous behavior, cheating on your husband, exchanging sex for money, stealing from family members and lying to everyone that has ever loved you, just to get high."

"I've repented for my sins and for who I was in the past," Gina boldly responds. "I've dedicated my life to trying to do right, including helping the victims the Alphas were sex trafficking. I even help run the addictions group at Andrews Memorial."

"You ran from your sin and your role in the downfall of this city," Raymond yells. "You allowed the gangs and those police in NAFA to go down, but you were given witness protection. Then you came back and were given a TV show and a podcast by Nubian Media. Why? Because you're a sinner that has sold her soul. The Bible says what profits a man to gain the whole world but lose his own soul."

"I've seen men like you before," Gina proclaims. "Men that think having a gun, or some powerful position gives them the right to look down on others. You know what those men did every time? They paid me to make them feel good. Look at you. As tall and strong as you are, you're nothing but a lost child. You're nothing without your mother. Your mother who murdered people right under your nose."

"Oh that's where you're wrong, whore," Raymond quips. "When my mother came back from Africa, after killing General Midnight and his demonic soldiers wrapped in the flesh of children, we had a revelation from God. That revelation was to clean this city up to help with God's return. God has been punishing this city for centuries, between the political corruption, the Flamingo Club, the drugs, closed businesses, dying economy. It was time we started doing the will of God, and taking out those who thrive on mocking what our savior and redeemer has done. The street children selling drugs, doing drugs, driving dirt bikes causing accidents and harassing hard working people at red lights to wash their windows. I mean seriously, these street kids are washing windows with squeegees. What about the rest of the car? Why can't they wash the car? So we did what any reasonable Christian would do, we went on a crusade in the name of Christ."

"You killed children," Gina corrects as Raymond frowns at her.

"No, we made sacrifices to the appreciation of God," Raymond yells back. "You weren't in Africa. You didn't lose your father to the demonic forces over there. You have been living with clean hands and a pure heart and all of this is your fault. If it wasn't for your involvement with Anna Cartwright, telling the world about the Alphas, General Midnight's operations would have continued to go under the radar, and everybody would have been at peace. But you opened your mouth. The Alphas were incarcerated. Paul Douglass was murdered, and General Midnight had to figure out how to continue his operation while the Flamingo Club continued to conduct business as usual without giving a second thought to what was coming in retaliation."

"What retaliation?" Gina screams.

"Bishop and Grace Andrews were murdered by General Midnight and his soldiers," Raymond screams back. "My father was murdered. Kesha's husband was murdered. Those kids raped my mother and were going to keep sexually assaulting her, then they were going to kill her. But she was given the strength of Sampson to kill each one of those children and General Midnight. Did the Flamingo Club thank her? No. Did they invite me in? No. But we had another play in the works."

"What are you talking about?" Kesha speaks up, not in a deep voice, but in a regular tone. "You know good and damn well you were never going to have a seat at the Flamingo Club table. That was never your role."

"Correct, my dear cousin," Raymond affirms loudly as the back door opens and Deacon Harris walks through, startling Raymond. Raymond turns and without thought shoots Deacon Harris twice with the shotgun. Deacon Harris falls backwards out of the doorway. "Shit!" Raymond panics as Deacon Harris squirms on the wooden steps and the back door's threshold. "I'm sorry, Harris, that was a mistake," Raymond says as he walks over to Deacon Harris, squirming in pain. "Great is his faithfulness, his mercies begin afresh each morning," Raymond says, standing above Deacon Harris before firing a shot into his chest, stopping him from moving. Hakeem, Kesha, Darrin, Gina and I all look on in silence as we notice the mercy killing Raymond just carried out for his mistaken shooting of Deacon Harris.

"Dear brothers and sisters, honor those who are your leaders in the Lord's work. They work hard among you and give you spiritual guidance," Raymond says to himself before turning his attention back to everyone at the kitchen table. The smell of gunpowder and blood has now mixed in the air with the faint scent of crabs along with the stench of urine and trash from the alley thanks to our open back door.

"Where was I?" Raymond says as he paces the kitchen, walking over to the stove and glancing at the food in the to go trays that came from the church's cookout. "Ah yes, I knew I would never have a seat at the Flamingo Club's table, but I was offered something greater. A place in the Dulaney Crime Family. All I had to do was take control from my dear cousin Kesha. I didn't plan for Hakeem to come back to Andrews Memorial, but things are always subject to change; it just takes the ability to adjust on the fly. Speaking of which, let's meet in the living room. Darrin, can you close that back door, and Tiffany, I need you to warm me up a plate. I want two of those ribeye steaks and those smoked collard greens," Raymond orders as he walks to the living room, picking up another shotgun out the duffle bag.

"You don't come into my home and give orders to my wife," Hakeem barks as Raymond points the shotgun at Hakeem.

"Shut up and get yo' uppity black ass in the living room," Raymond demands as Hakeem raises his hands as if he were surrendering. Raymond, Gina and Kesha quietly walk out the kitchen area and head to the white couch we purchased from Costco earlier this year. Raymond, briefly glancing at Darrin, pulls Deacon Harris out of the doorway and barks, "Hurry up," before walking into the living room and sitting on the white couch with the flower designs that used to be at my grandmother's home. Darrin, after finally closing the back door, joins Raymond on the white couch. As I open the microwave door, I notice Trinity's bottles of Tramadol and Tofranil sitting next to the microwave which was above the silverware drawer and next to our refrigerator. I open the microwave, and then place two of the ribeye steaks and collard greens on the white plate. I glance back and notice Raymond is still talking to Hakeem and Kesha, so I open the two bottles of Trinity's medication and begin breaking the pills apart in my hands and sprinkling the powder on the steak and greens. I place the plate in the microwave quickly, setting the timer for 2 minutes, and then wash my hands.

"The food ready yet?" Raymond yaps as I point at the timer on the microwave. I notice Darrin is seated right where we stash the handguns in the couch, as there's a knock at the door. Darrin attempts to answer the door, but Raymond demands that I go to the door and answer it. "Tell them anything is off in here and I will kill everyone in this room. You understand me, Jezebel?"

Raymond orders as I walk to the front door and open it partially. To my surprise, Aleem is standing outside with three members of the Knights.

"Are you ok, Sister Tiffany?" Aleem questions, trying to look past the blocked doorway. Full transparency, now I'm scared. If Aleem sees this situation on the inside, we're all dead. If I don't say anything, Raymond still might kill us. I look on silently as I hear Raymond in the background demanding I, "answer the man."

"Yes, of course," I respond in a shaky tone. My eyes dart from Aleem's eyes to the door, and then back to Aleem. Hoping that he would catch a clue to what I'm trying to hint at.

"We had several reports of gun shots, and a person said they saw someone drag a body from out the home to a large white van. Are you sure you're ok? Is Hakeem ok?" Aleem questions as I nod yes.

"I don't know what any of those reports were about," I respond, looking at Aleem's feet, and not making eye contact. "It didn't come from here."

"Ok, Sister Tiffany," Aleem responds. "If you need any help, give us a call." I start blinking my eyes rapidly at Aleem as he nods and glances back at the members of the Knights standing behind him. "Have a good night,"

Aleem says loudly as the group walks down the steps and onto the sidewalk.

I close the front door to the sound of beeping coming from the microwave. Raymond and Gina are both looking at me as I walk to the kitchen on unsteady legs to get the plate. I glance at the plate to see if the powder from the pills is visible, but they're completely absorbed in the steak and the collard greens. As I walk the plate out to Raymond, he asks that I set it on the coffee table and grab a seat on the recliner.

"Gina," Raymond calls out. "The bible says if you try to hang on to your life, you will lose it, but if you give up your life for my sake and for the sake of the Good News, you will save it. You have lived a life of self service, from being a drug addict, a prostitute, a bad mother, a horrible wife that caused your husband's death, doing that documentary about the police and the Alphas. You even came out of witness protection to get back into the spotlight. Then you, as a wolf in sheep's clothing, came into my church and tried to infiltrate our holy land. Today I charge you with death," Raymond states in a monotone voice before there's a deafening blast. As I try to put together what just happened, I see blood sprayed on the wall and my aunt's head rocked back, and there is a largehole in her blue dress.

"He killed her!" Darrin says as he looks like he's about to reach for the gun in the chair, but I shake my head no at him. Darrin yells, "You killed Aunt Gina! The hell is wrong with you?"

"She's the start of all of our problems," Raymond professes as he grabs the plate off the coffee table. I can see my aunt Gina's hand make small movements, and I think she's trying to lift her head back to a normal position. Is this one of those Marshawn Bell or Kenya delusions or is she really trying to hang in there and not die? "Tiffany, would you be a dear and get me a fork and knife?" Raymond requests and I walk into the kitchen in fear that he might shoot me in the back, or kill my son, or my husband. As I walk past Kesha, I notice that she's sweating profusely and trying not to overreact.

I return to the living room with the fork and knife, and notice Raymond has turned the TV on, and is flipping through channels. He lands on a channel showcasing a boxing match. Before I can take a seat, Raymond cuts several small pieces of steak, demanding that I take a piece, along with Darrin, Hakeem and Kesha. "Just want to make sure you didn't poison my food," Raymond says with an unnerving grin. The odd part to this is, I'm not sure if the pills will put me to sleep, cause a psychotic break or cause me to overdose and die. I snatch the piece of steak from him and begin to eat it; Hakeem and Kesha do the same. Raymond looks at Darrin and says, "After all this is over, I'm going to make sure you're raised the right way. The Andrews Memorial way."

"What are you talking about?" Darrin reacts. "You just shot hella people in our home and killed my aunt."

"They were sinners, boy." Raymond answers as he begins to eat the collard greens. "My birth mother was a sinner like your mom and real dad. Thank God for my spiritual mom, Monica, for making sure I was raised the right way. People like Hakeem want to reap the rewards of God but want to run from what God has ordained as righteous. I'm just trying to fix the deception your stepfather has caused."

"He is my father," Darrin proclaims as Raymond chuckles at Darrin. As Darrin attempts to look at Gina's body, Raymond requests that my son continues to watch the boxing match. As Raymond returns to eating, I feel my eyes grow heavy, and I notice that Hakeem and Kesha are yawning and rubbing their eyes. I never noticed how much they look alike until just now and begin to laugh to myself. If Jamar was still alive, the three of them would probably be considered triplets. As time begins to move slowly, Raymond cleans his plate and starts to yawn, and glances at the TV through glassy eyes. Through the blinds, I can see flickering blue and red lights outside, and when I look back at Raymond, he is sleep. I turn to my son, who's barely awake and signal for him to go outside. He points at Kesha and Hakeem sleeping on the couch, separated by Gina's body.

I try to move off the couch to get the shotgun from Raymond as he's sleeping, when I notice that my arms and legs are heavy, and I can't move. My eyes blink continuously, each blink a little longer than the last. Darrin attempts to get up as loud shouting and yelling is heard from a loudspeaker outside. Darrin changes the channel to the news, and we have a live look at the outside of our home with several police vehicles along with an armored silver and black tank-like vehicle that has the Baltimore City Police Department's decal on the side.

"If Raymond sees them outside, we're all dead," I whisper to Darrin. He nods in agreement and sneaks towards the front door. I fan for him to leave, and he attempts to gesture for me to follow him. I shake my head no, and then watch as the door opens and Darrin leaves out the house.

Chapter 40

I'm standing in the cemetery with my aunt Gina and Marshawn. The sky is cloudy but streaks of red and orange can be seen above and through the clouds. The air is still, and there's no noise from the community in the background. Glancing down I see a broken clock that has 12:34 blinking repeatedly on my grandmother's grave, the time she was pronounced dead at the hospital. I turn to look at the grave next to my grandmother's and I see the name Tina Simms, my aunt Gina's daughter. She took her life by swallowing pills in a bathroom back in 2016. Around that time, my aunt was active in her addiction, then again, she could have been getting clean. Who really knows the truth when it comes to addiction and recovery. All I know is my aunt has been clean from the heroin and the crack for the last few years.

"Saying goodbye is never easy," Gina says, looking down at Tina's gravesite before turning towards Kenya's grave. The grave is open and there's no casket inside.

"You know she's gone," Gina points out, walking to her grave. "By gone, I mean dead. She crossed over years ago, and it's nothing you could have done about it. Why are you carrying this guilt?"

"Because…" I pause to think before answering, "for once in my life, I was doing everything right. I owned a home. I owned a restaurant and a grocery store. Aunt Gina, I owned a bank. I was fighting Titan Industries and was winning. Then it seems like everything fell apart. It fell apart when I got married."

"Don't blame your husband for any of this," Gina explains. "Your husband has gone through a lot, just like you. You see the type of family he came from. The church he was raised in. Believe it or not, you probably was the most sane person he ever dealt with. Well, you and Pastor Donald Avery," Gina expresses as she points at Donald Avery's headstone.

"I'm not blaming him," I counter. "If it wasn't for Hakeem, the 10th Bank would have never gotten off the ground. We would have never been able to fight against Titan Industries. We saved so many black homeowners in the city. We financed so many black owned businesses in the city. We opened so many doors. But I feel like a failure."

"Why?" Gina questions. "Is it because of the gas and water line explosions that destroyed homes? That was going to happen. The pipes were outdated. You raised the money to make sure the underserved communities were able to get the pipes put down first. Mayor Hugo tried to serve the finance district and the thriving communities. Erica tried to use the water crisis as a method to gentrify areas like this."

"And she won," I admit, looking at my grandmother's grave. "I failed."

"You made a difference," Gina attempts to cheer me up. "Your grandmother's home was rebuilt, along with several homes in Ridgely Square, Westport and Mount Winans. Let's not get started on the work you did in Harlem Park, Walbrook, and so many other areas of the city. You did that. Nobody can take that from you."

"But all those people took the money and are moving out the city," I retort as Gina looks up at the discolored sky. The clouds are very still and moving extremely fast at the same time.

"You didn't fail," Gina returns. "This isn't denial, it's the truth. You did everything you could, raised enough money to be successful, and then life happened. Life that you can't control."

"Then why does it hurt so bad?" I ask, looking at Kenya's grave. "How many more of these graves will be filled with people that will die like Kenya, from hit and runs and violence in this city. I need to help them, but I failed. I even failed you."

"You failed me?" Gina questions in a playful tone. "Child, I came out of witness protection to spend time with you, and I did. I came out of witness protection to get to know your children, my family. Guess what, I did that too. I had a TV show and a podcast. Both were very successful. You didn't fail me; you gave me a second chance. I failed Tina as a mother. I failed Larry as a wife. I got a chance to see what Tina could have been, by watching you grow, hustle and become the legend you've become. Your resume alone is untouchable. You went from a single mother of 5 in a section 8 apartment to a successful home and business owner. You're a household name, and guess what… you didn't have to take off your clothes to achieve the success you achieved. You didn't need Hakeem or any man to be the thriving woman you are today. You earned the title, "The Mom of Baltimore," because of your hard work, and compassion."

"But you're dead," I say in a sad tone as Gina shakes her head no. "It's my fault. You came back for me."

"I made a choice," Gina dismisses my claim. "I was in witness protection, seeing all the beauty this country had to offer, but what I needed most was family. You gave that to me. It wasn't easy, and for a long time you gave me a hard time, and I deserved it for my past. Here's the thing, my past didn't define me. Yeah, I was a drug addict, yeah, I was a sex worker. What am I now?"

"Dead?" I answer in a confused tone.

Gina laughs, then says, "Yeah, but no. I brought down the Alphas and NAFA. I had a successful TV show and podcast. I'm a household name. I made amends for the things I could not change, and worked hard as shit to make a difference in the things I could. That's what you're doing. You gave your best friend a job at your grocery store. Your son will be working at the restaurant soon. Your husband will be pastoring one of the biggest black churches in America very soon. Because of the Tiffany Gibbons effect."

"My name is Tiffany Andrews," I correct.

"There was a season your name was Tiffany Gibbons," Gina continues. "Now you're in a season where your name is Tiffany Andrews. There was a season you was a sexual assault and molestation victim of your father, but you saved yourself that day in your basement with that gun. There was a season you faced homelessness, then you became a homeowner. Your friend, Sasha, was homeless, you opened the door for her into your home, until she decided to move out of your home and into mine. Seasons, Tiffany. Sasha left for a season, and now she's back. Hakeem left Andrews Memorial for a season and came back. If it wasn't for Hakeem's return, those people in that church would be stuck in the "bylaws" that make them a cult."

"What about the season where I tried to save the city, and failed?" I question.

"Who said the season has passed?" Gina answers. "You plant and water seeds in the right seasons. Then comes the harvest season. All the seasons don't happen at once. Your twins, Darrin and Desha, they're almost adults. There was a season when you breastfed them, carried them, changed their diapers, washed their clothes, read stories to them at night and helped them with their homework. Now look, Desha is traveling with a band and has colleges begging her to play for their school. Darrin is almost an adult and trying to find his way. He wants to work, he wants to drive, he wants to run the restaurant and the grocery store. He wants to run the bank if you let him. Seasons change, Tiffany, you just have to plant and water and trust that God will give the increase."

"What's the increase?" I ask as Gina points to a rose growing from out of the grass in the cemetery. "The increase is the harvest," Gina answers pointing at the rose that doesn't have a color. I know it's red, but I can't make it out.

"Jamar was in your life for a season," Gina adds. "In that season he gave you the gun that you used to kill your father. That was a seed planted, watered and the increase was you freed yourself from the person that victimized you."

"Come with me!" a voice yells as I look around to see where it came from. "Get up, we have to go," the male voice repeats as Gina vanishes and everything turns black, then my eyes open.

I'm back in the living room, as several people wearing tactical gear are in the home grabbing Hakeem, Kesha and me from the living room.

"My, my daughter, Trinity," I utter to one of the SWAT team members. "She's upstairs sleep. Please don't let her see any of this. Tell her I said it will be ok."

"Let's go, ma'am," the SWAT officer says picking me up and carrying me towards the door. His foot hit the coffee table making a loud screeching sound, causing Raymond to wake up.

"What are you doing?" Raymond questions as he reaches for the shotgun leaning against his leg. As Raymond grabs the firearm, two of the SWAT officers inside the home turn their black assault rifles towards him and begin firing multiple rounds, dropping him lifelessly to the couch.

"That's the end of his season," Gina says in the back of my mind. "Now it's time to cultivate the ground and plant a better harvest.

As the officer walks me outside and reunites me with Darrin, Kesha and Hakeem, we all hug and I say softly, "New Harvest."

Hakeem tightens his hold on me and says, "I like that. Let's rename Andrews Memorial to New Harvest Baptist Church."

"I love the name," Kesha says with a smile as Commissioner Mercer and Mayor Hugo walk towards us.

"I didn't think you could pull it off that fast," Mayor Hugo says to me with a serious look on his face. "You had the majority of the City of Baltimore turn their backs on y'all, but within the chaos of tonight, everyone is back on your side. There's a lot to process regarding this situation, but I would like to extend the invitation to join the Flamingo Club."

"No, thank you," Hakeem answers.

"We're going to go in a new direction," Hugo responds to Hakeem. "We want your wife and the 10th Bank with the Flamingo Club. I feel that with your sister and your wife at the table, this could be a great new start for everyone. Maybe the Flamingo Club having an influence with Andrews Memorial had too much of a negative impact on the church."

"Thank you," I answer. "I look forward to talking to you about my position in the Flamingo Club in the coming weeks. Right now, I want to focus on my family and getting the bank, restaurant and market back up to speed."

The mayor and the police commissioner turn around and walk towards a group of officers huddled near the armored tank.

Hakeem, Kesha, Darrin and I continue to hug as Kesha says, "Is this what it's like to have family moments? Not like the photo opportunities that dad used to organize, but those real heartfelt moments."

"Yeah," I answer confused by Kesha's question.

"Mind you, everything about our lives was based on how it looked for the church," Kesha explains, with a light-hearted tone. "Even my marriage was arranged. Hakeem left the church at 18 because my dad was going to have him marry some girl from Parker Memorial in Texas. What was her name, Hakeem?"

"Monet," Hakeem answers loudly.

"Monet, that's right," Kesha responds, snapping her fingers. "She's now Monet Dingle; she's married to the gospel singer Luther Dingle. Anyway, Hakeem, you and Tiffany have the church, I'm going to run the Ginger Hill Research Center. We're all good, right?"

"I think we might should do family counseling," Darrin jokes as we all chuckle.

"Any other ideas?" I ask.

"Yeah, the Woodstock Campus," Darrin continues. "Why don't we build more homes on the site. Then we can sell the homes on the campus to the people Erica gave the money to. We can have our own neighborhood, with a college campus and a prep school. The campus even has a homeless shelter, so we can help the homeless get on their feet."

Hakeem and I make eye contact and nod in agreement as my daughter Trinity is being brought out the house by police officers. Hakeem says, "I think that's a great idea and we should do it. I don't know about the family counseling thing right now; it's not like both our families are crazy…"

"We all know my family crazy," I express as Hakeem starts laughing loudly. Wait, *seriously?* Darrin and Kesha just chuckled, but why Hakeem laughing like that? I'm starting to feel some kind of way.

"They better not ask me to preach at Aaron's funeral," Hakeem says with a giant grin.

"Why?" Every last one of us questions at the same time.

"Because I'm going to start my sermon with an icebreaker. I'm going to go 'Who knows the statute of limitations for premeditated murder? You know, for a scum bag rapist. Sike, just kidding, Aaron's right here. He's already dead." Hakeem jokes as Kesha and Darrin start to laugh. Maybe I'm not the crazy one, maybe he's the crazy one.

"We're all crazy," Marshawn adds.

Chapter 41

The next few weeks were a different pace in Baltimore City. The park pools finally opened, along with the annual summer festivals like AFRAM and Artscape. Some of the restaurants, markets and companies that had to close due to the water crisis began reopening. I was able to partner with Mayor Hugo and Erica to provide some financial relief to many of the business owners. Of course, the hostage situation that my family endured with Raymond Nesmith helped put me back in the good graces of the citizens of Baltimore City.

Guy Dulaney was almost able to ask for a new trial for Carson Jessup; sadly, the racist prick of a religious leader never made it to court, as he was shot by a sniper while entering the courthouse. This sparked a lot of debates, the first being people blamed the murder of Carson Jessup on the copycat AFK. Some people even tried to say that there was a child's toy next to the shell casing from the bullet that killed the racist religious leader. The second debate was how would Carson Jessup be remembered. If the judge would have granted Carson Jessup a new trial, then the murder would have made him a free man, and every Right Hand of God Fellowship Church member that Carson turned in would have gotten a new trial or an appeal. The murder of Carson Jessup negated that whole idea. The other part to that debate was many of the people Carson Jessup turned on and helped incarcerate took plea deals, so they wouldn't be eligible for a new trial or an appeal without Carson Jessup going to trial first.

Monica Nesmith was transferred to a federal facility in West Virginia, but Hakeem and Kesha have refused to have any dealings with her. My aunt Gina's was the last funeral held at Andrews Memorial before the name was officially changed to New Harvest Baptist Church. The funeral had a large turnout, which isn't surprising when you think of all the lives my aunt impacted from 2017 until the day she was murdered. Mayor Hugo Titan gave her a mayor's citation to honor her life. Ms. Clair of Nubian Media agreed to pay for a headstone, but actually had a monument built at the grave site, based on a picture she found of Gina, my uncle Larry and their daughter Tina. Ms. Clair also created an in memoriam section at the station that had several pictures of Silk, the transwoman who used to be a radio personality for Ms. Clair's radio station but was fired for having sex with Ms. Clair's ex-husband. Silk was murdered by my father while sex working back in 2016.

Today, we celebrate the first Sunday service at the newly renovated New Harvest Baptist Church, which is Andrews Memorial, but a lot of the items tied to Hakeem's family were placed in a Glen Burnie storage unit. The 10th Bank and New Harvest Baptist Church have worked together to build more homes on the Woodstock Campus, and we even had discussions about having the Knights patrol the new community that we're going to rename Avery and Simms Crossings. Even the college and the prep school will be called Avery and Simms College. The New Harvest Baptist Church was able to absorb the Nesmith Suites, but we're unsure how we're going to reopen the hotel.

"Hebrews 12:11 says, 'No discipline is enjoyable while it is happening, it is painful. But afterward there will be a peaceful harvest of right living for those who are trained in this way,'" Hakeem begins preaching to a congregation with nearly 40 people in it. I'm sitting on the second pew of the church, in what used to be the VIP section. Darrin, Desha, RJ and Trinity are sitting about two pews behind me, looking on their phones and tablets.

"Brothers and sisters, can I be real a second?" Hakeem continues, "I really didn't want to preach again. I hated the idea of this calling. I didn't want to be in this building because of what it represented to my siblings and me. Then a kid named Duck was murdered by the Charm City Strangler, and I was asked to speak to those that were grieving from his death. One of the people grieving was my son, Darrin. Who can say no to their own child? But I was conflicted. I felt like God took so much from me. Jamar was murdered by Paul Douglass and Roland Wise back in 2019. People were dying from COVID-19, my church was burned to the ground, my wife's family home was burned down, my youngest daughter was traumatized from the fire-bombing. I helped with some legislation to secure black homeownership, but it was shot down in the state senate. I mean, there were a lot of losses attached to me. I thought I was being punished by God. Let me tell you something. It's important to know who you attach yourself to. Not just in the spirit world, but in the natural."

"When God created the sun, it was good," Hakeem continues. "When God created the water, the birds, the beasts, the fish, all those things were good. The word of God says that a man that finds a woman finds a good thing. The good thing in creation that God called good is the same thing that is said about finding a woman. When I found my wife, it was during some of the roughest of times. Her grandmother and her daughter died. Her niece committed suicide, the city had riots, thanks to the death of Tyrone Clinton and Kannard Lyles-Bey. But God blessed our relationship from the beginning all the way to this moment right now. I was bitter at God because things didn't go how I wanted. I wanted my parents to be more involved in my life. I wanted ministry to be better than it was at Andrews Memorial. I wanted my brother to be alive, sitting right in the same row as my beautiful wife. I wanted Duck to be alive, still having fun with Darrin. I felt that either God wasn't real, or I was cursed. But as the text states, no discipline is enjoyable."

Hakeem stops for a moment to drink water out of his glass cup before picking up the microphone and walking down the steps of the pulpit and standing in front of the pews. "This morning, my wife and I had breakfast, and I mean a big breakfast. The kids ate too. Don't worry, you don't have to call Child Protective Services, we fed Darrin, Desha, Trinity and RJ." Members of the congregation begin to laugh at Hakeem's joke. "Here's the thing, my wife and I started this game during our honeymoon in Jamaica of asking a random question to make you think. We still play the game from time to time. Today my wife asked, 'If you could bring back one TV show for one more season, what would it be. My answer was Awake. It was a show about a police officer that had a bad car accident. He wasn't sure when he was awake or when he was dreaming. In one reality his wife was alive, and the son died in the accident, in the other reality his son was alive, and his wife was dead. I used to love that show, but the reason why is because I hoped that I was dreaming and in reality, my parents were normal, my brother was a part of this ministry, and Kesha didn't have to take on so many tasks from a child up to now. We don't get what we want in this life, even as Bible believers. But God blessed me with a wife, my good thing. In that good thing, I now have 4 great children. I have a church I'm pastoring. I'm now in a position to help so many people with the shelter, the college, the school and the homes at the Avery and Simms Crossing.

"It wasn't easy to get here," Hakeem admits. "My aunt and my cousin turned out to be serial killers. We experienced a water crisis, that my good thing helped resolve. A lot of people lost their homes but were able to get paid a substantial amount of money and start new beginnings in other places. While I was against it for a long time, some things are not for me to decide, it's God's choice. My goal is to stay in his grace and mercy and to be obedient to his word and call. Today, while we stand on fertile ground, at the birth of this new ministry, New Harvest Baptist Church, I ask you to join me here at this altar for prayer. Let us plant seeds today for a beautiful harvest tomorrow."

As members get up from the pews to join Hakeem for prayer, an usher hands me an envelope with the words, we need to talk, written in black ink on it. As I open the white envelope, I notice a green army man toy and instantly realize that AFK gave it to the usher. The copycat AFK was the real AFK all along, and he killed Carson Jessup. This can't be good news for Baltimore City, and what could he want with me?

To be continued in The Confession: Bastards and Gentlemen

Letter From the Author

I'm glad to be at the close of this part of the story and doing the prep work for *The Transition*. Being honest with you all, this had to be the hardest book to write in the series for a couple of reasons. Reason number 1, we're 1 book away from ending this series. Characters like Tiffany, Darrin, Hakeem, Gina, Sasha and Erica have been around since 2018's *The Wake*. I had to make it a point to grow the characters. In *The Wake* Hakeem and Tiffany were both the morale anchor characters. You could always depend on those two to make the tough choices. Tiffany was/is the eyes and ears into this universe, so making her the morally secure character throughout the series didn't seem like the best idea. So at the end of *The Void*, I chose to make her more of a morally gray character. She's still the protagonist but having Hakeem as the morally just character fit perfectly, especially with Tiffany being the narrator and the eyes the viewer has to look through. While writing *The Legacy* I wanted to shift the moral point of view from Hakeem to Darrin. It was easy to do with the Action Figure Killer mis-directions. Then the church scene with Paul Douglass, Alex Tillman and Darrin made it easier for the reader to get behind Darrin. In this book, you feel for Darrin because of his interactions with Duck, Hakeem and Tiffany.

That brings me to reason number 2, writing such a big story with so many moving parts. The Andrews Memorial cult, the Charm City Strangler and the Water Crisis were tough topics to cover for any 1 book, so having them crash into each other to create a super problem was interesting. I didn't want to shy away from it, and purposely wrote myself into concerns on this. One of the challenges was Ms. Pugh and Monica Nesmith. I didn't want the two characters to come off sounding like each other. Ms. Pugh is a grieving grandmother, and a community leader. Monica Nesmith is a devoted church leader to a cult and surviving elder of the Andrews family. I thought about keeping the two separated, I also thought about making them the same character.

That brings me to reason number 3. I wanted to write the story with what logically made sense but would keep my audience guessing. Remember there's a satisfying end to this saga coming up in *The Transition*. I didn't want this book to focus on set up. *The Wake, The Void* and *The Legacy* were their own stories, continued an over-arching story, but didn't rely on the next book to tell each story. With *The Union*, Tiffany and Hakeem are married. Tiffany is secure in her role as a bank owner and community leader. Hakeem has the role of community leader, doesn't want the title of preacher anymore, and is grieving over his brother, parents and his life. Hakeem believes he's a failure and is holding everybody back, yet at times he knows he has to be the person to step up to make the tough decisions. He also knows that he has to be the role model/symbol that Darrin and Duck need for hope. That's why making Duck and Darrin the heart and soul of the story was important. With the changes to Hakeem's character, and Darrin's development, it only made sense to payoff Darrin's growth as the heart and the moral compass for Hakeem and Tiffany.

Choosing to write about a cult was a tough decision as well. I was born and raised in churches. My father was a deacon, my mother is a missionary, Sunday school teacher and some more stuff. That being said, I figured writing this story would be offensive to some of my devoted church friends, family members, loved ones and fans. This book was never an attack on any religion. It was more of the next step to show who Hakeem really is. When you strip away the titles of preacher, pastor and doctor, who is Hakeem Andrews? What makes him tick. Is it the guilt and grief from Jamar's demise? He lost an election he was guaranteed to win because of Jamar's murder. He learned how his parents died and he returned to Andrews Memorial just to see how much of a mess the church has become.

Hakeem is caught between resuming a role of pastor that he started to hate, or just continuing to work in the community. The Charm City Strangler indirectly forced Hakeem to take on the community leader role that he's been running from. Even the funeral that Hakeem is asked to preside over is a struggle, but he does it because of his love for Duck and Darrin.

The development in the writing doesn't stop there. We introduced some members of the Flamingo Club in this book. Mayor Hugo Titan, Kesha Stokes and James DeLuca are the newcomers that are members of the Flamingo Club. I took time to allude to other members, Neil Goldberg and Khin. Let's not forget that we learn that Erica Little is a member of the Flamingo Club, and she now owns and operates Titan Industries. The challenge starts with Erica capitalizing on the water crisis for Titan Industries' community redevelopment project. The story takes a weird turn when Mayor Hugo Titan desires for Erica and Tiffany to work together to solve the crisis. Erica and Tiffany have a clash of philosophies, yet they both believe they're doing the right thing.

Which leads us to Raymond and Monica. The two are dedicated to their family and the church. The problem with that is the two are dedicated to a philosophy that's hurting so many of their members and the communities in Baltimore. Even with access to the large campus in Woodstock, MD, Raymond and Monica were firmly against having the displaced residents stay at the campus. This was important for me to highlight because I wanted to show how dedicated Raymond and Monica were to the church's philosophy.

Explaining Kesha's reasoning for wanting to leave the church was perfect because it tracks with the damage that her parents did to her, Hakeem and Jamar in relation to the church. Yet, Kesha is doing the right thing, at least from her perspective, based on her side venture. I wanted that to start the arching problem in this story and the larger problem in the series because Kesha isn't just going against the church, she's actually going against the Flamingo Club and has dragged Hakeem and Tiffany into the situation.

I also want to point out Khin, Goldberg and the Dulaney Crime Family will all have significant roles in *The Transition*. I also want to point out AFK is back in the fold. What will his role be? You have to wait until *The Transition* comes out, but it will be worth the wait. I plan to release *The Transition* in the 4th quarter of 2024. The goal of 2024 is to continue to promote Bold Print Publishing, release some exciting new authors, and then release the close to this saga. I'm still working to develop the series into a live action version. There are a few versions of the pilot written. Stay tuned. Before I end this letter, I want to say thank you to so many people that contributed to this product. They include my wife Rebecca, my daughters Savannah, Sage and Shiloh, my uncle Tom Garland, Odessa Rose, Stacie Doi, Victoria Lake aka V, Devin Walker, and Moe Crosby, to name a few. I hope you all have enjoyed this story and I can't wait to see everyone's response to the conclusion to this series, *The Transition*.

http://www.kylesberkley.com

About the Author

Dr. Kyle Berkley is a husband and father from Baltimore, Maryland. After graduating from Fredrick Douglass High School in Baltimore City, Kyle attended Coppin State College with a major in history. During that time Kyle produced and wrote songs for hip hop, R&B, country, and gospel music artists. Kyle would later continue his education at Sojourner Douglass College and Morgan State University, where he earned his bachelor's and master's degrees in social work. Kyle also earned a master's degree in philosophy and a Ph.D. in Human and Social Services from Walden University. In 2012, Kyle and his wife, Rebecca, created a nonprofit organization called the 4 Us Initiative that provided safe housing for victims of domestic violence, homeless families, and preventive care for adolescents.

In 2014, Kyle was elected as a representative to the Baltimore City State Central Committee. Along with serving on the State Central Committee, Kyle has provided mental health therapy, grief counseling, and case management at Baltimore City shelters, hospitals, medical centers, transitional houses, outpatient medical, crisis response teams, The American Red Cross, and substance abuse treatment centers.

Kyle Berkley released his first novel in 2018 entitled *The Wake. The Void* was his second novel, and the first book in the Tiffany Gibbons Saga. In his free time, Kyle can be found cooking, playing video games with his 3 daughters, enjoying vacation trips with his wife, reading, and watching movies. Kyle is a huge history buff and comic book collector. Kyle also enjoys fishing, playing sports, weightlifting, engaging in casual debates on various subjects, comedy, helping people in need, listening to podcasts and spending time with his family.

The Wake: Renaissance Critiques

Ratings : 9.9/10 ⭐ In 2016, the fictional West Baltimore City community known as Ridgely Square was rocked to its core by several events and deaths. Through the eyes of Tiffany Gibbons, a single mother of five children, battling mental illness and trauma, you will witness the fall of a once prominent family and community–thanks to crime, corruption, gentrification, and family secrets. Read this fabulous book to know the whole story. This book is a combination of unique plot and engaging storytelling. The accessible language makes the book a compelling read. The author has a talent for creating a captivating narrative that keeps readers hooked! The smooth flow and balanced pacing of the book successfully enhances the reading experience, allowing readers to immerse themselves fully in the story without any interruptions. Also I appreciate the way the author has presented the characters. This book is certainly worth the buy and worth the read. It was an absolute page-turner. Once I started reading the book, I couldn't put it down. It was definitely a roller coaster ride for me. The cover page and title effectively reflect its content! Overall it was a mind blowing book. According to me, it's a must have book for your collection. I highly recommend this book to everyone.

A very heartwarming, a real dose of reality and a story that everyone can relate to. A must read and a must see.

- Comedian Big Gurl A.K.A Spicy from KSAL SHOW

Interesting ASF

-Matthew E Britt, CPRS

The Void Critiques

The Void Rating: 9/10 This book will make you want to keep flipping the pages and will make you desperate to know what is going to happen next. The book is absolutely intriguing, gripping and fast-paced. It will compel you to complete it in just 1-2 sittings irrespective of its length. The writing style of the author is marvelous. I mean I never felt like reading a book, it was all kinda happening in front of me (like a movie). The language used is easy to read. The characters are well developed and have been portrayed with utmost clarification and justified to their respective roles till the end. The cover of the book is wonderful and the title justifies the plot. I absolutely loved the book and would love to go through the future works of the author. I highly recommend this book to everyone.

"One of the best Baltimore stories, since *The Wire.*" - Moe Crosby of the Earth 2 Cosmic Cast

"Look what's cooking! If you live in Bmore or not in Bmore, this book is Bmore! Pick it up and read the damn book!" BlakBoxx Radio

"A compelling story about Baltimore City. Baltimore is a great city, but there are some areas that have been left to fend for themselves. Kyle Berkley does a wonderful job showing the neglected communities that have been taken over by the drug culture. Berkley's The Void puts on full display the negative effects drugs have had on certain neighborhoods in the city of Baltimore. Through the devastating life of the main character Tiffany Simms, we learn how drugs take a hold of not just the drug dealers, but whole families, the police force, state's attorney, and the community. Berkley is a remarkable storyteller. He doesn't shy away from the issues that make us uncomfortable. In The Void, he tackles them head-on, so readers get a true understanding how drugs destroy the lives of everyone."

Odessa Rose, best selling author for *Water in a Broken Glass* and *Kizmic's Journey*. Screenplay writer and director for *Stay Your Butt out of the Woods*. Member of the Black Writers Guild

The Legacy Ratings: 9.8/10 ⭐ The protagonist of the story is Tiffany Gibbons. She is a beautiful 35-year-old African American woman. It's been two years since she killed her child-molesting father by using a handgun. Now things in her world are looking much brighter. She has graduated from nursing college and purchased a restaurant and market that the residents of the community frequent regularly. She is also planning to marry the love of her life, Hakeem Andrews.

Hakeem is a local community leader turned-impromptu-pastor. But the Ridgely Square community isn't faring as well. Since the events that occurred two years ago, when Tiffany's aunt Gina and others exposed what was occurring in the underbelly of their community, it has been in the midst of a gang war and major unrest.

To know the whole story, you must read this fabulous book. The writing style of the author is fresh and interesting and will keep the readers stuck to the pages. The narration is magnificent and readers of all ages will love it. The book is very well written and the precision in the description of each and every scene is at the top level. The language of the book is easy to read and understand.

It is a fast-paced book and you can finish it in 2-3 sittings as it is absolutely a page-turner. The cover page of the book is wonderful and the title is interesting. Overall it is a fantastic read. I absolutely loved the story. I am really excited for my fellow readers to give this book a try. I am sure you all will love it.I highly recommend this book to everyone.

-Books With Benefits

As the third book in the series, Legacy continues important conversations about concepts such as gentrification, corruption, and gang violence within a narrative that keeps your attention. Tiffany Gibbons is a mother, entrepreneur, and a pillar in her community. Most of all, she is a character you can root for as she deals with past trauma, an active serial killer and harassment from Titan Industries and the Alphas.

-Bri of the Earth 2 Cosmic Cast

Void is a great build-up and then Legacy explodes. The twist and the turns and the roller coaster of emotions is NOT ok, in the best way. This would be one hell of a Netflix series in my opinion.

-Poetic Soul, author of *My Pain My Past My Progress*. Two-time winner of the PJJ Poetry Slam.

With Baltimore as its backdrop, in the same tradition as Homicide and The Corner, Dr Berkley spins a tale seemingly ripped from the same headlines. Touching on the institutional, structural issues to mental illness and family structure. No stone is left unturned. You see your family, the people in your neighborhood constantly echoing through the characters. Areas of gray and nuance that get lost in politics, sound bites and outrage. It's the humanity that many forget when speaking about many conflicts and communities.

-Wade Wilson, Hip Hop musical and visual artist. Tunebubble "Your Next Favorite Artist "June 2022. 2020-21 Trenton Film Festival Musical Short Nominee "Agent of Chaos"

Recent Projects: ChopHouse, Dystopian Daydream

The Union Critiques

The Union Ratings 10/10 ⭐ The book literally hooks the readers from the very beginning till the very end. I am really satisfied with the purchase. The writing style of the author is evocative and compelling. The language is quite easy to understand and the narration has been top notch. The flow of the book is smooth and hence it gives a perfect balance to the readers. The title and cover page of the book goes with the content. Overall, this book is a must-read and worth your time.

I highly recommend this book to everyone. You guys must go, give it a read without any further delay. I'm sure you're gonna love this book.

-Books With Benefits

In this latest installment of the Tiffany Gibbons Saga, author Kyle Berkley takes us on a wild dirt bike joyride through the crime ridden streets of Baltimore City. With the keen and intimate sensibility of someone who was born, reared, and still lives in the city, Berkley genuinely captures Baltimoreans and the issues that plague their neighborhoods. Full of compelling twists and turns, *The Union* explores the deadly underbelly of Baltimore's political arena, in which Tiffany joins forces with a secret, unholy alliance in her daunting and never-ending fight to save her family and Ridgely Square community, while trying to save herself.

-Odessa Rose, best selling author for *Water in a Broken Glass* and *Kizmic's Journey*. Screenplay writer and director for *Stay Your Butt out of the Woods*. Member of the Black Writers Guild.

This book is definitely a winner and shows your strength and versatility as a writer. It is soooo good!

-Karen Rodgers, Editor

If it ain't one thing happening in Ridgely Square, it's another," an apt quote for the next book in this series. Being a steward of one's community is an ongoing endeavor that Tiffany Gibbons knows all too well and it's starting to take its toll. As she navigates being newly married, she also faces a water crisis, another serial killer, a cultist church, and all the mental wear and tear that comes from everything else she's weathered. Through it all, she's still a character you'll root for because her focus is always on doing what's right even when there doesn't seem to be a right answer. Thankfully, this time she doesn't have to do it alone.

-Bri of the Earth 2 Cosmic Cast

2019 winner of the Women of International Business Award for The Wake

2023 finalist nominee for the Baltimore Crown Award for Author/Writer of the Year for the Void and Legacy

BOOKS BY THIS AUTHOR

THE WAKE

THE VOID

THE LEGACY

THE UNION

THE TRANSITION

COMING SOON

THE CONFESSION

COMING SOON